BLOOD FAVORS

BY
DONNA JOPPIE

DartFrog Plus is the hybrid publishing imprint of DartFrog Books, LLC.

301 S. McDowell St.
Suite 125-1625
Charlotte, NC 28204
www.DartFrogBooks.com

DEDICATION

To my sister, Charolette Chitty Crawford, and brother-in-law, Joe Crawford. Thank you for helping me with details of names of businesses, streets, and bridges from the years we lived in Houma. I cherished those many calls, not just for your help but also for the love we share, now more than ever after the passing of our dear Joe.

PROLOGUE

New Orleans
Spring of 1967

Dense clouds and constant rain sucked the color from the Crescent City coastline, leaving it a sickening gray. A slow-moving tanker stacked high with containers slipped past Jackson Square virtually unnoticed as residents went about their day, unaware of the tortured souls trapped inside the vessel.

High in the ship's wheelhouse, the captain nodded to a leather-faced man a few feet away.

The man left the wheelhouse, went to a remote section in the ship's bowels, removed a large duffel bag from a locker, and carried it to a metal door at the back of the vessel. He released the bolt on the door, tossed the bag into the room, and stepped in.

Four Hispanic men jumped from cots and backed away as the man approached, pinching his nose.

"Damn, it stinks in here." He picked up the bag and threw it at one of the men, knocking him to the floor. "There's soap and a change of clothes for each of you there. Get washed and changed before I get back." He turned to leave, then hesitated. "Do I need to remind you why you're here?"

There was no response.

"Don't play dumb with me. I know you speak English. Romeo, you seem to be the bright one here. Explain to your amigos what will happen if they don't follow orders."

The captor raised his head and drew back his shoulders. "My name is Ramiro García Montez. Not Romeo."

The man chuckled. "Answer my question, little man."

"If we don't do as you say, our wives and children will die."

A grin spread across the man's cracked lips. "That's right, and if any of you fail your assignment, it means you all failed."

"Please. You can't do that," Ramiro said, clasping his hands together.

The man approached him and chuckled in his face. "We make the rules, Romeo, so I suggest you convince your buddies to complete their assignments. Now get cleaned up!"

He left, locking the door behind him.

One of the men crumbled onto his cot, sobbing.

Ramiro went to him and placed a hand on his shoulder. "We must be strong, José, for our family's sake."

"But my son is not yet two, and my wife is carrying our second child. I can't let them die." He paused, then looked up at his fellow companions. "Maybe we can escape these men when we get off the ship and get back to save our families."

"No, José, we can't. Even if we got away, we don't know where they hid them. They will be killed long before we can reach them." Ramiro looked at each of the men. "The only chance we have of saving our wives and children is to do as we are told."

A long moment passed before one of the men took the bag from the floor and emptied the contents onto a cot. He went through the clothing, found what he needed, and went to the only water spigot in the room to wash.

One by one, the other men did the same.

Hours passed before the leather-faced man returned, followed by a man holding a rifle.

"Good. You're ready. It's time to get you off the ship. Keep quiet, or my friend here will shoot you and dump you in the river with the rest of the trash. Behave yourselves and follow me."

The man with the rifle stood back and followed the group out. He nudged them forward as the ship's crew members stepped out of the way or turned their backs. When the men reached the ship's deck, a church bell marked midnight in the distance. They were herded past the workers, down the ramp, and onto the dock before being told to stop.

"Keep quiet and stand in a row," the man ordered as four black automobiles drove out of a warehouse and stopped in front of them. The car door of the first vehicle opened, and one of the two men in the car got out.

"Which one of you is Ramiro Montez?"

Ramiro glanced at his companions and saw the fear in their eyes before raising his hand. He was grabbed by the arm and shoved into the backseat, and the man slid in beside him. As the car pulled away, Ramiro looked out the rearview window and locked eyes with José just as he was taken to the second car. He watched as long as he could because Ramiro knew this was the last time he would see José, or any of his companions, again.

CHAPTER ONE

Arizona

Rob Chambers fumbled for the light switch with his free hand as he balanced a cup of coffee and newspaper in the other. He entered his office and settled his body, still muscular and lean in his early thirties thanks to years of swimming, behind his desk and started to read his paper.

A man dressed in black with a ski mask over his face slipped from behind a tall bookcase and started wrapping a thin wire cord around the palms of his gloved hands. Moving silently to a position behind Rob's chair, he raised the wire above Rob's head and, in one swift move, looped it around his neck, choking him.

Rob clawed at the cord as the newspaper and coffee flew everywhere. Unable to free himself, he ran his hands up his attacker's forearms and jerked him forward as he threw his head back, striking the attacker in the face, causing him to loosen his grip.

Rob pushed against the desk with his feet, propelled himself backward, and landed atop his attacker. He thrust his elbows into the man's ribs and heard him gasp. Rob ripped the cord from his throat, flipped over, and wrapped the cord around his attacker's neck, then pinned him down with a knee.

Someone applauded across the room, and Rob released the cord. He got to his feet and pulled his attacker from the floor.

"Nice job," Senior FBI Agent Tom Neal said coolly from the doorway.

The attacker jerked the hood from his head, exposing his sandy blond hair and a growing red mark across his face.

"Dang it, Rob, you almost broke my nose."

Rob grinned. "You said to make it real."

"That was quite a show," Tom said, stepping into the room.

"Yeah, a painful one," Steve replied, carefully checking his bruised ribs.

"How's he doing?" Tom asked, jerking his chin in Rob's direction.

"My abused body thinks he's done great."

"How is he with firearms?"

"He's good, but that's not his strong suit. I focused more on other skills and even challenged him to learn a new language."

Tom chuckled. "How long did that take?"

"I'll be damned if he wasn't reading and speaking like a native in less than a month. Hell, it took me over three years to learn Russian, and I still have trouble writing it. If I didn't know better, I'd say he was cheating."

A slight grin crossed Agent Tom Neal's lips, and he glanced at Rob before responding. "So The Kid didn't tell you, did he?"

"Tell me what?"

"Rob has a photographic memory."

"So that's how you memorized all the Bureau's codes so fast!" Steve said to Rob, who shrugged in response.

"Codes?" Tom stepped closer. "Steve, you could go to prison for that. Our codes are classified."

"What are you talking about? Rob has clearance."

Tom looked at Rob and back at Steve and shook his head. "No, he doesn't. He's not with the Bureau."

Steve paused a moment, then began to chuckle. "Stop joking, Tom. We're standing in the middle of a former FBI training center. I had to get a special pass from you to get through the gate."

"I'm not joking. The Kid isn't FBI."

Steve's mouth dropped open as he looked from man to man. "Then who in the hell is he?"

Once again, Tom and Rob exchanged glances, but neither said a word.

"Damn it, Tom, say something! My career is on the line, and so is my freedom."

Tom Neal put a hand on the young man's shoulder. "Calm down, son. Nothing will happen if we keep quiet about this."

"Easy for you to say. For all we know, this place is bugged. The least you can do is tell me who Rob is."

"He's right, Tom," Rob said. "He deserves to know the truth."

"Then you tell him."

Rob stepped closer to Steve. "Which name would you like? I've had several."

"Let's start with the one your mama gave you," Steve scoffed.

Rob extended his hand. "Robert Chambers, but my friends call me Rob."

"Chambers, Chambers, Robert Chambers." Steve's eyes widened, and he pulled his hand back. "You're lying. Chambers was the lawyer and money launderer for the Rojas Martínez drug organization. The reports we got said Chambers drowned."

Hearing the name 'Rojas' brought Rob's memories rushing back. He'd been given the choice of laundering Rojas's drug money or watching his wife die. So Rob had done what Rojas wanted until his work as a money launderer was exposed, and he and Wanda had to run—not only from Rojas, but also from the FBI. They'd managed to stay hidden until Rojas, determined to kill Rob, found him at a safe house. With his own death imminent and his wife's life in jeopardy, Rob had been forced to bring the whole saga to an end in the murky water below an oil rig five miles out in the Gulf of Mexico. It was an episode of his life he tried not to think about.

"I posted that report," Tom said, the sound of his voice snapping Rob back to the present. "Hoover and I want the Rojas organization to think he's dead. Rob and his family are in WITSEC."

"WITSEC? The new witness protection program? I didn't know it was operational yet."

"The Kid and his family are among the first to be placed. Rob's knowledge of the Rojas organization is invaluable to the Bureau. We need him to testify when the remaining leaders are captured."

"Good for him, but why drag me into this?"

"I wanted him to have the skills to protect himself and his family in case the drug organization discovers he is alive."

"That's ridiculous. This is a secure base. Hell, there are guards everywhere you look."

"There is no such thing as secure," Rob said. "Wanda and I were on the run for almost a year when I called Tom and turned myself in. Rojas and his people found us in the safehouse Tom had placed us in. I was taken out of there to be killed, and Wanda almost died."

Tom glanced at Rob before responding to Steve. "We lost good people that day."

Steve dropped his head and shook it slowly. "I remember. Two agents died that night."

"After that experience, I thought The Kid should be prepared to defend himself and his family if it happened again. But giving him the codes was never part of the plan."

Steve stood inches from the older agent. "Then you should have told me who he was when you asked me to come."

Rob stepped between the two men. "Stop. If anyone's to blame for this, it's me. I asked Tom for training. If the organization learns I'm alive, they won't stop with me. They will kill my whole family."

"You don't have to tell Tom or me about this drug organization, Rob." Steve gave Tom a softer look. "We know exactly what they are capable of. The problem is, I'm not even supposed to know you are here. Hell, once they learn I've shared our codes, I'll spend the rest of my life in federal prison."

"I'm sorry for that. I never meant to cause you harm," Rob said.

"Look," Tom said, putting a hand on both men's shoulders. "Nothing is going to happen to either of you."

Steve started to chuckle.

"What's so funny?" Tom asked.

"I don't know why this just popped into my brain, but before I came out here, my girlfriend said if I ever stopped being an agent, I could always join her in selling Mary Kay. She keeps telling me they're going to be big. Maybe I should consider it."

Tom patted Steve on the cheeks. "Don't think so. You aren't pretty enough." He glanced at his watch. "I have a meeting with Hoover early tomorrow morning. I need to get to the airport."

"And I need to return to my unit," Steve added.

Rob crossed his arms and sat on the edge of the desk. "And I'm staying right here."

"You better be," Tom said. "I'll be in touch with both of you."

Rob heard the outside door close as Tom left. He glanced at Steve, who was curling up the cord they had used in training. "Steve, I'm so sorry I got you into this."

"I think it will be all right. Tom has a lot of clout with the director."

"You are fortunate to have such a close friend in his position looking out for you."

"Tom doesn't have close friends anymore. When he lost both his wife and son in less than a year, he shut everyone out."

"Not true. It's clear to see Tom cares for you."

Steve took a moment. "That's only because he helped raise me. I used to live next door to Tom and his family. His son Scott and I grew up together. He was my best friend. We even attended the same university."

"What happened to Scott? I know he was killed, but I don't know how."

"Our senior year of college, one of our buddies was getting married. About eight of us decided the best way to celebrate his bachelor party was a road trip to Mexico. I got the flu just before we left and had to stay behind. While the guys were in Tijuana, one of our buddies slipped away and bought pot, then bragged to the group that he had paid for it with a twenty-dollar bill wrapped around a roll of dime-store play money."

"And Tom's son went along with that?"

"Never. Scott was as straight and narrow as his dad."

"Then why was he killed?"

"The next night, the drug dealer and his thugs found the group, grabbed the guy who bought the drugs, and started beating him."

"Did the rest of them try to help?"

"They claimed they did, but I saw them right after they returned, and none had a mark on them. I think they panicked and ran. That is, everyone but Scott." Steve took a deep breath, exhaled, and closed his eyes. "The next morning, Scott and our friend who'd bought the pot were found with their throats cut, hanging from streetlamps on the town's main street. Their pant pockets had been turned inside out." Steve swallowed, opened his eyes, and looked at Rob. "Their hands were missing. Tom was told they cut them off as a sign to the community of what would happen to anyone that cheats them."

"That's horrible. But how did Tom find out the Rojas Martínez organization did it?"

"After we buried Scott, Tom spent months in Tijuana looking for the people who killed him."

"Alone?"

"Not exactly. Tom has a friend with the CIA down there. Apparently, this guy knew which organization ran Tijuana and the surrounding communities. Turns out, it was the same group that put you here."

Rob lowered his head. "I know what losing someone to them feels like. The organization killed my best friend, and I'll never be over it."

Steve took a long look at Rob. "I'm surprised Tom asked me to train you. As long as I've known him, he's never gone off-book like this unless . . ."

"Unless what? I've asked Tom several times why he's done so much to help us, but he's never given me an answer."

"He's doing it because you remind him of Scott. Not only are you built like him, but you're smart and seem to share a few of his characteristics. Has Tom said anything to you about that?"

Rob shook his head. "As you know, Tom is a man of few words. But once he did ask if I had gotten into this because I was protecting someone."

"Were you?"

"The organization said they would kill everyone close to me, starting with my wife, if I didn't work for them."

"And I'm sure they would have." Steve zipped up his supply bag.

"Why did you decide to become an agent?"

"As a kid, I thought Tom's job as a G-man was so cool. Every time he was home, I made a nuisance of myself, following him around and asking questions." Steve paused and cleared his throat. "After Scott died, I knew I had to be an agent, and I asked Tom to help me get an interview with the Bureau. He did, and now I'm here. Best decision I ever made."

"You're all he has left, Steve. Tom's not going to let anything happen to you."

"Or to you." Steve grabbed his bag and started for the door. "Good luck, Rob. It's been great getting to know you."

"Same to you. Be careful out there, and thanks for everything."

After Steve departed, Rob's mind returned to a phone call he'd received from Tom over two years ago.

Rojas knows you're helping us, Kid. He's coming for you. Get out now!

He recalled flying through the streets of Dallas with Wanda scrunched down on the floorboard of his car as he outran Rojas's men. It was only later he learned that his lifelong friend Joey, who was secretly aware of his connection with Rojas, had been tortured and murdered because of his closeness to Rob.

I'll die before I ever let Martínez or his people near my family again.

CHAPTER TWO

New Orleans

Deep in the center of the historic Garden District, a two-story building was a landmark for two reasons. The bottom floor was home to Savoy's Restaurant, a cherished Crescent City location known worldwide for its Creole cuisine. The top floor was famous, too, but for a very different reason.

As cooks and staff worked frantically below, a slim, immaculately dressed man in his early thirties sat holding a phone in one hand and tapping his fingers on his enormous mahogany desk. His tapping stopped when his call was answered.

"Jean-Claude DuMont calling for Señor Diego Martínez. Tell him it's urgent." DuMont heard Spanish spoken in the background before Martínez came on the line.

"Has my shipment been released?" Martínez demanded.

"It has not. You haven't completed all of your assignments."

"Three of the four are already done. I need that shipment."

DuMont rolled his eyes and admired the manicured nails on his free hand. "Sir, the agreement between Mr. Pascal and your predecessor precedes your demands. All shipments will be held until *all* assignments are completed."

"I know the agreement, DuMont. I'm the one who's been handling them since we started."

"That may be true, but after the unfortunate death of Carlos Rojas, things under your command have not been the same. Señor Rojas was meticulous with every detail, and each assignment was swiftly handled. You still have much to prove before earning Mr. Pascal's trust."

"Our arrangements may have been Carlos's idea, but I'm the one who found the people to carry them out and made sure they were completed."

The corners of DuMont's lips turned upwards. "So, if Rojas was the brains of your organization, what did that make you?"

"Careful, little man. Tell your boss the last assignment will be completed before tomorrow, and I want my shipment released to my men as soon as they arrive."

DuMont's intercom buzzed twice as the call ended, and he hastened to the adjoining office. "Yes, sir?"

"I take it our little drug lord doesn't appreciate being reminded of my expectations."

"Sir, I suppose it's difficult for some people to realize their place in the order of things."

Marcel Pascal chuckled. "True. We wouldn't be dealing with this riff-raff if Rojas were still alive."

"I agree. Rojas was far more professional and pleasant than his replacement."

Pascal glanced at his assistant. "I wouldn't put it past that power-hungry Mexican to have killed Rojas so he could take over."

"Sir, if that's true, he can't be trusted."

"I've already considered that, but their favors have eliminated many unwanted obstacles without being traced back to us. I think for now we give Martínez time to prove himself before I end our arrangement."

"I understand the value of the service, sir, but the man is insufferable."

"We don't have to like him to do business with him, Jean-Claude. Which reminds me—get our illustrious governor on the line. He needs to answer a few questions. While I'm on the phone, call downstairs and order a plate of softshell crabs for my lunch. My mouth has been watering all morning from the smell coming through the baseboards."

"Yes, sir. Right away."

*   *   *

Baton Rouge

Governor Parker Thompson stood with his assistant outside one of the capitol's conference rooms.

"Time to razzle-dazzle them, Lucas," he said. "If you want a career in politics, the skills of flirting and flattery are the shortest ways to fill your coffers. Every one of those old biddies is worth a fortune." Parker straightened his tie, then gave his assistant a sideways look. "Have you made the contact I requested?"

"The young lady will be waiting for you at Antoine's at nine this evening."

"The private room?"

"As always, sir."

"Perfect. I wasn't sure about this one."

"Sir. You're the governor. How could she possibly refuse?"

"You're worth your weight in gold, Lucas. Now, let's get this show started. I'll need a little nap before my rendezvous tonight."

His assistant pushed open the doors, and the chatter in the room stopped.

"Ladies, the governor of the state of Louisiana, the Honorable Parker Thompson." The assistant stepped aside, allowing the governor to make an elaborate bow as the room's occupants applauded.

Thompson dismissed his assistant and began circling the table. He kissed a hand here, a cheek there, and continued until he had personally greeted every member of the Daughters of the South committee. In minutes, he had them swooning. His reelection campaign wouldn't start for another two years, but that was no reason to miss an opportunity to collect donations ahead of time.

One never knows when you might have a few incidentals along the way, he liked to say.

"Ladies, thank you for filling these cold, dreary halls with warmth and beauty. I am so humbled and honored to be your servant." He beamed as laughter filled the room. "Please help yourself to sweet tea and cookies while we visit."

The group complied and began nibbling as they gushed over their host.

The governor was deep in conversation when his assistant came to his side.

"Pardon the interruption, sir. You have an urgent call."

"Lucas, tell Lyndon I'm with The Daughters of the South and cannot be disturbed."

The room filled with 'Oh my!' and 'Dear me!' as others giggled.

"It's not President Johnson, sir. The call is from the Garden District."

Thompson's toothy grin vanished. He exchanged a glance with his assistant and then got to his feet. "Ladies, I must beg your forgiveness. I promise to return to you as quickly as possible."

He turned to his assistant. "Lucas, I am giving you an executive order to take care of these lovely ladies until I return." He gave a short bow and made a hasty retreat.

Thompson rushed down the hallway to his office, closed the door, and picked up the phone.

"This must be important to pull you away from your lunch, Marcel."

"My lunch will arrive shortly, Parker. I hope, for your sake, you don't spoil it. Where are we on the contracts for the construction of the Super Dome? It's been a year since the bond was passed."

"You know how this works, Marcel. The committee must accept bids and thoroughly review them before they are awarded. After that, it could take as long as three years, maybe four, before the first shovel of dirt is turned. But rest assured, I will see that as many of your companies as possible are selected."

"Parker, I'm assured of nothing where you're concerned. I trusted you a year ago to get me the levee rebuilding contracts after Hurricane Betsy. You sat on your well-dressed ass and allowed Old Man Claymont's Slidell plant to take the lion's share of the program. All I got was scraps."

"Marcel, I did my best to sway the vote for your companies. But once it was placed in the hands of the Corps of Engineers, there was nothing I could do."

"Why was that, Parker? I lowered my rates like you suggested, and they still gave Crescent City Concrete the contract."

"That wasn't my fault, Marcel. How was I to know his reputation for being on time and quality overrode price in that decision?"

"Damn, it, Parker! The reason I made you governor was to get me every contract I wanted."

"I'm so sorry, Marcel. How can I make it up to you?"

"By making certain I get the levee maintenance contracts. I just learned that the Levee Board will be taking bids on the multimillion-dollar program in the next few months. I want that contract, Parker, and this time, you'll make sure I get it. If you don't, I'll find someone else to fill your chair in Baton Rouge."

"Now, let's not get all worked up, Marcel. As I recall, the old man who owned the plant died shortly after he won the rebuilding contracts. His company must be in trouble without him running the place."

There was an uncomfortable pause.

"Unfortunately," Marcel said finally, "it's more profitable now than when the old man was alive. Turns out his kid is better at running it than he was."

"Then, perhaps you should consider arranging for his heir to join him."

There was another pause at the end of the line.

"You may be on to something, Parker."

"You see, I am helpful."

"I'll decide that after I get the maintenance contract."

"I'll do my best, Marcel, but it may require you to step in and help."

"I don't have time. I'm dealing with some Yankee labor asshole trying to unionize my dock workers."

"Don't worry, Marcel. I'll take care of the board. Now, if that is all you need, I must get back to governing Louisiana."

"You don't run this state, Parker. I do, and don't you forget it."

The call ended.

CHAPTER THREE

Virginia

Agent Tom Neal entered the corridor to Hoover's office and glanced at the photos on the walls. He had seen them many times but never tired of the images depicting the FBI's history. The first photos dated back to 1924, when President Coolidge welcomed his newly appointed twenty-nine-year-old head of the Bureau. Others were of every president since Coolidge, standing next to J. Edgar. There were also international leaders, government officials, Supreme Court judges, and movie stars. Working under Hoover was no easy task. He was closed-minded about many things and would carry a grudge for years when offended. Despite this, Tom admired the man and knew he was as sharp today as he had been when Hoover welcomed Tom as a new recruit. That was over twenty-three years ago, just before the end of the war.

"Good morning," Tom said to Hoover's secretary. "Is he in?"

"Great to see you, Agent Neal. Mr. Hoover was just asking about you." She reached for her phone. "Sir, Agent Neal is here . . . Yes, sir." She hung up the phone. "Go right in."

Hoover looked over his dark-framed glasses and pointed to a chair when Tom entered his office. "I was beginning to wonder if you got my message."

"Sorry for the delay, sir. I was out of state, checking on our informant."

"How's my new program working?"

"Excellent, sir. However, he still has concerns about his family's safety. It's understandable, considering what they went through. And they are even more concerned now, with a baby in the family."

"Add more security if you think it will help. Your informant's knowledge of this organization is vital."

"Thank you, sir, I will. I'm sure the President is pleased to hear how much information Chambers has given us?"

Hoover leaned back in his chair. "Not in the slightest. He's so blinded by the Cold War and Vietnam that he's oblivious to the real danger sneaking into this country right under our noses. If we don't stop this new drug flow from entering, the loss of lives and cost to this country will be devastating. You know better than anyone what these drug organizations are capable of."

Tom exhaled, and his eyes glazed over. "Yes, sir, I do."

"I know it's hard for you to let someone else handle the case against the organization, but the Bureau has rules where family is involved."

"Yes, sir, I'm well aware."

"That's why I agreed to put you in charge of Chambers and put him and his family into WITSEC. I thought that would remove some of the sting of being sidelined from working the case."

"I appreciate that, sir."

"Good. Let's move on to why I called you in. I recall sending you to New Orleans after the Kennedy assassination."

"Yes, sir, you did."

"Well, I thought we were past all the wild conspiracy speculation around the assassination, but apparently we're not. I've been inundated with rantings from the New Orleans District Attorney, Jim Garrison. Have you heard of the man?"

"I met him several times during my trips to investigate Oswald's history in New Orleans."

"Good. That will give you a credible cover story." Hoover took a folder from his desk and gave it to Tom. "There have been numerous murders in and around New Orleans over the last eighteen months. Several of those killed were federal judges, government officials, and other business leaders."

"Isn't our New Orleans office handling this?"

"Supposedly they are, but this has been going on for too long, and they're not making a damn bit of progress." Hoover paused a moment.

"What do you know of the organized crime base down there?"

"Marcel Pascal has dominated every criminal element in Louisiana and most portions of the Gulf Coast for years. Whenever we think we have him, he wiggles out of it."

"That's because many local authorities and government officials in the area are under his control. That's why I'm sending you to New Orleans. I want you to make sure none of our people in that field office are on Pascal's payroll."

"Should I use the standard notification channels before I arrive?"

Hoover paused. "Hold off on that. I think you will get a better look at things if they don't know you're there."

"True, but what do you want me to say if they discover I'm in town?"

"Tell them I sent you undercover to investigate Garrison's conspiracy allegations. And Tom? One more thing. No one is to know about this. All the information you gather comes straight to me. Is that clear?"

"Very clear."

Hoover pointed to the folder. "You need to study every word in that file before you go. As soon as you're done, let me know, and my secretary will make the arrangements. She and I are the only ones who will know you're there."

"Yes, sir. I understand."

"It sickens me to think anyone carrying our badge is working for Pascal, but anything's possible where that man is concerned. Now get out of here. If there's a rotten egg in my basket, find it."

"Yes, sir." Tom got to his feet.

"See my secretary before you leave. She has something for you."

Tom retreated to the outer office, and Hoover's secretary handed him a large manila envelope. He opened it and removed one of several small black devices. "This looks like a pager."

"It's the advanced model. The range is extensive, and the display screen is larger to add code and symbols. I've placed those codes and their meanings in the envelope. Mr. Hoover insists you use the pagers to contact this office in an emergency and never use the Bureau's radio communication. There's extra in case one gets damaged." She took one from her center desk drawer. "I have one, and so does the director. Mr. Hoover's pager number and mine are on the list of codes. Don't hesitate to use them. If you can't reach him, contact me."

"He seems to have thought of everything."

"That's why he's the director."

"Point taken."

"Have a safe trip, Agent Neal."

*   *   *

Arizona

Rob sipped coffee at his kitchen table as he watched Wanda try to pry a scrambled egg-covered teddy bear from their seventeen-month-old daughter's arms. His thoughts wandered back to the day Sarah was born and he'd learned they were being moved from a safe house into this former FBI training complex in the Arizona desert.

The sound of his daughter's infectious laughter brought him back, and her hazel-green eyes met his.

"How did we get such a perfect child?"

"She's perfectly covered with egg, and so is her bear."

The phone rang, and he got up to answer. "Yes?" Rob listened for a moment, then hung up the phone. "Tom's at the gate."

"Did you know he was coming?"

"I didn't. He hasn't called in weeks." There was a knock at the door, and Rob went to answer.

"You're out early."

"I left Virginia at three this morning." Tom Neal removed his hat and entered. "Good morning, Wanda."

"Good to see you, Tom."

He reached over and tickled the baby's chin. Sarah threw out her arms and leaned towards him. "What does she want?" Tom asked.

"She wants you to take her."

Tom gave Rob his hat and the large manila envelope he was holding and took the child from her mother. "What do I do now?" he asked, keeping her at arm's length.

"Just hold her close to you."

Tom did, and Sarah laid her head on his shoulder.

"Wow," Rob said. "I thought I was the only man she liked."

"Tom," Wanda said, "she's getting her breakfast all over you."

"That's all right. I can't get over how much she's grown."

"Here, let me take her," Wanda said. "There's coffee in the kitchen if you're interested."

Sarah protested when Wanda took her from Tom and carried her to the other room.

"Let's go in the kitchen," Rob said. "I'll get you a damp cloth for your jacket."

Tom followed Rob and waited as he ran water onto a dishcloth. He brushed away the egg off his jacket as Rob poured coffee from the percolator into cups and sat them on the table.

"It's been so long since we talked, I was concerned Steve had gotten into trouble for training me."

"No, I've been busy. As far as the Bureau knows, Steve was never here."

"At least you have something to do. I'm going crazy doing nothing."

Tom gave him a sideways glance and put down the cloth. "Maybe I can help you with that. I need your help with something."

"Whatever it is, I'm in."

"Not so fast. This could get both of us in a lot of trouble."

"Will it help find the drug organization?"

"Possibly. That's what I'm here to find out."

"I thought you weren't allowed to work on the case?"

"I'm not. However, this new assignment I'm on could have ties to them. You know more about these people than the Bureau does."

"How can I help?"

"This conversation can't be shared, Kid. Not even with Wanda. Are you good with that?"

"If this will help keep her and Sarah safe, she will understand."

Tom picked up the manila envelope. "This is your last chance to say no. Once I open this, there's no turning back."

Rob nodded, and Tom opened the tab. He spread photos of crime scenes, victims, and artists' drawings on the table.

Rob turned them around and looked at each image. "Where were these gruesome photos taken?"

"They are murders that occurred along the Gulf Coast. Take a close look. At the bottom of the photos, I listed the names and occupations of each victim."

Tom arranged the photos into four groups, then took several index cards with dates and numbers from the envelope and matched them with each drawing and picture.

Rob looked up. "What does all this mean?"

Tom pointed to the photos. "Every one of the people in these photos was murdered within days of each other in or around New Orleans."

"Okay, but what makes you think these murders are connected to the drug organization?"

Tom tapped every drawing. "These men were executed. Their bodies were dumped within twenty miles or less of each murder. There were witnesses from a couple of the murders, and their descriptions match the first two men." He pushed another pair of images before Rob. "This one was shot by a cop after killing a witness at the courthouse before he testified against a Mafia hitman."

"What happened to the case?"

"No witness, no case. The suspect went free." Tom sat back, crossed his arms, and waited. "Is there anything about this that reminds you of your dealings with the organization?"

Rob read each note and studied every photo for several minutes. "Except for the witness, each victim appears to be an important official or community member."

"Keep going."

Rob started regrouping the photos by the occupations listed at the bottom of the images. "These four were politicians, three had connections to law enforcement, and two were trial witnesses. The rest were executives in companies. Do we know anything about those companies?"

Tom grabbed the envelope, took out a sheet of paper, and gave it to him.

"One was chairman of a steel manufacturing plant out of Beaumont. Another owned a food processing plant," Rob said, studying the sheet of paper. He glanced at Tom. "You seem to know about the victims. What can you tell me about these men in the drawings? It appears all are Hispanic, but I don't see any information on them."

"That's because we don't have any. Take the men in the drawing out of the equation and see what links the other killings."

Rob hovered over the table for several minutes. "The witness and district attorney killings make me think there are some crime boss connections. Their murders could be political or lead to control of some outcome, but I'm not sure what the food processing plant or the steel manufacturing executives have to do with the rest." Rob hesitated a moment. "We need to look at who would benefit most from their deaths."

Tom raised a finger and pointed it at Rob. "Now you're thinking."

"Thinking what? I don't understand where you're going with this."

"Kid, all of the murders of the witnesses, officials, and businessmen were done by amateurs."

"Amateurs? How did you come to that conclusion?"

"The killings were sloppy. There was evidence left all over the place, not to mention witnesses. And that's not all." He gathered the images and cards and slid them into the manila envelope, then took newspaper clippings from his jacket pocket and spread them on the table. "Take a look at these."

Rob read each clipping. "These people were killed almost two years before the other ones you showed me."

"Right. Now, look at the articles I clipped to the back."

Rob turned them over and started to read. "The same number of men were killed a few days later."

"That's right. The same MO as the first group you saw, and every person on the attached list of killings was Mexican. They were found within miles of the murders, each with a single shot to the back of the head."

"So, you think all these deaths are connected?"

"I do, and there have been two more scenarios like these dating back to 1964. What does it sound like to you?"

"Nothing I see here would benefit Diego Martínez or the organization. These look like Mafia killings."

"True. And if the men killed were white, black, or Chinese, I would agree this has nothing to do with the organization. But all of them were Mexican. I think that's the connection to the organization."

"Is there any way to get information on those men from Mexico?"

"I've tried, but it's almost impossible to get that side of the border to share any information. No one is willing to talk to us."

"Maybe they aren't Mexican. They could be from Colombia."

"Why would you say that?"

"Don't you remember when I was debriefed? Diego Martínez is from Colombia, not Mexico."

"I don't have your memory, Kid. I'll look into that."

Rob returned to the clippings. "If this has happened two times before, it could happen again."

"That's what I'm afraid of." Tom gathered everything from the table and placed it in the envelope.

"If this is all you have to go on, how are you going to stop it?"

"I had hoped these images might stimulate a memory that could help me."

"Sorry," Rob said, sighing. "I just don't see anything here that connects these killings to the organization. But now that it's locked in my brain, I'll keep working on it. If I come up with something, I'll tell you the next time you call."

Tom shook his head. "We can't discuss any of this over the phone. The Bureau records all of your phone conversations. Any information you have, we discuss in person."

Rob's brows raised. "Are you saying our phone is tapped?"

"It is. It's done to protect you."

Rob got to his feet. "Is our home bugged too?"

"Of course not," Tom said, rising from his chair. "Everything said or done inside your home is private. Tapping your phone is one way the Bureau is keeping you and your family safe."

"I appreciate that, but staying confined like this takes its toll."

"I understand. Hopefully we will capture the leaders of the organization soon, and you can get back to a normal life."

"That won't be possible until the drug organization is destroyed and these people are in prison for the rest of their lives."

"That's the plan, Kid. Time for me to go." Tom went to the door, and Rob followed. "Don't let Sarah grow up before I get back."

"I'll do my best. You be careful out there."

Rob watched him drive away before closing his door. He stood looking at the confines of their small apartment and his heart ached. Wanda had almost been killed, and now she and their daughter were forced to live in the middle of nowhere to keep them safe. He had to find a way to change that, but how? He couldn't risk the drug organization finding them.

CHAPTER FOUR

New Orleans

Caroline Broussard waved at the guard as she entered the Crescent City Concrete plant. She drove to the main office building, went up to the second floor, and was greeted by her secretary.

"Good morning, Miss Caroline."

"Good morning, Abigail. Has the bill for the satellite plant's backup generators come in?"

The secretary picked up a folder from her desk and followed Caroline into her office. "It came in this morning. The first payment is due on the fifteenth."

Caroline settled into her chair. "The fifteenth? That wasn't the agreement." She put her handbag in the bottom drawer of her desk. "I specifically told them to make it the first of the month. Get them on the phone. I need to straighten this out." Her assistant didn't move. "What is it, Abigail?"

She handed Caroline the folder.

"Here are the final invoices for the new site and the payroll figures you requested for the new employees at that location."

Caroline looked over the pages. "Looks like it's going to be tight around here until we win that contract."

"I pray that happens, Miss Caroline."

"So do I, Abigail. We need all the help we can get."

"I also made a copy for Mr. Broussard."

"Jack won't be in today. He's meeting with the governor, mayor, and several other business owners to try to set up some type of provision for government assistance for businesses in case another storm like Betsy hits us."

"Dear God." Abigail crossed herself. "If that happens, there may be nothing left to rebuild."

"We hope it won't, but Jack is trying to get something in place in case it does. Oh, there's one more thing. Jack asked me to arrange a meeting with our division managers tomorrow morning in the conference room. Tell them he is requesting suggestions on how to cut expenses in each department. We're going to need it so we can cover the new expansion."

Abigail hesitated for a moment. "I hope this doesn't mean we will lay people off."

"We are a long way from that. This new plant has strained our cash flow, but it's temporary. Stop worrying. We're going to be fine."

"I hope so. I'll make the calls and set up the meeting."

As her assistant left, a man wearing a company shirt walked in with a hard hat under his arm.

"Sorry to bother you, Miss Caroline. I need to speak with Mr. Broussard."

"Jack's out of town, Mark. What is it?"

"I just got word that the batch control panel on number Three West Seven unit was vandalized."

"Vandalized? How bad is it?"

"It looks like someone took a sledgehammer to it."

Caroline jumped to her feet. "Dear Lord. Do we know who did it?"

"No, ma'am. It happened either late last night or early this morning."

"Did anyone from the night crew see anything?"

"I just left the guard station, and he said there was a note from the night guard that a couple of guys stumbled up to the front gate last night and tried to get in. He had to call in some of the men to help run them off. Even with the extra guys, it took a while to get rid of them."

"Those men could have been sent to distract him. Have your men check the surrounding fences to see if they were cut."

"Yes, ma'am. I'll get every inch of our fencing checked."

"Have you notified the plant manager?"

"No, ma'am. When I saw what happened, I came here to report it."

"You get our fences inspected. I'll call the plant manager, and I will inform Jack when he's out of the meeting with the governor."

"Yes, ma'am." He rushed out the door.

Caroline picked up her phone and dialed the plant manager's office. "David, I need you to check all the panels on the lot. The number Three West Seven panel was vandalized last night."

She hung up the phone, closed her eyes, and sat in her chair. *This is the last thing we need right now,* she thought. *Without that unit, our production level is cut by a third.*

It was late evening when Caroline looked up and saw her husband walk in. "Can it be repaired?" she asked.

"Too soon to tell. The technician is working on it. Until it's fixed, that plant section is down."

"I know. What are we going to do?"

"Replacing the entire panel may be more cost-effective than waiting for it to be repaired."

"Jack." She sighed. "That would cost thousands. I've spent all day cutting every expenditure I could to cover the bill on our expansion."

"Sweetheart, this is the proverbial chicken or egg dilemma." Jack sat on the edge of her desk. "We've got to get that section up and running as quickly as possible."

"True, except either outcome will cost us more than we can handle now." She leaned back in her chair and shook her head. "When will the technician have an answer?"

"He said he should know by morning." Jack went to her and lifted her chin. "Whatever it is, we'll deal with it, honey."

She touched his face. "I know, but the timing is horrible. We need this plant running to full capacity before submitting our bid to the Levee Board."

"Let me worry about the plant. You do your magic and keep the bills paid."

"I'm afraid I'm almost out of fairy dust."

"You're as brilliant as you are beautiful, Caroline. You'll figure it out."

"I couldn't do this without you."

"Oh, I know." Jack kissed her on the forehead. "But it's nice to hear you say it."

She gave him a little shove. "Go fix that panel."

"And you get to work winning that contract. Remember what Papa said."

"How could I forget? Making concrete takes sand, money, and fortitude. Run out of one of the three, and you're out of business."

"Right, and fortitude is your middle name," Jack said with a grin.

*   *   *

Arizona

Rob opened the door to their apartment, breathing heavily and soaked with sweat.

"How many rounds did you do this time?" Wanda asked as she put Sarah in her playpen.

"Two."

"Two times around the whole complex?"

"Yes," he said between gasps. "I need something to drink."

Wanda followed him into the kitchen. "Stand back. I'll get you some water. I don't want you touching anything except a glass."

Rob gulped down the whole glass of water and handed it to her to refill. "I sure wish this place had a working swimming pool."

"I'm sure you do. Swimming has always been your stress relief."

"Swimming was much more than that. It cleared my head from all the clutter of memories," he said. "At least momentarily."

"I wish I could. I still have nightmares of us being found again."

"Apparently, you aren't the only one."

"What are you talking about?"

"As I circled the complex, I noticed twice the number of guards than I've seen before."

Wanda pressed her hand to her chest. "Do you think they know we're here?"

Rob took hold of her shoulders and looked into her troubled eyes. "Wanda, if there was a problem, Tom would have told us." The words were barely out of his mouth when the phone rang. He looked at Wanda again before answering it.

"I'm in Phoenix, Kid. I'll be there in about an hour."

"Has something happened?"

"We'll discuss it when I arrive." The call ended.

Wanda went to Rob as he hung up the phone. "Was that Tom?"

"He's on his way here from the airport. Why don't you make some iced tea while I jump into the shower? It's hot out there." He saw her chewing her bottom lip and knew she was worried. "Sweetheart, if there was a problem, Tom would have told us. I'm sure we're fine."

She exhaled. "All right. I'll make tea, but I'm packing some of our things in case."

He kissed her on the forehead and went to shower. After he dressed, he took Sarah from her playpen just as Wanda answered the phone in the kitchen.

"Thank you," Wanda said as Rob came up to her. "That was the gate guard. Tom's on his way in." She took Sarah and followed him to the door.

As they waited, Rob noticed her chewing her lip again. "If you don't stop, you won't have lips left to kiss."

A brief smile crossed her lips just as they heard a knock.

"It's good to see you, Tom. Come in."

Tom removed his hat. "Nice to see you, Wanda. How's this little lady?"

"Do they know we're here?" Wanda blurted out. "Rob saw a lot more guards around the post."

Tom glanced from her to Rob, then back to Wanda. "Everything is fine, Wanda. I requested more security so you would feel safer."

"You would tell us if we weren't, wouldn't you?"

"Of course I would." Tom reached over and tickled Sarah on the cheek. "I would never let anyone near her or either of you."

Sarah reached for Tom, and he took her willingly.

"I brought you something, little lady." Tom reached into his pocket and presented Sarah with a toy giraffe. She took it and hugged it to her body.

"That's so sweet of you." Wanda paused a moment. "I'm sorry for attacking you."

"I understand completely. May I borrow your husband for a while?"

"Of course you can. It's time I put this little girl down for a nap." Wanda took Sarah and went into the other room.

"Let's go to the training area, Kid."

The men walked across the complex to the row of buildings where the mock office was used for training and sat in chairs facing one another.

"Sorry about that, Tom. I shouldn't have told Wanda about the extra guards."

"Don't worry about it. Wanda has every right to be concerned."

"Are you here because of the information you showed me on your last visit?"

"I am. I did more digging and found nothing to connect the murders to Pascal or the drug organization, so I decided to turn my focus to the Hispanic men and see if I could find out who they were."

"How? The FBI has no jurisdiction in Mexico."

"We don't, but I know someone who does. I contacted this person two weeks ago and just got word he thinks he has something. He wants us to come and check it out."

"Tom, I can't go to Mexico. Someone from the organization will recognize me."

"I won't let that happen."

"You can't guarantee that, and I'm not leaving my family."

"I need you, Kid. That's the reason I increased the number of guards."

"I appreciate that, but this is a large compound. There's no way to guard every inch of this place."

"That's why I'm also bringing in four of the best agents I've worked with to stay with your family until we return."

"If the Bureau finds out, we will be kicked out of the program."

"They aren't going to know. These are retired agents. They won't say a word. Kid, I promise you. Your family will be in good hands."

"We were in good hands at the safe house when we were found, and those agents were killed."

"Yes, but there wasn't this level of protection. I can assure you, Kid. No one is getting near your family."

"What happens to us if the Bureau discovers I've left the country?"

"Listen, I understand your concern. And I just saw how afraid Wanda is of being found. But the only way to ensure she and your baby are safe is to end this organization and imprison everyone involved. I'm convinced the only way that will happen is with your help. When it does, you won't need the FBI's protection, and you can give Sarah and Wanda a normal life."

Rob sat looking at him for a time before he answered. "What do you need me to do?"

"You know more about these people and their business methods than anyone. I want you with me if we see or hear anything that connects these murders to the organization. Once we're done, I'll get you home before the Bureau knows we're gone."

"And if we're discovered, what happens to my family?"

"I'll make sure they're taken care of. Nothing's going to happen."

Rob paused, then nodded. "How long before we go?"

Tom checked his watch. "Three hours."

"Three hours?"

"Timing is crucial."

"I need to talk to Wanda about this."

"Then I suggest you get to it. I'll stay here and wait for my men."

Rob was deep in thought as he walked home from the training complex. He desperately wanted to end this. But even though he knew this was the safest place his family could be, the thought of leaving Wanda and Sarah terrified him.

When he got to his door, he took a deep breath and entered his apartment. He found Wanda, sat her down, and told her the reason for Tom's visit.

"Rob, this is insane. What if someone recognizes you? Is Tom trying to get you killed?"

"He assures me that won't happen."

"What about Sarah and me?"

"He's bringing in four agents whose sole job is to keep you and Sarah safe while I'm away."

Wanda took their daughter from her playpen and started to pace. Rob gave her time to process the information and didn't speak. After several minutes, she stopped and looked at him.

"Was this the reason for all that training you did?"

"I wanted to be able to protect us if we were found."

"Does he expect you will use it on this trip?"

"Probably not. Tom needs my knowledge of the organization to help him solve a case. I'm only there to observe."

"Just observe?"

"That's what he said."

"If observing helps end this madness, then I guess I agree. I don't want Sarah to spend all of her life behind these fences."

Rob went to her and wrapped his arms around her and their daughter. "Neither do I, sweetheart. This isn't the life I want for either of you. Sarah will need friends her age to play with. Not FBI agents. That's why I'm willing to go."

"You're right. I love you, Rob."

He kissed her. "And I love you."

"When do you leave?"

"In less than three hours."

She stood looking at him, then forced her lips into a smile. "Then we'd better get you packed."

A few hours later, Rob was putting Sarah down for a nap when Wanda entered the room.

"Tom's waiting for you at the door."

Rob kissed Sarah's cheek, then took Wanda in his arms and held her. "This may be the last kiss I get for a while."

"Then make it a good one."

He kissed her hard and long until Tom called out from the living room, "Kid, we have a plane to catch."

Rob released Wanda, and she followed him to the door.

"You bring him back in one piece, Tom Neal. Our baby needs her father."

"I'll take good care of him, Wanda. Come on, Kid, we can't miss this flight."

CHAPTER FIVE

Mexico

Sweat rolled down Rob's chest as he tried to remain still under a plastic drape in a tiny hair salon on the outskirts of Monterrey, Mexico. The small oscillating fan in the corner of the room did little to stir the hot air around the three people cramped inside.

"Ouch. You didn't tell me this was painful."

Tom chuckled. "Sit still, and she won't yank your ear."

Rob looked at the woman's reflection in the mirror. "*Perdón, senōra.*"

Tom got up and locked eyes with Rob in the mirror. "I didn't know you spoke Spanish."

"I didn't until Steve challenged me to learn a language during training. Considering who's after me, I thought Spanish was a good language to learn."

"Great thinking. We'll need it down here."

Rob's eyes shifted to the woman smearing color on his hair. "She knows what I look like. Are you sure we can trust her?"

"Positive. Leticia and I go way back. Now sit still and let her finish. We have a long drive ahead of us."

After another hour, Rob marveled at the results. "Damn. She does good work. I almost don't recognize myself. When this is over, I may keep the mustache."

"Your wife may have a say about that." Tom handed the woman a handful of pesos. "Time to go. We've been here long enough."

Rob unfolded his long legs from the chair and towered over Leticia as she placed a tube of mustache glue in his hand. Then he and Tom left the shop, got into the car Tom had rented using fake credentials, and drove out of Monterrey.

They arrived at a small fishing village on the edge of Tampico after midnight and parked near a darkened dwelling.

Rob scanned the area. "This place looks deserted."

"That's why it was chosen. Keep your eyes and ears open and your mouth shut. Understand?"

"Got it. Who are we meeting?"

"A longtime friend with the CIA." Tom took a large envelope from under his seat and handed it to Rob. "Hang on to this." He took his .357 from its holster, checked it, and carefully scanned the perimeter.

"I thought you said he was a friend."

"He is. But in this job, expecting trouble is the only way to stay alive." Tom holstered the gun and reached for the door handle. "Keep behind me, and no talking."

"Got it." Rob's eyes darted back and forth as they exited the car and approached the dwelling. As they neared the door, Tom motioned for him to step aside. He drew his gun and eased the door open. The room was dark and still, and Tom motioned for Rob to follow and went inside.

Suddenly, a hissing noise sounded, and a match flared beside a kerosene lamp. The light spread and revealed a portion of the room.

Tom holstered his weapon when he saw who blew out the match.

"It's been a while," the man said.

"It has. Good to see you, Sam."

"You too."

"Where's your guy?"

Sam motioned to someone in the shadows, and a short, pudgy Mexican man in his early twenties appeared.

"This here is Frank Sinatra Antonio Suárez. We call him Frankie." Sam chuckled. "Frankie's mama loved Ol' Blue Eyes."

"Does he speak English?"

"*Sí, señor,* I do."

Tom took the envelope from Rob. "I need you to look at these drawings and tell me if you recognize anyone. Can you do that, Frankie?"

"*Sí.*"

Tom took out three drawings and spread them on the table next to the lamp.

Frankie hovered over them for a moment then shook his head.

Tom lay three more on top of the first and waited. Frankie shook his head again. Tom picked up all the images and handed them to Rob before placing the next three on the table. He had barely placed the first one down when Frankie gasped and snatched it from the table.

"Please, señor, where is he?"

"Who is he, Frankie?"

"My cousin, Ramiro García Montez."

"What happened to your cousin?"

"Ramiro and his whole family were taken."

"Who took them, Frankie?" There was no response. Tom stepped closer. "You know who they are, don't you, Frankie? I can see it in your face. Tell me what happened."

"That night, *mi tía*, my aunt, ran to our house screaming and crying. She said men broke in and dragged him, his wife, and his daughters out of their home and took them away. She said she heard them shouting at Ramiro to stop fighting, or they would kill his family."

"Why wasn't your aunt taken?"

"They did not know she was there. She was in the *baño* and hid until they were gone."

"So, she didn't get a look at the men?"

Frankie dropped his head. "She didn't have to. Everyone knows who they are. They work for *jefe de los . . .*" His voice trailed off.

"What?"

"Drug bosses," Rob whispered. "Ask him how many bosses?"

Tom turned. "Keep quiet." He turned to Frankie and repeated the question. "How many bosses?"

Frankie peered past Tom to see who was in the shadows before he responded. "For a time, there were three. The big boss was named Carlos Rojas. Some say he is dead, but no one knows for sure. Then *La Muerte* took over, and now everyone is more afraid. The other one, we never see."

"La Muerte?" Tom asked.

"It means 'death,'" Sam replied.

Rob stepped forward and whispered, "It's them."

"Step back and keep quiet," Tom ordered, and Rob complied.

Tom placed the remaining images on the table. "Did that also happen to these men?"

"This one lived in the village of Manzanillo and was a friend of my friend."

"What happened to him?"

"*Desaparecidos.* Him and his family."

"All are gone," Sam explained.

Frankie went through the rest of the drawings. "I do not know these men."

"Did your cousin or the other man work for the drug lords?"

Frankie shook his head. "My cousin owned a small market near our homes. He sold bread, milk, and eggs. He never sells drugs. The other man was an ordinary worker like me. They work hard to care for their families."

Tom picked up the sketch of Frankie's cousin and put it in his hand. "You can give this to his mother. Tell her not to tell anyone where it came from. Understand, Frankie?"

"*Gracias,* señor. No one will know." Frankie studied the image for a moment. "Will we ever see him again?"

"I'm sorry, Frankie. He's not coming back."

Frankie dropped his head. "At least now we know."

Tom gathered the rest of the drawings and handed them to Rob.

Sam placed his hand on Frankie's shoulder. "Stay here while I talk with them. When I'm done, I'll take you home."

Frankie nodded, and the others left the hut.

Sam lit a cigarette as soon as they were outside. "Well, did that tell you anything?" he asked after blowing out a stream of smoke.

"It confirms a lot," Tom replied. "Now we know which drug organization took them and their families, and that they had no connection to the organization."

"What happened to those men?" Sam asked.

"They were all professionally executed in and around New Orleans."

"How did they get over there?"

"That's what we are trying to find out," Tom said.

"How are you going to do that?"

"Hopefully by finding someone who can identify the other men in the sketches."

"I would hold off on that if I were you. If the organization is involved, they don't like outsiders meddling in their business."

Tom nodded. "Sam, you've been working this circuit for years. How would you smuggle a group of hostages into the States if money wasn't an object?"

"How many are we talking about?"

"As many as four or five at a time."

The glow of Sam's cigarette danced on his lip as he spoke. "Any plane large enough to carry that many men and guards couldn't land just anywhere. They could truck them in if time weren't an issue, but that would mean dealing with border patrols." Sam paused. "You said New Orleans. That means they could have crossed the Gulf of Mexico by boat. But it would take a good-sized craft to carry that many men plus guards, and they would have to get past the Coast Guard patrols if they did."

Rob stepped out from behind Tom. "What if they were on a ship?"

Sam looked past Tom. "Tom, who is this guy?"

"He's not important. What about a ship?"

Sam kept his eyes on Rob for a time before responding. "Sure. You could easily make that happen down here for a price. Hell, the port of Heroica, Veracruz, has container ships arriving and departing all the time."

"Any chance you can check that out?" Tom asked.

Sam nodded. "Give me a little time, and I'll see what I can dig up." He took one more puff of his cigarette and then flicked it away. "Where can I find you?"

"Not sure. We are always on the move."

"That's good. Call me in a few days, and I'll tell you what I find."

"Will do."

Sam stepped closer to Tom. "That FBI badge is worthless down here. There's really nothing you can do about the organization taking those men and their families."

"Let's just say it's because of Scott."

Sam paused a moment, then nodded. "Yeah. I kind of figured that. Maybe it's time for you to let that go before it gets you killed."

Tom took a deep breath. "I can't. And like before, we have to keep this between us."

"As always. Just don't blow my cover."

"Thanks for your help, Sam. I'll call you in a few days."

"You got it, old friend. Just remember to keep your head down out here. Word gets out that you're Feds, you're dead." He strolled back into the hut without looking back.

"Let's go, Kid," Tom said. "It's a long drive back."

CHAPTER SIX

Mexico

Tom glanced at Rob in the passenger seat as he drove on the dark road that was miles from Santa Catarina.

"Where did the suggestion of the ship come from?" he asked.

"When Sam mentioned the Gulf of Mexico, it reminded me of something I did for Carlos Rojas. He insisted I get him access to docks along the Gulf coastline."

"Did you?"

Rob nodded. "I went to Galveston to find out who was in charge, but no one would talk to me. Later, I discovered why. Turns out most of the docks and shipping in and out of the Gulf Coast is under the control of the New Orleans Mafia."

"You mean Marcel Pascal. He runs his own drug business in Louisiana. I'm sure he would never agree to working with Rojas, though."

"Rojas never intended to compete with Pascal. It was only to gain a shorter, more secure route to transport his drugs into the States and supply customers outside Pascal's territory."

"Did you get access to the docks?"

"I couldn't get past Pascal's assistant. But Rojas wouldn't take that for an answer and came up with an offer he said Pascal couldn't refuse. To my surprise, it worked."

"I can't see Pascal changing his mind, no matter how much he was paid."

"Money was a factor, but the selling point was his offer of favors."

Tom glanced at Rob. "Favors? What kind of favors?"

"The kind that would put Pascal in prison for the rest of his life if they were traced back to him."

The words were barely out of Rob's mouth when Tom skidded to a stop on the empty road.

"That's it. The organization is kidnapping innocent people and using them to kill for the mob."

Rob closed his eyes and dropped his head. "I know. I came to that conclusion back at the hut." He raised his head and shook it. "Tom, I arranged it. All those people are dead because of me."

"You were forced into that situation, Kid. Rojas was going to kill your wife."

"But if we don't stop them, this will happen again and again."

"That's why we're here. When did that meeting about the dock access take place?"

"I wasn't included in any dealings with Pascal after he agreed to the first meeting. But I know it happened shortly before the FBI raided my office."

"Good. That gives me an approximate timeline."

"Now I have a question for you. How did you know I was laundering Rojas's drug money? I was extremely careful to keep everything hidden."

"Kid, nothing ever stays hidden. I was investigating the Kennedy assassination in Dallas when your name came up for two reasons. First was your client's involvement in the assassination, and second, as a person of interest in the drug organization investigation. Because of my son's death, Hoover wouldn't allow me near the case, but that didn't stop me from doing my own research on you."

"And what did you find?"

"You were squeaky clean until you appeared on that watch list. I had a hunch. If you were involved, there had to be a reason behind it, so I paid you a visit. My gut said I was right after talking with you and meeting your wife."

"I had to. There was no way out."

"I know, but now is your chance to help me put an end to this organization for good."

"I'm ready. Just tell me how?"

"We start turning over rocks and see what crawls out."

"Sam was right, Tom. You have no jurisdiction down here. What are you going to do if we find Martínez?"

"That's why I brought Sam into this. He has CIA resources behind him."

"But if Sam captures Martínez, won't you lose control of him to the CIA?"

"Yes, and that's a problem. I want the FBI to handle him."

"Could you get Martínez back if we prove he was killing for Pascal?"

"Proving anything concerning Pascal will be a problem. He has judges, government officials, and police in his pocket. So far, it's been impossible to prosecute him."

"Then how do we stop this?"

"I'll worry about pinning these murders on Pascal after we end the organization."

Rob shifted in his seat. "I'm sorry about what happened to Scott. No parent should ever have to go through that."

Tom hesitated a moment, inhaled deeply, and pulled back on the road. Nothing more was said for the rest of the trip.

Two days later, Rob paced restlessly in his hotel room in a town called Villa Sol. When he'd had all he could stand of the silence, he went down the hall to Tom's door and knocked. Nothing happened, and Rob rapped against the door again. He was turning to leave when it opened.

"I thought you were out."

"I was on the phone. Come in."

"Has something happened?" Rob asked as he stepped into Tom's room.

"Yes and no," Tom said, closing the door. "I was on the phone with Sam. Frankie's aunt is too frightened to meet with us."

"So, what do we do now?"

"We're moving to San Luis Potosi. It's Sam's base of operations, and it will be easier for us to communicate."

"Did he have any information on the ship idea?"

"Not yet. He expects to have something for us tomorrow."

"Shouldn't we at least try to show the sketches to people here? Maybe some of those men were from this area."

"Too risky. According to Sam, Villa Sol is overrun with Martínez's people. Get your things. We need to get out of here as quickly as possible."

Rob raced to his room, gathered his belongings, and met Tom coming out of his room.

"The sooner we're out of here, the better," Tom said, handing Rob the car keys and the envelope full of sketches. "Take this and my suitcase, and I will meet you at the car after I settle our bill."

Rob tucked the manila envelope under his arm and took their suitcases to the car. He was sliding into the passenger's seat just as Tom exited the hotel.

Once Villa Sol was far behind them, Rob picked up the envelope near his feet. "From what you told me about the murders, these men were operating alone when they attacked their victims."

"That's right."

"So why didn't they run instead of doing the killings?"

"What drove you to launder the organization's money?"

"They were going to hurt Wanda and others I was close to."

"Exactly. Like you, those men were willing to do the unthinkable to protect their families."

"Even though I did what I did, my best friend died."

Tom nodded and his tone softened. "For the first time in my career, I'm going against the Bureau's orders. I need to make certain Martínez and his organization pay for killing my son. It's time to stop them, Kid, even if it means breaking the rules."

The following day, Rob and Tom were sitting at a table in an outdoor cantina near their hotel when a boy ran up and handed Tom a note.

"For me?" Tom asked.

"Sí, señor."

Tom took a few coins from his pocket and gave them to the boy, who promptly ran away. Tom opened the note.

"Who's it from?"

"Sam."

"How the heck did he know we were here?"

"Good question." He pocketed the note. "Let's go. Sam wants to meet."

They drove to a remote cluster of abandoned buildings outside of town. Tom stopped before getting too close and scanned the area.

"Kid, it's time for a lesson. Look out there and tell me what you see."

Rob took a moment to check the area. "I see nothing but dirt and deserted buildings."

"Look closer."

Rob leaned forward. "Wait, I just saw a puff of smoke from a doorway."

"That's right." Neal took his .357 from its holster.

"What are you going to do?"

"Wait for them to make the first move."

Both men's eyes were glued to the doorway for several minutes before they saw Sam step from the shadows.

Tom holstered his gun and drove up to the buildings.

"I see you got my message," Sam said as they exited the vehicle.

"Who was that boy, and how did he know where to find us?"

Sam's lips curled up. "You know how it is. You make friends when you're in the field."

"And does this friend have a son?" Tom asked.

"As it turns out, she does."

Tom shook his head. "After three failed marriages, I would have thought you would have learned your lesson, Sam."

Sam chuckled. "Easy for you to say. You had the perfect wife."

"So how did the boy know where to find us?"

"My friend and her son live here, so I do my best to keep tabs on every stranger that comes to town."

"Your note said you have news."

Sam pointed to Rob. "Turns out your boy there was right. My

people tell me a couple of large shipping containers are on the dock with guards stationed around them."

"Do you think that's how the men are being transported?" Rob asked.

"I doubt it. I went there myself to check it out. There was no ventilation system on those containers. If anyone was in there, they wouldn't survive the heat. I'm guessing they contain drugs or some other contraband."

"If it's drugs," Tom asked, "any idea who they belong to?"

"It could be any number of dealers around here."

"Is there a way to find out where the containers are being shipped?"

"Not yet. I got their identification numbers, though, so once the containers are loaded, we'll have the vessel's name and know where they're headed."

"Let me know when you have that information, and I'll have it tracked when we return to the States."

Sam dropped the cigarette butt and ground it into the dirt with his boot. "I'll let you know." He reached into his shirt pocket and pulled out an empty cigarette package.

"Damn. I'm out. Can't do this job without my smokes. I'll be in touch."

"Thanks, Sam. I owe you."

"Yeah, and one day, I'm going to collect. Stay in San Luis Potosi. As soon as I know something, I'll find you." Sam disappeared behind the abandoned building.

Rob and Tom got into their car just as Sam's car barreled out from behind the building, passed them, and headed towards town.

Rob realized Tom hadn't started the engine. "What are we waiting for?"

"We need to let Sam get a few miles down the road before we go. One vehicle on a deserted road doesn't get much attention. Two traveling close together will."

"I was thinking about those containers. Even if we find out they are transporting drugs, we still don't know how they are getting those men into the country."

Tom started the engine. "True, or who actually owns the cargo." He turned the car around and drove slowly down the road. "Remember, Kid. One rock at a time."

Back in his room at the hotel, Rob spent hours thinking about Wanda and Sarah. Were they all right, and had the Bureau discovered he was missing? All these questions and more tormented him. He desperately wanted to hear Wanda's voice, but he knew that would be disastrous if their calls were monitored. Finally, he had all he could stand and went to Tom's door and knocked. Moments later, the door opened.

"Can I come in? The silence is getting to me."

"Of course. I was just reviewing my notes to see if I missed anything."

"Need any help?"

"I prefer to do this myself. Take a seat."

"No thanks." Rob paced for a moment, then stopped. "How much longer will we stay in Mexico?"

Tom looked up. "That depends on what Sam finds out at the docks. Why?"

"I'm just concerned for my family."

"I'm sure they're well."

"How do we know? We move around so much, no one knows where we are."

"It's safer for them and for us if no one knows. Relax, Kid. I'm sure your family is fine."

"I hope you're right." Rob went to the window, pulled back the thin curtains, and looked at the street. "Tom, something is happening! People are grabbing their children and running into buildings."

Tom rushed to the window just as two Jeeps slid to a stop in the middle of the street. Men with rifles jumped out and took positions across the street as others ran towards the hotel entrance.

"They're coming for us! Grab our paperwork."

Rob gathered papers and stuffed them into his shirt. Tom took a .357 Magnum revolver and several clips from a dresser and met Rob at the door.

"You have the papers?" he asked as he loaded the revolver.

"Got them."

Tom shoved the revolver in his hand. "Take this and do exactly as I say."

They exited the room and raced down the hall to the staircase. Tom raised his hand when he heard shouting from the lower level.

Rob tapped him on the shoulder, pointed to a window at the end of the hall, then rushed to open it. There was a two-story drop to a brick courtyard. The only way down was a rusty water pipe attached to the side of the building.

"Kid, you go, then cover me as I come down."

Rob swung a leg over the windowsill and looked back at Tom. "It may not hold us."

"Go. We're done for sure if we stay."

They heard footsteps and voices coming from the staircase. "Go!" Tom said.

Rob made his way down the pipe using the old brick on the side of the building as footholds. When he reached the bottom, he pulled the revolver from his belt and covered Tom as he lowered the windowpane and started to descend the pipe. Someone whistled behind him, and Rob spun around to find Sam motioning to him from the corner of the next building. He looked back just as Tom's feet hit the courtyard.

"Sam's here," Rob said, but before Tom could respond, glass shattered overhead, and the muzzle of a gun appeared through the broken window.

"Go, go, go!" Tom yelled. A spray of bullets peppered the ground and the walls of the surrounding buildings, following them as they ran after Sam.

Sam led them through cluttered alleyways and between buildings until they reached his truck.

"Kid, get in the cab!" Tom yelled.

Rob jumped in and turned to see Tom leap into the truck's bed holding his gun. He clutched the tailgate with his free hand as Sam sped between buildings and houses, swerving to avoid people and obstacles in his path.

Rob caught sight of one of the Jeeps several blocks back. "Sam, they're closing in!"

"Hold on!" Sam made one sharp turn, then another. He zigzagged through several streets before stopping in front of an abandoned building with a ragged canvas tarp draped over the front of it.

"Get out and pull back the tarp," Sam ordered.

Rob jumped out, grabbed the canvas, and tugged it open so Sam could pull in. He dragged the cloth down to conceal the truck and immediately heard the sound of a vehicle engine. He peered through a hole in the canvas and raised his hand to signal Sam and Tom to remain silent as a Jeep stopped in the middle of the road. The men in the vehicle stood with rifles raised, scanning the street. A moment later, one of the men motioned to the driver to move ahead, and they picked up speed and disappeared down the road.

Rob released the breath he was holding and whispered loudly. "I think we lost them."

"Not for long," Sam replied.

"Lucky you found this place," Tom said, climbing out of the truck bed.

"I've had to use it before." Sam glanced at him and started chuckling. "You surprised me, old man. I thought you were long past being able to shimmy down a drainpipe like that."

"I can do many things when bullets are flying. How did you know we were in trouble?"

"I was going into town to get my cigarettes when those Jeeps ran me off the road. I saw the guns and knew they were coming for you, so I turned around and headed to your hotel. I hid my truck and went through the alleys to get to your hotel."

"Thanks, man. This could have gone the other way if you hadn't."

"How did they find us?" Rob asked.

"The two of you stick out like a cornstalk in a rice field. The only way to ensure you stay alive is to get you out of Mexico."

"You're right," Tom said. "But how?"

"There's a little village called Las Golondrinas," Sam said. "We'll stop there so I can arrange a small plane to pick you up. There's a place about fifty kilometers from here that's flat and cleared enough for it to land. Just don't tell your friends at the Bureau about it."

"Deal. Let's go."

After Sam made his call, they drove for over an hour before Sam pulled off the road and drove through rough terrain to a remote area of flat land. The three men exited the truck as a small aircraft appeared overhead, and watched as it landed.

"Thanks, Sam. That was a close one," Tom said, extending his hand.

Sam shook it. "You've got to stop showing up here like this. We're getting a little too old to be running from bullets."

"You could be right." Tom chuckled. "I never thought your cigarette habit would save my life."

Sam let go of his hand and punched him. "Yeah, that reminds me. I still ain't got my smokes. Now, get out of here before those dudes find us."

"Thank you, Sam," Rob said.

"Take care of him, boy."

"I'll try."

"Let me know where those containers are going," Tom said as he and Rob got to the plane.

"You got it."

Rob looked down after they took off and saw Sam's truck driving away. He was grateful to be going home.

CHAPTER SEVEN

New Orleans

The applause ended, and Marcel Pascal leaned over to take his wife's hand as the lights brightened in their theater box. "Happy birthday, my dear. I hope you are enjoying the performance."

Camille Pascal kissed her husband's cheek. "It's wonderful! This was the perfect gift."

"You look just as lovely tonight as you did the day we met."

She shook her head. "Marcel, that was over forty years ago. I've had three beautiful daughters and enjoyed far too many bread pudding dishes from Commander's Palace since then."

Marcel patted her hand. "I see clearly, Camille. To me, you'll always be that dark-haired beauty."

Their moment ended when Jean-Claude stepped into the box.

"Sir. Governor Thompson is waiting in the hallway."

Pascal kissed his wife's hand. "I won't be long." He got to his feet and gave his assistant a look from his sparkling patent leather shoes to the top of his head.

"Nice suit, Jean-Claude."

The man's face lit up, and he drew his shoulders back as he stroked the lapel of his jacket.

"It's new. Thank you for noticing."

Camille reached over and took the young man's hand. "You look dashing, Jean-Claude."

"Thank you, Madame. A compliment from you is the highest form of praise."

"Stop flirting with my wife, Jean-Claude, and let's get this over with." Pascal entered the private hallway and found the governor waiting. "What's so important you must interrupt my evening, Parker?"

The governor flashed his best politician smile. "I'll be brief, Marcel, but first, congratulations on solving your Coastal Steel issue. I saw the news of the untimely passing of its chairman."

"He refused to pay tariffs on the Lake Pontchartrain Causeway contract. The new chairman is much more accepting. But that's old news, Parker. Why are you here?"

The governor looked up and down the hallway to ensure privacy before answering. "My life is in absolute turmoil, Marcel. My reputation is under attack, and that makes it impossible for me to serve the fine people of Louisiana."

Pascal shook his head. "Are you telling me you drove from Baton Rouge to New Orleans to ask me to clean up another of your petty messes?"

"This is far from petty, Marcel. I'm being forced to spend all my time defending my good name because of a minor indiscretion. People are calling me weak and a womanizer."

"Damn it, Parker, they're right! You wouldn't have these problems if you stopped bedding every brown-eyed, twenty-year-old female in Louisiana. Go home to your wife and deal with this yourself."

"I've tried, and nothing has worked." Parker leaned in. "I was hoping you could handle my little problem like you did the steel company chairman."

"You're not worth the hassle, Parker." Pascal looked past the governor to his assistant. "Jean-Claude, see the governor out."

The younger man stepped from the shadows. "This way, Governor."

"Marcel, please. I need your help."

Jean-Claude stepped in front of Parker. "After you, Governor."

*   *   *

Arizona

It was days before little Sarah would go near her daddy. The mustache was gone, but the dark hair and eyebrows confused her.

"I'll be so glad when this hair color grows off. It feels like being punched in the gut when Sarah pulls away," Rob told Wanda.

"She isn't the only one. It's almost like I'm sleeping with a stranger."

"It doesn't seem to bother you when we turn off the lights," he said, twitching his eyebrows up and down. He saw her cheeks blush red.

"I'm just glad you're home," Wanda said. She set her laundry basket on the kitchen table and began folding diapers. "You haven't said much about your trip. I realize Tom wants all this kept secret, but I'm part of this too."

"I know, but from what we hear was happening to families in Mexico, I'm not sure you want to know."

"You're probably right. I could barely sleep as it was, worrying about you. I was so afraid someone would recognize you down there."

Rob went to her and took her in his arms. "I'll do whatever it takes to keep them away from us, sweetheart."

"I know, but that doesn't keep me from worrying." The words were barely out of her mouth when the phone rang.

Rob released her and went to answer.

"What is it?" Wanda asked.

"The gate guard. Tom is coming in."

"I'll fold these in the bedroom and save him the trouble of asking me to leave."

As Wanda took Sarah from the playpen, Rob carried the laundry basket into the bedroom.

"I'll put Sarah down for a nap so you and Tom can talk."

Rob went outside to wait for Tom's car. As it came to a stop, he realized Steve was sitting in the passenger seat.

"Well, this is a surprise!" Rob said as Steve exited the car. "I thought I would never see you again."

"I changed my mind," Steve said, giving him a friendly punch.

"What's in the briefcase?"

"You'll see when we sit down."

Tom wiped the sweat from his forehead. "Let's go in. There's no sense standing out here in the heat."

They entered the kitchen, and Rob saw that Wanda had left a pitcher of iced tea on the counter.

"Take a seat," Rob said, bringing glasses to the table. He noticed Steve looking at him as he poured the tea.

"So, what's up with the new look?" Steve asked, but no one answered. "What's going on, guys? I can tell from the silence you've been up to something."

"Steve, you're here because you wanted The Kid's help. I suggest we get started with that."

After a short pause, Steve opened his briefcase, took a map and legal pad out of the case, and placed them on the table.

"Rob," he asked, "what do you know about the drug organization and Colombia?"

Rob glanced at Tom, then back to Steve. "I'm confused. I thought you said you weren't allowed to work on the organization's task force because of your friendship with Scott?"

"I'm not, but guys in my division are. I thought I could run a few things by you to see if you know anything I could pass along to them."

"Won't they question how you got the information?"

"I'll find a way around that. Do you want to help me or not?"

Rob and Tom exchanged glances again before Rob answered. "Sure. At least half of the product came from Colombia when I was with the organization."

Steve unfolded the map and spread it across the table. "Do you know how it was transported?"

"I don't. That process didn't involve me. Why are you so interested? Colombia is out of the FBI's jurisdiction."

"We have ways of tracking it if it's transported by air or ships."

Rob glanced at Tom again, and Tom gave him a nod. "I can't tell you that, but I know who was in charge. What do you know about Diego Fernando Martínez?"

"I know he's now the leader of the organization and a ruthless killer."

"All that is true, but do you know his background?"

"I don't. That's why I'm asking you."

"Martínez's family has owned coffee plantations all over Colombia for generations. That's why Rojas put him in charge of the growth and distribution of the product. After Rojas's death, Martínez took control of the organization, so I'm not sure he's still controlling growth and distribution. And from what we've heard, Martínez has become even more deranged than Rojas."

Steve looked up from his notes. "What do you mean by 'what we heard?'"

Tom raised a hand to stop him. "Stick to the questions we discussed, Steve, or we're leaving."

Steve paused a moment, then said, "What can you tell me about the other partner in the organization? The one who manufactures the drugs? We call him 'the chemist.'"

"His name is Juan Alejandro Varo," Rob said. "He really is a chemist. He creates the formulas and trains the people overseeing the cook houses."

"Is he as ruthless as Martínez?" Steve asked.

"Not the Alejandro I knew," Rob said, shaking his head. "He couldn't stand the sight of blood. In fact, he said it made him physically sick, which is ironic because his father and brother are renowned neurosurgeons in the capital. But you should know all this, Steve. I gave the Bureau all of this information during my debriefings."

"I'm sure you did, but your records are shielded from all but the highest-ranking department heads. I'm asking because three Academy classmate friends were gunned down near Laredo last week. That makes four people I've lost to this organization. It's personal, Rob. I need to help."

"I understand."

Steve pushed his notepad aside. "Killing is how this organization operates. How did you manage to get out alive?"

"He outsmarted them," Tom responded.

"I think it's time we do the same. Rob, is it possible any of the accounts or businesses you created are still in use?"

Rob glanced at Tom before responding. "I guess that's possible. I set up over sixty accounts nationwide, and five times the businesses, to channel the drug money."

"I know it's a long shot, but Martínez might have kept a few of the less obvious ones open. If he did, maybe we can track the money."

Tom shook his head. "Steve, The Kid has provided us with information on all the accounts and businesses."

"I'm sure he did, but there were so many he could have forgotten some of them."

"Not with his memory." Tom glanced at his watch. "If that's all, I think it's time for us to get to the airport."

Steve leaned back in his chair. "Something's going on here. It's as obvious as that dyed hair on Rob's head."

Tom started folding the map. "Your questions were answered, Steve. I see no reason to rehash information he's already given the Bureau."

"My friends are dying, Tom. Forgive me for being overzealous."

Tom slid the car keys across the table. "Go start the car. I'll be out in a minute."

Steve repacked his case, took the key, and got up from the table. "It was good to see you, Rob."

"You too, Steve."

Nothing more was said until Steve went out the door.

"He's suspicious," Rob said.

"Of course he is. Steve's one of the best agents we've had come up the ranks in a long time. I'll handle his questions from here."

"Have you heard anything from Sam about the containers?"

"I got a call from him before we flew here. He said they were loaded on a ship last night and left Veracruz this morning."

"Did he know where they were heading?"

Tom shook his head. "The first docking is in Florida. If they aren't offloaded there, the next stop is New Orleans before the ship returns to Veracruz."

"So, we wait to see where they land."

"That's the plan," Tom said. "The ship isn't scheduled to reach Florida until Thursday evening. I'll know within hours if the containers were taken off."

"If New Orleans is the destination, there could be more murders."

"That's what I'm afraid of. Have you remembered anything more concerning those favors?"

"Nothing yet," Rob said. "I've been racking my brain ever since we returned."

"Then there's nothing more we can do until those containers are off the ship. Maybe then we will find out what's inside them."

"Waiting is the part of your job I hate," Rob said.

"So do I, Kid, so do I."

CHAPTER EIGHT

New Orleans

Hungry patrons entered Savoy's Restaurant in droves, eager to feast on shrimp creole, redfish coubion, and other house specialties. However, in the office above, something less savory was occurring.

Jean-Claude slammed the phone into its cradle and expressed his displeasure loudly in French. He had not yet regained his composure when it rang again. He closed his eyes, inhaled deeply, and exhaled audibly before answering.

"The office. Jean-Claude speaking," he said in a calm, controlled manner.

"No one hangs up on me, fancy man," Martínez growled.

"Sir, if you want to communicate with this office, have your attorney call. What was that handsome man's name? Chambers? In any event, I will not be insulted by you again. Good-bye."

"The lawyer is dead!" Martínez interjected before Jean-Claude could hang up.

Jean-Claude returned the phone to his ear. "Dead? When did this happen?"

"He died with Rojas. Had he lived, I would have ripped every inch of his gringo flesh from his body."

"That's rather harsh. What did he do to deserve such a fate?"

"He betrayed us to the FBI."

"The FBI? Why wasn't Mr. Pascal informed?"

"This didn't involve him."

"Oh, but it does," Jean-Claude said. "When you do business with Mr. Pascal, whatever affects you can also affect this office."

"The lawyer has been dead for over a year, and nothing has happened to your boss. Now, let me talk to Pascal."

"I will see if he wishes to speak to you." Jean-Claude hit the hold button, pushed away from his desk, and lightly rapped on his employer's door.

"Come in."

"Sorry to interrupt, sir. There are two things requiring your attention. Diego Martínez is on hold, but as far as I'm concerned, he can wait. That man has no concept of social skills."

Marcel chuckled. "I could hear him yelling at you from here."

"Sorry, sir."

"What else?"

"I just received word that the Cresent City plant is back to full production."

"Damn it! I thought I made it clear I wanted that plant shut down until after the bid deadline."

"That is exactly what was ordered. I was just told the men I sent didn't do as thorough a job as they thought."

"Then make sure they feel my disappointment," Marcel said.

"Rest assured, sir, I will." Jean-Claude turned to leave, then stopped and faced his employer. "Oh, yes, I almost forgot. I just learned Martínez has withheld important information from you."

"What information?"

"Their attorney who initiated our contact was working with the FBI."

Marcel pounded his desk. "Why am I just hearing of this now?"

"I shared those exact words with Martínez, but he said it was none of your business."

"Which line is that little drug lord on?"

"Line two."

"Get out and close my door."

"Gladly, sir."

Marcel Pascal let the call sit a moment before picking up the phone. "Martínez! Why am I just now hearing that your attorney was working with the FBI?"

"It was my problem and did not concern you, Pascal. Even if it did, I was too busy securing our money and protecting our operation before the FBI took it from us."

"It's not his death that concerns me. It's his involvement with the Feds."

"His connection had nothing to do with you, Pascal. The lawyer was only there to offer our proposal. As you recall, he never participated in our meetings and knew nothing of the assignments or your request."

"If you ever withhold anything like this again, we're through. I managed to get along quite well before you came along, and I can do it again."

"There is no need to be concerned, Pascal. I will tell you when something happens from here on out. In fact, that is the reason for my call."

"Has someone else betrayed you?"

"Nothing like that. I'm calling to inform you of the six containers being shipped to you tonight."

"Not so fast, Martínez. Our agreement was for two at a time. You have no right to change that agreement without my approval."

"I had no choice. If I had only sent two containers, two-thirds of our distributors would be without product in less than a week. You will receive extra pay for the inconvenience this may cause."

"Your product shortage doesn't concern me, Martínez. Remove those containers from that ship."

"That is not possible. My containers are at the bottom of the shipment. The ship would have to be delayed for days in order to remove them. We are businessmen, Pascal. Sometimes we must bend the rules to be successful."

"No, I am a businessman, Martínez. You are merely a drug lord. We are nothing alike. This little stunt will cost you five times the agreed amount for the inconvenience you've caused."

"Five? That's too much."

"Pay, or I'll have my dock supervisor refuse all your containers."

"You can't do that, Pascal. It will cripple my business. What can I do to make this right?"

Marcel paused before answering. "Let me think about that. In the meantime, I'll accept your containers. But do this again, and our agreement is over."

Marcel hung up and pushed the button on his intercom. "Come in here." Within seconds, Jean-Claude reappeared at his door.

"Call the yard and tell our dock manager to expect a shipment of six containers from Mexico instead of two, and not to release them until he gets a direct order. It's time that damned Martínez understands what it means to be in business with a real businessman."

"I couldn't agree more."

Marcel glanced at his Rolex and got to his feet. "Damn it, that little drug pusher made me late. Call the Court of Two Sisters restaurant and tell my guest I'm running late."

"Yes, sir. Right away."

Marcel didn't return to his office until the following morning. As soon as he entered, he tossed his hat on Jean-Claude's desk. "I want to speak to Parker now."

"Yes, sir. Right away."

Marcel went to his office and dropped into his chair as his intercom buzzed.

"Sir, the governor is on line two."

Marcel grabbed the phone. "Parker, I should have fed your sorry ass to the gators a year ago."

"Calm down, Marcel. Why are you upset?"

"I met with one of the Levee Board members last night. He said a majority of the Board members have strong ties to the Broussards and are likely to vote their way and give them the maintenance contract."

"Marcel, the Broussards have been an outstanding family in New Orleans for years. Any attempt to slander their good name would have the opposite effect. The only way to ensure you win that contract is to stop Crescent City from submitting a bid."

"That isn't likely. Crescent City hasn't missed a bid in almost forty years. I need you to stop them from getting the contract."

"Sorry, Marcel, I can't. I have newspaper and television reporters, senators, and state representatives demanding my resignation over this little, uh, peccadillo with the young lady. Those leeches are sucking the life out of me. I've barely had time to breathe, much less stop Crescent City from doing anything."

"Parker, you're a waste of good oxygen. It's time I put someone else in that chair."

"We've been friends for too long, Marcel. You wouldn't do that."

"I am not your friend, Parker. The only reason you are there is to benefit me. Do you know what I do with people who fail?"

"You eliminate them. But Marcel, please. It may take a little time, but I'll do everything I can to keep Crescent City from getting the votes to win." There was no response. "Marcel, are you there?"

"That's just it, Parker. I don't have time. I'll just have to handle this myself."

"Really. How? Never mind. It's best if I don't know. Can I still be governor?"

"For now, but only because I don't have time to deal with you."

"Thank you, thank you."

Marcel Pascal hung up the phone and pressed the button on his intercom. "Get our little drug lord on the line. He owes me after that last call, and I need to collect." He released the button, leaned back in his chair, and laced his thick fingers across his chest. "It's time to stop being soft."

*   *   *

Arizona

Rob hung up the phone and went into the small living room where Wanda was putting away Sarah's toys.

"Tom's on his way in."

"So soon? Do you know why?"

"I don't."

"Am I going to have to leave so you can talk?"

"Sweetheart, Tom feels the less you know, the less you'll worry."

"Well, he's wrong. It's what I don't know that drives me crazy. Will you at least talk to him about it?"

"Of course I will."

"I'll let it go this time, but after this, I want to be included." She took Sarah and left the room.

Rob went out to meet Tom. "What's going on, Tom? This is the second time you've been here this week."

"We need to talk in private."

"Okay, but you should know Wanda is tired of being excluded from our conversations."

"It's for her own good."

"I understand, but everything we do affects her and Sarah. She has a right to know."

"Some things, maybe, but not this."

"If it's that serious, we should talk out here."

"It's too hot. Get in the car. I'll turn the air back on."

Rob slipped into the passenger side as Tom got behind the wheel and started the engine. He turned up the air conditioner and settled in.

"What's this about?"

"The container ship is scheduled to dock in New Orleans tomorrow evening. If Martínez picks the containers up, it proves he's working with Pascal."

"How will you know? Martínez is too smart to show up in person or have his name on the paperwork."

"True. That's why I need you with me in New Orleans."

"We just got back from Mexico. Besides, we still don't know what's in those containers."

"Yes, we do. Sam called and said when the containers were being loaded in Mexico, one of the locks broke, and a pallet of drugs fell out. The guards ordered the dock crew to reload them, then secured the doors and stayed with the container until it was on the ship."

"Are you sure it was drugs?"

"Sam was able to get a sample of one of the broken packets after the guards left."

"What was it?"

"Some new concoction more potent than anything we've seen before."

"That still doesn't tell us the drugs belong to the organization."

"True, but on the chance they do, I need you there to identify whoever picks them up."

"Martínez is sure to have new people working for him by now, Tom. I was on the run for over a year, you know."

"Yes, but with a shipment this valuable, he'll only send his most trusted crew."

Rob was silent as he mulled over Tom's response.

"This won't be like Mexico, Kid. You'll be a distance away, watching them with binoculars. Once you get a look at who's picking up the shipment, I'll put you on a plane and get you back to your family."

"And who's keeping watch over Wanda and Sarah while I'm gone?"

"My people, same as before."

"There's sure to be hundreds of workers unloading that ship, and who knows how long it will take? That's a lot to deal with for only two of us."

"I've got that covered. My people will be there when the ship docks, and they will keep watch as the containers are offloaded. I want you there when they're claimed. If it turns out to be the organization's crew, my people will track them back to Martínez."

Rob took a moment to absorb this information. "I'll go on one condition."

"What's that?"

"No more hair dyes."

For a fleeting second, he saw Tom smile.

"You have my word."

Rob leaned back against the seat to think. "When do we go?"

"A car is coming for you at 5:00 p.m. The driver will have a packet containing your airplane ticket and cash for the trip."

"Where will you be?"

"I'll be waiting for you at the Creole House Hotel on Barataria

Street. A room is reserved for you under Martin Penn. Kid, this is our best chance of catching these guys."

"How are you justifying this trip to New Orleans with the Bureau?"

"I don't have to. I'm following orders. That is, except for involving you."

"How did you manage that?"

"Bureau business. Not your concern."

Rob nodded. "Okay. Unless there's more, I need to tell Wanda I'm leaving again."

"Wait. Get that sack from the back seat. There's a stuffed puppy dog inside for Sarah."

"Are you trying to steal my daughter's affections?"

"Maybe." Tom waited for Rob to get the sack. "Don't worry about your family, Kid. I'm not going to let anything happen to them."

Rob waited for Tom to drive away before turning around. When he did, he saw Wanda standing at the door with Sarah. He took the toy from the bag and held it out to Sarah as he approached.

"What's that?" Wanda asked.

"Tom got Sarah a gift."

"You're leaving again, aren't you?"

He took both of them in his arms. "I am."

"When?"

"At five this afternoon."

"Are you sure about this?"

"Sweetheart, I've already told you I'll do anything to keep you and our daughter safe. If helping Tom does that, I have to go."

She looked at him for a moment, then kissed him. "It's time for Sarah's nap. If we're quiet, we could have a little time to ourselves before you go."

"Time for what?"

"For you to show how much you will miss me."

Rob kissed her. "I love you, Mrs. Chambers."

It was almost five when Wanda walked Rob to the door with his suitcase. He put it down and wrapped his arms around her.

She tilted her head as she looked up at him. "How long will it be this time?"

"I'm not sure. I hope to be back before you miss me."

"Too late. I already do."

Rob reached for the gold locket around her neck and ran his finger across it. "Do you remember when I gave this to you?"

"How could I forget? It was the day we learned we were going to have Sarah."

Rob snapped it open. "If something happens to me, remember what's behind our pictures."

Wanda sighed. "Don't make me repeat this again."

"Wanda, it's important.

"The account numbers of our Zurich account and the contact information of our banker." She snapped the locket closed and dropped it down the neck of her dress. "You're coming back, Rob. I'm not going to need it."

He pulled her close and was about to kiss her when someone knocked. Rob held her for several more seconds before opening the door.

"Sir, are you ready to go?"

"I'll be there in a moment," Rob said to the driver. He took Wanda in his arms, kissed her, and held her tight. "I'll be back as soon as I can, sweetheart. I love you."

"And I love you."

Rob released her and went to the car. He turned back and looked at her standing in the doorway until she was out of sight.

CHAPTER NINE

New Orleans International Airport

A few minutes after his plane landed, Rob carried his suitcase outside to find a taxi. It didn't take long for his shirt to become glued to his back from the evening's heat and humidity. Finally, he waved down a Yellow Cab, and it stopped in front of him.

"Where to, boss?" the driver asked.

"Creole House Hotel on Barataria Street," Rob said, tossing his suitcase into the back seat.

In less than an hour, the taxi started up the long, narrow ramp of the Huey Long Bridge. Rob got an eerie sensation of impending doom looking down at the vast black snake of the Mississippi River. The only thing separating the river from the city of New Orleans was the miles and miles of the levee system.

Once across the bridge, the cab maneuvered the streets until it stopped in front of a white plantation-style house with tall, dark wood shutters. A black wrought iron fence surrounded the manicured yard of the hotel, where a sign was lit up with lights proclaiming The Creole House. The house reminded him of one from *Gone with the Wind*.

"That'll be $4.75," the driver said. Rob paid the man, and he drove away.

Rob felt like he had stepped back in time when he entered the hotel. Had it not been for the man behind the counter, he would almost swear he was checking into *The Twilight Zone*.

He went to his room, unpacked, and stretched out fully clothed on the bed to wait for Tom. He had just dozed off when someone knocked. Rob opened the door and was surprised to see Tom in jeans and a work shirt instead of a suit. He handed Rob the same shirt and walked into the room.

"Hope you packed your jeans?"

"I did."

"Put them on. We must blend in with the dock workers."

"Is the ship here?" Rob asked as he unbuttoned his shirt.

"It arrived a few hours ago, and the containers were about to be unloaded when I left."

"Who's watching it?"

"I have people there. Get dressed. I can answer your questions in the car."

"I'm done," Rob said as he threaded his belt through the loops of his jeans.

"Let's go."

They exited the hotel and got into Tom's car.

"Who are these people helping you?"

"Two friends of mine who are local agents."

"Tom, what are you doing? They can't know I'm here."

"Relax. I've known these two for over twenty years. My wife and I made repeated trips to New Orleans to be with Willard, or Wiley as he prefers to be called, and his wife while their five-year-old son was in a coma."

"What happened to him?"

"Somehow the boy got too close to a kid hitting baseballs and was struck in the head with the bat. We weren't sure he would make it for weeks."

"I'm glad he survived."

"Yes, but the damage was done, and he's never matured much past the age he was hit."

"That has to be devastating," Rob said.

"It was, for both Wiley and his wife. Since it happened, every time Wiley gets stressed, one side of his face starts to twitch." Tom paused for a second. "If it hadn't been for Wiley, Phillip, and their wives when I lost my wife and Scott, I'm not sure I would have made it."

"They sound like good friends."

"The only reason I'm telling you this is so you know we can trust them." Tom shifted in his seat. "Let's get back to business. I called Sam and asked him to monitor the docks for more guarded containers. If there are any, we know this is their port."

"Tell me exactly how this is going to happen if I recognize some of the organization's men?"

"We track them to see who they are selling the drugs to and track the money back to Martínez, like Steve said."

Rob thought for a moment. "It would be interesting to see where and how they are handling the drugs." His train of thought was broken when he heard an unfamiliar buzz.

"What's that?"

"A message." Tom reached down to his belt, unclipped a small black object, and glanced at it as he drove.

"When did the FBI start using pagers?"

"This isn't an ordinary pager. I'm using it because I can't use our service radio. If I do, the local office will know I'm here."

"I thought you said you were sent here by the Bureau?"

"I was, but that's classified. Take a look," Tom said, turning the pager so Rob could see.

"It looks like a phone number with symbols and more numbers. Is it some kind of code?"

"That's exactly what it is." Tom returned the device to his belt clip. "The number tells me the phone number to call, and the symbols are code for who's calling and what action to take."

Rob chuckled. "This is like something from a Dick Tracy comic book."

A rare smile crossed Tom's lips. "Yeah. I guess it is."

Minutes later, Tom parked behind a black pickup, almost invisible in the dark. A slim, short man stepped out of the shadows when Rob and Tom exited the car.

"I got your message, Phillip. What's happened?"

Phillip glanced at Rob. "Who's he?"

"He's good. I've cleared him. Now, what happened?"

Phillip eyed Rob for a moment before answering. "Two moving company trucks arrived on the docks about twenty minutes ago."

"Moving trucks? That's unusual."

"That's why I paged you."

"Where's Wiley?"

"He's keeping watch on the stash. Before we go, put these on." Phillip handed each of them a cap.

Rob placed the hat on his head. "Have you seen any sign of hostages?"

"Not yet," Phillip said. "My guess is if there are any, we won't see any sign of them until the ship is unloaded. Too many workers close to the ship." Phillip gestured to Rob. "Can he take care of himself?"

"He's trained."

"Good, because this could get dicey."

Rob glanced across the road from the docks and saw a long line of houses that looked to be at least a century old.

Phillip tapped Rob on the shoulder. "Stop sightseeing. Time to go."

The two men followed Phillip down the fence line to an opening cut into the chain-link and slipped through. Then the three men darted between buildings until they reached row after row of containers and tarp-covered goods.

Workers were all over the docks. Some were on forklifts moving pallets, and others were in tall cranes offloading containers as workers on the ground guided them with ropes and chains. The men continued moving until Phillip pointed to a man crouched behind a stack of wooden pallets.

Phillip pulled a tarp from a small piece of machinery and bundled it up. "You two grab something to carry."

Tom and Rob found what they could and followed Phillip with their heads down until they reached the stack of pallets. They put down the stuff they were holding and ducked behind the pallets next to the hidden man.

"What's going on, Wiley?" Tom whispered.

"The moving van's doors have been opened, but so far, that's it."

"Where are the drugs?"

"See the two big armed guys leaning against those containers? A few minutes ago, the men from the vans walked up to them and talked for a while before disappearing somewhere on the docks." Wiley passed a pair of night vision binoculars to Tom. "The guards look Latino to me, but I can't be sure from this distance."

Tom raised the binoculars. "Have they opened the containers yet?"

"Nope."

"Looks like that's about to happen. Two forklifts just pulled up, and one of the guards appears to be opening the locks."

"Damn." Tom passed the goggles to Wiley. "Take a look."

"That's the biggest load of drugs I've ever seen."

"Do we have enough men to follow those vans after they leave the docks?" Tom asked.

"Yep. They are parked outside the gate."

"Did you tell them to record every place they stop and take photos?"

Wiley shook his head. "I got it handled, Tom."

Rob inched next to Tom and watched as pallets of drugs were transported to the vans. "Tom, if those drugs belong to Martínez," he said, "he's multiplied their production capabilities."

"And this is only one shipment," Phillip said. "Imagine what's coming in by other methods."

Wiley gave Tom a nudge. "How did you know they were shipping them here?"

"It happened by accident."

"Some accident," Phillip said. "The question is, how do we stop it?"

"That's why we're here." Tom handed Rob the binoculars, and he watched until the last pallet was loaded.

Tom nudged him. "See anyone you recognize?"

"Nope." Rob passed the glasses to Tom.

"Looks like they're about to drive away." Tom lowered the binoculars. "Wiley, check on your people and make sure those drugs are being followed."

Wiley started to get to his feet but suddenly fell back, moaning.

Tom caught him. "Are you all right?" he whispered.

"It's my back. Guess I've tackled too many bad guys in my day. Don't worry, I'm good."

"No, you're not."

"I'll go," Phillip said and slipped away.

"Dang it, Tom. Let me do my job," Wiley said.

"I'm sure you can. Where are your other men?"

"Phillip will send them in as soon as we go. It's too dangerous to have all of us here at the same time."

"There could be hostages on that ship," Tom whispered.

"I doubt it," Wiley said. "If there were, they would have already off-loaded them. It's almost daylight and too easy to spot."

"You could be right, but I still want to be notified if anything unusual happens."

"You got it."

Tom gave Wiley the binoculars before he and Rob retraced their steps to the car and returned to the hotel.

After a couple hours' sleep, Rob and Tom met for coffee in a tiny café. Tom's pager buzzed. He took it from his belt and looked at it. "Stay here. I need to make a call."

When Tom left, Rob replayed the events of last night in his head. *This is my fault,* he told himself. *Those drugs are here because I set this in motion.* Rob remained deep in thought about that time in the past until Tom returned.

"That was Wiley. The ship left this morning for Veracruz."

"Any sign of hostages?"

"Not this time."

"What about the van?"

"They drove through Shreveport and were heading toward Texas."

"That's more confirmation the drugs belong to the organization. Rojas only wanted the use of the docks because it was a safer, faster way to get the drugs into the country."

Tom took his cup and downed the rest of the potent brew. "We need to get back. Wiley and Phillip have lined up people to help us. We are meeting them tonight."

"Are they all with the FBI?"

"Not this group. Let's go. We have a lot of work to do before we meet them."

CHAPTER TEN

New Orleans

It was dark when Tom parked on Barrack Street. He and Rob walked several blocks around Jackson Square until they came to a multi-storied building.

"This is where we're meeting Phillip and Wiley, but we're not going in this way. Too many people around for us to use the front door."

Rob looked up at the name painted on the brick. "Jax Brewing Company. Tom, this is a working plant. There must be people inside. I can hear machinery."

"I didn't pick this place. Wiley did." They continued down the street a couple of blocks before Tom darted between two buildings.

"Stay close," he said. "We're doubling back."

Rob followed him down the alleyway and saw they were only yards away from the levee bank. They went up the embankment and made their way back to the brewing company.

They were almost there when Tom's pager vibrated. He took it from his belt clip and looked at it.

"Do you need to find a phone?" Rob asked.

"We don't have time. I'll make the call after we're done."

A few minutes later, they reached the back of the brewing company, and Tom pointed to a rust-covered door. "That's how we're getting in."

Tom did a quick check of their surroundings before knocking. A small window opened, then shut. The door was unlocked, and they entered.

"Stay close," Phillip said as Rob and Tom slipped inside. "No talking until we're in the meeting room." He locked the door behind them and led the way.

Rob followed Phillip and Tom into a large room filled with a strong, hoppy smell of beer and workers dressed in smocks and paper caps who were monitoring the line of bottles clanking against each other as the machines filled them.

Phillip started up a staircase, and Rob and Tom followed. When they reached the third floor, Phillip made three short raps on the wooden door, and it opened. Wiley was waiting on the other side.

"Before you go in," Wiley said, "I need to tell you how this works. We aren't using names."

"Then how do we address each other?" Tom asked.

"With these." Wiley took two pieces of colored cloth from his shirt pocket and gave Tom the strip of black fabric and Rob the yellow. "Everyone here, except for Phillip and me, has a cloth of a different color hanging from his shirt pocket."

Rob looked down at the yellow fabric in his hand. "I hope the color doesn't reflect your opinion of me?"

Several of the men in the room chuckled.

"It's yours because none of us would take it," said a man with a blue cloth dangling from his pocket.

Tom tucked the cloth into his shirt pocket. "Unusual method."

"It was Phillip's idea when we started the group," the man said. "We've been doing it this way for four years. Just use the color instead of a name."

The man with a green cloth stepped forward. "We had to do it this way until we knew we could trust each other. You've got no idea how corrupt this city is."

"He's right," Blue added. "You'd have better luck finding a virgin on Bourbon Street than an honest cop, judge, or politician in this city. Hell, the whole state." He looked at Tom. "Wiley and Phillip said you need help with something big coming here."

Tom stepped into the middle of the room. "It's not coming, it's already here. We have reason to believe the mob has allied with one of the largest drug organizations in Mexico and is importing large quantities of drugs through your docks. We also think many of the murders committed in and around New Orleans over the last year and a half were committed by the Mexican organization as part of the payment for using those docks."

"People are killed here all the time. What makes you think these people are doing it?"

"During the last year and a half, I'm guessing you've noticed an unexplained increase in the deaths of prominent people such as judges, senators, business executives, and trial witnesses?"

"Sure," Green said. "But what makes you think these murders are connected to Pascal and the drug organization?"

"Because of the number of Hispanic men professionally executed within days of each murder."

Blue stepped forward and pointed a thumb toward Green. "He and I worked on some of those cases. What makes you think those killings are connected?"

Tom paused and glanced at Rob. "Sorry. That's classified."

Green stepped forward. "Hell it is! Look, we're risking our lives being here. If you want our cooperation, we need to know what you know."

Wiley placed a hand on Tom's shoulder. "He's right. We need these guys. Just answer their damn questions."

When Tom hesitated to respond, Rob stepped forward. "He has an informant who worked for the drug organization."

Tom spun around. "Kid. Stop talking."

Green shook his head. "How do you know your informant is telling the truth?"

"I know because he and his family were almost killed on my watch," Tom said.

"And he was the one who set this plan in motion," Rob replied.

Wiley stepped next to Tom. "Look, guys, Phillip and I have known Black for decades," he said, indicating Tom Neal with a jerk of his chin. "You can trust him. So, if you're in, raise your hand. If anyone wants out, we're all out."

Tom and Rob watched as one man after another raised a hand.

"Good," Wiley said. "Now that everyone's in, it's time to tell our new friends who they are working with." Wiley pointed at Blue and Green. "I'm sure you figured out these two are cops. They are veteran detectives with the New Orleans Police Vice Division. Then we've got these two. Orange is with the DA's office, and Red is a senior member of the mayor's office. All of them are former military and know how to handle themselves if needed."

"Now that you know who we are," one of the vice detectives said, "fill us in."

Tom exchanged a glance with Rob, then turned to the group. "Two containers of drugs from Mexico were unloaded on your docks last night."

"That's nonsense," challenged Orange. "Marcel Pascal runs all the drug operations around here. He wouldn't allow that to happen."

"He's right," one of the vice detectives said. "Someone is lying to you."

"He's telling the truth," Phillip said. "Wiley and I were there. The four of us watched the contents of the containers being packed into moving vans and transported out of state."

The detective looked around at his companions before replying. "So, you're saying Marcel Pascal is allowing this drug organization to use his docks, and they are paying for access by having their people kill for him?"

"Not exactly," Tom said. "We believe the men doing the killings were all abducted by the drug organization and forced to kill because the organization has their families."

"And you think the Hispanic men who were executed were the hostages?" said one of the detectives.

"I do."

"Damn it. If you're right, pinning this on Pascal will be almost impossible."

"That's why we need your help," Tom said.

"How many men do you have working on this?" the man from the mayor's office asked.

"For now, Wiley, Phillip, and the two of us."

The two detectives exchanged glances with each other before one spoke up. "Wait a minute. Aren't you FBI?"

Tom glanced at Rob before answering. "I am."

"Then why are you asking for our help when you have an entire FBI regional office at your disposal?"

All eyes in the room were fixed on Tom.

"At the moment, I prefer to handle this with you instead of them," he said.

The questioning detective glanced at his partner, then crossed his arms. "Sounds like you think you have a rat in your ranks."

Phillip exchanged glances with Wiley, then looked back at Tom. "Is he right?"

"Pascal knows every agent in that office. He will know we're on to him if he sees them snooping around."

"You're good at avoiding answers." Blue exhaled audibly. "What can we do to help?"

"I have contacts in Mexico who will notify me when another shipment is loaded. If it takes the same route as the last, it will stop in Florida, then be offloaded here."

"What if the drugs are taken off before they get here?" Blue asked.

"Then you're off the hook. If not, we only have three days to prepare before the ship arrives from Florida."

"I know I'm asking all the questions here," Blue continued, "but my partner and I are on the streets fighting this stuff every day. How do you plan to stop this?"

"We trace the drug money back to the drug lords and take them out. Once that's done, the drug shipments, and hopefully these murders, will stop."

"That could take a while. In the meantime, how will you know if there will be more killings?"

"We won't until we see the hostages taken off the ships."

"Okay. Say you see the hostages," Red with the DA's office said. "Are you expecting us to just stand by and let innocent people die until you are able to track the drug organization down?"

"Absolutely not," Tom said.

"Then how do you plan to stop any more killings from happening?"

"I'm working on that." Tom looked straight at the detective, challenging him. "If you have a better way of handling this, I'm eager to hear it."

The detective glanced at his partner before turning back to Tom. "I'm not sure there is one. Sounds like you're doing your best with what you've got. How do we fit into this?"

"I need you and your partner, Green, to help us find men we can trust to follow the drugs and the money once it's sold."

"What about the rest of us?" asked Red, the man from the DA's office.

Tom gestured to Rob. "We need someone here to look into the people who were killed and see if there is a link to Pascal. Knowing why those men were targeted will help us determine who could be next. My associate will give you the information we have on every person who's been murdered."

"How will we know the next shipment is coming?" Red asked.

"You will hear from Wiley or Phillip when I get the call," Tom replied. "Now, if there are no more questions, let's get started."

Rob huddled in a corner with two men while Tom spent the rest of the time with Wiley, Phillip, and the two detectives. When the meeting ended, everyone scattered like cockroaches into the night.

Tom and Rob retraced their route to the car without speaking.

"Do you suspect someone in this FBI office is on Pascal's payroll?" Rob asked as Tom got behind the wheel.

Tom took a moment to respond. "I'm not sure. I was sent here to look into that." He started the car and pulled away from the curb. "Hoover doesn't want anyone in the local office to know why I'm here."

"What about the two men you have working with us?"

"Wiley and Phillip can be trusted, but it wouldn't hurt to have someone here without any connections to this area. Someone we already know."

"Tom. We can't involve Steve. You saw his reaction when he discovered who I was after training me. I don't think he will want any part of this when he finds out you brought me here."

"Steve will be all in once he understands who we're after and why. Take my word for it."

CHAPTER ELEVEN

New Orleans

Rob drove to the airport with Tom seated next to him two days later. A look of shock came over Steve's face when he saw Rob behind the wheel.

"Are you two out of your mind? What the hell is he doing here?"

Tom motioned to the back seat. "Keep quiet and get in."

Steve tossed his suitcase onto the seat and got in. "I think both of you are off your rocker," he said as Rob pulled away from the curb.

"We need him, Steve."

"If you aren't concerned about our careers, you should at least be concerned about Rob and his family. This could get them tossed out of the protection program."

"Turn around, Kid. We're taking Steve back to the gate."

Rob glanced at Tom before hitting the turn signal. As he pulled into the turn lane, he felt a tap on his shoulder.

"Never mind. Tom went through a lot of trouble to get me here, so whatever this is must be important." Steve leaned forward in his seat. "But no more secrets. Do this again, and I'm out."

Tom glanced over his shoulder. "I'll make a deal with you. If you want out after I tell you why he's here, I'll drive you to the airport myself."

"Fair enough. Start talking."

Tom turned in his seat to see both men. "The Kid and I made a trip to Mexico several weeks ago and discovered cargo containers full of drugs being transported by ship from a port there to one here in New Orleans."

"That explains the new hair color the last time we were together. And why you refused to answer some of my questions."

"Do you want to talk or listen?" Tom snapped.

"Sorry. Keep going."

"While we were there, The Kid recalled a meeting he arranged between the organization and Marcel Pascal to discuss the Rojas organization's access to Pascal's docks. A deal was struck, and now not only are drugs being transported into the States, but people are being killed as part of the payment."

"Are we talking about the same drug organization that killed Scott?"

"From what we learned in Mexico, it is. But to be certain, I brought The Kid here to see if he could identify the people claiming the drugs."

"So he's only here to observe."

"That's it. There wasn't anyone from the first shipment The Kid recognized, but he's going to get another chance. I received word last night that six containers of drugs and hostages left the port in Mexico a day ago."

"Why do they have hostages?"

Tom explained what they had discovered on their trip and the connections to the killings in New Orleans.

"Dang," Steve said, shaking his head. "So you're saying the organization is kidnapping people to commit the killings ordered by the New Orleans mob?"

Rob glanced at Steve in the rearview mirror. "That's right. Rojas referred to them as favors. I know because I negotiated the deal."

"Damn it. That means it's going to be impossible to trace the killings back to Pascal."

Tom opened the glove box and took out a packet as they approached the Huey P. Long bridge. "Exactly." He handed Steve a pager and set one aside for Rob.

"What's this?" Steve asked as he examined the box.

"It's your pager." Tom removed two sheets of paper and handed one to Steve.

"This looks like some sort of new code."

"It is. It's a list of symbols and numbers to add to the phone numbers you enter into the pager. As you can see, each set has a meaning. Start memorizing it."

"How did you get these things?"

"They're a gift from the director. Kid, I'll give you your list when we stop."

Steve looked at the page of numbers and symbols. "Well, Rob won't have a problem memorizing these, but I'll need a few days."

"Make it quick. There will be no radios used to communicate. The local office can't know we're here. Hoover is concerned some of the agents may be on Pascal's payroll."

"That's crazy! What are we supposed to do for backup?"

"That's why I needed you."

"Dang, this just keeps getting worse."

Rob chuckled. "You said you wanted the truth."

"Kid, stop at that grocery market," Tom said. "I need to use that pay phone to page Wiley."

Rob parked, and Tom got out. Steve leaned forward and rested his arms on the front seat. "While Tom's on the phone, we need to talk."

"About what?"

"About all these trips you and Tom are taking. Who's paying for you to be here? I know the Bureau isn't."

"What do you mean?"

"I told you about Tom spending weeks in Mexico after Scott's death. Now he's taken you there, as well as brought you here," Steve said. "There's no way the Bureau's funding this, so it has to be coming out of Tom's pocket."

Rob turned and looked over his shoulder. "What are you asking?"

"Look, Tom's finances are none of my business, but if he keeps spending money at this rate, he won't have a dime left to retire. I guess what I'm trying to say is, I want to pitch in."

"There's nothing for you to be concerned about. Tom has more than enough to cover everything we need."

"But where's the money coming from, Rob? I've been with the Bureau long enough to know no one retires rich."

Rob didn't answer.

"I'll be damned," Steve said. "The money is coming from you?"

"Not exactly. Let's just say we found a way to finance things."

"How? From what I know about this witness program, you go in with nothing but the shirt on your back. So where's the money coming from, Rob?"

Rob paused before answering. "The Bureau has every account I set up for the Rojas organization in the States and offshore before I went on the run. As I understand it, all the accounts were seized. Except, that is, for one offshore account."

"What happened to that offshore account?"

Rob turned back in his seat.

"Look, you said you would tell me the truth, so talk," Steve said.

"I was pretty beaten up when Tom got to me," Rob said, twisting in his seat to face Steve. "After what happened to us in the safe house, he thought it best to keep me hidden until he could negotiate a deal with Hoover to put us in the witness protection program and bring me in. Tom and I doubted my family's safety because the program was new and untried, so we set up some insurance in case the Rojas organization found me and took us captive again."

"What kind of insurance?"

"Before Tom brought me in, I moved the money from the offshore account and placed it elsewhere. The only time it's been touched was to finance these trips."

Steve fell against the seat, laughing. "I love it. We're hunting the drug organization with their own money."

"Exactly." Rob looked up and saw Tom returning. "You can't say anything about this, Steve. Not to Tom or the Bureau. If you do, it's over for all of us."

"Don't worry. You have my word."

"Let's get going," Tom said after settling in the passenger seat.

Steve leaned forward. "How long do we have before the next shipment arrives?"

"Four, maybe five days after it leaves Mexico if the ship takes the same route as the last one."

"Dang it, that's not much time to figure this out. How are we supposed to deal with the drugs and prevent those hostages from killing anyone?"

"We have a plan for tracking the drugs," Tom said. "But the only way to prevent anyone from being killed is to find out who the targets are before it happens."

"How are you going to do that?" Steve asked.

"By learning what Pascal has to gain by their deaths," Rob said.

"That could take weeks. How will we do that in four or five days? And by the way, who is Wiley?"

Tom told Steve about Wiley, Phillip, and the men at the meeting.

"That makes me feel a little better. I thought we were it."

Tom's pager sounded just as they parked in front of the hotel. "Steve, bring your suitcase. You'll have to wait to get settled in, though. I need both of you with me when I make this call."

Tom picked up his phone as soon as they entered his room. "What is it, Wiley?"

"I got a call from our guys in the DA's office. He has something for us and asked to meet."

"Where and when?"

"As soon as you can get to Audubon Park Zoo. He'll be waiting for us in the gorilla exhibit."

"What's the address?" Tom snapped his fingers and pointed to Rob before repeating the address. "On our way," he said.

"Make sure you're not followed," Wiley said, and ended the call.

"This is it, Steve. Are you sure you want to stay?"

"I love the zoo. Let's go."

"Kid, get a map from the hotel desk on our way to the car."

"Will do."

The two men were in the car when Rob exited the hotel empty-handed.

"Hey," Steve called out from the back seat. "Where's the map?"

"They were out. The only map they had was on the wall."

"How will we find the zoo?"

"I looked it over and know where to go."

Tom started the engine. "Which way, Kid?"

"Turn left at the next block."

Steve settled back in his seat. "How do you memorize a map with one look?"

Rob didn't answer. He directed Tom across the city to Audubon Park. "We have ten minutes to get to the gorilla exhibit."

"Then we'd better hurry," Tom said as he parked.

Tom paid for their tickets as Rob located a map of the park.

"This way," he said once Tom had their tickets, and took off walking, followed by Tom and Steve.

They found Wiley waiting near a bench. His right eye started to twitch when he saw Steve.

"Who's he?"

"One of us," Tom replied. "You can trust him."

"Maybe I do, but Orange won't. He needs to stay out here."

"It's all right, Tom. I'll keep an eye on the entrance," Steve said.

The three men walked into the darkened, cave-like entrance and made their way to the large glass window of the exhibit. The gorilla was lounging near the glass, watching them, but Orange was nowhere in sight.

"Are we early?" Rob asked.

"You're right on time," Orange said, coming up behind them. "Just wanted to be sure you were alone."

"This must be important for you to call a meeting in broad daylight," Wiley said.

"Our guy with the mayor's office and I think we found the connection between the murder victims and Pascal." He handed Tom a large manila envelope. "The witnesses were killed to keep them from giving testimony that would incriminate Pascal's hitmen. But when the politicians apparently refused to do his bidding, Pascal had them killed and put people he owned in those positions."

Rob shook his head. "If you found this, why couldn't the police press charges?"

"They won't because there's no proof. No one here is brave enough to testify against Pascal."

"That's convenient," Tom replied.

"Yeah," Wiley added. "It happens a lot down here."

"There is one murder I'm confused about," Rob said. "The steel manufacturing chairman. He was in Beaumont, not New Orleans."

"True, but his company did a lot of business along the Gulf Coast. There are a number of reasons he and Pascal could have butted heads."

"Did your research give you any indication on who Pascal's next targets might be?" Tom asked.

"Not yet." Orange glanced at his watch. "I have to go."

"Thanks for your help," Tom said. "We'll stay back so you can get away from here. It's safer for you if we're not seen together."

"Thanks. I was going to suggest that. I'll let Wiley know if we find anything else," Orange said, then disappeared behind a door marked *Employees Only*.

Wiley watched the man leave before approaching Tom. "Was any of that news to you?"

"It's more a confirmation of what we suspected." Tom glanced at the large envelope. "Hopefully, this will help us determine who's next."

"While you're reviewing that, I'll notify the group to meet tonight so we can prepare for the shipment and hostages coming in. We need to figure this out before there are any more bodies to bury.

CHAPTER TWELVE

New Orleans

Caroline looked up from her work when Jack came into her office. "Please tell me you have good news."

"I do. The repaired panel is working perfectly."

"Thank God," she sighed.

"I also had our people check the other units to ensure they were working properly after picking up the slack to keep up production."

"And?"

"They're fine." Jack pointed to the ledger. "How's that going?"

"We made payroll, paid for the repairs, and even managed a small profit. This scraping by will be over when we win that contract."

"Speaking of that," Jack said, rubbing his hands together, "I'm going to pick us up some po-boys after we close so we can work on the proposal here instead of carting all your ledgers and files home with us."

Caroline placed her pen on her desk. "Jack," she whispered. "Was I wrong to push you into building our new plant?"

"Don't do that, sweetie. You had valid reasons for doing it."

"It made sense on paper, but now we're struggling to make ends meet. I'm beginning to think we should have waited."

"Stop it, Caroline. The new plant was a great idea. It will put us head and shoulders above everyone else."

She paused, then picked up her pen. "Thank you. Now that leaves me with the next difficult decision."

"Which is?"

"Do I want a shrimp or oyster po-boy?"

*   *   *

New Orleans

Tom, Rob, and Steve spent all day reviewing the information Orange had given them without coming up with any leads as to who might be the next targets. That night, all three of them went to the meeting at the brewery. As soon as they entered, all eyes were on Steve.

"Who is this guy?" one of the undercover cops asked.

"He's from our West Coast office," Tom said. "We can trust him."

Steve was handed a pink strip of cloth. "What am I supposed to do with this?" he asked.

Wiley took it from him and tucked it into Steve's shirt pocket. "Tonight, you're called Pink."

Steve looked down at the cloth and shook his head. "If you say so."

Tom stepped into the center of the room. "I assume all of you have been updated on the shipment and hostages coming in."

One of the detectives stepped forward. "Wiley said there were six containers of drugs this time. That is going to require a lot more men to follow them."

"Can you handle it?" Tom asked.

Green looked at his partner with the blue cloth. "We'll make sure it's done."

"Do we know where the last drugs went?" Orange asked.

"I can answer that," Blue said. "We tailed them from Louisiana to Lindale, Texas before any money changed hands. The next stops were Temple and San Antonio, and then what was left of the cargo was split up and transferred to three small trucks."

Orange shook his head. "So, you're saying you lost sight of the money."

"Not all of it. The trucks we were following met up with a black Buick near Elk City, Oklahoma. Four large duffel bags were transferred from the truck to the car. Green and I were certain it was cash and followed the Buick. We tailed it to a small office building in Jackson, Oklahoma, leased to the Mid-Continental Transportation Company."

The hairs on the back of Rob's neck stood straight up. "Wait a minute. Are you certain it was Mid-Continental Transportation Company?"

"Positive," Blue answered. "When we returned, I ran the company's name and address through our system."

"What did you find?" Tom asked.

"Not much. The report said the company started less than three years ago. The odd part is there are no tax records on file or records of any employees."

Rob caught Tom's eye and whispered, "That's because there aren't any."

Tom motioned for him to be silent before speaking. "And you saw them carry the bags into the office?"

"Sure did. We think this Mid-Continental company is nothing more than a dumping spot because they locked the door behind them and left empty handed. My guess is it's just a holding location until things cool down and someone else picks up the money."

"What makes you think that?" Orange asked.

"We tracked down the building manager and asked for the information of the person leasing the office. He gave us a P.O. box in Albuquerque, New Mexico, which is listed as the headquarters of the company."

Tom shook his head. "All we have is another dead end."

The man from the DA's office stood. "Maybe not. You asked us to look into possible reasons Pascal is targeting people. Well, Red and I think we found something. After Hurricane Betsy, President Johnson approved a fifteen-billion-dollar package to rebuild our coastline and levee system. Our research indicated that Pascal pushed, or paid off as many people as possible, to get *his* companies the contracts to do the reconstruction."

"Was he successful?"

"Not by a long shot. All Pascal got was around four hundred thousand dollars. Four hundred thousand was nothing when the winners of the contracts got millions."

Tom crossed his arms. "I'm sure Pascal was furious, but what does that have to do with what's happening now?"

"Fifty million of the fifteen billion was allocated to maintaining the levee system, and the bids for that contract will open soon."

Tom unfolded his arms. "Who makes the decision on those contracts?"

"The New Orleans Levee Board."

"So, who's most likely to keep Pascal from getting it?"

"It could be many people. Competing company owners, Levee Board members, and the Corps of Engineers. Even the city council members have a say in the final decision."

"That's too many people. Is there some way to narrow that down?"

"That's what we've been trying to do, but unfortunately, it's too early to make that decision."

Green raised his hand. "While Orange is working on that, my partner and I need to discuss how many people we'll need to track the next shipment."

The meeting went on for hours. When it finally ended, Rob, Tom, and Steve headed back to the hotel.

"Rob, I heard what you whispered to Tom back there," Steve said from the back seat. "Sounds like you know something about Mid-Continental Transportation Company."

"It's one of the corporations I created to hide the Rojas organization's money."

"That means the organization is still using it," Steve said.

"It seems they are," Tom added. "But for now, I'm more concerned with stopping the next batch of killings than shutting that company down."

Steve scooted forward in his seat. "I'm afraid there's not much we can do if we don't know who the targets are."

"If we don't discover that soon, the only chance we have of saving the targets is to follow the hostages when they get off the ship and pray we can stop them before they kill anyone."

"That's a big *if*, Tom," Steve added.

"True, but at this moment, it's the only option left."

"We could always call in the regional office, stake out the docks, and arrest all of them when they offload the hostages," Steve said.

"Absolutely not," Tom said. "Then all we wind up with are the hostages, drugs, and a few of the organization's people. Pascal will simply move the ships to a new location and start the process all over again. This is our best chance to follow the money *and* catch Martínez." Tom paused a moment and glanced in his rearview mirror at Steve. "There's one more thing you should know. Hoover doesn't want the regional office to know I am here."

Steve leaned in. "Why?"

"He sent me here to investigate the local office to make certain none of them are on Pascal's payroll."

"Now I understand why you got me here." Steve sat back in his seat. "You could have told me this earlier, Tom."

"Would it have changed your mind about staying?"

"Probably not."

"Good, because we need you."

The following day, Tom, Rob, and Steve were delving deeper into all of the people involved in the upcoming maintenance contract when Tom's pager buzzed. He glanced at the face of the pager and went to the phone.

"Who is it?" Steve asked as Tom was dialing.

"Wiley." Tom motioned for him to be quiet.

"Got your code. What's happened?" Tom asked when Wiley answered.

"I just got word that the ship is tying up at the dock."

"I was told it wouldn't be here until tomorrow."

"Whoever said that was wrong. It just came in."

"Then we need to move fast. Have you told the detectives to get their people in position?"

"Phillip is on the phone with them now. He's also calling the rest of the group."

"Have Phillip remind everyone to bring their walkie-talkies," Tom said. "We have to be able to communicate when this goes down."

"Will do."

"How fast can you get to the docks? We have to be there when they bring the hostages off."

"We're going as soon as we hang up the phone. I was told it will be a while before anything happens because the ship can't dock until another vessel moves out of the way."

"Good. That gives us more time to get everyone into place."

*   *   *

The hundred-year-old grandfather clock in the hallway struck six as Caroline left their bedroom and found her husband fighting with his bow tie in front of the gold-trim foyer mirror.

Jack threw up his hands when he saw her approaching. "Whoever dreamed up these dang things should be hung."

Caroline giggled as she brushed his hands aside. "Jack Broussard, I've shown you this at least a dozen times. My mama taught me this before I was ten." She straightened the finished bow and stepped back to admire her work. "There. It's perfect." She moved so he could see his reflection in the mirror.

"So glad I married a southern girl."

She gave him a peck on the cheek. "Shall I count the ways?"

He gave her a wink. "What else did your mother teach you?"

"Definitely not what you're thinking. Now let's go."

"I have a better idea. Let's skip the ball and stay home."

"We can't. Three members of the Levee Board are joining us tonight. We need them on our side when the decision comes to a vote."

"We bought a table for twelve. Who else is coming?"

"Some of our old friends, to keep you from going out of your mind."

"Thank you. I hate these things."

"It's business, Jack. Put on that Broussard charm and act like you're enjoying yourself."

"I'll try, but we're coming home as soon as it's over."

Caroline glanced at the clock. "With pleasure. Now let's go."

*　*　*

New Orleans Docks

Rob twisted in the passenger seat of Tom's car and exhaled loudly. "We've been sitting here for hours. Are we certain this is the right ship?"

"Relax, Kid. We are certain it's the ship. All we can do now is wait." Tom had barely gotten his words out when his walkie-talkie buzzed.

"Blue reporting. We have two black sedans with tinted windows entering the gates."

"Read out the plates."

"Three, six K, as in kilo, seven, four, two, and three, six K, as in kilo, seven, seven, one."

Tom glanced at Rob, and he nodded.

"Wiley. You got that?" Tom asked.

"Roger. I see them. They just pulled in."

"Any sign of hostages?"

"Not yet. Wait a minute. I see a man with a rifle behind two men coming down the gangplank."

"It's happening," Rob whispered.

"Talk to us, Wiley," Tom ordered.

"Looks like they are splitting up the hostages and putting one in each car. Heads up, guys. They're leaving."

Tom pressed the button on his walkie-talkie. "Blue, the cars are coming your way."

"Affirmative. I see headlights approaching the gates. Both cars just turned east. Orange, you should be seeing them soon."

"Got them. It doesn't look like either car is turning off this road."

Tom broke in. "Red, they're coming your way. Pull out now and stay ahead of them until they get to Green."

"You got it."

Several minutes passed. "Coming up on Green."

"Okay. Turn into a driveway and let the cars pass you. Green, sit tight. They will be passing you soon."

"We have a problem," Green said. "The second car just turned down my street. If I turn around now, he'll know I'm following him."

"Damn it. Don't move. Steve, where are you?"

"Relax, Tom. Phillip and I are on our way."

"Make it quick or we'll lose him. The first car just passed us. We'll follow him from here."

Several minutes passed with no communication. Tom picked up his walkie-talkie and pressed the button.

"Steve, do you have the car?" No reply. "Damn it, Steve. Answer."

"We got him, Tom. The driver must have circled the block to make sure he wasn't followed."

"Thank God. Don't lose him."

"Same to . . ."

"Steve . . . Are you there? Steve!" When Tom didn't get an answer, he tossed his walkie-talkie into the back seat. "We must be out of range."

Rob glanced at Tom when he saw the car getting farther ahead of them. "Why are you slowing down?"

"I don't want them spotting us." They approached a busy intersection. "Okay, Kid. This is where it gets tricky. You keep your eyes on them while I focus on traffic." Tom entered the lane of cars and allowed two automobiles to get between them.

As they followed the car, Rob took note of the street signs they passed. "This is Canal Street. The busiest part of the city."

"I know. Keep your eye on them, Kid. We can't lose them."

The car ahead of them turned off, and Tom held back to allow another automobile to slip into the stream of traffic before he made the turn. The car they were tracking then turned onto another street, and Tom followed. "Where are we now?"

"Royal Street," Rob said. "The car appears to be slowing down in front of that building with all the lights."

"What is that building?"

"According to the sign, it's the Monteleone Hotel," Rob said, leaning forward to get a better look. "The sign's announcing The Patrons of Rex Carnival Gala."

"What's that?"

"Rex is the main parade during Mardi Gras season. Tom, the car's turning into the alley next to the hotel. This must be where it's happening."

"I see him. Look down there as I drive past to see if they stopped."

"It's stopped next to a side door of the hotel."

Tom pulled to the curb and parked. "You stay here."

"Where are you going?"

"To get as close to that car as possible to see what's happening." Tom got out and slipped into the alley.

Rob waited a moment, got out, and stood back as people in formal attire strolled past him and entered the hotel. After several minutes, Tom rushed back.

"What happened?" Rob asked.

"Get in."

Both men quickly got into the car.

"I saw the hostage get out dressed as a waiter. Before he went in, one of the men from the car handed him a gun."

"What are we going to do?"

"You're staying here and I'm going in."

Tom grabbed an extra clip from his glove box before getting out and rushing into the hotel. He went to the reservation desk and flashed his badge. "Where are all your waiters wearing white jackets working tonight?"

The young man's eyes widened. "B-- Banquet Halls A and B," he stammered. "It's the Rex Gala."

Tom rushed down the hallway and entered the room. "Damn," he whispered when he saw hundreds of people in formal attire and almost as many waiters in white jackets. Not knowing who the target was made this an impossible task. All he could do now was try to locate the hostage before he carried out his assignment.

*   *   *

At the front of the banquet room, a man approached Caroline as she stood beside her table.

"You're looking lovely tonight, my dear."

"Oh, thank you, Raymond. You look quite dashing yourself."

"That's kind of you. I'm not usually addressed in such flattering terms."

"Of course not, Raymond," Jack said as he joined the two. "You're a lawyer. Now, sit down and stop flirting with my wife."

"Relax, Broussard. It's the price you pay for marrying such a beautiful woman."

The teasing banter continued as more guests arrived at Caroline and Jack's table.

At the back of the banquet hall, a Hispanic waiter slipped in from a side door and stood against the wall. His hands shook as he took a folded piece of paper from his pocket and opened it, then scanned the room. When he found what he was searching for, he crumpled the page and hurriedly stuffed it into his jacket pocket.

The waiter noticed that other, real waiters were placing used dishes and utensils on a nearby cart. He grabbed an empty tray off the cart and began working his way to the front of the room, occasionally gathering a dish or utensils from a table as he went. He stopped when he got to the center row at the front of the room and stood motionless for a long moment.

The waiter purposely dropped a few pieces of silverware from the tray and looked around to see if anyone noticed. When he saw no one was paying attention, he got down on one knee and placed the tray of dishes on the floor. Sweat ran down his face despite the room being air-conditioned. He looked at the table before him, crossed himself, reached under his jacket, and jumped up, sending the tray and dishes sliding across the tiled floor.

"Gun! He's got a gun!" screamed a woman at a nearby table.

A man at the table lunged forward just as the waiter fired his gun. The man crumpled onto the woman beside him. Just as the waiter was about to fire again, he was grabbed from behind and thrown to the floor by two men in tuxedos.

The room erupted in chaos as people ran for the exits, leaving the two men holding down the unarmed waiter as he sobbed on the floor.

Tom pushed through the frantic mob and found the Mexican lying motionless, pinned down by the tuxedo-clad men. He turned his attention to the victim and saw a man and woman working frantically to loosen the man's tie and open his blood-soaked shirt.

"FBI. Get out of my way!" Tom shouted.

"You, get back," the woman said as she worked on the victim. "We're doctors. Make yourself useful and call for an ambulance."

"They're on their way," a man rushing to join them said. "I'm the hotel manager. How can I help?"

Tom presented his badge. "Find the people at this table and every table surrounding this one and hold them. They need to be questioned."

"I'll do my best," he said and hurried away.

Tom got down on one knee next to the victim. "Who is he?"

"Jackson Broussard," the man working with the woman said. "Please, step back and let us do our work."

Realizing the victim was in good hands, Tom turned his attention to the shooter. He showed his badge to the men holding him. "FBI. I need to talk to him."

"Fine," said one of the men, "but he stays where he is."

Tom took a pair of handcuffs from his belt and handcuffed the waiter before sitting him up.

"Do you speak English?" Tom asked.

The man slowly raised his head but said nothing as tears fell from his cheeks.

"I'm trying to help you. You have to talk to me before you're taken away," Tom said, but the man only shook his head. "At least give me your name."

"Ybarra."

Tom looked up and saw police officers approaching and Rob coming up behind them.

"Ybarra, I am Agent Tom Neal. You must not talk to anyone but me. Understand?"

The Mexican looked at him but didn't reply.

*　*　*

Rob had almost reached Tom when hotel security stopped him.

"This is a crime scene. You need to back away."

Tom held up his badge. "Let him through. He's with me."

Rob tried to step around the hotel security but was blocked. "Let the medical team through, then you can go."

Rob moved back as several men rushed by pushing a gurney. From where Rob stood, he could see a woman wearing a gown covered with blood, looking pale and confused. Off to the side, he saw the police officers lift the waiter from the floor and start his way. One of the officers stumbled over an overturned chair and fell, taking the waiter down with him. Rob saw something fall from the waiter's jacket as the men righted themselves and got to their feet. The officers didn't notice and took the shooter away.

The hotel security guard dropped Rob's arm. "Okay, you can go."

Rob didn't hesitate. He scooped up the paper the waiter had dropped and quickly stuffed it into his pocket before going to Tom. "Is he going to make it?" Rob asked, looking at the victim, who was being loaded onto the gurney.

"It doesn't look good." Tom shook his head. "Dammit. I was less than twenty feet away when I heard the shot." He paused for a moment, then turned to Rob. "What happened to the car in the alley?"

"Someone opened the side door, shouted something, and the car took off. What can I do here?"

"Find out what hospital they're taking the victim to and get back to me. We need to get to the shooter before he's questioned by the local police."

Rob exited the hall, rushed through the crowd, and got to the ambulance just as they were helping the woman inside.

"Wait," he shouted. "The FBI wants to know where you're taking him."

"Ochsner Hospital," a paramedic said. "Stand back. We have to go."

Rob stepped back as sirens blared and the ambulance pulled away. Tom was coming out as Rob turned to go back inside.

"I have the name of the hospital," Rob said.

"Good. Let's go."

CHAPTER THIRTEEN

Police Station

Rob and Tom were nearly run over by two officers attempting to control a belligerent man as they entered the Fifth District police station. On their way to the desk, Rob noticed an officer sitting on a bench next to a man in a nice suit and handcuffs who was obviously intoxicated. A fourth officer brushed past them, holding on to a makeup-caked woman who seemed well acquainted with the officer gripping her arm.

Tom flashed his badge at the officer behind the desk. "Who's in charge of the hotel shooting?"

The balding, overweight policeman squinted. "Dang, you boys got here quick."

"Answer my question."

"Detective Miller."

"Where is he? I need to speak to him."

The officer picked up the phone and dialed a number. "Detective Miller, the Feds are here. They want to talk with you about the Monteleone Hotel shooting."

The officer kept his eyes on Tom as he listened.

"Yep, that's exactly what I said." He listened for another moment, then hung up the phone. "Go down this hallway," he told Tom and Rob. "Detective Miller will find you."

Rob and Tom entered the hallway and saw a sour-faced man wearing a rumpled shirt and a loose necktie approaching. He stopped several feet away from them and crossed his arms.

"He doesn't look pleased," Rob whispered.

Tom presented his badge. "Are you Miller?"

"Depends. Who are you?"

"Senior Agent Tom Neal."

"What's your interest in the hotel shooting?"

"We suspect the shooting is connected to a gang we've been tracking."

"How did you know the shooter was here?"

"Doesn't matter, detective. Where is he?"

Miller paused a moment. "You're wasting your time."

"Why? Has something happened to him?"

"He's fine. The guy doesn't speak English." The detective uncrossed his arms. "But if you insist on trying, he's all yours until my interpreter arrives. Then you have to leave."

"Sounds fair."

Miller looked at Rob. "Who's he?"

"My interpreter."

"Really? You should have told me that earlier."

"I just did."

Miller's eyes moved from one man to the other before taking a step. "He's this way."

The detective took them down a long hallway to a set of doors. Miller opened one of them, and they entered. The room was dark and had a large glass window that allowed them to see the handcuffed man sitting at a table. He was rocking back and forth with his head bowed. Miller flipped a switch near the glass window, and they heard the Mexican mumbling over the speakers.

"He's been doing that since he got here," Miller said. "Good luck getting anything out of him."

Tom motioned to Rob, and they left the observation room and went back to the hallway.

"Could you understand what he was saying?" Tom whispered.

"He was mumbling, *I failed, I failed.*"

"When we go in, tell Ybarra to only respond in Spanish."

"How do you know his name?"

"He told me at the hotel. Remember, Miller will listen to everything said in that room, so be careful," Tom said, opening the door.

Rob took the chair across the table from the despondent man, keeping his back to the observation window. Tom stood at his side. Rob leaned forward and whispered to the man in Spanish.

"Ybarra, I'm Rob, and this is FBI Agent Tom Neal. You need to speak only Spanish. Do you understand?"

At first, the Mexican didn't respond. Then he stopped his rocking and slowly raised his head.

"You were at the hotel," he whispered in English.

Rob shook his head and whispered. "*No inglés*, Ybarra."

He nodded.

Tom whispered, "We know you and another man were brought here by ship and were told to kill someone. Do you know who the other man was supposed to kill?"

Ybarra shook his head before responding in Spanish.

Rob turned to Tom and whispered, "He said they didn't tell them anything until they were put in the cars."

The Mexican started sobbing as he spoke.

"What is he saying?" Tom whispered.

"He's saying, 'I failed, I failed. My family will die.'"

"I don't think we're going to get much out of him," Tom whispered.

Rob leaned back and motioned for Tom to get closer. "Block me from the view of the window. I need to show him something."

Tom nodded and casually closed the gap between them.

Rob leaned forward, took something from his pant pocket, unfolded it under the table, and slid it in front of Ybarra.

"Where did that come from?" Tom whispered.

"It fell out of his pocket when he was taken from the hotel."

"That looks like a table diagram."

"It is." Rob tapped the table with an X marked on it. "Is this how you knew where your target was sitting?" he asked in Spanish.

"Sí."

Rob guardedly flipped the page over to reveal a photo of three people standing in front of a large building: an older man in the middle, the shooting victim on one side, and the woman from the hotel on the other. All were smiling.

"Do you know why you were sent to kill this man?" Tom whispered, tapping the photo of the victim.

Ybarra started to cry and shake his head, mumbling.

Rob turned to Tom. "He keeps saying, 'I failed, I failed.'"

"Dang it, Ybarra," Tom whispered. "You didn't fail. This man is probably dead by now."

Ybarra lifted his cuffed hands and ran his finger across the photo. He said something in Spanish, then pushed the image away.

Rob's eyes widened as he turned to Tom and whispered, "The man wasn't the target. He was told to kill the woman."

Tom held Rob's gaze for a moment. "We have to get to that hospital," Tom said just as someone tapped on the glass behind them.

Rob grabbed the paper from the table and slid it into his pocket.

"They're telling us to leave," Tom whispered. "Tell Ybarra not to talk to anyone except us. We will try to find his family. I'll get back to him as soon as I can."

Rob suspected Ybarra understood what Tom had said but whispered everything to him in Spanish to make sure. Ybarra nodded just as the door opened.

"Did you get anything?" Miller asked, entering the room.

"You were right," Tom said. "He doesn't want to talk."

"We'll see about that. My interpreter's here. Time for you to go."

"Take good care of him, Miller. I want to find him healthy when I come back."

Miller looked annoyed. "Of course. Anything to support the Feds. Now, get out of here."

Tom and Rob left the interrogation room and rushed to the front desk. "We need directions to Ochsner Hospital."

The officer took a map from a drawer, unfolded it, and tapped a thick finger on a spot. "You're here on Magnolia Street." He slid his hand across the city and stopped. "Ochsner Hospital is here on Jefferson Highway." He reached over and picked up a pad and pencil. "It's a long way from here, so you better write this down."

Tom glanced at Rob.

"I got it," Rob said.

"Thanks," Tom said and started for the door.

As soon as they were in the car, Rob began giving directions. They had driven for several blocks when a traffic light changed, forcing them to stop.

Tom struck the steering wheel. "Damn it. Every second we waste gives Pascal time to locate the woman."

"Has Steve paged you?"

"Not yet. I'll reach out after I know we have the woman secured."

They finally reached the hospital, and Tom and Rob raced to the front desk.

"Where is Jackson Broussard?" Tom said, flashing his badge.

"You said Broussard?"

"Yes, Broussard. First name Jackson."

"Let me check." The receptionist picked up the phone and made a call. "The authorities are here to see a patient named Jackson Broussard." She glanced at Tom for a second. "Thank you," she said and hung up. "Mr. Broussard is in surgery."

"Where will I find Mrs. Broussard?"

"Uh, I'm guessing the waiting room on the third floor of the surgery wing."

"Where are the elevators?"

She pointed to the hallway to her left, and Tom and Rob ran in that direction.

When the elevator doors opened on the third floor, Tom and Rob stepped out into a corridor packed with people, many of them still dressed in formal attire. They pushed through the crowd to get to the waiting area.

Fortunately, Rob was taller than most people and could scan the room. A middle-aged woman standing alone caught his eye. She wasn't dressed as finely as everyone else, but she appeared to be the only person in the room who was genuinely distraught. Rob made his way through the groups of people to her.

"Excuse me, ma'am. I'm looking for Mrs. Jackson Broussard. Is she here?"

The woman looked up and blotted tears from her eyes with a handkerchief. "Miss Caroline is changing her clothes." She glanced past him. "There she is now."

Rob turned and saw a woman wearing a light blue shirt, capris, and flats approaching them. She looked more like Mary Tyler Moore from *The Dick Van Dyke Show* than the socialite he had seen at the hotel. She was holding her rolled-up beaded gown and heels as she went through the crowd, nodding to one person after another as she made her way to them.

"Give me those, Miss Caroline. I'll take care of them."

"Thank you, Rosie. I didn't know who else to call."

"I'm always here for you, Miss Caroline. Have been since you were a little girl. You know how much I love you and Mr. Jack."

"And we love you, Rosie. You're all the family we have left."

"That's not true. You have Mr. Moretti."

"Dear God, you're right. I need to call C.J."

"Not to worry. I already have."

"How did you get his number?"

"He gave me his card after your daddy's funeral. He wanted me to call him in case you needed him."

"Thank you, Rosie. I can't think straight right now."

"Miss Caroline, this gentleman was asking for you."

Caroline looked up at Rob just as Tom joined them. "I think I remember you from the hotel. Are you with the police?"

"No, Mrs. Broussard. I'm Agent Tom Neal with the FBI, and this is my partner." Tom opened his wallet and showed his credentials. "It's imperative we speak with you privately."

"Why? I've already told the police everything."

"Mrs. Broussard, I insist."

She frowned. "Sir, I'm not going anywhere. My husband is across the corridor fighting for his life."

Rob stepped forward. "Ma'am, we aren't asking you to leave the floor. Your friend can come, too, so she will know exactly where to find you if there is news about your husband."

Caroline looked at Rosie before turning back to Tom. "All right, but only for a few minutes."

Rob led the trio through the crowd and continued down the hallway until he found an unpopulated spot.

"I'll come for you if I hear anything, Miss Caroline."

"Thank you, Rosie."

"How long has your husband been in surgery?" Tom asked.

"Three hours. They come out and give me updates every hour or so. I think it's their way of assuring me he's still alive." She took a breath. "My Jack's a fighter. He's going to get through this."

"I'm sure he's getting the best of care, Mrs. Broussard," Tom assured her.

"Jack has never harmed a soul in his life. Why would someone do this to him?"

Tom paused a moment before responding. "Mrs. Broussard, your husband wasn't the target."

"What are you talking about? That man pointed that gun right at him."

"He wasn't aiming at your husband, Mrs. Broussard. He was there for you."

Her mouth dropped open. "Me? Oh my God. Are you saying I'm the reason Jack was shot?"

"Mrs. Broussard, do you know why anyone would want to harm you?" Tom asked gently.

"What? No!" She wiped her eyes and looked at Tom. "You seem to know so much about this, you tell me."

"What do you know about the New Orleans Mafia?"

"It's run by Marcel Pascal." She scrunched her forehead. "Everyone in this city knows that."

"Do you know why he's after you?"

She paused a moment. "Pascal's not after me. He's after Crescent City Concrete. It's the largest concrete plant in the state. Pascal tried to force my father to pay tariffs for years, but Papa refused. Pascal's tried for decades to run us out of business, but none of his devious plans have worked." She paused for a moment. "My father passed away two years ago, and now I run the company. It belongs to me."

Rob exchanged a glance with Tom.

"Don't look so shocked. Yes, I own and operate a concrete plant."

"Sorry, Mrs. Broussard," Rob said, knowing his surprise had been written on his face.

"Your reaction is why we decided to make Jack the face of the company. He's a brilliant negotiator and people manager. I'm the numbers person, and the visionary. Truthfully, I began running the company years before my father's death. He was ill and struggled with the stress of everyday decisions. Jack and I kept it a secret because our company had just been awarded the contract to provide most of the concrete to rebuild the levees after Hurricane Betsy. We could have lost the contract if the Corps of Engineers discovered I was head of the company instead of Papa."

"If your father died two years ago," Rob said, "why is Pascal after you now?"

"There's a levee maintenance contract coming up worth millions, and Pascal knows our company has the best chance of winning it. He's already tried to sabotage our plant once, and when that didn't work, I guess he decided killing me was the only way he could win."

"What do you mean by 'tried to sabotage the plant?'" Tom asked.

"A couple of weeks back, a section of our plant was vandalized to cut our production capabilities. Jack managed to have it repaired without the extravagant cost of replacing our systems. Fortunately, we were back to full production within a few days. When his plan didn't work, my guess is Pascal did this."

Suddenly, a buzzing sound interrupted their conversation, and Tom took his pager from his belt clip. "Kid, escort Mrs. Broussard back to the waiting room and stay at her side until I return," he said, then turned and started down the hallway.

"Let's get back, Mrs. Broussard."

They were walking down the hallway when Rosie and a nurse came rushing toward them.

CHAPTER FOURTEEN

Ochsner Hospital

Rob and Caroline followed the nurse to a door marked *Cardiothoracic Surgery, Gregory Duplantis, Specialist*. Rob recognized the man the moment they went in. He was the man dressed in a tuxedo working on Mr. Broussard at the hotel. The doctor came around his desk and glanced at Rob before speaking to the nurse.

"Thank you, Edna."

"Is there anything else I can do for you, Doctor?"

"Yes. Please escort this gentleman back to the waiting room."

"Sorry, Doctor. I can't leave Mrs. Broussard's side."

"I beg your pardon?"

"He should stay, Gregory," Caroline said. "Apparently the authorities feel I need a bodyguard."

Rob ignored the doctor's glare and stood by the door.

"Please have a seat, Caroline."

She didn't move. "Gregory, don't you dare bring me in here to tell me Jack died."

"Jack is in recovery, Caroline. Now, will you please sit? You look exhausted."

She closed her eyes briefly, exhaled, and sat.

The doctor sat beside her and took her hand.

"Before you say anything, Gregory, thank you for caring for Jack at the hotel. Had you not, he wouldn't be alive."

The doctor shook his head. "I'm just grateful that you asked Margo and me to sit at your table. You should know it's a miracle Jack has made it this far."

She looked into his eyes. "What do you mean by this far? Are you saying I could still lose him?"

The doctor looked down for a moment. "I've known you too long to sugarcoat this, so I'm going to talk to you like you are a fellow surgeon. The bullet nicked Jack's liver and destroyed one of his kidneys. The good news is his remaining kidney is functioning, and we were able to save his liver."

"If that's the good news, I'm afraid to hear the bad."

"The bullet lodged against Jack's spinal cord. I had to call in three of the top specialists in the city to help me remove it."

She took a breath. "Then Jack's going to be all right?"

"Honestly, we don't know. You need to prepare yourself, Caroline."

"Prepare for what? You said you removed the bullet."

"We did, but there's a strong chance Jack's spinal cord was damaged." The doctor took a breath. "He may never walk again."

She shook her head. "No! I refuse to accept that. Gregory, you have to do whatever it takes to make sure he does."

"We have, Caroline. There's nothing more we can do. The greatest risk to Jack now is infection. Once we're past that hurdle, you should thank the good Lord he lived."

"I do, but how long will we have to wait before we know if he'll be able to walk?"

"That could take weeks, even months. You must stay hopeful, Caroline. There is still a good chance he will have full use of his upper body."

"I'm a numbers person, Gregory. Give it to me in percentages."

The doctor took a deep breath. "I'd say Jack's chances of using his upper body are about 60 to 70 percent in his favor."

"And walking?"

"Less than 10 to 20 percent chance of ever using his legs again."

She looked at him without responding, then closed her eyes.

The doctor patted her arm. "You must be positive when you're around him, Caroline."

She opened her eyes and looked at him. "And how do I do that?"

The doctor shook his head.

Rob watched the interaction with the doctor, and his thoughts returned to what he and Wanda had endured. They'd survived their involvement with Rojas and Martínez, but his best friend hadn't. Rob had worked hard to suppress his grief and remain strong for Wanda. He sensed Mrs. Broussard would do the same for her husband.

*   *   *

Tom found a phone a few floors down, dropped in several coins, and dialed. He waited for the signal, then entered the pay phone number and a code before hanging up. He looked at his watch several times before it rang.

"Were you able to stop it?"

"By a hair," Steve said. "A second later and we would have been too late. What about you?"

"The target's alive, but not because of us. Who was your intended victim?"

"He's a labor union organizer. We followed the car to an old movie theater in a community called Chalmette. There was a large crowd going in, so we went around back. I saw the Mexican entering and followed him. Phillip went in through the lobby," Steve said. "When I got inside, I realized it was a dock worker gathering about unionizing. When I saw the shooter aim his 9mm at the guy on stage, I tackled him, but he got off a shot."

"Was the target hit?"

"Nope. The bullet took out a large spotlight overhead and sparks and glass flew everywhere. Phillip grabbed the target and took him off stage to safety." Steve started to chuckle. "When that shot took out that spotlight, those dock workers almost trampled each other getting out of that place."

"What about the guys in the car?"

"We were too busy inside to worry about them. What about you?"

"Our guy shot the wrong person. He hit the husband instead of the wife."

"The target was a *woman?*"

"Yes, and still is. Her husband jumped in front of her just as the gun fired. I wasn't close enough to stop it."

"Is the husband going to make it?"

"Not sure. It doesn't look good." Tom shut his eyes for a second as he recalled the scene. "Where is the shooter and your target?" he asked. "I need to question them."

"Phillip called the undercover cops, and they placed the target in a safe, guarded location. The detective took the shooter someplace else. They said the Mexican wouldn't live long in lockup if Pascal's involved."

"Damn it. My shooter is in police custody. How quickly can you and Phillip get to Ochsner Hospital?"

"Let me ask."

Tom could hear talking in the background.

"Phillip said almost an hour."

"Get there as fast as you can. The Kid's on the third floor with the woman. Her name is Caroline Broussard. The husband's name is Jack. Or Jackson."

"Where are you going?"

"To the police station to make sure my shooter is safe." Tom hung up and ran.

*　*　*

Garden District

The lights above Savoy's Restaurant burned brightly despite the late hour.

Pascal picked up a glass paperweight from his desk and hurled it across the room. "Jean-Claude! Get that worthless drug lord on the line!" Several minutes passed before his assistant ran into his office.

"Sir, Martínez is on line one."

Pascal grabbed the phone. "You worthless piece of shit!"

"Careful Pascal. What has you so angry?""

"Both assignments are very much alive. And to make matters worse, your shooters were caught. Where was your backup?"

"Backup? What backup?"

"Damn it, Martínez. Are you telling me you had no one backing these men up?"

"Every assignment you requested has always been filled. There was never a need for backup."

"You idiot. Our agreement is over."

"Wait, wait! You can't do this, Pascal. Let me fix this."

"You had your chance, Martínez. I never want to hear from you again."

"But what about my shipment?"

"Consider it my payment for having to clean up this mess."

"You can't do that."

"That shipment is in my possession, Martínez. I can do whatever I damn well please."

"I am sending men to fix this, Pascal. And when it's done, I'm taking my shipment."

Marcel Pascal paused momentarily, then leaned back in his chair as a smile crossed his lips. "Instead of fighting over this, I suggest we make a wager. I'll even make it easy for you. Instead of two assignments, we'll only focus on one. My most pressing concern is the Broussard woman. If you eliminate her before my people do, you get your shipment. If my people get to her first, the shipment is mine, and I never have to see you again."

"If that is the only way I get my shipment, then yes. We have a deal."

"Good. I suggest you move fast, or this will be over before you arrive."

*　*　*

Mexico

Martínez rushed out of his bedroom in his underwear and found his guard asleep in a chair outside his door.

"Gonzales, wake up!"

The man fell out of the chair.

"Find Salvador! Tell him I will cut off his feet and yours if I don't see his silver-tipped boots in front of me in less than an hour."

Gonzales ran down the hallway.

Martínez returned to his bedroom and slammed the door. He grabbed his pants and cursed as he dressed.

Win or lose, Pascal. No one takes my shipment, he thought. Someone rapped at his door. "Did you find him?" Martínez yelled.

The door opened. "Salvador is coming, boss. He is coming."

"Get everyone up. No one is sleeping tonight!"

*　*　*

New Orleans

Tom had an eerie, unsettled feeling as he sped down the quiet New Orleans streets between dark and daylight. It appeared the city was populated by two different worlds of people and at the moment, night dwellers were giving up their hold on the city. Most residents spent all their lives not knowing the other world existed.

Tom arrived at the police station and found that a policewoman had replaced the night desk officer. Her hair was twisted into a knot so tight it looked painful. He stood across from her, waiting as she held a phone to her ear, filling out a form.

He cleared his throat to get her attention, but she never looked up, so Tom took his badge from his pocket and placed it on her paperwork. She glared at him as she continued her phone conversation.

"Yes, ma'am," she said. "I'll have one of the detectives give you a call." She hung up and pushed his badge off her papers. "Can I help you?"

"I need to see the prisoner brought in last night from the Monteleone Hotel shooting. His name is Ybarra."

She pulled out a clipboard. "Ybarra, Ybarra. He's not here. Looks like he was taken to Central a few hours ago."

"And where is Central?"

"1400 South Dupre Street."

"You got a map?" She reached into a drawer and was starting to unfold it when Tom snatched it from her hand and started for the door.

"Hey, you can't take that!"

"Send the bill to FBI headquarters."

Tom unfolded the map when he got behind the wheel. He started the engine as soon as he located Dupre Street and pulled away. The roads were almost empty, so Neal ignored most traffic lights to get to the building as fast as possible. Despite his best efforts, it still took him nearly an hour.

"I'm here to see a prisoner who came in a few hours ago," Neal said, showing his badge to the officer at the desk.

"What's the prisoner's name?"

"Francisco Ybarra. He's a suspect in the Monteleone Hotel shooting. Detective Miller is in charge of the case."

"Wait here."

"Where are you going?"

The officer didn't look back.

Tom felt his gut twisting. He shifted from one foot to the other until the thin officer returned. He wasn't alone.

"I'm Lieutenant Conti. I understand you're with the FBI."

"I am. I need to see a prisoner named Francisco Ybarra. He was transferred here last night or early this morning."

The lieutenant and officer exchanged glances. "You need to follow me," the lieutenant said.

Tom felt the knot in his gut tighten as he followed the lieutenant through several hallways to a set of unlocked doors.

"These doors are unlocked. Why put a prisoner here?"

The lieutenant didn't respond. He simply pushed the doors open.

Tom entered and saw a sheet-covered body. The lieutenant lifted the sheet. "Is this the man you're looking for?"

Tom looked down. Ybarra's throat had been slit from ear to ear. "How did this happen? He was only here for a couple of hours."

"He was alone in the showers when it happened."

"Where were the guards?"

"A guard was posted outside the shower entrance. When Ybarra didn't come out, the officer went in and found him on the floor in one of the stalls."

"Who else was in the showers?"

"No one. The officer said the showers were empty when he went in."

Tom lifted the dead man's chin, exposing the gaping gash. "Well, he sure didn't do this to himself. Where's the weapon?"

"There wasn't one."

Tom's eyes narrowed as he looked at the officer. "Where is the guard who was watching him?"

"He's being debriefed across town." The lieutenant shrugged. "Sometimes, things like this happen."

Tom spread the sheet over Ybarra. "Yeah, apparently a lot around here."

"Is there anything else I can do for you, Agent Neal?"

"No. I think you've done enough."

Tom rushed to his car and started back to the hospital. If Pascal could get to Ybarra in lockup, Rob and the woman wouldn't stand a chance at the hospital.

CHAPTER FIFTEEN

Ochsner Hospital

Jack was moved from recovery and placed on the Intensive Care floor of the hospital. Caroline was at his side. Rob wasn't family and was not allowed in, so he stood near the door that accessed the ICU floor.

Rob made use of his time by making mental notes of the names and faces of every nurse, doctor, orderly, and family member entering and exiting the unit. He also noted the routines of the staff by checking his watch each time someone new appeared. It was apparent the team knew each other well from their friendly exchanges.

An attractive nurse who looked to be in her early forties came out the door.

"Excuse me, nurse." Rob glanced at her name tag. "Nurse Bennett. Is it possible for me to see Mrs. Broussard?"

"I need to see her too," said a male voice behind them.

Rob turned and made a mental note of the man, who was of medium build. He looked to be in his early fifties, with sprinkles of gray in his hair.

"I'm sorry," Rob said. "Who are you?"

"C.J. Moretti. I'm a close friend of the family. Who the heck are you?"

Rob positioned himself between the man and the nurse. "Sorry, sir. Mrs. Broussard isn't allowed visitors."

"That's ridiculous. If I can't see Caroline, neither can you."

Nurse Bennett stepped between the two men. "Gentlemen, please. No one is allowed except family and hospital staff."

Moretti looked at Rob. "You aren't a doctor, and I know you're not family. Are you police?"

"I'm not on anyone's payroll."

Moretti turned back to the nurse. "Miss, I've spent all night on a plane to get here. Could you at least tell Mrs. Broussard I'm here?"

Before she could answer, Caroline pushed through the doors and flung her arms around his neck. "I heard that Philly accent all the way from Jack's room. I'm so glad you're here."

Rob stepped away as they embraced again.

"Rose called, and I got here as fast as I could." He took her hand. "How is he?"

"It's bad, C.J. The bullet was lodged against his spine. They are saying Jack may never walk again."

"Dear Lord. I'm so sorry. What happened to the scum that shot him?"

"He's in police custody."

"Good. Why on earth would he shoot Jack?"

Caroline glanced at Rob before answering. "I was told Jack was shot by mistake."

"A mistake? That's crazy. Who was that guy after?"

Rob stepped forward. "Mrs. Broussard can't answer that."

Moretti looked at Rob. "Then who can?"

"Agent Tom Neal is in charge of the investigation."

"Agent? Why is the FBI involved in this?"

"Again, all questions must be answered by Agent Neal."

"So, when can I speak to this Agent Neal?"

"I don't know."

Caroline patted C.J.'s shoulder. "I know you're concerned, but I think it's best to let the authorities handle it. Just knowing you came means more than you know."

"I'm not going anywhere, Caroline. I'm staying right here for as long as you need me."

"You can't do that. You have a family and a company to run."

"I can handle my plant from here. And Sadie told me to stay as long as you needed me."

"You married a good woman, C.J."

"Yes, I did. Since I'm not allowed in to see Jack, what can I do for you at the plant?"

"I'm really not sure. My mind is in such a blur. All I can think about is Jack."

"Don't worry. I'm well acquainted with running that plant. Those years I spent working for your papa were some of the best of my life."

"If Papa were here, he would say the same about you."

"When do you think I'll be able to see Jack?"

"I don't know. I'm fortunate the hospital is letting me stay."

C.J. glanced at Rob. "What about him?"

"He's Agent Neal's partner. His name is . . . is . . ." Her brow furrowed as she looked at Rob. "I just realized I don't know your name."

"Kid. You can call me Kid."

"Kid, this is C.J. He's our dear friend from Philadelphia." Caroline pressed her hand to her mouth to suppress a yawn and glanced at them with weary eyes. "Sorry, I need to get back to Jack. Please try to be nice to each other."

"I'll go, but if you need anything, Caroline, call me at the plant. I'm going there right after I have a word with Mr. Kid."

"I insist you stay at the house. Rose needs someone to fuss over right now."

"Don't worry about me." C.J. kissed her hand. "You take care of Jack. I'll be in touch."

She hugged him and went through the doors leading to the patients' rooms.

When she was out of sight, Moretti turned to Rob. "When will Agent Neal return?"

"I don't know."

C.J. took a card from his wallet and scribbled a number on the back. "Give him my card and tell him I want to talk to him. The number on the back is Caroline's office at Crescent City Concrete. He can reach me there."

Rob took the card and read both sides before tucking it into his shirt pocket. "I'll see he gets it."

"This family is important to me, Mr. Kid. I need answers."

"I will give Agent Neal your message."

Tom parked in the hospital parking lot and removed his spare 9mm

Parabellum handgun and a clip from his glove box. He loaded the weapon, holstered it, and exited the car. As he approached the hospital entrance, he noticed a van parked near the front door with *May's Florals, New Orleans' Finest* on the door. A young man took two large vases of flowers from the back of the van and went through the door of the hospital.

Tom was about to go in when he heard someone whistle. He spun around with his hand on his gun.

"Easy," Steve said as he and Phillip approached. "Did you secure your shooter?"

"Not here," Tom said, beckoning Steve and Phillip to follow him to the side of the building.

"I was too late. My shooter's throat was slit in lockup before I arrived. That means they know he failed. I'm certain they'll be coming here for the woman."

Steve glanced at Phillip. "What do you want us to do?"

"Hold back for at least five minutes, then come in."

"How do we find you?"

"Go to the information desk and ask for Jackson Broussard's room. Wherever he is, the woman will be nearby. I told Kid not to leave her side. Did one of you get word to Wiley?"

Phillip nodded. "I called and told him to meet us here after we talked to you."

"I hope he gets here soon. I've got the feeling this is going to take all of us. Stay alert."

"Roger that," Steve replied.

*   *   *

Steve and Phillip waited at the side of the building for several minutes after Tom went in.

Phillip scratched his head. "If Tom doesn't want us to be seen together, how will we know where to find Broussard without showing our badge?"

Steve gave him a wink. "I have an idea. Follow me." He walked to the back of the van, opened it and reached inside. He took two vases of flowers and handed them to Phillip. The bouquets were so large you couldn't see the man holding them. Steve took another bouquet from the van and closed the doors. "Let me do the talking."

"Go slow. I can barely see anything through these flowers."

They went in the doors to a woman seated at the information desk.

"Can I help you?" she asked.

"Yes, ma'am. May's Florist with a delivery for a . . ." He pretended to look at the card tucked in the bouquet. "Mr. Jackson Broussard."

The woman looked at her clipboard. "I'm sorry, Mr. Broussard is in the Intensive Care unit. You will need to leave the flowers at the desk."

"Right, what floor is that?"

"The fifth. Take the elevators at the end of the hallway."

"Thank you." Steve nodded to Phillip and got into the elevator. But instead of going to the fifth floor, they exited on the third without the flowers.

*   *   *

Up on the fifth floor of the hospital, Rob glanced at his watch and realized he hadn't slept in over twenty-six hours. He pushed away from the wall and started pacing to help stay alert and noticed Tom coming up the corridor.

"What are you doing out here?" Tom grumbled. "I told you to stay with the woman."

"I was ordered off the floor." Rob saw the stress in Tom's eyes. "Did you find Ybarra?"

"He's dead."

"Dead? How did that happen?"

"No one seems to know."

"Have you heard from Steve?"

"His target is safe, and the shooter is being guarded somewhere out of the hands of the police."

"Well, at least that's some good news."

Tom pulled him aside and handed Rob his extra revolver. "Hide it under your shirt. Careful, it's loaded."

Rob took the gun, slid it under his belt, and covered it with his shirt. "Steve showed me how to handle it."

"This isn't training, Kid. Let's go. We have to protect the woman."

"We aren't allowed in."

"Oh, yes, we are."

Rob followed Tom through the door to the nurse's desk and saw Nurse Bennett's expression.

"Sir, I've already told your friend you can't be on this floor."

Tom presented his badge. "I'm not asking for permission. Do you have a floor plan for this floor?"

She thought for a moment. "I have a fire evacuation plan for this floor. It will show every door and exit."

"Perfect. I need a copy."

"Let me see what I can do." She stepped away, and Tom turned to Rob.

"Where is the woman?"

"She's in her husband's room."

Nurse Bennett returned with a sheet of paper. "Here is a copy of the plan."

Tom took the paper and looked it over. "I see the main door here and what appears to be a side door to the hallway down there to the right," he said, pointing in that direction.

"Yes," the nurse said. "That hallway leads to the service elevators."

Rob looked over Tom's shoulder and pointed to something on the page. "What's this?"

"That's the fire escape. It's at the end of the hall on the left."

"Can I keep this?" Tom asked.

"Sure." The nurse looked up at Rob. "Does he need one too?"

"No need. Where is Mrs. Broussard?"

"She's in 2A with her husband."

Tom gave Rob the floor plan. "Look this over in case we're separated."

Rob scanned the page and then gave it back. "Got it."

"Find 2A and stay with Mrs. Broussard. I need to locate Steve and Phillip."

Tom went to the end of the hallway and disappeared through the doors.

Rob entered 2A and found Caroline sleeping in a chair beside her husband. Jack Broussard looked pale and had several tubes coming out of him. The machines were making so much noise that Rob wondered how Caroline could sleep. He positioned himself by the open door to wait for Tom's return.

As he stood there, Rob noticed the regular nurses going from room to room with a clipboard or tray of medication. One of the doctors he recognized was leaving the floor, brushing past two men in white coats without acknowledging them. Rob watched closely as the two men stood off to the side. They never spoke to the nurse at the desk, but just looked around and whispered.

As Rob was focusing on them, Tom came into the room.

"I have the floor laid out, and Steve and Phillip are in place. I need you to watch the back hall entrance in case they come in that way. I will stay here with the woman. We have to be ready for anything."

Rob didn't respond.

"Kid, did you hear what I said?"

"Tom, they're already here," Rob said in a low whisper.

"Where?"

"See those two men talking? They aren't the regular doctors."

"Go to the nurse's desk and tell the nurse to spread the word to the staff to stay calm and clear the hallway as fast as possible."

Rob leisurely approached the nurse's station and asked Nurse Bennett for a pen and paper. She gave it to him, and he wrote, *Everyone here is in danger. Quietly spread the word to the regular staff to slip out of here as normally as possible and take cover.* He slid the note to the nurse and tapped the word *regular* as she read it.

She looked up at him with eyes as large as saucers, nodded, and casually left her desk.

Rob returned to the doorway of Jack Broussard's room, and he and Tom watched Nurse Bennett make her way from one person to another. She was about to approach the two men in white jackets when Rob cleared his throat loudly. She glanced at him. He shook his head, and she went to other staff members. One by one, the staff disappeared down the hallway. Nurse Bennett glanced at Rob and Tom before slipping behind her desk.

"Stay here with the Broussards and secure the door," Tom whispered.

Rob entered the room and closed the door but discovered it didn't have a lock. He went to the large window separating the room from the hallway, closed the curtain, and whispered to the sleeping wife. "Wake up, Caroline, wake up."

She lifted her head. "What?"

"Men are coming for you."

"Jack. What about Jack?"

"It's you they're after, not him. Duck below the window and follow me to the door."

Caroline kissed her husband and was almost to Rob when they heard shots fired.

Rob grabbed her and pressed her against the wall behind him. "Don't move." He cracked the door to see Tom firing near the nurse's station. Tom glanced at him after several rounds, pointed to the hallway behind him, and motioned for them to go.

Rob shielded Caroline with his body as they rushed from the room. They were almost in the hallway when he heard Tom shout.

"Use the pager!"

Rob glanced back as a spray of bullets hit Tom, and he slumped to the floor. Before Rob could react, Steve appeared behind the shooters at the end of the hallway and opened fire. Rob saw Nurse Bennett crouched behind her desk, and their eyes met. "Take care of him!" he shouted before heading down the hallway in the direction of the service elevator.

They were almost there when someone Rob recognized from his past came around the corner. Rob pushed Caroline behind him and faced the man.

"How can this be?" the gunman said, standing before him. "I was told you were dead."

"Let her go, César. She's done nothing to you."

"Maybe not, but she is why I'm here. Killing you is a gift. It will make the boss very pleased to hear you are really dead." He pointed the gun at Rob's head. "*Adiós, gringo.*"

A shot rang out, and the gunman crumbled onto the floor. Rob touched his head and looked down at his blood-soaked shirt.

"There's more coming," Wiley said as the right side of his face twitched. "I'll cover you to give you time to get her out of here."

"We have nowhere to go!" Caroline shouted.

"Fire escape," Rob said.

"Move!" Wiley shouted before ducking into a doorway for cover.

CHAPTER SIXTEEN

Ochsner Hospital

Rob remembered the fire escape from the diagram and rushed Caroline to it. He raised the window and lifted her onto the platform before climbing out behind her. He released the ladder, and they started down as gunfire rang out above them and police sirens wailed below.

When they hit the pavement, Rob grabbed Caroline's hand and they joined the frantic masses exiting the hospital. When they reached the street, Rob saw a city bus coming to a stop at the end of the block.

"Hurry. That bus is the quickest way out of here," Rob said, taking Caroline's arm. When they were a few feet from the bus, Rob slowed his pace. "Stay calm and act as normal as possible."

Caroline boarded first, then Rob. As he took coins from his pocket for the fare, he noticed the driver staring at him.

"Hey, man, are you hurt?"

Rob looked down at his blood-splattered clothing. "A friend had an accident, and we brought him to the hospital."

"What's going on over there? I never saw so many police."

"Not sure. I think a car was backfiring and someone called the cops."

"Well, in this city, you never know."

Rob nudged Caroline forward. They were halfway down the aisle when the sight of a Hispanic man boarding the bus caught Rob's eye. He didn't want to draw attention to Caroline, so he kept moving her down the aisle.

They found two open seats, and Caroline slid in next to the window and Rob sat next to her. The man passed them and sat a couple of rows behind.

"Keep your head down and don't say a word," Rob whispered as the bus pulled away from the curb. The bus continued for several blocks before it made another stop. Several people got off, and others got on, taking up every seat in front of them. A teenage girl loaded with shopping bags was the last to get on. After dropping coins in the box next to the driver, she made her way down the aisle.

The bus started moving again, and Rob heard the girl talking to someone behind him.

"Excuse me, mister. Can you let me in? That seat by the window is the only one left."

Rob heard the man grumbling and bags crumpling behind him. It was quiet for several minutes when the girl spoke again.

"Those are some fine boots, mister. I especially like those shiny metal toe caps you have on them. My boyfriend would love a pair of those. How much do they cost?"

There was no reply.

"Mister, we'll be here a while, so you might as well answer me. How much did you pay for your boots?"

"These were handmade, and the toe caps are silver, not metal. They cost more than your boyfriend makes in a year," the man said in a Spanish accent.

"Well, there's no call to be nasty," she replied. "But if you're that rich, why are you on this bus?"

He didn't answer. Rob took the gun from his belt but kept it hidden under his shirt.

Caroline leaned over and whispered. "Is he one of them?"

"We have to assume he is."

"What are we going to do?"

"Stay calm and hope he gets off before we do."

Two stops later, the teenage girl gathered her things and got off the bus.

The bus turned onto Loyola Avenue, and Rob whispered to Caroline, "We're getting off. Keep your eyes forward and calmly exit the bus."

Rob stood and blocked the aisle as she got up and moved toward the front.

"Is he following us?" she whispered.

"I don't know," Rob said as they waited for people ahead of them to exit.

"We should return to the hospital," she whispered. "You saw all the police. It's safer there than here."

"Stop talking and keep moving."

Rob motioned her forward as soon as they left the bus and kept glancing backwards to see if they were followed. They had walked for several blocks when Rob spotted a bus station ahead. He took hold of Caroline's arm and started walking towards it.

"Stop walking so fast," she said, pulling free of his grasp. "My legs aren't as long as yours. Just tell me where we're going and let me walk there on my own."

"I'm getting you out of town."

"I'm not leaving Jack."

"Yes, you are. Your husband isn't safe as long as you stay in New Orleans. You have to do this for him."

Caroline reluctantly entered the bus station with him. "Where is your next bus going?" Rob asked when he got to the ticket window.

"I have one leaving for Houma in fifteen minutes."

"Where is Houma?"

"It's about sixty miles southwest of here. The trip takes three hours because of the stops."

Rob noticed the ticket lady looking at his blood-stained shirt.

"I'll take two one-way tickets." Rob paid the lady and took Caroline to the end of the counter.

"I need to wash this blood out of my shirt. You go to the ladies' restroom and stay there until I call you. Can you do that?"

"Of course I can. I'm not a child."

Rob walked her to the door of the women's restroom, then went into the men's. He had just finished washing the blood from his face and shirt when he heard the station intercom announce, "Bus 54 to Houma now boarding."

He hurried out of the restroom and so did Caroline. "When we get on, go as far back as possible," Rob said. "The fewer people sitting behind us, the better."

They got on, and Rob scanned the passengers as they went down the aisle to the back of the bus. After they were settled, he mentally noted every person's face as they boarded and found a seat. To his relief, none were the man with the silver-tipped boots. Finally, the driver closed the doors, and they pulled away from the bus station.

"We're going to be on the road for several hours," he whispered. "I suggest you get some rest."

"How do you expect me to sleep?"

"This may be your last chance for a while. I suggest you take it."

Caroline glared at him briefly, crossed her arms, and turned to the window.

After a time, Rob looked over and saw that she had fallen asleep. He slipped the pager from his pocket to check the screen but saw no message.

Rob replayed the vision of seeing Tom shot and prayed he and all the rest of them had survived. If they hadn't, there would be no one to help him and Caroline.

*   *   *

The fifth floor of the hospital was overrun with people. In addition to the minor wounded staff, and the severely injured FBI agent, there were also several covered bodies scattered about the floor.

The police were questioning everyone who was on the floor during the shooting but were mainly focused on the three FBI agents involved. When they finally released Steve, telling him to stay nearby, he found Wiley and Phillip and pulled them aside. "How much did you tell them?" Steve whispered.

"As little as possible," Phillip responded. "What about you?"

"The same." Steve leaned in next to Wiley. "How did you get on the floor without us seeing you?"

"I saw a group of men huddled together in the parking lot when I arrived. I suspected they were up to something, so I went to the back entrance and used the stairs instead of the elevator. Good thing I did because I would never have seen the man slipping down the hallway."

"Good call," Steve said. "Did you hear about the Broussard's shooter?"

"What about him?"

"He got his throat slashed in lockup this morning."

"That was fast." Wiley looked up and saw three men in dark suits and fedoras approaching. "Heads up, guys. It's Ashcroft."

"I was wondering how long it would take him to show up," Phillip added.

"Careful what you say," Steve whispered. "We can't let him know why Tom's here."

"Good luck with that. You haven't met Ashcroft."

Senior Agent Ashcroft stopped before the three men and looked them up and down. "Would one of you be so kind as to tell me why I had to hear from the police that two of my agents were part of this fiasco?"

Phillip glanced at Steve, who gave Phillip a nod.

"Wait just a moment," Ashcraft said as he glared at Steve. "Why do *my* men need *your* permission to answer my question? Who are you?"

"Agent Steven Harrell on assignment from the Arizona office."

"Show me your credentials."

Steve retrieved his wallet and presented his badge and ID.

Ashcroft's forehead furrowed. "Why wasn't I notified you were coming?"

Steve shrugged. "I guess we got here before my paperwork did."

"We? Who else is here?"

Steve cursed himself for slipping. "I'm here to assist Senior Agent Tom Neal from the Virginia office."

Ashcroft crossed his arms and glared. "Doing what? Neal finished his work on the Kennedy assassination investigation months ago." Ashcroft looked up and down the hallway. "Where is Neal?"

The three men exchanged glances before Steve answered. "He's in surgery."

"Is it serious?"

Steve took a breath. "Yes, sir. I'm afraid it is."

Ashcroft turned back to his agents. "And how did the two of you get involved in this?"

Wiley shifted his weight from one foot to the other. "Just a coincidence, boss. Phillip and I have known Tom Neal for over twenty years. He asked us to meet him here so we could catch up."

"That's preposterous," Ashcroft scoffed. "There was a reason Neal had you meet him here. What was it?"

Wiley looked at Steve and Phillip, then back to Ashcroft. "Tom's the only one who can answer that."

Agent Ashcroft poked his finger at Wiley and Phillip. "If I find out the two of you are working a case for Neal without my permission, I'll dismiss you both."

Detective Miller walked up before Wiley or Phillip could respond.

"Well, well, well. Thank you for coming, Ashcroft. You saved me a trip to your office."

"For what reason, detective?"

"Last night, one of your agents and his interpreter insisted on questioning my suspect in the hotel shooting. And now I learned that same agent and your men were in the middle of this."

"Which of my agents are you referring to?"

"He said his name was Neal."

"Tom Neal?" Ashcroft replied.

The detective leaned back and chuckled. "You don't know anything about this, do you? Damn it, man, have you lost control of your department?"

"I assure you, Miller, I have everything in check. The Bureau does not need to inform you of our actions. Now, if you will excuse me, this conversation is over."

"Don't give me that crap, Ashcroft. Anything that happens in this town is my business."

"Then do your job and figure it out." Agent Ashcroft turned to his agents. "I expect a full report of this incident on my desk by the two of you before the end of the day," he said, and marched off with two men in suits behind him.

Miller watched Ashcroft walk away, then shook his head. "Now that your joke of a boss is gone," he said to Wiley, Phillip, and Steve, "why don't the three of you tell me what really happened?"

"First, I have a question for you, detective," Wiley said. "How did Broussard's shooter wind up dead in lockup this morning?"

"Don't change the subject," Miller said. "That prisoner has nothing to do with this."

"Oh yes, he does," Steve replied. "The suspect that shot Broussard was in your custody when someone slit his throat. And it looks like this group showed up to finish the job."

"How long have you been in New Orleans?"

"A couple of days."

"How is it all these people started dying when you arrived?" Miller asked.

"This was in the works long before I got here, detective. This would have been worse if we and Agent Neal hadn't been here to stop them before they reached Broussard's room."

"Are you saying these men were here to finish off Broussard?"

"Come on, Miller," Wiley said. "Why else would these guys shoot up a hospital?"

Miller locked eyes with Wiley. "I'm a cop, not a fortune-teller. Maybe they had another reason. We'll never know, since you didn't leave any of them alive so I could question them."

Wiley shrugged his shoulders. "How many people do you think they would have killed if we hadn't stopped them?"

Miller ignored him and went to one of the sheet-draped bodies. He lifted a corner of the sheet and looked at the body. "What can you tell me about these men?"

"They're all from Mexico," Wiley replied.

"What does that have to do with this?"

"Broussard's shooter was from Mexico too," Phillip added. "There's a pattern here, detective."

"I'll have the lab run prints and see if we can identify them. Give me a call when your friend gets out of surgery," Miller said. "I want to talk to him."

"That may be a while," Steve replied.

"I don't care how long it takes."

"What about Broussard?" Phillip asked.

"I'll assign men to protect him. In the meantime, I need the three of you to stay in town."

"We aren't going anywhere," Wiley added.

"See that you don't," Miller said and walked over to join some of his officers.

Wiley turned to Steve. "Does Tom know who killed the shooter who shot Jack Broussard?"

Steve spoke softly. "He didn't say."

"Pascal has people everywhere. Some are behind bars, and others are guarding them. You'd be amazed at what a carton of cigarettes will get you."

"With Tom out of commission, it's up to us to keep the only shooter we have left and his target alive," Steve said. "The last thing we need is for the police to know we have them."

"I'll go check on them and get back to you," Phillip said.

Steve turned to Wiley. "Where are the drugs?"

"On the docks, but a crane showed up around dawn and stacked all six containers on top of other containers, making it impossible for anyone on the ground to open them. I have a man watching them in case something happens."

"What about guards?"

"There aren't any."

Steve stroked his chin. "That's strange. Those drugs are worth millions."

"The drugs aren't our only problem. One of us needs to stay here and watch out for Tom. He's in no condition to protect himself if this happens again."

"You're right. We'll take turns keeping an eye on him."

"But Miller said he would have his people on the floor," Phillip added.

"I don't trust Miller to protect Tom or Broussard. Look what happened to the shooter. His throat was cut while he was supposedly being guarded."

"What about the woman and The Kid?" Phillip asked. "Any idea where they went?"

Steve shook his head. "No more than you. Wiley, you were the last to see them. Did he say anything to you?"

"There was no time. I hope your guy knows what he's doing?"

"He does. He's been through this before."

"Not here, he hasn't," Wiley said. "Phillip and I will talk to the remaining shooter and see what he knows."

"While you take care of that, I'll be here. I'm not leaving Tom," Steve said.

"Let us know how he's doing."

"Don't worry. Tom's too stubborn to die."

CHAPTER SEVENTEEN

Houma

It was late afternoon when the bus driver made an announcement. "Everyone not going to Morgan City, gather your belongings and exit the bus. Those of you that are going on can get out and take a break. We have an hour layover in Houma before continuing to Morgan City."

Rob started to move and realized Caroline was asleep against his shoulder. He nudged her. "Time to go."

She jerked back and rubbed her face as if to erase the contact. "What did you say?"

"We're in Houma." Rob stood and stepped into the aisle. "We are getting off."

She scooted out of the seat. "When can I go back to New Orleans?"

Rob pressed a finger to his lips, then whispered. "Not here." His pager buzzed, and Caroline gave him a questioning glance.

"What is that?"

Rob removed the small box from his pocket, looked at the numbers on display, and returned the pager to his pocket. "It's our lifeline. I need to find a phone."

As they stepped off the bus, Rob looked around. The Houma station was small compared to the one in New Orleans, but despite its size, it was busy. As he was ushering Caroline forward, Rob noticed a bayou separating the station from the town.

He tried to take Caroline's arm, but she glared at him and pulled away.

"You don't need to hang on to me."

"Fine, but stay close."

They entered the bus station and found rows of adults sitting and children running everywhere.

"Too many people in here. We need to find a phone somewhere else."

They left the station and crossed the street, then walked past several blocks of homes before seeing a bridge. They went across and found themselves in town. They passed a dress shop called Palais Royal, a furniture store, and a small shoe repair store.

"Let's see if this shop will let me use their phone," Rob said, opening the door for Caroline.

"Welcome to City Shoe Service," the little man behind the counter said. "What can I do for you?"

"Sorry to bother you," Rob said. "Our car broke down and I need to find a phone."

"That's too bad. The nearest pay phone is next to the entrance of Woolworths. Take a left and go down three blocks and you can't miss it. It's across the street."

Woolworths was easy to find. It was the largest store in the block. Rob opened the door and followed Caroline inside. To their right were display tables, sales staff, and shoppers. To their left was a long counter with signs displaying brands of soft drinks, banana splits, hamburgers, and other food choices.

"You need to eat," Rob said, "and I need change."

Caroline took a seat on a stool at the counter, and he sat next to her.

"What can I get ya?" said the woman behind the counter.

"How is your tuna salad?" Caroline asked.

"Not as good as my burgers."

"Then I'll take a burger, no onions or cheese. Just fries and a Coke."

The woman turned her attention to Rob. "And you?"

"I'll have the same, but add cheese to mine." Rob took out a twenty-dollar bill and handed it to the lady. "Take it out of this and give me three dollars in change for the pay phone."

"Don't move from here until I get back," Rob whispered to Caroline as soon as the lady stepped away.

"Who are you calling?"

"My contacts."

"When you get off the phone with them, call the hospital and check on Jack."

"I can't, but I will ask my people to check on him." Rob put a figure to his lips when the woman returned and handed him bills and coins.

"I'll be right out front. Stay here until I get back."

He left Caroline and went back outside to the phone. He dropped several coins into the slot, entered Steve's pager number, then put in the pay phone number after the tone and hung up.

Rob paced back and forth in front of the large windows for several minutes, peering inside to check on Caroline while he waited for the phone to ring. Having Steve's page was a relief. At least he knew someone was alive. All he could do now was pray Tom had also survived.

A man walked by just as the pay phone rang. Rob waited until he had passed to answer. "Steve, is that you?"

"Yeah, man. Are you all right?"

"A bit frayed around the edges but fine."

"Have you found a safe place to stash the package?"

"Not yet. We're about sixty miles out of town, but I'm not sure it's far enough to be out of reach."

"Understand."

"Any news on the injured supervisor?"

"He's still being worked on."

"What are his chances?"

"I don't know the answer to that."

"We can't lose him, Steve."

"I know."

"Who's in charge of things while he's out of commission?"

"For now, it's me." There was a short pause. "Sorry, I have to go. Check back when you've found a place to store the package. It's important I know where it is and where you are."

"Wait. What about the damaged package we left behind?"

"Nothing new to report. It's just as you left it. Take care of things there."

"I will. You do the same."

Rob hung up the phone, but instead of going inside, he dropped more coins into the slot and dialed another number. He closed his eyes when it was answered.

"Hello?" Wanda said.

Rob didn't respond.

"Hello. Is anyone there?"

He desperately wanted to tell her he loved her but knew he couldn't take the chance that someone was listening. His heart sank when she hung up.

Rob took a moment to compose himself before he went back inside. Their food arrived just as he took his seat.

"Did you ask them about Jack?" she whispered.

Rob nodded and reached for his drink. "He's just as you left him. Nothing has changed."

She closed her eyes and exhaled. "Thank God for that. How soon will your people be here to take us back?"

"They aren't coming, Caroline."

"They have to. I need to get back to my husband."

"Not so loud," he said as he looked from side to side. "You can't go back until we know it's safe."

"And how long is that going to take?"

"You will know as soon as I do. For now, can we eat in silence while I figure this out?"

She ducked her head and hissed, "What do you mean, figure this out? I thought the FBI *trained* you to handle situations like this."

"Not exactly." He glanced around before whispering, "I'm not with the Bureau, Caroline."

Her mouth dropped open. "Then what the heck are you?"

"A lawyer. At least, I was."

Caroline leaned back. "A lawyer? Oh, my God. We're going to die."

"Shh, not so loud."

She closed her eyes and shook her head. "My life is in the hands of an amateur."

"I may not have a badge, but I'm no amateur. I've survived something like this before." He pulled her plate in front of her. "Stop talking and eat. You're going to need your strength." He picked up his burger. "We both are."

She paused for a moment before responding. "I don't mean to sound ungrateful. I'm just scared and worried about my husband."

His tone softened. "You should be. Now, eat before your food gets cold."

She spun her head. "Would you please stop ordering me around?" she said in a raised whisper. "I'll eat when I'm ready."

Rob raised his hands in surrender, then picked up his hamburger and took another bite. After several minutes, she did the same. When he finished, he looked over and saw she had eaten less than half of her food.

"If you're done, we need to find a place to stay," Rob said as the woman behind the counter returned.

"Would you like another Coke?" she asked.

"No, thanks, but I have a question for you."

The woman picked up his plate. "Ask away."

"We are looking for a place we could stay for a few days?"

"That's easy. The Thatcher Hotel is across the street from the court-house on Goode Street. It also has a restaurant. It's too pricey for my taste, but you may like it."

"We would prefer a place that isn't in the middle of town."

"Then try the Sugar Bowl Motel. It's on West Park Avenue, about half a mile from here."

"Sounds like that will work. We don't have a car, though. Is Houma big enough to have taxi service?"

The woman glanced at Caroline and then back to him. "Heck, no. When we want to go somewhere, we use pirogue service. The closest one is next to the shrimp plant down from the bus station."

Caroline began to snicker.

Rob glanced from her to the clerk. "You're joking, right?"

The woman chuckled as she picked up Caroline's plate. "I can spot a Texas boy a mile off."

* * *

Garden District

Pascal was selecting a Cohiba cigar from his humidor when Jean-Claude entered his office.

"What is it?" he asked as he ran the carefully rolled tobacco under his nose.

"Martínez is on hold. He seems very upset."

Pascal snipped the end of his cigar. "I bet he is." He struck a match and lit the Cohiba.

"Shall I say you're unavailable?"

A cloud of smoke escaped from his lips. "Give me a moment to enjoy my cigar, then put him through."

"Yes, sir." Jean-Claude exited, closing the office door behind him.

Several minutes passed before Pascal's intercom buzzed. He took the cigar from his lips and picked up the phone. "What is it, Martínez?"

"I need my shipment, Pascal. My people are running out of product to sell."

"We've had this discussion, Martínez. And so far, you have failed twice to complete the task. First the hotel, and now at the hospital."

"How was I to know the FBI was guarding her?"

"It's your job to know. As far as I'm concerned, that shipment is mine. Good-bye, Martínez."

"Not so fast, Pascal. It isn't over until the woman is dead, and to make sure, I'm coming to handle it myself. After I kill her, I'm taking my shipment."

Pascal took several puffs of his cigar before responding. "Not if I get to her first."

He hung up the phone and smiled as he savored his cigar.

* * *

Ochsner Hospital

Once again, the fifth floor of the Intensive Care Unit was overrun, but this time, it was with painters and maintenance crews who were patching the floors and walls and cleaning them of blood.

Steve stood by the nurse's desk as a patient was rolled from a room down the hallway. "Where are they taking all the patients?" he asked the nurse behind the desk.

"The hospital director has ordered us to move every patient from this floor except for Mr. Broussard and your Agent Neal."

"Did he give you a reason?"

"I was told it was at the request of the police."

Steve saw Wiley and Phillip walking toward him.

"Where's everyone going?" Wiley asked as orderlies pushed beds past him.

"Not everyone. Broussard and Tom will be staying here. Miller's orders."

"Any news on Tom?"

"He's in recovery," Steve said.

"How bad was it?"

"One bullet took out Tom's spleen, and the other hit the femoral artery in his thigh. Had the nurse not gotten to him as quickly as she did, he would have bled out before the shooting stopped."

"Have you heard from our guy and the woman?"

Steve touched his finger to his lips. "Not out here." He motioned for the two men to follow him into an empty room.

Steve closed the door. "All I know is they are out of the city."

"You got any idea why Tom would bring a rookie into a case like this?"

"I assure you he has skills. Why all the questions, Wiley?"

"Whoever's after her has done a heck of a job trying to take her out, and I doubt they're going to stop."

The conversation ended abruptly when the door to the room opened and a nurse came in.

"You men need to step out. We need to set up this room for a patient."

The three men stepped out into the hallway as Tom was rolled into the room they'd just vacated. Once Tom was settled in the room, Steve, Wiley, and Phillip went in, and Steve went to Tom's side.

"Tom, can you hear me?"

"Give him a minute," Phillip said. "I'm sure they have him knocked out."

"We might as well take a seat," Wiley said, settling into a chair. "This could take a while."

"What happened when you went back to your office?" Steve asked.

Wiley glanced at Phillip before answering. "We got our butts chewed, but that's nothing new."

"Yeah," Phillip responded, "but you're going to need to be careful. I overheard Ashcroft tell his assistant to call headquarters and find out why you and Tom were here."

Tom's eyelids fluttered, then barely opened. "Wh . . . where are they?" he whispered in a raspy voice.

All three men rushed to his side.

"Damn, old friend," Wiley said. "I thought you were invincible until now. You nearly died on us."

Tom's eyes roamed from man to man. "Where is the woman and The Kid?"

Philip placed a hand on Tom's foot. "Tom, let us worry about them. You need to heal."

Tom tried to pull free of the sheets. "Got . . . got to find them."

Steve grabbed Tom's arm. "They're fine, Tom. Stop moving before you rip something open."

Nurse Bennett came into the room, carrying a tray. "What's going on in here?"

"He's trying to get out of bed," Phillip answered.

She put down her tray, picked up the syringe that was lying on the tray, and injected the needle into Tom's IV. "This will keep him down."

Steve noticed her arm was bandaged. "That was sure brave of you to go to him when all those bullets were flying," he said. "Thank you for saving him."

The nurse returned the syringe to the tray. "I'm no hero. Every one of you are. Who knows how many staff and patients would have been killed if we hadn't been warned?" She pulled Tom's sheet across his chest and tucked him in. "You should all go. He'll be asleep for hours."

Steve shook his head. "Sorry, we can't leave. We need to be here in case it happens again."

"There are six policemen on this floor and others at every hospital entrance. I think we're safe." She scanned the faces of the men. "I'll agree to one of you staying, but that's it. He needs to rest."

"Okay," Steve replied.

"We'll go for now," Wiley said, "but if we hear something is going to happen, we'll be back."

"Fair enough. I'll be at my desk watching to make sure at least two of you go." The nurse took the tray and left.

Steve looked at the two men. "She's tough."

"Did you get any information from the shooter or the target as to who's behind this?"

"The union guy mentioned having a run-in with a couple of Pascal's men a couple of days before the theater attack," Phillip said, "but nothing like the other night."

Steve chuckled. "After seeing those dock workers running from that movie theater, I think it's going to be a while before they attend any more union meetings."

"Phillip and I decided the union organizer was safer in Chicago than here, so we put him on a plane this morning," Wiley said. He handed Steve a note. "That's his contact information. He's agreed to cooperate any way he can."

Steve folded the paper and put it in his pocket. "Call our Chicago office and have them keep an eye on him. We don't want Pascal getting to him up there."

Wiley nodded. "Consider it done."

"What about the Mexican shooter?"

"We managed to get him calmed down enough to tell us his family was taken about three weeks ago," Phillip said. "The poor guy's terrified they're going to kill his wife and kids."

"Did he say who took them?"

"Some drug organization down there that runs the place."

"Keep him secure. We need him to testify and identify the men who took him from the ship."

Wiley eyed Steve. "You look like crap. Phillip can stay with Tom while I go to the office and arrange to have the Chicago office meet the union guy's plane. I'll check on the Mexican, then come back to relieve Phillip."

Steve twisted his stiff back. "I'm good."

Wiley scoffed. "No, you're not. We've been doing this since you were a snot-nosed brat. Get out of here."

"All right, but page me if something comes up."

"Now you sound like Tom. We better go before that nurse storms in here and throws us out."

Steve nodded and was the first to leave the room. He needed food and a phone before he could even think about resting, so he took a cab to the French Quarter and asked the driver for a good place to eat. He was dropped off at the Acme Oyster Bar.

"What can I get for you?" questioned the dark-skinned man behind the counter.

"I'll take a dozen oysters on the half shell and a bottle of hot sauce."

"Jax, Old Milwaukee, Falstaff, or Schlitz with that?"

"Do you have Coke?"

"Man, nobody drinks a Coke with oysters."

Steve grinned. "Usually I agree with you, but not today. Just a Coke, thanks." He turned and looked around. "Any chance you've got a pay phone in here?"

The bartender pointed across the room. "There's one under the restroom sign."

"Perfect. I'll be at that table near the sign."

"Suit yourself. Most people avoid that table."

Steve went to the phone, dropped in a few coins, waited for the pager tone, dialed the pay phone number, and hung up. He returned to the table as his oysters and Coke arrived. He had downed several oysters when the phone rang. Steve jumped up and answered it.

"Got your page," Rob said.

"Can you talk?"

"I can."

"Where are you?"

"A town called Houma. It's about sixty-five miles southwest of New Orleans."

"I didn't know there was anything but swamp south of New Orleans. Are you sure you weren't followed?"

"I think we were at first, but we lost him. How's Tom?"

"It was close, but the docs say he'll recover."

"That's great news."

"How's the Broussard woman?"

"She's determined to get back to New Orleans. Any news on her husband?"

"Nothing's changed. The doctors are still keeping him sedated."

"Any word on whether he'll walk again?"

"I don't think they know."

"Damn, I was hoping to give her some good news."

"He's alive. Just tell her that."

"Where should we go from here?"

"Stay where you are until Tom's coherent enough for me to talk to him."

"All right, but Caroline's not going to wait long. She's determined to return to her husband."

"She doesn't have a choice."

There was a short pause. "Steve, I need to ask you something," Rob said.

"Sure, what can I do?"

There was another pause, then Rob said, "If something happens to me, I need to know someone will look after my family."

"Rob."

"Don't, Steve. . . I know these people."

"Yeah. So do I. Would you like for me to call Wanda?"

"You can't. Tom said the Bureau had our phone bugged. Maybe you can get word to her by one of the men Tom has watching them."

"I'll have Tom do it as soon as he can talk."

"Have whoever contacts her tell her the truth. She'll understand more than anyone what Caroline is going through because she's lived it."

"I will."

A moment passed without either man speaking.

"I was angry at Tom for asking me to train you, but now I'm glad I did," Steve said.

"So am I. How are things going with Tom out of commission?"

"We're doing our best. I hope, for your sake, we're making the right calls."

"I know you are. Take care of Tom."

"Don't worry about him. He's got a good-looking nurse hovering over him."

"Ahh. I see you've met Nurse Bennett."

"She saved his life."

"Thank God for that." Rob sighed. "It's been a long day. Caroline is asleep in the next room, and I need to rest."

"Keep your eyes open and stay out of sight. From what I understand, Pascal's tentacles stretch everywhere."

"I think you're right."

"Page me every chance you get. Tom's going to want constant updates from you."

"I will."

CHAPTER EIGHTEEN

New Orleans

Just before midnight, a man wearing jeans, a T-shirt, and a baseball cap pulled low on his forehead went to the door of a ninety-year-old Victorian home on Prytanis Street. He ducked his head to conceal his face before he knocked. A figure appeared on the other side of the leaded-glass window in the door, and the man pressed a note against the glass.

"Place it under the mat," said the person behind the door.

The man bent down, slid the note under the mat, then quickly disappeared into the night.

Jean-Claude tied the cords of his red velvet robe before opening the door and retrieving the note. Then he locked the door and read the message.

"Oh, my," he said and rushed into his study. He picked up his turn-of-the-century, gold overlay phone from his Queen Anne desk and dialed.

"Sir, I'm sorry to bother you so late."

"What is it, Jean-Claude?" Pascal said with a yawn.

"I just received word that Diego Martínez has at least a dozen men in New Orleans."

"Have them followed. I want to know every move that little weasel makes."

"Yes, sir. I'll see to it at once."

"And wake the governor. Have him meet me at The Court of Two Sisters tomorrow at 5:00 p.m. Tell him not to be late."

"As you wish." Jean-Claude hung up the phone, removed an alligator-embossed notebook from a hidden compartment in his desk, and dialed his phone.

*   *   *

Houma

Rob knocked on Caroline's door the following morning. "Are you ready?" he said through the door.

"Where are we going?" Caroline asked, opening it.

"To get something to eat and then do some shopping. I spoke to my people last night, and they said for us to stay here for a while."

"How long is a while?"

Rob shook his head. "If I knew, I would tell you."

"Did they say anything about Jack?"

"He's still sedated, but nothing has changed. Let's go."

Caroline didn't move. After a moment, she narrowed her eyes and glared at him. "I'm done waiting for your friends. I need to get back to New Orleans so I can be there when Jack wakes up."

"I understand your frustrations, Caroline, but your being there puts him and everyone in that hospital at risk."

"Not if the police and your people are doing their jobs."

"The FBI *was* there, Caroline, and you know how that turned out. It's best for you, Jack, and everyone if you stay away."

Caroline crossed her arms. "You think I'm heartless, don't you?"

"Not heartless. Just strong-willed and understandably concerned about your husband. But the only way to get safely back to him is to do exactly as my people say."

"You have far more faith in them than I do," she muttered and walked out the door.

Rob shook his head and followed her.

They walked to a restaurant the motel clerk recommended, and a woman wearing a brown dress and apron greeted them.

"Welcome to the Pit Grill. Take a seat anywhere you like."

Rob found a booth at the back of the room, and they settled in.

The waitress handed them the menus and asked, "What can I get you to drink?"

"Coffee with cream," Caroline answered.

"I take mine black," Rob said. "We need a minute to look over the menu."

"Sure, take your time. I'll have your coffee right out."

Rob glanced at the menu after she left, and when he looked up, Caroline was staring at him. "What is it?" he asked.

"I just realized I spent the night in an adjoining room with a man I don't know. Is Kid your name or a nickname?"

Rob paused a moment before responding. "For now, let's just say it's both."

Her eyes remained on his. "Why is a lawyer with a secret name working with the FBI?"

"It's a long story, Caroline. One I'm not at liberty to tell. Can we just leave it at that?"

"Well, it would be nice to know who you are if I'm being forced to stay with you."

Rob chuckled as he shook his head. He didn't respond.

Caroline pushed back into her seat and closed her eyes. "Look, I know I'm strong-willed. I have to be. I'm responsible for a plant that has over five hundred employees."

"That's a major task for anyone, Caroline."

"What you really mean is for a woman."

"I didn't say that."

"You didn't have to." She picked up her menu. "Jack is great at managing the operations and dealing with the public, but the ultimate success or failure of the company is on my shoulders."

"I didn't mean to insult you, Caroline. I was only trying to get you to understand how dire a situation you're in. You are one wrong move away from losing everything," he said, and saw her eyes widen.

"Oh, my God. You're right. I forgot all about the proposal."

"What proposal?"

"The levee maintenance contract I told you about. I've been so concerned with Jack that I forgot about it."

"Can't someone in your office handle it for you?"

"My bid isn't finished. Even if it was, it's in our safe, and Jack and I are the only ones with the combination."

"I can contact my people and have them give the combination to someone you trust at your company, and they can finish it."

"You don't understand. There's more to this than just submitting the bid. The Levee Board's decision is not only based on the merits of the bid but also on the people behind it." She shook her head. "Jack is in a hospital in critical condition, and as far as the Board knows, I have disappeared. If I don't get back and take control of my company, the committee will award the bid to Pascal."

"You just said they base part of their decision on the people's character. Surely they know who Marcel Pascal is?"

"This is Louisiana. Pascal owns the governor and most of the officials. My plant is the only one large enough to compete against him." She leaned forward. "There's no way I'm going to let Pascal take it after what he did to Jack."

"How long before the bidding process closes?"

"Less than four weeks."

"Maybe we can get you back before then."

"I can't risk that. Contact your people and tell them to come for us *now*."

Rob started to respond but stopped when the waitress returned with coffee.

"Now, what can I get you two?"

Rob looked over at Caroline, and she shook her head. "I think we're good with the coffee," he said.

"All right, then. Let me know if you change your mind."

As soon as they were alone, Rob leaned forward. "Caroline, we aren't going anywhere until we're told it's safe. Now finish your coffee. We both could use a change of clothing."

Rob drank his coffee quickly and got to his feet. "Stay here," he told Caroline. "I'll pay the check and have them call us a cab."

Rob went to the register, paid the bill, and requested a taxi. When he returned to the table, Caroline was gone, and the waitress was cleaning the table.

"Do you know where the lady at this table went?"

"I don't know. She could be in the restroom."

"Could you please check?" The waitress gave him a questioning look. "She wasn't feeling well," Rob said. "I'm concerned."

"Okay, sure."

Rob shifted from one foot to the other until the waitress came out. "She's not there."

Rob rushed out the door of the restaurant and went to the curb. He scanned up and down the street, but there was no sign of Caroline. He rushed back to their motel and checked the rooms. Both were empty.

"Damn it, Caroline, where are you?" he muttered, exiting the motel.

Rob took off toward town and came to the same bridge they had crossed on their way in from the bus station. He got to the other side and stopped in front of the courthouse, scanning both ends of Main Street, searching. He finally spotted Caroline crossing the street several blocks down from him. He took off after her, dodging people on the sidewalk as he ran.

Rob was almost to her when Caroline entered a department store. He hurried in and found her talking to a saleslady at a counter.

"Excuse me, Miss. I need to speak to this lady," he said, taking Caroline's arm.

The clerk looked from him to Caroline before stepping away.

Rob took a breath. "What the heck are you doing?"

Caroline jerked free of his grasp. "I was trying to get to the bus station. Then I remembered I had no money, so I came in here to see if I could use their phone to make a collect call to my secretary."

Rob shook his head. "Caroline, *no one* can know where you are. It's too dangerous for you to be out here alone."

"We're in Houma. No one knows me here."

"It's not the people of Houma I'm worried about."

Caroline crossed her arms and closed her eyes. "I'll give your people two more days to straighten this out, then I'm returning to New Orleans, even if I have to walk."

Rob knew it would be a miracle for this to be over in two days, but he didn't share that with her. Instead, he said, "I'll discuss your return with my people the next time we talk."

"Fine, but I'm going back in two days with or without their help."

"I'll pass that along." Rob looked around the store and saw it had a women's and men's department. "Since we're here, let's pick up a few things."

She looked down at her clothing. "That would be nice."

"Why don't we ask that saleslady to help us?"

"This is the women's department. You need to go to the men's side of the store."

"After what happened at the restaurant, I'm not letting you out of my sight."

"I told you, two days. I'll keep my word."

"If you don't, you'll wear those same clothes until we return to New Orleans."

Rob went a few aisles over to the men's clothing but continued to glance back to make sure she was there.

*   *   *

"Men," Caroline said to the saleslady.

"The poor things can't help it."

"You are so right." Caroline pointed to several items in the display case, and the saleslady got them for her.

A short time later, Rob returned with a couple of bags and removed his wallet to pay for Caroline's items. Caroline gathered all their bags and waited for him near the door while he was getting his change. One of the bags slipped from her grasp.

"Let me get that for you," said a man coming up from behind her.

"No, thank you. I can manage." As she bent down to retrieve the bag, her heart skipped a beat. The man was wearing expensive boots with silver-capped toes. It was the man from the bus.

Caroline dropped her bags and started to run, but he grabbed her.

"Kid!" Caroline screamed as the man lifted her off the floor. "Kid, help!" she shouted.

The man almost had her to the door when Rob leapt on them from behind, taking all three to the floor.

Caroline scrambled away and watched as the two men tumbled into a display of mannequins, toppling them over and shattering glass shelves. Suddenly, the man from the bus rolled on top of Rob, pinning him down, and grabbed a long shard of glass. He tried to force it into Rob's neck, but Rob took hold of his hands and pushed back with all his might.

Caroline picked up the leg of a broken mannequin and swung it like a baseball bat, striking the man in the head with a loud thud. He rolled off of Rob, and she was drawing back to hit him again when Rob scrambled to his feet and grabbed her arm.

"He's unconscious. We have to get out of here. He won't be alone."

Caroline dropped the plaster leg and followed Rob to the back of the store, where people were hiding behind the counters.

"Where's the exit?" Rob asked a woman. She pointed.

Rob grabbed Caroline and raced into the back room the woman had indicated. "Stand over there," he said, pushing Caroline towards the wall. Rob opened the large metal door and looked out. He heard the sound of someone behind him and spun around to find a woman holding the hands of two small children.

"I have to get my kids out of here," the woman pleaded. "There are men out there with guns."

"Go," Rob said, allowing the mother and her children to leave. As he and Caroline followed, the wail of police sirens could be heard. Rob took Caroline's hand, and they ran for several blocks until they reached an abandoned building surrounded by a chain-link fence.

"We need to get out of sight."

"Why don't we flag down one of those police cars and tell them what happened?" Caroline said, gasping for air.

"We can't. I wouldn't put it past Pascal to have some of them on his payroll." He spotted an opening in the fence and pulled her through it. The structure was deserted and in various stages of demolition.

"Kid, are you sure this place is safe?"

"It's safer than being on the street." Rob stood her in the shadow of a wall. "Stay here. I need to make sure we weren't followed."

"Where's your gun?"

Rob patted around his belt. "Damn. I must have lost it in the fight."

"How are you going to protect us?"

"By not getting caught."

Rob went to an opening in the fence a few feet away and scanned the street. As he was looking, Caroline came up behind him and grabbed his shoulder.

"Kid, the man who grabbed me was wearing silver-tipped boots."

"He must have followed us into the bus station and saw which bus we boarded."

"What are we going to do?"

Rob paused a moment. "We have to get out of Houma."

"How?"

"Not sure, but I know we can't stay here."

They left the structure and made their way back to the courthouse. The police had set up roadblocks on the main street to check cars and people on foot before allowing them to cross the bridge.

He and Caroline joined a group of pedestrians that had already been checked and started over the bridge. Halfway across, Rob pointed to a boat tied to a dock next to a large building south of the bus station.

"That's how we're getting out of here," he whispered.

Once off the bridge, they crossed the street, walked past the bus station, and kept going until they came to a business with *Blum & Bergeron's Shrimp Plant* painted on the side of the corrugated metal building.

"The woman at Woolworths wasn't kidding. There really is a shrimp plant in the middle of town," Rob said. "We need to hurry. We have to get on that boat before it leaves."

They crossed the street and entered the lot next to the building with row after row of shrimp-covered tables. Two men were hauling large ice chests from a fifteen-foot wooden boat painted white. The vessel's stern was covered with ropes, and netting hung from a tall pole near the small wheelhouse and was gathered at the base of the pole in a neat pile.

As they got closer, Rob noticed a third man with a clipboard speaking to one of the men offloading the ice chests.

"How's the shrimping?" the man with the clipboard asked.

"C'est bon," said the little man, dumping the chest's contents onto a scale.

"Is that all of it?"

"Yep," said the other worker, who was wearing a shirt bearing the logo of the shrimp plant. "Pauley got a good load this time. I'll take it in after you total it."

Rob waited until the plant employee left before approaching the remaining two men. He walked up just as the man with the clipboard was handing the shorter man a wad of money.

"Excuse me," Rob said. "Is this your boat?"

The man with the clipboard nodded to the shorter man, who stuffed the money into the pocket of his baggy pants.

"Why do you ask?" said the little man.

"We would like to go for a ride."

The little man looked at the plant manager and then back to Rob. "This ain't no party boat, mister. It's a shrimp boat."

"I'll pay you thirty dollars."

"Man, don't hand me no wolf tail," the little man said.

"Sorry, what is a wolf tail?"

The man with the clipboard chuckled. "That's Cajun for pulling my leg."

Caroline came to Rob's side and whispered, "I think those men just crossed the bridge."

Rob took out his billfold. "I'll pay you forty if we leave now."

The little shrimper did a jig. "Man, for forty dollars, I'll take you anywhere you want."

"We have to go *now*," Rob said.

Pauley grabbed two of the empty chests. "Then you gotta help."

Rob grabbed the chests from Pauley and carried them to the boat.

He and the shrimper loaded the last of them quickly, then Rob lifted Caroline onto the vessel.

Pauley rushed to the wheelhouse and started the engine.

"Untie them ropes from the bulkhead," Pauley shouted.

Rob untied the ropes, tossed them onboard, and jumped on just as the boat pulled away from the dock. He began quickly stacking ice chests on top of one another.

"Caroline, get behind the ice chests and duck down."

"What about you?"

"I'll find another place to hide. Hurry before they see you." She got behind the stack, and he placed chests around her to close her in. The only place left to hide was in the small three-sided wheelhouse with Pauley. Rob went in and sat on the floor next to Pauley.

"Look, mister, if you got trouble with the police, I ain't taking you no place," Pauley said, looking down at Rob. "I got enough problems."

"I assure you it's not the police. If you want us off, at least wait until we are out of town, please."

"If it ain't police, we ain't got a problem."

"Thank you."

Rob remained hidden as they puttered past the bus station. As soon as they were past, he stood up slowly and glanced around Pauley to see four men running to the water's edge, pointing to the shrimping boat. Rob recognized one of them as the man with the silver-capped boots who had tried to take Caroline.

All he could do now was pray Pauley was taking them someplace they wouldn't be found.

CHAPTER NINETEEN

New Orleans

Marcel Pascal sat at his private table at The Court of Two Sisters restaurant, checking his watch as he sipped his gin and tonic. "He's late," he said to his bodyguard.

"Perhaps the governor was detained?"

"Jean-Claude would have sent word if he was. If he's not here by the time I finish my drink, I'm leaving."

"Yes, sir. I'll make sure your car is waiting."

The door to the private room opened, and Governor Parker Thompson walked in.

"I am so sorry, Marcel. I had a pressing matter and couldn't get away."

"Oh, really? What was this one's name?" Pascal waved his hand. "Never mind, take a seat."

Parker took a chair. "Can I order a drink?"

Pascal pointed to the man at the door.

"I'll take a whiskey sour," said the governor.

The man nodded and left the room.

Governor Thompson turned to Pascal. "What is so important that you had to wake me in the middle of the night?"

"I need to know your progress with the Levee Board."

"Not much has changed since our last conversation, Marcel."

"Damn it, Parker. How is that possible? Jack Broussard is in the hospital on death's door, and Caroline Broussard is missing. That should be enough to sway all the votes in my direction."

"Oh, that," Parker said as Pascal's man returned with his drink. The governor took a sip. "How could such a horrible thing happen?"

"Don't be coy, Parker. Answer the question."

"This requires timing, Marcel. If I had swooped in so soon after such a tragedy, I would look like a vulture pouncing on the dead before the body has cooled."

"I don't care how you're perceived. Your job is to make sure Crescent City Concrete is out of the running."

"I understand," the governor said, "but there were Board members at their table the night of the Rex fundraiser. I'm sure they are still reeling from seeing it happen. If I try to sway them now, I will look heartless." The governor took another sip from his glass. "Do you think Caroline Broussard will return?" he asked.

"Not if I can help it."

"Marcel, the bid submission ends in less than four weeks. I think it's in your best interest to ensure she doesn't return until it's over."

"I don't need you telling me how to do my job, Parker. I'll take care of her. Your job is to see I get that contract."

"It is my first priority, Marcel. I will make that happen."

*   *   *

Houma

Rob waited until they were out of town before allowing Caroline to leave her ice chest fortress.

"Do you think they saw us?" Caroline asked as he took down the structure.

"It's possible."

"What should we do?"

"That depends on where we're going. Let me talk to our captain."

As Rob took the forty dollars from his wallet, he realized his cash was almost gone. He went to the wheelhouse and gave the shrimper the money.

"Thanks, Pauley. You did us a big favor back there. You can drop us off whenever you're ready."

The Cajun stuffed the money into his worn jeans and shook his head. "From the angry looks of the men behind the bus station, it's better you keep on the boat with me than go anywhere close to them."

"You're right."

"Why are they after you?"

"It's a long story, Pauley." Rob needed to change the subject. "Where are we going?"

"To my house in Dulac." The grin reappeared. "My Yvette makes the best gumbo in all of Terrebonne Parish. We feed you, and then you can go on your way."

"I appreciate that, but the boat ride is more than enough."

"Can't do that. When my Yvette hears you pay me forty dollars, she will kill me if she doesn't feed you."

"We don't want to cause you any trouble, Pauley."

"No trouble. Yvette just gonna drop a few more shrimp and rice in the pot, and we got plenty."

That wasn't the trouble he was referring to, but Rob thought it best not to explain.

*   *   *

Garden District Office

"What do you mean they got away?" Pascal shouted into the phone.

"Boss, we followed the Mexicans all the way to Houma. We saw one of them go into a store, and next thing we knew, police were everywhere."

"Where did they go after that?"

"We followed them onto a bridge and saw the Mexicans watching a shrimp boat. When the boat passed under the bridge, we saw why. The woman and a tall man were on the boat trying to hide."

"Did you get the name of the boat?'

"It was the *Miss Yvette.*"

"Did the Mexicans see the name?"

"I'm sure they did. It went right in front of them. Do you want us to keep following them?"

"Yes, but if they grab her, take them and her out. I'm not losing this bet." Marcel hung up and then pushed the button on his intercom. "Jean-Claude, get in here."

The assistant appeared at his door. "Yes, sir."

"Get hold of our people in Terrebonne Parish and find out who owns a shrimp boat named *Miss Yvette*. Dupre said the woman and a man were on that boat as it left Houma."

"Yes, sir. Right away." Jean-Claude spun on his heels and raced out of the room.

*   *   *

Ochsner Hospital

Steve was almost to Tom's room when he heard shouting.

"I don't care! You can't hold me against my will!"

Steve rushed in and found a doctor a few feet away from Tom, who was gripping the bed as he fought to stand on his feet.

"What's going on in here?" Steve said as he went to Tom's side.

"It seems Agent Neal thinks he's well enough to leave."

Steve grabbed Tom just as his legs gave way. The doctor rushed to his side and helped Steve put Tom back in the bed.

"Damn it, Tom. Keep this up, and you'll never recover," Steve said.

"That's what I was trying to tell him," said the doctor as he reconnected the monitors.

"Kid needs my help," Tom replied, then groaned.

"He's fine at the moment. Now be still and let the doctor get you connected."

"Have you talked to him?"

Steve's eyes shifted to the doctor, then back to Tom. "I'm not telling you anything unless you promise to stay in bed."

Tom took a breath and flinched in pain. "That's extortion."

"More like common sense."

The doctor stepped to the door. "Nurse," he called. "I need help in here."

Nurse Bennett rushed in.

"Check his tubes and IVs while I examine his incisions."

"What happened?" she asked.

"He got out of bed. I'm increasing his pain meds and some of his other medication for the next twelve hours, and I'm giving you a directive to sedate him if he tries this again," the doctor said, then left the room.

"You heard the man," Nurse Bennett said to Tom. "Try this again and I'll put your bedpan in the freezer."

Steve chuckled quietly when he saw Tom lock eyes with her and smile.

"What's your name?" Tom asked.

She pointed to her name tag. "I thought reading was a requirement for the FBI."

"I mean your full name," Tom said. "I'd like to know the person threatening me."

"Suzanne. Suzanne Bennett." A grin crossed her lips. "But you can call me Nurse Bennett." She turned to Steve. "I'll be back with his meds. Make sure he stays put."

"Yes, ma'am."

Tom pointed to the door when she left. "Close it."

Steve did and returned to Tom's bedside.

"When did you talk to The Kid?"

"Shortly after they brought you here after surgery."

"Are they safe? Where did they go?"

"Relax. You're going to bust a stitch."

"Stop coddling me and talk."

"They're in a place called Houma," Steve said. "He said it's southwest of New Orleans. So far, they're fine."

Tom coughed and turned pale from the pain. It took him a long moment to regain his composure before he could speak. "Page him."

"I will, but it might take him a while to call us."

"I don't care. Do it."

"I was told I needed to stay here and keep you in bed."

"I'm too exhausted to go anywhere. Page The Kid."

Steve went to the hospital's first floor and found a pay phone. He dialed Rob's pager, entered the pay phone number, and hung up.

As he was waiting, a man came to use the phone. "Don't bother," Steve said, stepping between the man and the phone. "It doesn't work."

"Okay, thanks." The man walked away.

Steve looked around and found a hospital pamphlet. He turned it over, wrote *OUT OF ORDER*, propped it on top of the phone, and leaned back against the wall.

An hour later, he redialed Rob's pager, but this time, he entered his pager number and code to reply. Then he hung up and returned to Tom's room.

"Did you talk to him?"

"He didn't return my page."

"Something happened to them."

"Tom, stop jumping to conclusions. He's probably just not near a phone."

"Does anyone else know you're talking to him?"

"Only Wiley and Phillip."

Tom nodded. "Where are we with the drugs on the docks?"

"Oh, they're still there, only now they are stacked on top of other containers."

"That seems a little strange?"

"I'm guessing Pascal had it done to keep them from being unloaded."

A slight grin crossed Tom's lips. "If that's true, I'm sure Martínez isn't happy about it."

"That's my guess."

"Is the shooter safe?"

"Yes. Wiley is checking on him now."

"We need him alive. After losing Ybarra, he's the only one who can testify as to why he was brought here."

"We're doing our best." Steve looked around. "What happened to Phillip?"

"He left to answer Wiley's page." Tom flinched in pain and gripped the sheets. "You should try to page The Kid again."

"I don't have to. I left my pager number."

Tom closed his eyes for a moment, then opened them. "How is Broussard doing?"

"He's awake, but not much more than that."

"Have you questioned him?"

"I tried, but he doesn't know anything," Steve said. "He just keeps asking for his wife."

"What did you tell him?"

"I told him we moved her to a place out of town to keep her safe."

"I hope you didn't tell him she was the target."

"I left that out." Steve leaned forward in his chair. "Tom, you need to rest. We're doing everything we can to handle this."

Tom shook his head. "I know you are, but I won't breathe easy until we get The Kid and the woman out of this mess." Tom groaned. "I promised The Kid's wife I wouldn't let anything happen to him."

"Rob and I talked about that. He asked me to get word to her about what happened but said not to call because their phone line was being monitored."

"It is."

"He suggested we contact the men you have watching them and have them tell her."

"No. Wanda should hear this from me. I'm the one who pushed him into this. He would be safe at home with his family if it hadn't been for me."

"Tom, stop being so hard on yourself. You didn't force Rob into anything. He chose to come."

"I know, but it still feels like it's my fault."

Before Steve could respond, a nurse entered the room.

"Time for your meds," she said, handing Tom a small paper cup containing pills.

"Where's Nurse Bennett?"

"Her shift ended."

"When is she coming back?"

"Not until tomorrow morning. Is there something you need?"

Tom glanced at Steve before responding. "No, I was just wondering why she wasn't here." He took the cup and dumped the pills into his mouth, then took the glass of water the nurse held out.

Once Tom had swallowed the pills, the nurse turned to Steve on her way out. "He needs to rest."

"I'll be as quiet as a mouse," Steve promised.

She left, closing the door behind her.

The sun was setting when Tom's eyes fluttered open. He glanced over and saw Steve in the chair next to his bed. "Have you heard from The Kid?"

"Not yet."

"Something's wrong."

Before Steve could answer, Wiley came in.

"Got some bad news, Tom," he said.

"What happened?"

"They got to our shooter. He's dead."

Steve got to his feet. "I thought we had people watching him."

"We did, but apparently someone leaked his location."

"Where were the men guarding him?" Steve asked.

"Dead. Whoever did it used a silencer. No one in the hotel heard or saw a thing."

"How did they get in the room?"

"Looks like they were let in. There was an untouched cart of warm food in the room."

"Someone had to have seen something," Steve said.

"If they did, they're not talking."

"Damn it," Tom roared, pounding the bed. "Keep looking. Steve's right. Question every person in that hotel if you have to. Someone had to see something."

"Where's Phillip?" Steve asked.

"He's at the hotel managing the scene. My guess is this is Pascal's way of cleaning up the mess the drug organization left."

"I agree, but we need proof," Tom spat.

The room went silent for a moment.

"Are The Kid and the woman still in Houma?" Wiley asked.

"Last we heard," Steve replied.

Wiley stepped closer to the bed. "Tom, I think it's time to bring them in."

"I was thinking the same thing until this happened. Now I think it's safer where they are than here. Who else knew where the shooter was stashed?"

"The undercover cops you met at our meetings," Wiley replied. "But I can assure you they had nothing to do with this."

"Then how was he found?" Steve asked.

Wiley shrugged. "Could have been the hotel clerk, housekeeping staff, anybody. Pascal has ears everywhere."

"We need to find out how this happened."

"I'll head there after I go by my house to check on Melanie."

"What's wrong with Melanie?" Tom asked.

"Our boy is having a bad day. He's been having a lot of them lately."

"I'm sorry, Wiley. That has to be rough."

"It is, but we'll get through it. I'll page Steve if Phillip and I come up with something at the scene."

When the door closed, Steve stepped close to the bed. "What do we do now?"

"I'm not sure. Try to reach The Kid again. I need to know they're all right."

CHAPTER TWENTY

Dulac

The shrimp boat bumped up against old tires tied to the dock a few yards from Pauley's small home next to the bayou.

Rob scooped up the rope from the stern of the boat and was about to jump off when Pauley called out to him.

"Toss the rope to my boys. They know what to do."

Rob looked up and saw two boys running up to the boat. He tossed the line to the younger boy as the older one jumped on board, grabbed the line from the boat's bow, and jumped off to secure the vessel to the dock.

"Some crew you got here, Pauley."

"That big one is T-Boy," Pauley said, pointing to the older boy, "and the little one is Dudley. They have been helping on the boat since they could walk." Pauley went to the side of the boat and shouted orders to his boys in French.

"He has a family. We can't stay here with them," Caroline whispered as Rob helped her off the boat.

"I know. I'll ask for directions out of town, and we'll go."

"I see my Pauley caught more than shrimp this trip," said a woman coming up behind them.

Pauley and their two boys came to her side. "This is my Yvette," Pauley said. "My missus. She ain't just pretty. She's smart too."

Yvette elbowed him in the side. "Welcome to our home. You just in time for supper."

"Thank you, Yvette," Rob said, "but we can't stay."

"*Mais non*," Pauley said. "Nobody going nowhere. You got to eat."

Rob glanced at Caroline and saw her shrug her shoulders. He turned back to Pauley. "Thank you, Pauley, but then we must go."

"Yvette, you take the lady in while I get the coolers in the shed."

Yvette glanced at Caroline's clothing. "Poor thing looks like she's been drug down the road." She took Caroline's arm. "You come with me, and I'll let you get washed up."

Caroline smiled. "That sounds wonderful."

Pauley looked up at the sky. "Boys, there's a storm coming. Get the boat ready." The two young men turned and ran back to the boat.

Rob glanced at the blue sky and wondered what Pauley was talking about.

"Why are you in such a rush to go?" Pauley asked. "Does it have somethin' to do with what happened in Houma?"

"It does," Rob said. "Those men are dangerous, and it's not safe for you and your family to be around us. We will find some place around here to hide."

"That ain't gonna do you no good. Everybody here knows everybody else twenty miles from here. This ain't no place for you to hide. Besides, there's a storm coming."

Rob looked up again. "Pauley, the skies are clear."

The little shrimper held up his weathered, calloused hand and attempted to flex his swollen joints. "These never lie. A big one is coming for sure."

Just then, the boys returned and stood next to their dad.

"In that case," Rob said, "can I use your phone?"

"You could, but we ain't got one. The closest one is at Leland's Grocery. After we eat, T-Boy will fetch my friend Sammy. He's got a car and will come running to help when I tell him Yvette's made gumbo."

"Sounds great. Thank you, Pauley."

The two men entered the small shotgun house, and Rob looked around. It was warm, inviting, and spotless, despite looking generations old.

"Take a seat," Yvette said, filling bowls with rice and gumbo at the stove.

"Give T-Boy the first bowl," Pauley said. "He needs to fetch Sammy as soon as he's done."

"What for?"

"Our friend here gotta use the phone at the grocery."

Yvette placed a steaming bowl in front of the boy and handed him a chunk of French bread. "You best eat up. You ain't got much time."

"Yes 'm," the boy said as he bit off a large chunk of bread.

"Where's Caroline?" Rob asked.

"Your missus is changing. I gave her some of T-Boy's things he grew out of. The rest of you take a seat. Gumbo is best when it's hot."

Rob decided to let them believe he and Caroline were married. The less they knew, the better.

Pauley swatted his wife's bottom when she set his gumbo in front of him.

"Pauley, we got company." She laughed and nudged him, then returned to the stove as Caroline came in wearing clean jeans she had rolled up above her ankles and a freshly pressed shirt she tied at her waist. All eyes were on her as she approached the table.

"Ou wee," Pauley said. "You look nice."

Color flushed Caroline's cheeks, and she smiled. "Thank you for the clothes, Yvette. It's nice to feel clean again."

"Our pleasure," Yvette said. "Now, set yourself down and eat."

T-Boy grabbed a large chunk of French bread and got up from the table. "I go now, Papa."

"Make it fast and tell Sammy he better do the same if he wants some of your mama's gumbo."

"Yes, sir," he said and ran out the door.

Caroline tasted the gumbo. "*Très bien*, Yvette."

A broad smile spread across her face. "*Merci, mon amie.*" Her expression changed when she heard a buzzing sound. "What's that?"

"It's something that lets me know someone is trying to reach me," Rob said, taking the pager from his pocket.

"I didn't know there was such a thing," Pauley said. A moment later, they heard an automobile horn. "That be Sammy. You ready?"

"I am," Rob said, getting to his feet.

"Tell Sammy I'll have some bread and gumbo ready for him when y'all get back," Yvette said.

Pauley scooped up another spoonful of gumbo before going to the door.

As Rob and Pauley stepped off the porch, T-Boy went into the house. Rob got in the tattered backseat of the rusted 1950 Chevy sedan and let Pauley sit up front next to the burly, unshaven man behind the wheel. He was grateful the windows were down because the driver's body odor permeated the car's interior.

Pauley and the driver talked in Cajun as they traveled the shell-covered road. Several minutes later, Pauley turned and glanced at Rob.

"I told Sammy your boat broke down near the intercoastal canal and you need to call somebody to get you."

"Thanks, Pauley." As they drove, Rob noticed the smattering of houses and sheds, most of which backed up to the bayou just like Pauley's did. They stopped at an unpainted building with a faded sign perched above the porch.

"We here," Pauley said. "Sammy will take us back when we're done."

Pauley was greeted by the grocer and several locals as soon as they entered.

"*Comment ça va?*" the grocer said. "What you need, Pauley?"

"I'm good, but my friend here needs the phone."

"Sure. You know where it is."

"Thank you," Rob said, then started in the direction Pauley pointed.

"I'll be here catchin' up with these old men till you be done."

"We ain't old," one of the men told Pauley.

"Yes, you are, Hebert."

Rob left the men to their banter and went to the phone at the back of the store. He dialed Steve's pager, entered the number of the grocer's telephone, and hung up. He could hear the laughing and talking up front as he waited. It felt like an eternity before the phone rang.

"Why haven't you been returning my pages?"

"Couldn't. The package was almost taken in our last location, and we've been on the move."

"Where are you now?"

"A place called Dulac, but leaving soon. Can't risk being found again. Any news on 2A and our friend?"

"2A's awake and asking for his wife. Other than that, he's the same. Our friend is being hardheaded and almost impossible to keep down."

"I'll take that as a good sign."

"You should know we lost the other hot sauce we had stashed away."

"Damn it," Rob said. "Who found it?"

"Don't know. Impossible to know who to trust down here."

"Understand. We need to return the package as soon as possible."

"Can't. Too unstable here after what happened to the sauce."

"I can't keep it here. I'll just have to keep moving."

"I'm afraid so, at least until we get a handle on this. Keep checking in. If you don't, I'll have to tie our friend to the bedpost."

"I doubt that will work for either of you."

"I'm sure it won't. Take care out there."

"I will."

Rob realized the chattering at the front of the store had stopped when he hung up the phone. Then he heard what sounded like multiple people walking around, and his heart skipped a beat when he heard Spanish being spoken. He peered around the shelving and saw a man wearing silver-toed boots. The same man who had grabbed Caroline.

"I'm looking for a man called Pauley Guidry," the man said.

Rob's heart lodged in his throat when he saw Pauley approach him. "Don't do it," he whispered.

"Why you ask?" Pauley said. "Does he owe you money?"

"It's none of your business, little man."

"Ya, it is. I lent that coonass twenty dollars two weeks ago, and he ain't paid me back."

The man with the silver-tipped boots looked at the Frenchman. "Guidry left Houma today with a man and woman on his boat." He tapped Pauley's forehead. "Tell me where he lives, and I'll give you the twenty bucks myself."

Pauley turned to one of the men in the group. "Theriot, you know where Pauley lives?"

The Cajun took off his cap and scratched his balding head. "Can't say I do, Robichaux."

"LeBlanc, do you know where he lives?"

"Can't say I do either. Maybe Pauley at his other job."

"What job?" the man asked.

"I heard he works for a tugboat company out of Houma. Maybe that's where he is."

"I saw him leaving town with the two people on his boat myself," the man said, poking his finger into Pauley's chest. "You seem to know so much. You tell me where he lives."

"How would I know? I never been to his place."

"If I find out you're lying, I'm coming back for you."

Pauley pushed his hand away. "Well, take your time. I ain't going no place." He stepped around the man and went to the counter. "André, where is my boudin? If I go home without it, my wife gonna kill me."

"You know where it stays, Robichaux. Get it ya self. I'll put it on your bill."

As Pauley started for the back of the store, the man grabbed him by the shirt and jerked him back.

"Remember what I said, little man."

Pauley pulled away and went between the row of shelving to the back where Rob was standing. "We gotta get out of here before somebody tells them where I live," he said in a low voice.

Rob peered around the corner. "Looks like they're leaving. Is there another way out?"

"There's a back door."

"Let's go," Rob whispered.

Pauley entered a storeroom and then went out a side door. A large water cistern was next to the building, and the two men hid behind it.

Rob inched out and saw the men climb into a couple of two-tone pickups and spray shells from the road as they sped away in the opposite direction of Pauley's home.

When the trucks had disappeared from view, Rob and Pauley ran to Sammy's Chevy and jumped in. Pauley shouted at the driver in French before closing his door.

Sammy started the old Chevy, made a U-turn, and raced back to Pauley's house as Pauley jabbered to him in Cajun.

"What are you telling him, Pauley?" Rob asked.

"I told him bad people were after us, and we gotta get home before they find us."

"Does Sammy speak English?"

"No, just French."

"Pauley, you have to get your family out of here before those men find you."

"What about you and your missus?"

"We'll find a place to hide."

"No. You come with us. We have friends in Golden Meadow. From there, you can get back to Houma."

"We can't go to Houma. We'll hide here until they're gone."

"Where? The best way out is by boat, and that's with us."

Rob paused and nervously rubbed the back of his neck. "You're right. We'll go with you."

Sammy skidded to a stop in front of Pauley's house. As Pauley said something to the driver, Rob jumped out and ran to the house. He rushed in and found Caroline in the kitchen with Yvette and the boys. "Caroline, they're here."

"Oh God! We can't let them find us here."

The words were barely out of her mouth when Pauley came through the door shouting in French, followed by his sons running out the back door.

"My boys are putting extra fuel cans on the boat."

"Would somebody tell me what's going on?" Yvette asked, throwing down her dishtowel.

Pauley took his wife by the shoulders. "Some bad people are looking for me and them, Yvette. We gotta leave before they find us."

She glanced from her husband to her guests. "What did you all do?"

"I'll tell you later. Right now, you gotta get all the food, clothes, and supplies you can out to the boat," Pauley said. "Then close the shutters on the windows and lock the doors. It needs to look like we ain't here."

"I ain't doing nothing till somebody tells me what's this about."

"All Pauley did was help us, Yvette," Rob said. "It's us they're after."

"Why?"

"Marcel Pascal is trying to have me killed, Yvette," Caroline said. "Mr. Kid isn't my husband. He's trying to protect me."

The woman crossed herself. "Sweet Jesus. We gotta get out of here."

Caroline took her hand. "What can I do?"

"Come with me." The ladies went to the back room, and Rob and Pauley ran to the boat.

As soon as they were on board, Rob draped tarps over the name and marking of the boat, then loaded the gas cans and coolers the boys had carried to the dock. Then the boys ran back to the house to get more. Rob put the baskets of clothing and supplies the boys brought onto the boat and Pauley stowed them away.

When they were done, the women boarded, and Pauley started the engine. Rob and the older boy untied the lines, and the vessel puttered away with Pauley's family huddled together in the wheelhouse, looking back at their home as it slipped out of sight.

The shrimp boat traveled up the bayou within view of the road. Rob saw the two-tone pickups stop, and several men jump out. He grabbed Caroline and took her to the opposite side of the wheelhouse.

"Hold on and stay out of sight," he said, crouching beside her as low as he could. He was sure they would be seen until Yvette and the boys stepped in front of them, blocking them from the men running up to the water's edge.

CHAPTER TWENTY-ONE

Dulac

Later that evening, the grocery owner was sweeping the porch when one old regular who had been there earlier returned.

"Hey, Marquette," the grocer said. "I was about to close up. Didn't expect to see nobody after what happened today."

"Thought I'd come and see if you know what happened after I left."

"I don't know any more than you. I'm closing so I can get home to my family." The words were barely out of his mouth when two younger men appeared. "I'm closing, Latour. What do you need?"

"Mostly answers. Some men passed by my house asking about Pauley. They scared my missus so bad she locked herself and our kids in the bathroom."

"Yeah, mine too," said the other man. "We saw them going to other folks' houses on our way here."

"Best we get inside before they see us talking," the grocer said. He entered his store, and the others followed. "Hope y'all didn't say anything about Pauley," he said, leaning the broom against the wall.

"We didn't. Why are they looking for him?"

"Don't know. When you see people, tell them to say nothing about Pauley or his family. Everybody needs to stay inside their homes till they leave."

"You're right. We best get back to ours. If something happens, let us know."

"I will." He nodded. "Take extra care of your folks till these people go back to where they come from."

"My shotgun is already near the door," Latour said. "Take care, *mon ami*."

"All you too."

The screen door had barely closed behind the two men when they came running back in.

"They just pulled up outside your store," Latour said breathlessly.

The old Frenchman named Marquette got behind the counter when the man with the silver-tipped boots walked in, followed by four of his men.

"Get over here, old man, and sit," the man ordered.

The old Frenchman did as he was told.

The Mexican glared at the grocer. "Where's the little man with the big mouth I saw earlier?"

The grocer chuckled. "Look around. We are all little men. Who are you talking about?"

The Mexican grabbed him by the collar of his shirt and pulled him close. "The one you called Robishit."

"You mean Robichaux," the grocer replied.

"That was Pauley, and you know it. Tell me where he is."

"How do I know? After he got his boudin, he left."

The Mexican pulled his pistol and pressed it to the grocer's head. "Tell me, or I'm blowing your head off."

"Wait!" shouted Marquette. "Don't shoot, don't shoot."

The Mexican released the grocer and went to Marquette. "Where is Pauley?"

"None of us know, but Sammy does. He was waiting to drive Pauley home when you were here."

"How do I find this Sammy?"

"His place is one, maybe two, three miles down the road. Look for the big ugly dog on the porch. You find the dog, you find Sammy."

The Mexican gave orders to his men in Spanish. One took a position next to the door, and another went to the end of the counter. Before he left, the Mexican turned back to the grocer. "If you're lying to me, I'm coming back and killing all of you." Then he stomped out the door, followed by two of his men.

*   *   *

Ochsner Hospital

Tom heard Nurse Bennett talking to someone in the hallway seconds before three men in suits and fedoras entered his room.

"I see you survived," said a tall, pale-skinned man, looking down at him.

"So, I was told. You must be Ashcroft."

"Why wasn't I notified you were in New Orleans?"

"That's hard to do when confined to a hospital bed."

"I'm not stupid, Agent Neal. You were here for days before this happened."

"True," Tom said, "but I felt there were more pressing matters needing my attention than making a courtesy call."

"You know the procedure. I should have received paperwork informing me of your arrival."

"Ashcroft, I've made dozens of trips to New Orleans after the assassination. There was no need for paperwork."

"The Kennedy investigation is over. Why are you here?"

"Hoover sent me here to investigate leads brought to him by your district attorney, Jim Garrison."

The senior agent crossed his arms. "I'm head of the regional office. I should have been informed. Now I have not only you but also another out-of-town agent getting two of *my* agents involved in a gun battle at this hospital."

Before Tom could answer, Steve, Wiley, and Phillip entered the room. Ashcroft glared at his men. "And here they are now. I need answers, Agent Neal. Why are you here?"

"I've already told you, Ashcroft, but since you don't believe me, let's get Hoover on the line and let him explain."

Ashcroft's eyes widened, and his pale skin turned a shade of gray. "No need to bother the director. Besides, you aren't able to do much investigating lying in that bed. But if I hear you are dragging my men into something without my approval, I'll contact Hoover myself. Is that clear?"

Tom nodded. "Thanks for dropping by."

Ashcroft pushed past his two agents and Steve and left the room.

Steve shook his head and went to Tom's side. "I'm having a hard time liking that man."

"So am I. I'm just grateful he didn't call my bluff about phoning Hoover."

"Wait a minute," Wiley said. "You told us the director sent you."

"He did, but for a different reason." Tom glanced at Phillip and Wiley. "Look, if you have doubts about helping us, I'll understand."

"No way," Wiley said. "Ashcroft is too scared of Pascal to do anything about him. This could be our only chance at actually taking him down."

"Heck," Phillip added, shrugging, "Wiley and I are already on Ashcroft's hate list because we don't kowtow to him like the other agents in our office."

"We're grateful to you both," Tom said. "We can't do this without you."

"Now, with that out of the way," Wiley said, slowly lowering himself into the chair, "have you heard back from your guy?"

"They ran into trouble in Houma and had to relocate to Dulac," Steve said, "wherever that is."

Phillip chuckled. "It's a small community south of Houma, about fifteen minutes from the Gulf. Has he been down there before?"

"Not that we know. Why?" Steve asked.

"If bayou people like you, you've got a friend for life. If they don't, it's best not to stick around."

"Let's hope they stay out of sight," Tom said. "Has anything happened at the docks?"

"The containers haven't moved," Phillip said, "but something else is happening that might explain why."

Tom tried to push himself up but quickly realized it was a bad idea. "What?" he said through clenched teeth.

Phillip came closer to the bed. "One of my informants told me a bunch of Mexicans are searching for someone in the same area where The Kid and the woman went."

Steve said, "Sounds like Pascal is backing off and giving Martínez a chance to clean up his mess."

Phillip shook his head. "I don't think so. My informant tells me Pascal's people are keeping an eye on them."

"Could be Pascal doesn't trust them," Steve said, glancing at Tom.

"Damn. This keeps getting worse by the minute," Tom said. "Now The Kid has Martínez and Pascal after them."

"What do you want us to do?" Wiley asked.

"Find The Kid and Mrs. Broussard before they do."

"What about the drugs?" Wiley asked.

"I'll worry about the drugs later," Tom told him. "Phillip, contact your informant and tell him to let you know if he hears anything else."

"I'll give him a call right now," Phillip said and left the room.

"While Phillip's contacting his informant, I'll call one of the guys working on the drug organization's case from my office," Steve added. "Maybe he will know what's happening down here."

"Be careful, Steve," Tom said. "We don't want your office to know you're working on this."

"I know how to handle it," he said, and left the room.

Wiley stepped closer and put his hand on Tom's foot. "You need to take a break, old friend. Let's talk about something else before you have a heart attack."

Tom took a deep breath. "You're right. There's nothing we can do until they return anyway." Tom grimaced as he pulled the sheet up to his chest. "Tell me about Melanie and little Kyle. How are they doing?"

"Melanie is my rock. How she manages to handle Kyle and me without going crazy baffles the heck out of me. As for Kyle, he isn't little anymore. He's fifteen now and strong as an ox. It's hard on Melanie because, as big as he is, he still has the mind of a five-year-old," Wiley said. "A couple of years back, his disposition changed. Don't know if it's hormones or something else, but he went from being a sweet little boy to a moody and angry teenager." Wiley dropped his eyes and laced his hands together. "A few months back, I came home and found Melanie out cold and bleeding on our living room floor."

"That's terrible. What happened?" Tom asked.

"She said Kyle was playing with his train set and asked to watch *Captain Kangaroo*. When Melanie tried to explain the show wasn't on right then, Kyle got mad and threw his metal train engine at her."

"Geez, Wiley. Is she all right?"

"Yeah, after an X-ray of her head and five stitches to close the gash. That's when I knew it was time for him to be in a place with trained people to care for him."

"What did Melanie say about that?"

"What do you think? She said no. He's still her little boy."

"What are you going to do?"

"I've got to protect my wife. I found a place for kids like Kyle, but it's in Lake Charles. It took some work, but Melanie finally agreed to see it. When we were there, she saw how Kyle responded to the staff and some boys his age living there, and she finally admitted I was right. The problem is, it's three hours away, and she doesn't want to be that far from him."

"Surely there are centers closer to your home?"

"There are, but none we can afford. You have no idea how much those places cost, Tom. But I've got to do it, for Melanie's sake."

"Let me help you, Wiley."

"Thanks, but you've got your own troubles to deal with." Wiley groaned as he pushed himself out of the chair.

"What's going on with you? You don't look well."

"That's funny coming from a man with more stitches than my grandma's quilt. I'm fine, don't worry about me," Wiley said, forcing a smile. "I hate to leave you alone, but I'd better go check in at the office before Ashcroft comes back here looking for us. Page me if you need me."

"I will."

Several minutes later, Steve returned.

"What did you find out?" Tom asked.

"No one has heard of anything happening here."

"I'm not surprised. Did The Kid tell you what happened to them in Houma?"

"Just that they barely made it out."

"And now Pascal and Martínez are looking for them. Damn it. I need to be out there so I can get them back."

"Tom, you can do that from your bed. You're still in charge of the operation. Tell me what you need, and I'll do it."

"Start by locating my gun. I feel naked without it. And where's my pager?"

"I have your gun locked in my suitcase at the hotel."

"And my pager?"

Steve reached into his pants pocket and gave Tom the device. "I made sure they gave it to me before you went into surgery."

"Good. I'm going to need it while you're in Houma."

"I'm not leaving you here unprotected."

"You're not. Phillip will be back by the time you return with my revolver."

"All right. I'll be back as soon as I can."

Tom lay silent for a moment after Steve left, then whispered. "We're coming, Kid. I need for you to stay alive. I can't lose you too."

CHAPTER TWENTY-TWO

South of Dulac

The shrimp boat puttered through a bayou lined with trees and dense vegetation until eventually the landscape changed to thinning grass and weeds. Instead of houses, there were shacks or camps built on pilings. Soon, those disappeared, too, and they came to open water. Rob noticed the skies getting darker with dense, angry-looking clouds. The wind was blowing, forming huge waves with whitecaps that pounded the boat, rocking it back and forth. He saw Yvette gather her boys and have them huddle beside Caroline. She covered them with a tarp and got under with them. Rob joined Pauley in the wheelhouse.

"How long will it take to get to Golden Meadow?"

"Too long. My uncle and his family got a camp not far from here. Hope we can get there before this storm hits, 'cause it's gonna be bad."

"We've already put your family at risk, Pauley. The last thing I want to do is endanger more of your relatives. Is there any place you can drop us off?"

"Only place close to here is the landing to the Healer's Settlement."

"Let us off there, and you go on without us."

"I don't think so. It will be dark soon, and the path to the village is hard to see."

"You have to let us off, Pauley, I insist."

"If that's what you want, I'll get you as close as I can."

"Thank you. And one more thing. If those men find you, tell them I forced you to help us. That's something they'll understand."

"If you are sure about this, okay." Pauley spun the wheel of the small craft into a canal.

"How far is the settlement from Golden Meadow?"

Pauley chuckled. "It depends on which way you go. The people in the village will help. Just tell them you are Pauley and Yvette's friend, and they'll take good care of you."

A big gust of wind rocked the small craft, followed by another, as lightning flashed across the sky.

"We almost there," Pauley yelled over the thunder. "As soon as you're off the boat, you best run as fast as you can to the settlement before the rain hits. The swamps ain't no place for you and Miss Caroline."

Rob looked at the cypress trees lining the banks. The wind had increased, making the moss on the branches fly like sheets of gray lace and the tall grass around them lay flat like green shag carpet. Pauley slowed the engine when they reached two wooden pallets nailed atop cypress stumps.

"This is where you get off."

"If that's the landing, where's the trail?"

"Look for the markers," Pauley shouted over the rushing wind. "They will lead you in. You gotta jump. It's too rough for me to tie up."

A wave hit the side of the boat, spraying water over its deck.

Rob grabbed the little shrimper's hand. "Thank you, Pauley."

"Never you mind. You just get to the settlement."

Rob went to get Caroline as she hugged Yvette and the boys. "We have to jump."

Yvette grabbed his arm. "Take care, *mes amis.*"

"We will."

Rob lifted Caroline and jumped onto the makeshift landing. He set her down and held onto her arm as he looked back at the shrimp boat and gave Pauley one last wave.

Large raindrops like soft-boiled eggs began pounding them. It quickly became difficult to see anything at all, much less a marker.

"Where are we going?" Caroline shouted, cupping her hand over her eyes.

Rob peered into the trees and rain-swept grass. "Not sure. Hold onto my belt, and don't let go."

She grabbed his belt, and they stepped off the small landing. The surface beneath them felt like walking on a thick, soggy sponge.

A bright bolt of lightning flashed across the sky long enough for Rob to see a faded red cloth hanging from a cypress branch.

"I see a marker," he shouted over a deafening roll of thunder. "Follow my steps, and don't let go." Another flash of light ripped through the sky, giving the swamp an eerie glow.

Caroline wrapped her arms around him as thunder rolled. "Get us out of here," she yelled.

Rob took her hands from his waist and put them on his belt. "Hold on." He took several steps before something hit his leg. He reached down and found a long, slender branch about two inches thick in his path. He picked it up, ripped off the twigs and leaves, and used it to test the ground for sinkholes as they moved forward.

They had only gone about twenty feet when the sky lit up again, allowing Rob to spot another red marker. "We're going the right way," he shouted over the thunder.

They moved faster, using the branch to ensure his footing. By the time Rob found the third marker, the lightning had moved further inland, the wind had calmed down, and they were in a steady downpour. When the rain finally ended, it only took a few moments before an unmistakable buzzing hum descended on them like a net.

"Mosquitoes!" Caroline shouted and started slapping the insects that were covering her face and body.

"Run!" Rob said, tossing the branch and grabbing her arm. They had only run for a short distance when Caroline fell.

"They're eating me alive," she yelled, then began spitting bugs from her mouth.

Rob wrapped his arm around her waist and carried her with one arm, covering his mouth and nose to keep from inhaling the blood-sucking insects with the other hand.

He saw lights between the trees in the distance and realized someone was coming. "I think I see people," he said behind his hand.

"What are we going to do?"

"Keep moving forward. It's too dangerous to get off the path. Stay behind me and do as I say."

When the people were near, Rob heard a woman speaking in French. He and Caroline stood still as several of the men formed a circle around them.

"Lady, don't move!" the woman shouted just before Caroline took a step backward and screamed.

"My leg, my leg!" Caroline yelled just as a rifle fired so close to them that it made their ears ring.

Rob grabbed hold of her just as someone dropped a grass garland over her head.

"We don't have much time," the woman said, draping a garland around Rob's neck. "Lay her down."

Rob gently lowered Caroline to the wet grass and watched as the woman placed her lantern next to Caroline and removed a knife from her belt.

"What are you doing?" he said, grabbing her arm.

"Cottonmouth," the woman replied with a strong Cajun accent. "Let go of me. I am trying to save her life."

Rob looked past her and saw a man holding a giant black snake by the tail. He tossed it away as the woman ripped Caroline's pant leg up to her thigh, took a sash from her waist, wrapped it several times above Caroline's knee, and tied it off. She reached into a pouch hanging from a cord around her neck and smeared something into the puncture wounds above Caroline's ankle. Then she wrapped the wound with clean strips of cloth and took a small glass vial from another pouch and put it to Caroline's lips. "She must drink. It will ease the pain."

Again, Rob grabbed her hand. "What is that?"

The woman looked up at him. "The bite punctured a vein. Mama Rue said to give this to her to slow her heartbeat and make her sleep." Rob released her hand, and the woman poured the contents of the vial into Caroline's mouth. Then the woman got to her feet and spoke to the men in French.

Two men stepped forward and got on either side of Caroline and lifted her up as she went limp. They allowed her feet to dangle, almost touching the ground.

"I told them to keep her heart above her legs," the woman said. "Come, we don't have much time."

"How did you know about the snake or that we were here?"

The woman looked up at him. "Your questions will be answered after we get the lady to Mama Rue."

"She needs a hospital, not someone called Mama Rue."

"Your lady would die before we could get her to a boat."

"Does anyone have a car?"

"No roads, no cars. Best that you stay close, mister. You are big but no match for the swamps."

"I need to get to a phone."

She said something in French, and the people around her laughed. "We have no need for phones in the swamps. Everybody we care about is here. Stop talking. We must get to the village before the storm returns."

"All right, but I'm taking her to a hospital as soon as possible."

The woman ignored his comment as they made their way deeper into the swamps.

Rob suddenly realized he could still hear the mosquitoes, but they weren't biting him. He lifted his garland and inhaled a pungent odor that burnt his nostrils. He glanced at the people around him and saw they were also wearing garlands.

"Citronella," the woman said. "It works for mosquitoes, but it does not work for snakes."

Rob heard dogs barking in the distance and saw what looked to be a clearing ahead. As they got closer, he noticed a village of small wooden dwellings scattered about an open patch of ground. Behind the houses were massive, moss-bound oak and cypress trees. He saw people standing in doorways holding oil lamps as they entered the camp. All the people except the men carrying Caroline ran to the homes and disappeared behind closed doors.

Rob followed the woman and the men holding Caroline past a large cast-iron pot in the center of the clearing to a tiny house flanked by four large oak trees. The house was painted such a brilliant white it appeared to glow in the dark. Oil lamps hung from hooks on the porch, and Rob noticed a dim light inside a window.

A black cross was nailed over the door, and others were placed on either side of every window. A brass bell hung from an iron hook attached to one of the porch posts. Rob was taken aback when a large white owl perched atop an old wooden rocker screeched and flapped its wings.

"That is Chouette Blanche," said the woman as they stepped onto the porch.

Rob stepped in front of the woman. "I need to know more about this Mama Rue before you take her in."

"Mister, the lady is dying. Mama Rue is the only one who can save her."

"I've heard stories about this religion, magic, cult, or whatever you call it. I'm not letting your Mama Rue use voodoo on her."

"Then she will be dead before morning."

Rob looked at Caroline and saw she had turned pasty white. He looked down at her leg, which was now three times its normal size.

"Mister," the woman urged.

"All right, but if anything happens to her. . ."

Just then, the door to the cabin opened, and a little old woman bent over a cane hobbled out. She went to Caroline and pointed to one of the lanterns. The younger woman took a lamp from its hook and held it near Caroline's face. The old woman got up next to the light, and Rob saw her face. It was weathered and wrinkled, and he gasped when he saw that her eyes were cased in a gray film.

"She's blind. How is she going to help?"

The old woman looked his way, chuckled, and said something in French.

"Mama Rue said she sees more than you will ever see with two good eyes. She also said that if you don't get out of the way, the woman will die in less than an hour."

Rob hesitated a moment, then stepped aside so the men could carry Caroline inside. He stood near the door, watching as the men placed Caroline on an old wooden table covered with handmade quilts. Every wall of the small structure was lined with shelves filled with glass jars and clay containers. Above his head hung numerous clusters of dried plants, herbs, and flowers. A cast-iron stove in the corner of the room held a large black pot boiling some type of mixture.

He saw the younger woman take the healer's hand and put it on Caroline's wounded leg.

"*Tout le monde,*" the old woman ordered.

The younger woman turned to Rob. "She told us to go."

"I'm not going anywhere."

"We must. Mama Rue never allows anyone in the room when she prays."

"Prays? Caroline was bitten by a poisonous cottonmouth snake! She needs more than prayers!"

The moment he finished speaking, the room was bathed in a flash of light, followed by deafening thunder. The two men who had helped carry Caroline in turned and ran past him and out the door.

"Come," said the woman. "The second storm coming will be worse than the first."

"Who are you? And how do you know there's a second storm?"

"My name is Monique. Do not worry about your lady. She is well cared for. Now come. We don't have much time left to cross the clearing."

Reluctantly, Rob followed Monique out and had just stepped off the first step when the old woman yelled from inside the cabin.

"*Arrêtez!*"

Monique grabbed Rob and pulled him back onto the porch just as a lightning bolt struck the large iron pot a few yards away. The force of the electricity knocked both of them down, and the thunder that followed was so loud it shook the tiny house.

Every hair on Rob's body stood straight up, and the scent of sulfur filled the air. He looked over at the woman lying next to him. "Are you all right?"

"*Oui.* I mean, yes. I'm good."

"How did you know that was going to happen?" he asked as he helped her to her feet.

"I didn't. Mama Rue ordered us to stop."

Rob looked back at the cabin behind him. "How?"

"*Allons!* There is no time to talk."

She rushed down the steps, and Rob followed. They were pelted with what felt like stones instead of raindrops as they ran across the open area to a small cabin.

"You stay here," Monique said, leaving him at the door. She raced across the compound to another dwelling and went inside.

Another flash of lightning hit, and Rob rushed inside and closed the door. The one-room cabin was lit by a kerosene lamp on a small table. Next to the lamp was a pitcher of water and a large bowl. In the corner, a potbellied stove heated the room. Next to it was a wooden crate filled with kindling. The bed was covered with quilts, and a large nightshirt lay on top. Rob picked up the shirt and held it against his frame. To his amazement, it was exactly his size.

"How did they know we were coming?" he whispered.

Rob took the pager from his pocket and checked the dial. *No signal.* He turned it off and placed it on the table. *I hope this old woman knows what she's doing,* he said to himself. *It's impossible to get Caroline anywhere tonight.*

CHAPTER TWENTY-THREE

Houma

Steve drove down the main street, looking for a place to get answers. He saw a large five-and-dime store, parked, and went in. There were several people seated at the soda fountain counter, and he joined them. The woman behind the counter looked like she had been there for decades and was chatting with everyone she served. He saw her take her order pad out of her apron pocket as she approached him.

"What can I get you?" she said as she took a pencil from behind her ear.

"I'll just have coffee."

"That's it?"

"For now."

She frowned, returned the pencil to her ear, and went away. Moments later, she returned with a dark, steaming cup of coffee and a small pitcher of cream. "Sugar?"

"No thanks, but there is something I'm curious about."

"What's that?"

"I heard you had quite a commotion here a couple of days ago, and I would like to ask you about it." Suddenly, the woman's whole demeanor changed, and Steve detected a smile.

"Sure, but it didn't happen here. It was at Dupont's Department Store a few doors down," she said, pointing to her left.

Steve took a sip of the coffee and did his best to not grimace. It was strong. Really strong. He poured in a hefty dose of cream. "Sounds like you've got the inside scoop. What happened?"

The woman leaned in. "I wasn't there, but my friend Jenny was. She said this couple was in the store buying some things when some for-eign-looking guy grabbed the woman and tried to drag her out the door. Before he could do it, though, a man flew over the counter, tack-led the creep, and started pounding him."

"Wow, that's awful."

"It was, but it got worse. Jenny said they broke everything in sight. Glass was everywhere. Then the foreign guy grabbed a big chunk of glass and was about to cut the man's throat when all of a sudden, the lady grabbed a mannequin's leg and knocked the guy out cold!"

"Really? Well, good for her," Steve said. "But why did Jenny think the guy was foreign?"

"Not sure." The waitress shrugged. "But Jenny said he had dark hair and tan skin and was wearing fancy boots. We don't see people like that down here."

"What happened to the couple?"

"Jenny said they ran to the back of the store with some of the other customers before more of them foreign-looking guys showed up with guns."

"Your friend must have been terrified."

"She was. Jenny and other store clerks hid behind counters until they left."

"Did your friend see where the man and woman went?" Steve asked.

"Nope, but I heard they got on a shrimp boat down at Blum & Bergeron's Shrimp Factory."

"They left town on a shrimp boat?"

"They sure did. I'm guessing those same bad guys saw it, too, because they went to the shrimp factory and beat poor Henry half to death until he told them who that boat belonged to."

"Did the police catch any of them?"

"Naw," she said, picking up his empty cup. "They got away."

"That's some story," Steve said as he took a ten-dollar bill from his wallet and placed it on the counter.

"I'll get your change."

"It's yours if you tell me how to find the manager of the shrimp factory."

She eyed him for a moment before replying. "Why are you so interested in this?"

"That couple are friends of mine. I'm worried about them and want to bring them home."

"How do I know you aren't with those bad guys?"

Steve held out his arms. "As you can see, I'm not foreign. I need to find my friends before those bad guys do."

The waitress looked deep into Steve's eyes. "Okay then," she said finally. "I'll meet you at the door."

She came around the counter, and he followed her out the door.

"Go past the courthouse," the waitress said, pointing down the street. "Cross the Lafayette Street bridge on the right. From there, turn right, pass the bus station, and keep going. If you roll your window down, you'll smell the shrimp drying before you see the factory on the right."

"Thanks for your help."

"Hope you find them."

"So do I."

Steve followed the woman's directions and parked near the shrimp plant. He walked to the back of the plant and saw a man with a water hose spraying down a large scale. He noted the man's battered face as he got closer.

"Excuse me. Are you the manager? I have questions about an altercation that happened here a couple of days ago."

The man shut off the nozzle on the hose. "Who are you?"

Steve presented his badge. "I'm with the FBI."

"You must be talking about the beating?"

"Yes, I am. Can you tell me what happened?"

"A bunch of scumbags showed up and almost beat Henry and me to death."

"Do you know why?"

"They wanted to know who owned a shrimp boat that left with some people on it."

"Did you tell them?"

"If I hadn't, I wouldn't be standing here right now. Poor Henry, the manager, wouldn't tell them, and they beat him really bad, knocked him out cold, and started on me. They would have killed both of us had our guys not run out with chains and shovels."

"Is the manager here?"

"Nope. Henry's home nursing cuts, bruises, and a couple broken ribs."

"What can you tell me about the boat and its owner?"

"Like I told Police Chief Fakier, Pauley Guidry owns the boat called *Miss Yvette.*"

"How well do you know Mr. Guidry?"

"We've been buying Pauley's shrimp for years."

"Do you know where Pauley lives?"

"He's from Dulac and has a wife and couple of kids, but that's all I know. If you don't mind, I gotta get back to work."

"Thanks for your help. I hope you and Henry are better soon."

"You need to lock those dudes up. We never want to see them again."

"I'll do my best to make that happen."

*   *   *

Ochsner Hospital

Phillip was sitting next to Tom when a pager buzzed. "Not mine," he said after checking the device in his pocket.

"It must be mine," Tom said, pointing to his bedside table. "It's in the drawer."

Phillip got the pager and handed it to Tom.

"It's from Steve, and he's added three X's. Take down the number and get back to me as quickly as possible."

Phillip jotted the number down and left the room.

Tom looked at the number again. "Damn it, Kid. Please be all right."

*   *   *

Phillip went to a pay phone at a nearby gas station. He dialed the number Steve had sent, and it only rang once before it was answered.

"Who's this?" Phillip asked.

"Steve. I just learned our people were attacked in Houma."

"Are they all right?"

"I think so. I heard they left town on a shrimp boat but aren't out of the woods yet. It seems part of the same group that attacked the hospital found out who owns the boat. We need to get to them before they do."

"If they know, so does Pascal."

"Are you on your way back?"

"No. Tell Tom I'm going to someplace called Dulac. I'm not sure what I'm getting into, and I need backup."

"No problem. Do you know how to get there?"

"I'll get directions or a map."

"I'll get back to Tom, and either Wiley or I will head your way." Phillip hung up and rushed back to the hospital.

"What did Steve say?" Tom asked as soon as Phillip entered his hospital room.

"He said our people were almost captured in Houma, but they managed to get out of town on a shrimp boat."

"Did he find out where the boat was going?"

"He said Dulac. It's where the owner, a guy named Pauley Guidry, lives. The problem is that the people who are after them know too. Steve's on his way there and asked for backup."

"Page Wiley and tell him to get down there as fast as possible. I need you here in case they try to page us. It's too risky to make calls from my room."

Phillip ran from the room.

*   *   *

Garden District

It was late that evening when Pascal left his office and got to his car.

"Long day, sir?" his driver asked.

"Too long. I'm eager to be home."

Just as the driver was about to close his door, Jean-Claude ran down the sidewalk.

"Jamerson, wait. I must speak to Mr. Pascal."

The driver opened the door and stepped away from the automobile.

Pascal frowned and shook his head. "Whatever it is, it can wait. I'm done for the day."

"I understand, sir, but this is important."

Pascal closed his eyes for a moment and blew out a rush of air. "What is it?"

"I just received a call from Dupre."

"Did he finish off the woman?"

"Not exactly?"

"Damn it, Jean-Claude. What did he say?"

"He discovered where the shrimper lived and went there to look for the woman. When he arrived, he learned that Martínez's people had gotten there before him."

"Are you telling me Martínez's people have the woman?"

"No, sir. She and the man with her escaped with the shrimper. The good news is Dupre confronted Martínez's men on the road and took many of them out."

"I don't care how many he killed. He needs to find that woman."

"Sir, I have Dupre on hold. What should I tell him?"

"Find out where he is and tell him to stay put. It's time to bring Jerome in."

Jean-Claude clasped his hands together. "Sir, may I speak openly?"

"Make it quick. I would like to get home before midnight."

"I know you have impeccable judgment."

"Apparently not, or I wouldn't be in this mess."

"Sir, every time Jerome is involved, he leaves behind far more bodies than the task requires, and we have more to cover up."

"True, but millions are on the line, Jean-Claude. The only way to guarantee we get that money is to ensure Caroline Broussard never submits her bid. Do as I said and make that call to Jerome. I'm not going to let that pompous little drug lord win our bet."

"Yes, sir. Right away."

*   *   *

The Healer's Settlement

The long night of pounding rain and lightning continued well into the morning.

"Storm or no storm, I have to check on Caroline," Rob said to himself, taking his shirt and pants from the back of a chair near the potbellied stove. He dressed and ran through the rain to the little white house. Just as he reached for the door handle, the door opened, and the old woman shoved the end of her cane into his chest.

"*Non,*" she said with a shake of her head. "*Non.*" She pointed to his cabin with a crooked finger before shutting the door in his face.

He paused a moment, then reached for the door handle again.

"Mister, stop," called Monique from across the clearing.

Rob turned and saw her standing at the open door of her cabin.

"You must let Mama Rue work. Go back to your cabin and wait. There is nothing you can do."

"I have to get her out of here."

"Not in this storm. If you try, both of you will die."

He looked at the woman and saw she was being pelted by rain.

"Mister, please. You will see your lady as soon as Mama Rue says you can."

"I'll give her until noon, then I'm going in." He saw Monique shake her head before she disappeared behind her door.

Rob heard the old woman shouting from inside her cabin. *Chouette Blanche, gètte lé!*

A moment later, a large mass of white flew at Rob's face, screeching and flogging him with its wings. The bird forced Rob away from the door and went to rest on the rocking chair. It spread its massive wings and looked at him.

"You are the strangest guard dog I've ever seen," Rob muttered.

Suddenly, the bird launched at him, forcing Rob off the porch.

"Okay, I'm going." The bird seemed to understand and took up position in front of the door. "This isn't over, my feathered friend. When I return, I'm going in."

The creature screeched at Rob, and he jumped off the porch and ran to his hut. Once inside, he went to the window and looked out at the white cabin. The owl hadn't moved. A moment later, he heard knocking at his door. He opened it and saw a man running through the rain to a nearby cabin. A basket covered with a plastic cloth and a hot coffee pot wrapped in cloth were on his doorstep.

He took them in, unwrapped the coffee pot, and sat it on the stove. Inside the basket were two covered pots. He lifted the lid to one and was greeted by the delicious aroma of red beans and rice. He checked the second pot and found it contained warm corn muffins atop two fried eggs and a generous serving of grits. He placed the beans near the stove and filled a plate with eggs, grits, and muffins.

As he savored the delicious meal, the sound of the rain pounding on the roof of the cabin was deafening.

How did Monique know I was checking on Caroline? Rob wondered, lifting another spoonful of grits to his mouth. *She sure couldn't have heard me with this rain going on. There are a lot of strange things happening here.*

CHAPTER TWENTY-FOUR

The Healer's Settlement

The rain continued until noon. When it stopped, Rob dashed across the soaked clearing to the white cottage, fully expecting to be confronted by the watchdog owl. But to his surprise, it was gone. Just as he was about to open the door, it swung open. Instead of the owl or Mama Rue blocking his entrance, this time it was Monique.

"I'm not leaving here until I see her."

"*Il peut entrer,*" the old woman said from inside the cabin, and Monique stepped aside to let him in.

Fear spread through Rob's body when he saw Caroline drained of color and motionless.

"She's dead! You told me Mama Rue could save her." Before he got an answer, Caroline's eyelids fluttered open.

"Kid," she said with a raspy whisper.

Rob took her hand. "Thank God. I thought I had lost you."

"I feel like you did."

Rob looked at the two women standing next to him. "Is she going to be all right?" The old woman answered his question in French, and he turned to Monique.

"Mama Rue said your lady has a strong spirit. It will take some time, but she will recover."

"How much time?"

"The cure cannot be rushed, Mister. It takes as long as it takes."

"You don't understand. Every day we are here puts us and you in danger."

Mama Rue pounded her walking stick on the floor and started to speak.

"She told you not to worry. The storm was sent to delay the evil chasing you."

Monique glanced at the old woman as she spoke again. "She says to tell you Pauley and his family are safe. They reached his uncle's camp and are doing well. The ones who are chasing you will not find them because she has prayed for their protection."

"Who told her about Pauley and the people after us?"

"No one. Mama Rue knew of your coming weeks ago."

"That isn't possible. We only met Pauley a few days ago."

The old woman chuckled and started to speak.

"Mister, your aura called out to Mama Rue before you arrived. She said she knows that you and your lady are deeply in love, just not with each other. Mama Rue knows that you were given the role of the lady's protector."

"Then she knows why I have to get her out of here before we are found."

Mama Rue rested her hand on Rob's shoulder as she spoke.

"She says to tell you as long as you are here, you are under her care and protection. In time, that will change, and when it does, she will tell you to go."

"I don't understand how she knows all this."

Monique smiled and pointed upward. "Mama Rue draws her knowledge from above."

"And what about you? I've noticed that you seem to be able to communicate without words."

"That is because we share the same blood. Mama Rue is my great-great-great grand-mére. Of all her many children and grandchildren, I was chosen to carry on her work from an early age, but there is still much I must learn from her before I can take her place."

"Great-great-great grandmother? How is that possible?"

Monique laughed. "You will see many things you will think are impossible the longer you stay, but for us, they are not. We are blessed to have Mama Rue. She is why our people have survived so long in this place. You coming here was not by chance."

"For me, it was. I never knew this place existed."

Mama Rue looked into Rob's eyes, pressed her aged hand against his unshaven face, and whispered, *"Ton énergie est forte."*

"She said your energy is strong."

The old woman continued speaking in French.

"She asked that you sit by Caroline's side and send healing thoughts to her."

Rob took a moment to process everything he was told before pulling up a chair beside Caroline and sitting.

He spent the next few hours at her side as the women worked around him. The humidity from the rain made the tiny house almost unbearable. Rob felt as if his skin was melting, and to make matters worse, Monique and Mama Rue kept adding strong-smelling elements to the kettle boiling on the potbelly stove.

Caroline's eyes flew open, and she cried. "My leg, my leg is on fire!"

Mama Rue pulled Rob from the chair and nodded to Monique. She uncovered Caroline's leg. It was swollen from her toes to above her knee and had turned a horrible shade of red.

Rob watched as the younger woman unwrapped the bandage and wiped away a foul, greenish matter, revealing two puncture wounds that appeared to have been cut open.

The old woman mumbled something, and Monique went to the end of the bed and took hold of Caroline's foot. Mama Rue placed her hands above Caroline's knee and began to chant in French as she pressed down.

Caroline screamed and started slapping Mama Rue's back, almost knocking her over.

Rob grabbed her arms and held her down. "What is Mama Rue doing?"

"The poison has been contained, but she will lose her leg unless it is removed."

He watched in horror as a thick mixture of blood and vile matter oozed from Caroline's wounds. Mama Rue slid her hands farther down her leg and pressed again. Caroline screamed again and then fainted.

Monique wiped away the residue as Mama Rue continued to push on her leg for a while, then stopped.

"Why are you stopping?" he asked. "Caroline's leg and foot are still swollen."

"She needs to rest. Mama Rue will continue the process later."

"How long will this take?"

"Several days."

"How will you know if you've gotten it all?"

"We will know when the redness and swelling disappear. Soon after, Miss Caroline's strength will return." Mama Rue mumbled something. "She says she knows this is difficult for you to watch, but it is the only way she will recover."

Monique went to the kettle, dipped some liquid into a cup, and returned to Caroline. "It is time for you to go. Once we give her this mixture, she will sleep, and we will bathe her. If anything changes, I will come for you."

Rob stepped away and watched Monique spoon the mixture into Caroline's mouth. Mama Rue pounded her walking stick on the floor, then pointed to the door. He raised his hands in surrender. "Okay. I'm going."

Rob went out to the porch, and the door shut behind him. He stood there, inhaling fresh air as he looked around the settlement. People were busy cleaning up tree limbs and debris and repairing the damage to their homes from the storm's fury.

The large kettle that had been struck by lightning appeared to have survived. Rob noticed a woman was mixing something in it with a large wooden paddle. A breeze blew in his direction, and he realized she was making lye soap.

Rob looked beyond the kettle and noticed an old man sitting in front of one of the cabins dipping a chicken into a small pot. Then he started plucking at the feathers. Young girls were hanging the clothing their mothers scrubbed over washtubs, and as Rob observed them, a man carrying several strings of catfish entered the clearing. He approached the old man who was plucking the chicken and held up one of his strings of fish. The old man shouted something in French, and an old woman appeared at the cottage door with a bowl of eggs, which she exchanged for the fish.

Suddenly, everyone stopped what they were doing and started whistling, clapping their hands, and shouting in French. Rob stepped off the porch to see what was happening just as a man with a large alligator tail draped over his shoulder appeared, followed by two boys carrying bloodied burlap bags. He could see the man and the boys grinning, nodding, and waving to everyone as they passed. *Mama Rue was right,* Rob thought. *Everything they need is here in the swamps.*

He was about to go back to his cabin when a boy about ten carrying a covered pot approached him.

"*Pour la dame.*"

"Sorry, I don't understand."

The boy pointed to the white cabin. "*Pour la dame.*"

Monique came out of the cabin and took the pot from the boy.

"*Merci beaucoup,* Samuel."

The boy grinned, ducked his head, and ran across the clearing.

Monique lifted the lid on the pot. "Chicken soup for the lady."

"It smells wonderful."

"It tastes even better than it smells." She carried the pot into the cabin and closed the door.

I don't care what Mama Rue says. Every day we're here puts these people in danger.

*   *   *

Dulac

Steve drove to a small grocery store outside of town and went in. The robust conversation going on in French ended as soon as he was noticed.

"What can I do for you?" said the man behind the counter.

Steve took out his badge and presented it to the man. "I'm with the FBI and need to ask you some questions."

"Why? You lost?" one of the old men huddled around the stove asked. The other men in the group started to laugh.

"I'm looking for someone named Pauley Guidry."

"You and everyone else," another in the group spouted. "What you want with Pauley?"

"I need Mr. Guidry's help to find a couple he brought here from Houma."

"Why?" asked the grocer. "Those people brought us a bunch of trouble."

"What kind of trouble?

"Lots of bad people showed up looking for them. A guy in the first bunch put a gun to my head and said he was going to shoot me if I didn't tell them where Pauley lives."

"Who were they?" Steve asked.

The man shrugged. "Don't know. Never seen them before, but they spoke to each other in Spanish."

"So what happened?"

"They went door to door looking for Pauley at first. When that didn't work, they went down the road to look for one of Pauley's friends. After they found him, they left. We thought we were safe, then a few hours later, another bunch showed up looking for Pauley."

"What other bunch?"

"The ones sent by *le boss de la Mafia.*"

"Did you say Mafia?"

"Sure did." The men in the grocery started to mumble among themselves.

"How did you know it was them?"

"Everyone in Louisiana knows."

"What happened then?" Steve prodded.

"They blocked the road just outside of town and started a gun battle with the first group of guys who came here looking for Pauley. When the shooting stopped, one of them came in here and said he would kill us next if we didn't tell him where Pauley and the woman went."

"What did you say?"

"I told them we knew nothing about a woman. The last time we saw Pauley, he only had a man with him. After that, they went down to Sammy's."

"Who is Sammy?"

"He's an old boy who lives down the road," the grocer said. "Sammy drives Pauley from time to time 'cause Pauley doesn't have a car."

"Did they find Sammy?"

The old Frenchmen stood. "Sure did. But he's okay. I went down to make sure he was all right after the last bunch left."

"How do I find Sammy?"

The grocer came around the counter. "Take a left on that road out there and go till you see a rusted Chevy sedan parked in the front yard of his house."

Steve's pager buzzed. He took it out and looked at it. "I need to use your phone."

The grocer pointed to the back of the store. "On the wall next to the cooler."

"Thanks." Steve went to the phone and dialed Wiley's pager. He entered the grocer's number, hung up, and went back to the front of the store.

"That was quick," the grocer said.

"You'll get a call from an FBI agent named Wiley. Please tell him Steve said he couldn't wait, and I want him to come to your store, and you will tell him where I am."

"Where are you going?"

"To find Sammy. After what you told me, I had better find my friends before the big boss's men get them."

"*Bien sûr*," the grocer said. "But when you get to Sammy's, don't get close to the house. He's got a big, mean dog that will rip your head off if he gets ahold of you."

"Thanks for the warning."

"You best be careful around Sammy. After what's happened, he won't take kindly to strangers."

"Good to know."

"And if you find Pauley, tell him to let us know he's okay. We all worried about him."

"I will. Thanks for your help."

Steve followed the directions and found the rusted Chevy parked in an overgrown yard in front of a weathered house. He remembered the grocer's warning and parked several yards from the house and watched as a large, brown mongrel sat up from a tattered sofa on the porch. The dog was watching him but seemed content, so Steve opened his door and eased out of the car. As soon as he did, the dog launched off the porch and ran for him. Steve jumped back into the car just in time to see the dog jerked off its feet by a chain around its neck just a few feet from his door. The dog scrambled to its feet, pulling against the chain, snarling and barking.

"Bull," shouted a large man wearing a tattered sleeveless under-shirt and baggy jeans who was coming out the screen door carrying a shotgun.

Steve raised his hands as he got out of the car. "I'm not here to cause trouble, Sammy. I just want to ask a few questions."

"*Quoi tu veau?*"

"Do you speak English?" Steve shouted over the barking dog.

Sammy kept the gun pointed at Steve and didn't answer. "Bull!" Sammy yelled, and the slobbering dog stopped barking and sat down, staring at Steve intently. Sammy dropped down on the tattered sofa and laid the shotgun across his lap as he and the dog watched Steve's every move.

The standoff lasted for over an hour before Wiley arrived and exited his car, sending the dog into a new volley of snarls and barking.

"Looks like you could use some help," Wiley said, approaching Steve's door.

"Glad you're here."

"What's going on?"

"This guy was the last one to see our people, but he only speaks French. One of us needs to keep an eye on him while the other returns to the store and gets someone to translate."

Wiley stepped away from Steve and raised his hands. "*Bonjour mon ami. Pas ici pour vous faire du mal.*"

"I'll be damned," Steve said, coming to his side. "I didn't know you spoke French."

"I'm from a small town not far from here called Galliano. My grandmother only spoke Cajun French and taught all her grandchildren so she could talk to us. What do you want to know?"

"Ask him if he knows what happened to our people and his friend, Pauley."

Steve listened as Wiley and the Cajun communicated.

"He said he took Pauley and the man with him to the grocery so the man could use the phone. While he waited for them in his car, a group of men with guns showed up. It wasn't long before Pauley and the man came running from behind the grocery and told him to get them home as fast as he could."

"Does he know where they went?"

Wiley asked the question in French.

"He said Pauley and the man talked about Golden Meadow, but he doubted they would have made it there because of the big storm that came through that night."

"Ask him if he told the men with guns about Golden Meadow."

Wiley translated the request, and the Frenchman began waving his hands as he spoke.

"What's wrong?" Steve asked.

"He said he told both groups of men the same thing because they were going to kill him and his dog if he didn't talk."

"How long ago was this?"

Wiley asked, then turned to Steve. "They are at least a day and a half ahead of us."

"How far is Golden Meadow from here?"

"By car, less than an hour. Not sure how long it would take by boat."

"Damn it. We have to find them before it's too late."

CHAPTER TWENTY-FIVE

The Healer's Settlement

Rob spent the next two days helping with repairs around the settlement and going back and forth to check on Caroline. On one of his visits, he walked into the little white cabin with an armload of kindling and was surprised to find Caroline sitting in a chair.

"I'm glad to see you're getting your strength back."

"So am I. That was horrible."

"I'm sure it was. Where's Mama Rue?" he asked, placing the wood into a crate.

"She and Monique left about an hour ago with several empty baskets."

He pulled up a chair. "They must be looking for more stuff to make that foul-smelling brew," he said, pointing to the kettle.

She laughed. "It is bad, isn't it?" She took a deep breath and exhaled. "I owe you an apology."

"For what?"

"For acting like a spoiled brat and running away in Houma. You were almost killed, and now I've put Pauley, Yvette, and their boys in danger."

"None of that was your fault, Caroline." A smile spread across his face. "Well, except for the spoiled brat part."

She laughed softly. "Okay, I deserve that."

"What brought about this attitude change?"

"I don't know if it's Mama Rue's medicine or bad dreams, but I kept seeing that horrible moment when Jack was shot over and over again." Tears ran down her cheeks. "Except now it's in slow motion." She closed her eyes and shook her head. "I could see the bullet as it left the gun and when it pierced Jack's body. This is all my fault. That bullet was meant for me, and now Jack may never walk again." Caroline covered her face with her hands.

"He was protecting you, Caroline. Jack knows this wasn't your fault."

She lifted her tear-stained face. "It's not just that. My focus has always been more on the business than my husband."

"I'm sure he doesn't see it that way."

"How would you know? You're as bad as I am. You're risking your life to save mine, and it's not even your job."

Rob thought for a moment. "I know this sounds crazy, but helping you is my way of protecting my family. Don't get me wrong. I'm as anxious to get back to them as you are to Jack. But I'm not putting you at risk to do it."

Their conversation ended with the sound of a clanging bell. Rob went out and found Monique striking the bell on the porch.

"What's going on?"

"I must gather our people."

Rob glanced across the clearing and saw people coming from all directions. Mama Rue stood on the last step of the stairs, motioning everyone to come closer. He could see the concern on their faces as Mama Rue spoke to them in French.

"What is she saying?" he asked.

"The evil men are coming. She tells the people to go to their hiding places and stay there until the bell rings again."

Mothers started scooping up children and running as fast as possible into the trees and tall grass outside the settlement. Some men helped older residents out into the overgrowth behind their cabins. Moments later, the men returned to the clearing with firearms, clubs, machetes, whatever they could use as weapons. They gathered in front of Mama Rue and listened as she shouted orders in French. When she finished, the men scattered.

"What did she tell them?"

"They were told not to show themselves unless she gives the order."

"Monique, are these men coming for us?"

She turned and looked at him. "They are. Come, we must get Miss Caroline and you to a safe place."

"What about Mama Rue?"

"She is staying here."

"I'm not leaving her alone."

Mama Rue turned and shook her head. At that moment, a man who looked to be in his twenties ran up to them, holding a rifle. He propped the gun against the porch, took one of Mama Rue's arms, and motioned to Rob to take the other. They helped Mama Rue back onto the porch, and she pointed to the trees.

"This is Daniel," Monique said. "He is here to carry Miss Caroline."

"I can do that," Rob said, rushing into the cabin.

"What's happening?" Caroline asked as he scooped her up in his arms.

"They're coming for us." Rob carried her out and stopped beside Mama Rue. "Are you sure you want to stay?"

She nodded and patted his arm.

"Mister," Monique said. "We must go now."

Daniel looked at Monique, and she pointed to the area outside the clearing. He grabbed his rifle and started out ahead of them. They followed him across the clearing and into the thick growth of cypress trees and moss-covered oaks outside the settlement. They stopped before a large oak, and Daniel motioned to Rob to follow him. Rob set Caroline down gently and found Daniel behind the tree, holding the end of an old rope ladder.

Rob looked up and saw wood planks nailed together to form a small platform high up in the tree.

"I go first," Monique said. "Then I can help Miss Caroline when she reaches the top. You follow as soon as the ladder is free. We must hurry. The evil one is nearing our settlement."

Rob took hold of the rope ladder as Monique started up. "Tell Daniel I can handle this. He needs to get back to his family."

"I am his family," Monique said as she reached the platform. "We are to marry at the next new moon. Now, help Miss Caroline."

Rob started to lift Caroline up but she pushed his hands away. "What are you doing?"

"I'm going to carry you up over my shoulder."

"No," Monique protested from the platform. "The ladder is old. It will not hold both of you."

Caroline took hold of the ladder. "I can do this on my own," she said, gently placing her injured foot on the first rung and slowly starting to climb.

Daniel stood next to Rob and helped hold the rope ladder until Caroline reached the platform.

Monique looked down at Daniel. "*Gete toi. Je t'aime,*" she said. He blew her a kiss, grabbed his rifle, and disappeared into a large patch of grass nearby.

"Hurry, Mister. We are out of time."

When Rob reached the top, there was barely any room left for him. "How is Daniel getting up here?"

"He is staying below to guard us. Hurry, pull up the ladder, then stay low so we will not be seen."

Once the ladder was secured, Rob ducked down and peered between branches and moss. He could see the clearing and Mama Rue on the porch of the little white house, hunched over her walking stick. The village dogs started to bark as heavily armed men entered the clearing, led by a man dressed in black. Rob got extremely uneasy when the man in black walked up to Mama Rue. Rob turned and was letting down the rope ladder when Monique grabbed his arm.

"What are you doing?" she whispered.

"Someone needs to protect her."

"Mama Rue does not need your protection. You serve her best by staying here."

"All right, but I still need to go down so I can hear what they're saying."

"It will do you no good unless you understand French."

"Then how will I know if she needs help?"

"If she does, I will tell you. I will hear everything from here."

"How is that possible? We are too far away from her."

Monique exhaled. "In situations like this, Mama Rue shares her eyes and ears with me. She does this so I know what to do for her and our people."

Rob stared at her for a moment before responding. "Then tell me everything that's said, or I'm going down to help her."

Monique shook her head. "I will, but you must stay here and keep quiet."

Rob glanced at Caroline and saw the shocked expression on her face, then turned back to Monique. "You have my word." He watched as she took a deep breath, turned her face towards the clearing, closed her eyes, and started describing everything she heard.

*　*　*

The Clearing

Mama Rue said nothing to the man dressed in black as he looked around the settlement.

"Old woman, where are your people?" he asked again.

"I sent them away to keep them safe."

He laughed. "No one is safe from me, old hag. If you do not give me the woman and the man you are hiding, I will have my men drag your people from the swamps and slaughter them one by one in front of you. Then I will kill you."

Mama Rue chuckled. "I have lived a good life for almost a hundred and fifteen years, Jerome. The Great One will take me when *He* is ready, not you. The only reason I am here this long is to see to the needs of my people. But that is something you will never understand, *chéri*, because you care for no one but yourself."

A grin crossed his lips. "I see you know my name."

"I know much more about you than your name."

Jerome took his knife from the sheath strapped to his leg and switched it from one hand to another. "If that is true, old woman, what am I holding in my hand? It is plain to see you are blind." His men started to laugh.

Mama Rue lifted her cane and struck the boards at her feet. "Your knife does not scare me, Jerome."

"If not my knife, then maybe something else will." Jerome returned the knife to its sheath, pointed to the fire under the iron pot, and then to three of his men before returning his attention to Mama Rue.

"Now watch, old woman, as my men burn your settlement down."

Mama Rue's eyes never wavered from his as she began to chuckle.

The three men picked up broken branches near the iron pot, lit the ends in the fire, and then looked back to their leader. He pointed to the cabins.

When the men started across the clearing, Mama Rue turned to the trees and shouted, *Chouette Blanche. Attack!* A wave of white descended on the men, clawing and shrieking as it attacked them.

One was slashed across his face, another's back was ripped open, and the last man dropped his burning branch and ran back to the safety of his group. The owl continued its attack until Mama Rue called out to the bird, and then the creature came to rest next to her with its wings outstretched possessively.

"As I said, I see everything, even the fear in the eyes of your men. But you have more to fear than my owl, Jerome."

"I fear no one, old woman, least of all you." He started towards her, and she pointed her cane at his feet. He stopped instantly, as if his feet were glued to the ground.

"I am not the one you should fear, *mon chéri*. The one you should fear is represented by the golden crucifix hanging around your neck. Your mama hoped it would draw you away from your wicked path. But you chose the darkness and have become the child of the devil."

Mama Rue lowered her cane and let it fall to her feet, then raised her hands and started to pray.

The men with Jerome started to mumble behind his back.

"Quiet!" Jerome said. "You have more to fear from me than this old witch."

As he spoke, Mama Rue's prayers got louder and louder and turned into chants.

"Take your machetes and rip her to shreds," Jerome shouted to his men.

Mama Rue pointed a crooked finger at the men, and they froze. "If you do not leave now, you will be forever lost in the swamps. I have asked the Mighty One to send the fog to cover your path." She waved her hand toward the men to release them, and they ran from the clearing, screaming in fear.

"Your spells have frightened my men," Jerome said, "but I am stronger than them or you, old woman! Soon you will tire, and I will cut off your head, take the woman from the swamp, and do the same to her."

Mama Rue stomped her foot. "Look down at your feet and see the thin white mist is collecting. That is His work, not mine. All your life, you have mocked the One your crucifix represents. To prove His might, I asked that He give you a sampling of what will come to you if you do not change your ways and follow Him."

Suddenly, the golden crucifix around Jerome's neck turned a fiery red, and he screamed out in pain as his skin sizzled from the heat of the chain and the pendant.

"Stop, stop!" he screamed.

"Your flesh is burning, Jerome, and soon it will burn all the way to your bones. The only way to save yourself is to leave this place at once. If you do not, you will die where you stand."

"Damn you, old woman!" he cried. "Release me, release me, and I will go."

Mama Rue waved her hand and Jerome's feet were freed. He began jumping and screaming, then ran from the clearing into the dense fog.

His cries could be heard for several minutes until they stopped.

*　*　*

Rob turned to Monique. "If I hadn't seen this myself, I would never believe it. I thought you said Mama Rue was a healer?"

"She is, but her family before her were not."

"What does that mean?" Caroline asked.

"Many, many years ago," Monique explained, "Mama Rue's people were taken from Haiti as slaves. The slave traders did not know that her grandmother was a mambo queen until the captain and ship's crew became ill a few weeks into the journey. Fearing the slaves would overtake the ship, the captain ordered his crew to kill them. Mama Rue's grandmother told the captain she had cursed not only him and the crew, but also all of their families at home. She said they would die unless she and all the enslaved people aboard the ship were released from their chains and fed."

"What did the captain do?"

"He did as he was told, and she lifted the curse. When they reached New Orleans, Mama Rue's grandmother and mother were allowed to leave the ship without chains. News of what happened traveled all over New Orleans, and her grandmother and mother never spent one day as slaves. They were given a fine home, and her grandmother reigned as the voodoo queen of New Orleans until her death, and then her mother took her place."

"So why did Mama Rue give up that life?"

"When she was a child, she became friends with the son of a Baptist missionary family that arrived in New Orleans. As time passed, Mama Rue was trained in the old ways, but that didn't stop her friendship with the boy. As years passed, that friendship turned into love. She knew her mother would never allow her to marry an unbeliever because she was destined to be the next mambo."

"Did the boy know who she was?" Rob asked.

"He did, but he told Mama Rue his faith in the Mighty One was stronger than anything her mother's powers could do to them."

"What did they do?" Caroline asked.

"One night, Mama Rue used what she had learned from her mother and drew from her new faith in the Mighty One to create a potion to put her mother to sleep. Later that night, she and her beloved left New Orleans and hid in the swamp."

"How did they survive?" Rob said.

"By using Mama Rue's gifts and knowledge. For years, her mother's followers looked for her in the swamp. Each time they were close, she called upon the powers of the swamp to protect them, and they were never found," Monique explained. "Eventually, her mother died, but Mama Rue and her beloved stayed in the swamps and built the cabin she uses today. Soon the people learned of her gifts and brought their sick and injured to her for healing. Word of her healing powers traveled, and people from near and far came to her for help. She was paid with food and fur pelts. Some stayed and built cabins around her. These people taught her and her beloved the skills they needed to survive," Monique said proudly. "That is how our settlement was formed. Mama Rue gave up the old ways, and her faith grew strong in the Mighty One."

The sound of Mama Rue's pounding her foot on the porch caused Monique to look her way.

"I am being told I have said enough. Mama Rue has sent the fog back into the swamp, and it is time for us to return to the clearing."

Rob shook his head. "This is hard for me to believe."

"Maybe not in your world, but faith and nature are our way of life. The Mighty One has always provided and protected us. We are safe in His hands." Monique dropped the rope ladder and looked over the edge of the platform. "I see Daniel is ready. Mister, you go first, and we will follow."

When they reached the ground, Rob carried Caroline back to the clearing and put her down next to Mama Rue.

The old woman cupped Caroline's face with her hands and spoke to her in French.

"Mama Rue says your strength will be completely restored by morning, Miss Caroline," Monique translated. "And you will have no scars to mark your injury."

Monique paused as Mama Rue continued.

"She wants you to know the one you love is eager for your return."

Caroline glanced at Monique. "Please ask her if Jack will walk again."

Before Monique could ask, Mama Rue answered.

"*Que la foi, íamore, iespoir sont tout ce dont vous aurez besoin pour faire un miracle.*"

"Please tell me what she is saying."

"Faith, love, and hope are all you need to make miracles."

"I don't understand."

Monique shook her head. "Have faith in the Mighty One, Miss Caroline. Love your husband with all of your heart and hope will turn into miracles."

Mama Rue turned from Caroline to Rob and continued to speak in French.

"She says you were born with many gifts," Monique told Rob. "Unlike most babies, you swam before you walked. Water is your home as much as land."

"How could she know that?" Rob asked.

Mama Rue chuckled, patted his cheek, and then placed her hand against his forehead as she spoke.

"She knows of your memory," Monique translated. "In the days ahead, you must use it and all your gifts to save others, as well as yourself."

Mama Rue shook her crooked finger at him.

"She warns you of the powers of the mighty Mississippi. The river chooses who to swallow and who she will spit out."

"It sounds like she's telling us it's time to go?" Rob said.

"She is," Monique replied.

Mama Rue spoke again.

"Do not go to Golden Meadow. She says the evil one from today has sent people there, and many from across the Gulf are also there looking for you."

"Then where should we go?"

Mama Rue turned her attention to Monique and looked deeply into her eyes. The younger woman nodded and looked at Rob.

"Daniel and I will take you to my aunt, Emeline, in Napoleonville. Mama Rue insists you contact no one until she sends you a sign."

"But I need to let my people know we're alive."

Mama Rue pointed her finger at him and raised her gravelly voice as she spoke.

"She is saying if you do, it will endanger you and Emeline. She says to keep Emeline close and wait for her sign."

The scowl on Mama Rue's face softened and turned into a smile as she spoke.

"She said, 'Go, dear boy, and be the protector you were called to be. It is your greatest gift.'"

Rob looked into Mama Rue's gray, overcast eyes. "Thank you for all you've done for us. I won't speak to anyone until you send us a sign."

Mama Rue embraced him for a long moment, then took his arm and pointed to her cabin. He helped her in, and she closed the door. Rob stepped off the porch and returned to Monique.

"I gave my word to her, Monique, but I know my people are worried and searching for us."

"You must abide by your word, Mister. She would never have made that demand without reason. Nor would she allow Emeline to be put in your care if she did not trust you would honor her demand."

"How are we getting to Napoleonville?"

"We walk."

"We're going through the swamp?"

"Have no fear. Daniel knows the way. You must go to bed early. We will leave before daylight." She turned to Caroline. "Tonight, you will stay in my cabin. I have the clothing and shoes you will need for the journey. We will start at first light."

Monique took Caroline's arm and guided her across the clearing to her cabin. Rob went to his dwelling, but instead of entering, he stood in the doorway to get one last look at the settlement and saw the people returning from their hiding places and heading to their homes.

As he watched, he recalled all that had been done for them and what he had seen since they arrived. *How do I tell Tom about this place without sounding crazy?*

He had barely finished his thought when he saw the door to Mama Rue's cabin open. She stepped out and looked straight at him.

I understand, Rob thought. *I will not share the location of this place with anyone.* Mama Rue nodded, returned to her cabin, and closed the door.

How did I know what Mama Rue was thinking without either of us saying a word? It's like this place exists in a different world.

CHAPTER TWENTY-SIX

The Healer's Settlement

The settlement was dark when Daniel gave Rob and Caroline foul-smelling garlands to wear around their necks. Rob glanced back at the white cabin as they were leaving the clearing and saw Mama Rue on her porch. He paused, and they exchanged one last long look before she went in and closed her door.

"She was telling you good-bye," Monique said, coming to his side.

"I know. I heard her praying for us."

"Now you understand why we have no need for phones. Come, we have a long way to go before nightfall."

Shortly after leaving the settlement, it became apparent that this would not be an easy journey. Daniel hacked through dense vegetation as Rob removed debris and helped the women navigate ankle-deep mud.

Daniel stopped them several times during the journey to avoid snakes, the occasional alligator, and large rat-like creatures that Monique called nutrias before allowing them to continue.

They reached a small community just before dark. One of the villagers noticed them and ran up and down the row of houses, shouting in French. Before long, people came from everywhere to welcome Monique and Daniel.

Rob and Caroline stood back as Monique and Daniel spoke to the people who came to greet them. Several turned and looked at Caroline and him during their conversations, and Rob knew they were being discussed. Finally, Monique left the group and came to speak to them.

"We will be staying here tonight. You will have fresh rainwater for a warm bath, food, and a comfortable place to sleep."

"That's wonderful news," Caroline said. "I have mud up to my knees."

"I agree," Rob added. "Does anyone here have a car? I'll be happy to pay for gas."

"There is no need. We are going by boat."

"Please thank them for us," Caroline said.

"I already have. I told the people Mama Rue would hear of their generosity as soon as I returned. Now, go with these families and rest. We leave at first light."

When Rob and Caroline approached the vessel the next morning, it reminded Rob of Pauley's boat and how he had risked so much to help them. Now, another shrimper was doing the same. Rob would never forget the kindness of these people.

Rob and Daniel untied the line to the dock, and the boat puttered away in the early dawn. The wake of the shrimp boat reached the shoreline, causing a large egret to take flight and search for food elsewhere.

The vessel was bigger than Pauley's and had an enclosed wheelhouse. Rob ducked as he entered and joined Monique, who was standing beside the man at the wheel.

"Monique, please thank your friend for helping us."

"You can thank him yourself, Mister. Henri speaks English."

Rob laughed softly. "Sorry, Henri. I should have known better than to assume you didn't. Thank you for your help."

"There is no need, Mister. Mama Rue has done much for my family and others in our village. It is my honor to do this small thing for her."

"How long will it take to get to Napoleonville?"

"Four, maybe five hours. This will be a much easier trip than the one you made from the settlement."

"I'm sure it will be. Thank you again, Henri." The man nodded, and Rob left the wheelhouse to join Caroline at the stern of the boat.

They docked hours later at a cluster of buildings in a town called Cut Off. Rob jumped off and tied the back of the boat to the pier as Daniel tied the stern. He helped Monique and then Caroline onto the dock.

"Why are we stopping here?" Rob asked. "I thought we were meeting your aunt in Napoleonville?"

"We are," Monique said, "but she does not know where to meet or when we will arrive."

As she walked away, Caroline leaned over to Rob. "Did you hear that? She is using a phone. You need to go with her and tell your people to come get us. I have to get back to Jack."

"You heard Mama Rue, Caroline. She said no contact with anyone until she sends a sign."

"I know what she said, but we aren't in her village anymore. I haven't seen or heard anything about Jack in over a week. He needs me."

"I understand, but I gave her my word." Rob glanced past her and saw Monique returning. "When it's time, I'll make the call."

"Aunt Emeline is on her way," Monique said. "You will be in good hands with her the rest of the way."

"Aren't you coming?" Caroline asked.

"Daniel and I must get back to the settlement. This is the harvest season of healing plants. Mama Rue and I must gather them before it is too late. If we do not gather enough, many people in our village and others will suffer. Do not worry. My aunt will take good care of you. She will hesitate at first, but she will do as Mama Rue asks."

"If she is going to be uncertain about this, why is Mama Rue sending us to her?'

"Emeline is blood. That connection allows Mama Rue to see through her eyes, as she did with me."

Rob took a moment to take this in. "So Mama Rue can do this with other family members?"

"That is how it works, but this is not as unusual as you think. Ask any mother. They awaken in the middle of the night before their infant cries. As the child grows, the mother can sense when her child is in danger before it happens. The same holds true for siblings. Emeline has a sincere heart. She and Mama Rue are many decades apart in age, but close in spirit."

"That may be true, but I don't want to force her into doing anything against her will."

"Once I tell her the request is from Mama Rue, she will agree."

"So, you can also read her mind?"

Monique smiled. "Not always, but I am still learning."

Almost an hour passed before a car pulled up near the docks and a woman in her early sixties got out. Monique rushed to greet her.

"*Ma chérie*," Emeline said, taking her into her arms. "It's been far too long since I've seen you, child."

"*Comment ca va, Tante Emeline?*"

"*Tre bien, ma chérie.* I am blessed." Emeline leaned back and looked into the younger woman's eyes. "*Comment va Mama Rue?*"

"She's well and sends her love."

Emeline looked past her niece to the others in her group. "And who do we have here?"

Monique reached out for her fiancé's hand. "This is my Daniel. We are to marry soon."

The aunt grabbed the young man and wrapped her arms around him. "I'm so happy to meet you, dear boy."

Monique giggled. "He only speaks French, *Tante* Emeline."

Emeline repeated her greeting in French, and the three contin-ued their conversation for several minutes. Afterwards, Emeline and Monique approached Caroline and Rob.

"It seems I've been asked to help you."

"Yes, ma'am," Rob said. "That is what I understand."

"You should know I've never done anything like this before."

"*Tante* Emeline," Monique said, joining them, "Mama Rue asked that you keep Mister and Miss Caroline hidden until she sends you a sign. When it happens, Mister will know what he is to do." Monique laid her hand on Rob's arm. "Remember, contact no one until you see the sign. It is the only way to keep you and my aunt safe."

"I assure you I won't."

Emeline turned to Monique. "And you're sure Mama Rue put them in *my* care?"

Monique took her aunt by the shoulders. "There is nothing to fear, *Tante*. Mama Rue will be watching."

Emeline blew out a gust of air. "That is good. Did she tell you where I should hide them?"

"Do not take them to your home. That is all I know." Monique kissed her aunt on each cheek. "*Au revoir, Tante.*"

Monique hugged Caroline and Rob, then she and Daniel got on the boat. They waved one last time as the shrimp boat puttered away.

When they were out of sight, Rob turned to the nervous aunt.

"I'm sorry you were put in this position, Emeline. I would say we would go on our own, but Mama Rue insisted we stay with you."

"So I've heard." She started to wring her hands. "Now, all I have to do is figure out where we should go."

"I have a suggestion," Rob said. "Why don't we get in your car and start driving? Maybe something will come to you then."

"That's as good an idea as any. Let's go."

Rob got in the back seat, and Caroline sat next to Emeline.

"If I had known this would happen yesterday, I would have stayed in church all day and prayed," Emeline said. "Wait a minute. . . Thank you, Lord!" She raised her hands.

Rob leaned forward in his seat. "What happened?"

Emeline turned and looked over her shoulder. "It's Monday. I know the perfect place for us to hide." She started the car and pulled onto the road.

"Where?" Rob asked.

"Donaldsonville. It's a good hour's drive from here."

"Are you sure it's safe?" Caroline asked.

"It's the safest place you can be. You'll understand when we get there."

"Aren't you the least bit curious as to why you were asked to hide us?" Caroline asked.

"If Mama Rue wanted me to know, she would have had Monique tell me. Maybe it's safer this way for all of us."

*   *   *

Ochsner Hospital

As Steve and Wiley entered Tom's room, he raised up on one elbow as far as his IV line would allow. "Did you find them?" Tom asked.

"We didn't," Steve answered, "but neither did anyone else."

"Who was hunting them?"

"Apparently, some of the drug organization group *and* Pascal's men," Steve answered.

Wiley went closer to the bed. "We heard groups swarmed the town one after the other."

Tom glanced from man to man. "If they aren't in Dulac, where are they?"

Steve shrugged. "We don't know."

Tom grimaced before easing back on his bed. "We have to find them," he said, trying to conceal his pain. "It's been over a week since we've had contact. Something happened to them."

"Easy, Tom," Wiley said. "We've done all we can do."

"You have, but I haven't. I put The Kid in this mess. I have to get him out of it." Tom threw off his bed sheet and ripped the heart rate monitor from his chest.

Steve grabbed his hands. "What the heck are you doing?"

"I'm getting out of this bed."

Nurse Bennett came rushing into the room. "What do you think you're doing?" she said, prying Tom's fingers from his IV tube.

"I'm getting out of here."

"No, you're not! You need to calm down before you have a stroke."

Tom looked up at her. "Stroke? How old do you think I am?"

Nurse Bennett took his shoulders and pressed him down on the bed. "Keep behaving senile, and I'll sedate you and have you transferred to the nearest old folks' home." She turned her attention to the other men in the room. "What are all of you doing here? I told you one person at a time. I want all of you out right now!"

"They aren't going anywhere," Tom protested. "I need them."

"Agent Neal, you may be the boss in your world, but I give the orders on this floor. If you don't calm down, I have the authority to keep them off this floor for good."

"You can't do that. You have no idea what's at stake."

"All I care about is you," Nurse Bennett said. "If you rip everything apart, I'm not sure the doctors will be able to piece you back together."

"You don't understand. I have to get out of here."

"Not on my watch. Try this again, and I'll have you strapped to this bed."

Steve, Phillip, and Wiley remained silent as they watched the two argue. This was the first time any of them had seen someone challenge Tom.

Finally, Tom exhaled. "All right. You win. I'll stay in this bed, but only if you allow them to stay."

She crossed her arms and glanced at the men before looking at Tom. "They can stay, but if you try this again, I'll make sure you see none of them until you're released. Understand?"

The corners of Tom's lips turned up for a split second. "You're tough."

Nurse Bennett's smile lasted longer. "You have no idea."

*   *   *

Rob and Caroline had been riding with Emeline for an hour when Emeline pointed to her left and said, "We're here."

"Where?" Rob asked. "All I see are trees."

Emeline turned left onto a shell road. "You'll see in a moment." She continued on the road for several minutes and stopped in front of a small building with a tall steeple.

"This is a church," Rob said.

"Sure is. No one will be here until later this week."

"You should park on the far side of the building so your car won't be seen from the road."

Emeline nodded and parked the car behind two large trees.

"You two stay here while I look around," Rob said. He circled the building, checked the back door and windows, but found they were locked. When he got back to the car, the women were gone.

"Damn it," he muttered under his breath and went to the front of the church, where he found Caroline standing on the steps.

"Dang it, Caroline, I told you to stay in the car. Where's Emeline?"

"Inside. She needed a restroom."

"But everything is locked. How did Emeline get in?"

"She opened the door and walked in," Caroline said.

His eyes grew wide. "It was open?"

"Sure was."

"We need to get inside before someone sees you."

Rob followed Caroline inside and looked around. The humble structure had four rows of pews separated by a middle aisle. The benches faced a platform with a meager podium. A piano stood at the side of the stage, flanked by eight chairs. None of the windows had curtains, and the walls were painted white. What looked to be a handmade wooden cross hung on the wall behind the podium with a crown of thorns draped over the top. Unmarked doors were on each end of the platform.

"Sorry, I was about to burst," Emeline said as she exited one of the doors.

Rob pointed to the other door.

"Oh, that's the pastor's office."

"Sounds like you've been here before."

"Many times," Emeline said.

Rob entered the cramped office and found a desk, a chair, and a bookcase constructed of cinder blocks and two-by-fours. A phone sat atop a stack of books and papers on the desk. He desperately wanted to dial Steve's pager but instead picked up the phone, put it on the seat of the chair, and pushed it under the desk to keep Caroline from finding it. Then he closed the door and returned to the ladies.

*   *   *

Mexico City

"Damn you, Salvador!" Diego Martínez shouted. "You told me you knew where she was."

"I thought we did. We searched every inch of that town, but they weren't there. Did Pascal's people find her?"

"If he had, he would not wait to tell me he won our bet." There was a long pause. "I think it's time I come and handle this myself," Martínez said.

"What do you want me to do?"

"Hide our men someplace away from Pascal's city, then get back here as fast as possible. I'll gather every man I can spare and have them waiting for you when you arrive. I will take them to Texas and hide some of them with the rest of our men."

"Boss, why do we need so many men to find this woman?"

"Forget the woman," Martínez said. "Pascal would not honor our agreement even if I killed her in front of him. I need these men to take back my shipment. Now, do as I say and get back here as soon as possible. It's time I take back what is mine."

*   *   *

Garden District

Jean-Claude waited patiently for Pascal to sign several documents. He was almost done when the phone on Jean-Claude's desk rang.

"Take it here," Pascal said. "That could be Jerome."

Jean-Claude answered. "Yes. Who may I say is calling?"

Pascal looked up to see Jean-Claude roll his eyes and press the hold button.

"It's him, and he's in quite a mood."

"I don't give a damn what kind of mood he's in. Give me that!" Pascal jerked the phone from his assistant's hand and pushed the button. "Did you take care of her?" he said into the receiver.

"Not exactly."

"Damn it, Jerome! I told you the Broussard woman was with the shrimper and I even told you where he lived. What happened?"

"They were gone by the time we arrived. I tracked them to a settlement in the middle of the swamp but couldn't find them."

"Did you burn the place down?"

"I tried, but a witch was protecting the settlement."

"Are you telling me you cowered to a woman?"

"Not any woman, Pascal. This witch was powerful!"

"Why didn't you kill her?"

"I couldn't. The old hag cursed us. I had to lead my men back to safety before we were lost to the swamp."

The phone shook in Pascal's hand as he cursed the man on the other end of the line.

"I don't care how many witches curse you. Get it done, Jerome."

"I will find her, but you should know if I kill the man with her, the FBI will be hunting us."

"Not if his body is never found. Do you think you can handle that?"

"I will if that's what you want."

"Don't make me repeat myself, Jerome. I'm not happy with you as it is."

"I have never failed you, Pascal."

"The woman's still alive, isn't she? Find her, or you will never work for me or anyone else again," Pascal said, then ended the call.

*   *   *

Emmanuel Gospel Church

Rob came out of the pastor's office and found Caroline waiting for him.

"Is there a phone in there?" she asked.

"Look for yourself," Rob said, opening the door and standing at the edge of the desk to block her from going around and finding the phone.

"This is crazy. There should be a phone in here."

"We aren't calling anyone even if there were."

Caroline walked out and slumped down on the front pew. "I am so tired of this madness. We can't keep running like this, Kid."

"Once we know it's safe to return to New Orleans, I'm sure we'll go." Rob looked up and saw Emeline approaching.

"Was this a good hiding place?"

"A great choice, Emeline." Rob glanced at the two women. "Both of you look exhausted. Why don't you take a pew and get some rest?"

"What about you?" Emeline asked.

"I need to keep watch."

"That's ridiculous. You are as exhausted as we are."

"I agree with Caroline," Emeline added, settling herself in a pew.

"I'll be fine." Rob went to the last pew and took a seat. After a while, he got up, went as softly as he could to keep the plank floors from creaking, and looked out the windows to check the area.

He found a pipe less than two feet long on one of the windowsills and guessed it was used to support the window when it was open. He was about to return the pipe but thought it could come in handy if a weapon was needed, so he held onto it instead.

He carried it to the pews where the women were sleeping and sat on the floor at the end of Caroline's bench. He held the pipe in his lap and watched for several hours until silence and fatigue overcame his resolve, and he drifted off.

CHAPTER TWENTY-SEVEN

Emmanuel Gospel Church

The sound of the floor creaking woke Rob, and he sprang to his feet with the pipe raised, ready to strike.

"Hold on, hold on," said a large, dark-skinned man with hands raised in surrender. "I mean you no harm." The man's eyes shifted to the women. "Miss Emeline? Is that you?"

"Hello, Ezra."

"My Lord, Miss Emeline. What are you doing here this time of night?"

"My friends are in trouble, Ezra, and this was the safest place I could think of."

"Safe from what?"

"Who are you?" Rob asked with the pipe still raised.

"I'm Reverend Ezra Johnson, pastor of this church."

Rob lowered his hand. "Sorry, Reverend. I didn't know who you were. Did you know your door was unlocked?"

"This is the Lord's church. Our door is always open. If it's okay with you, I'd like to put my hands down."

Rob laid the pipe on a pew. "If you don't mind, could we stay here awhile?"

"Visitors are always welcome."

Emeline went to the end of the bench. "What are you doing out so late, Ezra?"

"I was on my way home after my shift at the plant. I saw a car behind the trees and came in to check."

Emeline pressed her hand to her stomach when it started to growl.

"When was the last time you had something to eat?" Ezra asked.

"None of us have eaten since breakfast."

"Then you all should come home with me. My Martha will fix you some supper and give you a proper place to sleep."

"Thank you," Rob said. "But we can't be seen together."

"Why not? Because I'm Negro?"

Emeline placed a hand on his shoulder. "He didn't mean it like that, Ezra. He's only trying to protect you and Martha."

"Protect us from what?"

Emeline glanced at Rob, and he shook his head.

"Sorry, Reverend, it's safer for you if you don't know."

Caroline spoke up. "Let's just say we're running from the evil one and his legion of demons."

Ezra's eyes went from person to person before responding. "So, those demons are the reason you're here?"

"They are," Caroline said. "And they will stop at nothing to get to us." She dropped her eyes. "I mean me."

"Are you familiar with Matthew 10:28?" the pastor asked. "It tells us not to fear those that can kill the body but can't kill the soul."

"Maybe not," Rob said, "but I'm fearful of what these people will do to Caroline, Emeline, and you if they find us."

"Sir, the Good Lord appointed me a shepherd of this church twenty-one years ago. A day will come when I will be asked if I gave shelter to the homeless, fed the hungry, or comforted the weary. So, you see, helping you will go well with my soul."

Rob smiled. "You could have been a great lawyer. That was a great closing argument."

Ezra laughed. "No, thanks. I chose the higher road."

"Having been one, I agree."

"Well, if you won't come home with me, the least I can do is get you some food. These ladies need to eat."

Before Rob could respond, Emeline stepped forward. "Thanks, Ezra. I'm starving."

"All right," Rob said, "but please tell no one we're here."

"I won't. I promise."

"Here," Rob said, reaching into his pocket. "Let me pay for it."

Ezra shook his head. "No, sir. I just got paid," he said, and walked out the door.

Rob turned to Emeline. "Are you sure we can trust him?"

"I've known Ezra since he was fourteen years old. He's as honest a man as you will ever know."

Almost an hour passed after the pastor left. Rob went back and forth to the window at the front of the church checking, but there was no sign of him. When Rob returned the last time, only Emeline was sitting on the pew.

"Where's Caroline?"

"She's in Ezra's office."

Rob rushed in and found Caroline holding the telephone. He took it from her hand and hung it up. "I told you, no calls."

"You lied to me. There *is* a phone."

"No, I didn't lie. I just didn't tell you there was one."

"I know Mama Rue told *you* not to call, but she said nothing about it to me."

"Damn it, Caroline! Have you forgotten what happened to you in Houma? Those people are out there hunting you."

"I was only going to call the hospital."

"That's exactly what Pascal wants. I'm sure he has people at that hospital just waiting for you to call."

"I didn't think of that."

Emeline appeared at the door to the pastor's office. "I heard something at the front door."

"Get in here, lock the door, and don't come out until I tell you."

Rob retrieved the pipe on his way to the front of the church. He looked out the window and saw a blur of white flying against the door.

"Emeline," Rob called. "Come here."

He heard the floor creaking as the ladies approached.

Rob pointed to the window. "Is that what I think it is?"

Emeline went to the window and looked out.

"That's Chouette Blanche, Mama Rue's owl."

Rob opened the door, and the feathered creature flew into the church and went to rest on the podium.

"How did that owl know we were here?" Caroline asked.

"Mama Rue must have sent her," Emeline replied.

The bird stretched its wings and flew to the first pew, then hopped from pew to pew, until it flew to the door. It flapped its wings and started striking the door with its claws.

"Looks like she wants out," Caroline said.

"She does," Emeline added.

Rob eased the door open, and the bird hopped out. But instead of flying away, it turned and looked at him for a moment before spreading its wings and disappearing into the night.

Emeline stepped next to Rob. "I think you just got your sign."

"I think I did. I could swear I heard Mama Rue speaking to me when that bird locked eyes with me."

"What did she say?" Emeline asked.

"She said it was time."

Caroline rushed to his side. "That means we can tell your people to come get us."

Rob went to the office, dialed Steve's pager number, entered the church phone number, and hung up.

It felt like an eternity before it rang.

"Hello?" Rob said.

"Dang it, man," Steve answered. "We thought something happened to you. Where have you been?"

"You wouldn't believe me if I told you."

"Where's the package?"

"It's safe and ready to be delivered."

"Good, because it's time to get it and you back. Where are you?"

"North of Donaldsonville on Smoke Bend Road. It's a small white church. You'll need to look closely because there's a row of trees between the road and the church."

"Who else knows the package is there?"

"Two people, but they can be trusted." Rob felt someone tap him on the arm. He glanced at his side and saw Caroline pointing to the phone. "How are the others there?"

"Alert and asking questions about your package, but nothing new to report."

"Let me pass that on," Rob said, then repeated the information to Caroline before returning to his call.

"And the other one?"

"Making life miserable until he gets you and the package back. Stay where you are. I'll page you when I'm heading your way."

"Sounds great. How safe is it for us to return?"

"Not sure. Keep your heads down until we get there."

"Are they coming for us?" Caroline asked as soon as he hung up the phone.

"Yes, but it may take a while."

"I don't care as long as we're going back."

"Hey, where are you?" Ezra shouted from the front of the church. "I could use some help."

Emeline stepped out of the office. "We're here," she said rushing out of the office to lend a hand. "Let me help you with those bags."

"White Castle Hamburger House was the only thing opened this late," Ezra said. "They smelled so good I had to get a couple for myself."

"Thank you," Caroline said when he handed her a drink and one of the sandwiches. "I'm starving."

Rob's pager buzzed. He took the small device from his pocket to read the numbers.

Ezra stepped closer to get a look. "What is that thing?"

"It's our lifeline." He held up the device. "Those numbers are a message."

"Mercy, what will they think of next?"

"Does it say where they are taking us?" Caroline asked.

Rob looked at Ezra.

"I think we need to let them talk, Miss Emeline," Ezra said, picking up his sandwiches and drink. "Why don't you and I take our supper to the piano?"

Caroline stepped closer to Rob and whispered, "Please tell me we're going to New Orleans. I have to get back to Jack."

"I'm not the one making that decision, Caroline."

"You don't understand. I have to get back. Jack needs me, and so does my company. I'm done with running. It's time to end this mess."

"The only way that may happen is to let Pascal have the contract," Rob said. "Maybe that's enough to get him to leave you alone."

"I can't do that. If I give in to Pascal, he'll take over every building project in Louisiana."

"One thing at a time, Caroline. Let's focus on keeping you alive, then we'll work on the rest. Let's get back to the others." He motioned for Ezra and Emeline to rejoin them. "Finish your food and take a seat. I'm going to turn off the lights until my friend arrives. There's a good chance he may be followed."

"I can stand on the porch and wait for him," Ezra offered.

"That's too dangerous."

"Then I'll sit in my truck and see who turns off the main road. When I do, I'll let you know."

Rob gave that some thought. "All right, but make sure you're not seen."

Ezra chuckled. "My skin is almost as dark as my work shirt. Nobody is going to see me. What kind of car am I looking for?"

"I don't know."

"I'll let you know when I see anyone turn off the main road."

"Do you really think Pascal's men will follow them?" Caroline whispered.

"We have to assume they will."

CHAPTER TWENTY-EIGHT

New Orleans

Pascal's phone rang next to his bed.

His wife rolled over and shook him awake. "Marcel. Wake up and answer that thing."

"Damn it," he mumbled after answering. "This better be important, or I'll have your head."

"Sorry, sir," Jean-Claude said. "I would never disturb you this time of night unless it was important."

"Then get on with it so I can get back to sleep."

"I just received word that twenty or more Hispanic men arrived in Cameron, Texas an hour ago."

"What makes you think it's Martínez's men?"

"One of our people with Wildlife and Fisheries was in the area and saw them. He said they were armed and were using vans to transport them."

Pascal chuckled. "This sounds like something that little weasel would do. You said they were spotted about an hour ago?" he asked, looking at his alarm clock.

"Yes, sir."

"That doesn't give us much time. Get Jerome on the line. If these are Martínez's men, they will be coming here. I think it's time I end this once and for all."

"But what about the favors?"

"As far as I'm concerned, it's over. Keep track of those vans, Jean-Claude. I want them stopped before they get to my city."

"It's being done as we speak."

"Contact Jerome and tell him to gather his men and wait for my call." Pascal tossed back his sheets. "Meet me at the office within the hour."

"Yes, sir."

*   *   *

Emmanuel Gospel Church

Rob gripped the pipe as he scanned the area outside the window. All had been still for over an hour when suddenly Ezra jumped out of his truck and ran through the door of the church.

"I just saw a car turn off the main road."

"Take the women to your office and lock the door," Rob said.

"Let's go, ladies. We're about to have company." Ezra ushered the women to his office and shut the door.

Rob raised the pipe and listened by the door. He heard shells crunching under the vehicle's tires, then the car stopped, and moments later Rob heard someone coming up the steps. The door opened slowly, and he was about to strike when Steve stepped inside.

"Man, you have no idea how glad I am to see you," Rob said.

"Me too. Can you put that pipe down? You're making me nervous." Steve looked around. "Where's the woman?"

"You can come out," Rob called.

Ezra came out alone. "Is it safe?"

"It is."

"Praise the Lord." The pastor hurried down the aisle with an outstretched hand as the women followed. "It is good to meet you, friend," he said to Steve.

"Steve, this is Reverend Ezra Johnson. The lady next to him is Miss Emeline. They have taken great care of us."

"Good to meet both of you. Sorry to cut this short, but I have to get these two out of here."

"No, no, we understand," Ezra said.

Emeline wrapped her arms around Caroline. "Take care, *ma chérie*." She glanced up at Rob. "And the same goes for you, young man."

"We'll do our best," Rob said. "You shouldn't go home for a few days, Emeline."

"Don't worry about Miss Emeline," Ezra said. "She can stay with Martha and me for as long as she likes."

"Thank you, Reverend," Rob said, shaking his hand.

"You have been quite the guardian angel," Caroline added as she hugged him.

"I'm no angel, Miss Caroline. I just offered shelter in a storm. I'm going to keep praying for you both."

"Say a word or two for the rest of us?" Steve added. "We could use all the help we can get."

"Consider it done."

Rob went to the door and scanned the area. "It's clear."

Steve darted out to start the engine of the Ford Cortina. Rob took Caroline's hand, dashed out, and put her in the back seat before getting in the front with Steve.

"Get down on the floor, Caroline," Rob said, turning back just in time to see Ezra close the church door.

*   *   *

Garden District

Pascal hurried into the office and found Jean-Claude already at his desk. "Have they crossed the state line?"

"Yes, sir. I just got word they are on Highway 14 east of New Iberia."

"Did you reach Jerome?"

"He's waiting for your call."

"Get him on the line."

Jean-Claude dialed the number as Pascal waited. He snatched the phone from his assistant's hand as soon as the call was answered.

"How soon can you get your men to New Iberia?" Pascal demanded.

He listened a moment, then frowned. "Forget about the woman, Jerome. There's a caravan of vans heading to New Orleans. It appears our friend from Mexico is trying to sneak into town with reinforcements," Pascal said. "Before you eliminate them, make sure Martínez is one of them, then dispose of the bodies where they will never be found. Call me as soon as it's done." Pascal handed the phone to Jean-Claude. "I need coffee. Lots of coffee. This is going to be a long day."

"Sir, it's already made."

*　　*　　*

Rob watched every vehicle coming and going as night turned into day.

"Can I get up now? My legs are going to sleep," Caroline pleaded.

Rob glanced over his shoulder. "All right, but stay in the middle, away from the windows."

"Where are we going?" she asked.

Steve glanced at Rob, then turned back to the road. "I left before that was decided."

Caroline scooted forward. "Maybe it's time we find out?"

Steve glanced at Rob and saw him smile. "You're right. Keep an eye out for a pay phone."

They drove several miles before stopping at a gas station.

"Stay with her while I make the call," Steve said as he got out of the car. He went to the pay phone on the side of the building.

Caroline scooted forward in the seat. "We need to talk. Hear me out before you answer."

Rob turned and looked over his shoulder. "What's this about?"

"I'm going to New Orleans no matter what your friend is told." Rob opened his mouth to protest, but Caroline held up her hand. "I'm not done," she continued. "I have to get back to New Orleans to submit my bid before the deadline for the levee maintenance contract runs out."

"That isn't going to happen, Caroline."

"Kid, you don't understand. I have to win this contract. If I don't, hundreds of my hardworking people will lose their jobs. I could lose my plant, and Pascal wins. Then every new build in the city and the levee repairs will be forced to use his inferior concrete. That will be disastrous for everyone."

"What's wrong with his product?"

"He uses more sand in his mix because it's cheaper than cement and gravel. Over time, the finished product cracks and breaks apart under pressure."

"How do you know that will happen?"

"When the soil under New Orleans is damp, it's stable, but when it dries out, it shrinks and cracks apart, and so do foundations."

"That doesn't sound good."

"It's not. At least a third of my business is repairing homes and buildings built with Pascal's concrete, and that's just *my* company. To make matters worse, an enormous sports arena called the Superdome is scheduled to be constructed in New Orleans. It's supposed to hold over seventy-thousand people. Add that to a compromised levee system, and you can see why I must do all I can to keep Pascal from getting those contracts."

"I understand why the bid is so important to you, but even if you don't get the contract, can't you trim down and survive until another opportunity comes?"

She dropped her head. "A year ago, that would have been possible, but I used most of our reserve capital to build a remote location to cut the travel time from our main plant. The saving of fuel and man hours will allow us to be the more competitive bid."

"Now I understand why Pascal is after you."

"Jack opposed the decision, but I kept pushing and pushing until he gave in." She paused and glanced out the window. "Then this happened, and now everything is falling apart. If I lose the company, I'm afraid I won't be able to afford the care Jack will need to recover."

Rob turned back around in the seat. "I can see how that would add another layer to your problem. I can't make any promises, but I will talk to the man in charge. Maybe there's something we can do to help."

*　*　*

Ochsner Hospital

Tom woke up and realized he was alone. A short time later, Phillip came in with two large cups of coffee.

"How did you get those?" Tom asked.

"Your Nurse Bennett was at the desk."

"I'll have to thank her. It's going to take one this size to shake off my sleeping pills." He took a sip. "Have you heard from Wiley?"

"I did last night. He told me the containers had been moved from the dock into a warehouse."

"That sounds like Pascal is planning on keeping them," Tom said. "If he does, we'll have a war on our hands."

"I'm afraid you're right."

"Any news from Steve?" Tom asked.

"Not yet, but there's a problem," Phillip said. "Ashcroft called a meeting of all the agents this morning, and I have to go."

"You're right. The last thing we want is Ashcroft asking more questions."

"I'll be back as soon as I can."

After Philip left, the silence was deafening. This was the first time Tom had been alone since he was shot. An orderly brought him a breakfast tray and helped him sit up so he could eat. Tom took a couple bites of toast and pushed it away. He checked the time and saw it was just a little after 8:00 a.m.

"To hell with this," he muttered. "I'm getting out of here."

Tom threw off the sheets, pushed the tray stand aside, and cautiously eased himself off the bed. It felt like his insides were ripping apart the moment his feet hit the floor. He became light-headed and had to grip the side of the bed to keep from passing out.

After several minutes, the shock of being vertical eased, and Tom took his car keys, wallet, badge, and revolver from the drawer of his bedside table. He was grateful the hospital staff hadn't found his belongings after Steve returned them to him a few days earlier.

Phillip walked in just as Tom was removing the monitors taped to his chest. "What the hell? Get back in that bed!"

"I thought you were at your meeting?"

"I was almost there when Steve paged me. He wants to know where to take them."

"Have you heard back from my contacts?"

"Not yet. Tom, you're as pale as a ghost. Get back in bed."

"I can't I need to call them myself. I've been in that bed long enough as it is. I have to get out of here. Hand me my clothes and shoes, Phillip. After I'm dressed, I need you to drive me to a pay phone."

"Tom, you're going to burst your stitches open."

"I don't care. I'm leaving here even if I have to do it with my butt hanging out."

*   *   *

"What took so long?" Rob asked when Steve finally returned.

"I was waiting for Phillip to call me back. But to my surprise, it wasn't Phillip, it was Tom."

"What? He knows better than to call from his hospital room."

"He didn't. He left the hospital."

"Why would the hospital release him so soon?" Rob asked.

"They didn't. Tom just walked out."

Caroline leaned forward. "Did he tell you where we're going?"

"To a house on Neely Street in Jefferson Parish, wherever that is."

"Get me a map," Caroline said. "I can get you there."

Steve went back to the gas station and brought her a city map. A few minutes later, she leaned over the seat and held it up for Rob to see.

"That's Neely Street," she said, tapping the spot with her finger, "and we will enter the city here. You can figure it out from there."

"How well do you know that side of town?" Steve asked as he pulled back onto the road.

"As I recall, it's a little run-down, but it's near Jack's hospital."

Rob and Steve exchanged glances.

"Did Tom give you the house number?" Rob asked.

"It's 817 Neeley. I'll do a drive-by to check it out before we go in."

Steve glanced at Caroline in the rearview mirror and saw her smiling. "You've got to get back on the floorboard when we get near the city," he told her.

"I'll ride in the trunk if it gets me closer to Jack."

Rob gave Steve directions as they drove. 817 Neeley was a little brick house with a single-car garage and bars on its windows and door.

"What are these people afraid of?" Steve asked as he drove past. "I've never seen so many homes with bars."

"You will see a lot of that in older neighborhoods," Caroline said from the floorboard.

"Go to the end of the block and let me out," Rob said. "I'll double back and check it out."

"Good idea."

Steve went down the street, and Rob jumped out. He returned to the house on foot and circled the property before returning to the car.

"How does it look?" Steve asked as he got in.

"The backyard is fenced, with tall shrubs blocking the view from all directions. All the windows have bars, and the back door is locked. How are we supposed to get in?"

"My fault. I forgot to tell you about the ceramic frog. Tom said it was near the door?"

"I saw it."

"There's a combination lock built into the bottom of the frog. Open it, and the key is inside. Once you're in, open the garage door and let us in."

"No problem. What's the combination?"

Steve gave him the numbers, and Rob went back. He retrieved the keys, opened the back door, and stepped into the kitchen. The walls were covered with wallpaper featuring lemons and limes, and the appliances were avocado green.

Rob went past the kitchen table to a small living room with paneled walls and a rug covering the scuffed linoleum floor. A well-used sofa was against one wall, and an oversized, padded rocker sat in the middle of the room facing a small television resting atop a coffee table against the opposite wall.

He went to the hallway and found several doors leading off it. The first was a closet. The second led to a bedroom with a double bed. Across the hall was the bathroom. Everything in it was pink except the faded shower curtain, which had large pink flowers. The next door opened into a room with twin beds pushed against the walls. Every room was impeccably clean.

Rob opened the last door at the end of the hallway and entered the small garage. He pushed the door up and pressed himself against the wall as Steve pulled the car inside. There was barely enough room to pull the garage door down once the car was in.

"Hope we don't have to make a fast exit," Steve said, sliding past the car door. "It will take time just to get behind the wheel."

"At least we have a place to sleep," Caroline said, getting out of the car.

"Hope you like pink, yellow, and green," Rob said, following her into the hallway. Rob showed Caroline the first bedroom. "This one is yours. We'll take the one across the hall. The bathroom is across from your room."

"What are we supposed to do now?" she asked.

"Nothing until Tom arrives," Steve replied on his way to the kitchen.

"Why don't you get some rest?" Rob said. "You've barely slept."

Caroline shook her head. "Not until I take a bath." She paused a moment. "It's good to be close to Jack."

Rob sighed. "Caroline, I hope you realize seeing him is out of the question?"

"He's right," Steve shouted from the kitchen.

"At least I'm here," she said. She went to the bathroom and looked in. "Whoever built this house really loved pink."

Rob laughed. "You haven't seen the kitchen." He entered the kitchen and found Steve looking in the refrigerator.

"Dang, there's enough food to feed an army," Steve said.

"Where are Wiley and Phillip?"

"Not sure where Phillip is, but Wiley was at the docks when I left. Tom said the containers were moved from the dock into a warehouse."

Rob saw a phone on the kitchen wall behind the counter and went around to pick it up. "It works."

"I know," Steve said, biting into an apple. "I've already paged Tom and sent the *all clear* code. Nothing left to do now but wait."

"I'll take the first watch," Rob said. "You were up all night."

"Yep, same as you. Wake me if you hear anything." Steve took another bite of the apple and disappeared down the hallway.

Rob went from the kitchen to the living room and closed the window curtain. He returned to the kitchen, went around the counter towards the window, and stared at the phone on the wall for a long time before picking it up. He heard the tone, then dialed two digits before hanging up.

What am I doing? he thought. *I can't risk the Bureau discovering I'm not there. I just hope Sarah doesn't forget me before I get home. God, I miss them.*

CHAPTER TWENTY-NINE

The Van Caravan

"You're getting too close," Martínez shouted to his driver.

"I have to, or I'll lose them."

"No, you won't," Martínez said, looking down at his map. "I know where they're going. You'll come to a crossroads soon, but stay on Highway 14."

Martínez's driver stopped when he saw a man standing in the middle of the road waving his arms.

"Looks like that driver lost his load of cinderblocks," Martínez said.

"Boss, the road is blocked to Highway 14, and that man is telling us to take a different road."

Martínez looked at his map. "Go the way he's pointing. I am sure he told the vans to do the same. It will take us longer, but we will still reach the city before dark."

They drove for several minutes, then Martínez's driver saw something in the road ahead. "Boss, looks like the vans have stopped?"

"Stop," Martínez said. "Back up, back up." The car sped in reverse. "Okay, this is far enough. Pull into those weeds as far as you can to keep anyone from seeing our car."

"What's happening?" his driver asked.

"That's what you're going to find out. Stay in the tall grass and get as close as you can without anyone seeing you."

"Not even our people?"

"Not anyone. Go!"

"But who will guard you?"

Martínez snarled as he removed his pistol from its holster. "Do as I say, or I will shoot you where you sit."

The driver jumped out of the car and struggled through the tall grass near the swamp's edge until he was close enough to see two pick-ups parked nose to nose, blocking the road ahead of the vans.

Four men stood in the beds of the trucks with rifles pointed at Martínez's men, who were exiting the vans and taking cover around them.

The driver watched as a man dressed in black stood in the middle of the road between the trucks and the vans. He motioned for the men in the trucks to lower their weapons. "Which one of you is Diego Martínez?" he called.

"Who is asking?" shouted someone from the vans.

"I am Jerome. Are you Martínez?"

"Why do you ask?"

"My employer has a message for him."

"What is the message?"

Jerome shook his head. "I can only tell Martínez."

"Look around," said the man from behind the first van. "I have over twenty armed men with guns pointed at you. Now, give me the message, or I'll tell my men to fire."

Jerome glanced back at the people behind him, then turned to the one speaking from the van. "You must be Martínez. Only a stupid man would expose his hand before playing his cards."

"What are you talking about? We have you outnumbered."

"Not exactly."

Jerome raised his hand, and suddenly the roar of engines came from both sides of the road. Eight large jeep-like vehicles with oversized aircraft tires emerged from the densely wooded swamp on both sides of the road, carrying men with automatic rifles.

Martínez's driver had to scramble into the water and hide behind a cypress tree to shield himself from the volley of bullets. When they stopped, he peered out and saw the road was covered with the bodies of Martínez's men.

"Make sure all of them are dead," Jerome shouted to the men on the jeeps as they climbed down from the vehicles. "And check the vans to see if they will run."

Men climbed into the vans and reported three of the four vans were still operational.

"Load the bodies in the vans and take them to the swamp drop," Jerome ordered. "Make sure you prop the doors open before you push the vans into the bayou. Tow the disabled van and dump it with the others."

The driver crawled out of the water and slithered back through the grass to reach his boss.

"I heard gunfire," Martínez said. "What happened?"

"They're dead! Boss, all of our people are dead."

"That's not possible. All twenty of them?"

"Yes. They are all dead. Strange machines came out of nowhere loaded with men and automatic rifles. They killed them all."

Martínez started to chuckle. "That means my plan worked. I knew Pascal would find out we were here. Now he thinks he killed all of us."

"Boss, you knew our men would die?"

"This is war," Martínez said. "Sometimes, you must sacrifice a few to get back what is yours. I wanted Pascal to think he won. Now I can slip in and take back my shipment before he realizes he was the one who was tricked. Get in the car. We must meet Salvador and his crew before Pascal realizes I have outsmarted him."

*   *   *

The Safehouse

The following day, Tom opened the screen door at the back of the house on Neely Street and tapped on the door. He heard movement inside and tried the doorknob. It was locked. "It's Tom. Let me in."

Steve opened the door, and Tom stepped in slowly, gripping his side. "Where are they?"

Rob entered from the hallway, and Caroline followed. Rob quickly placed a chair in front of Tom. "You look terrible. You should sit before you pass out."

Tom smiled for a split second, then grimaced as he lowered himself into the chair. "It's great to see you, Kid. For a while there, I thought I had lost you."

"We came close a time or two but glad to be back."

"I should never have pushed you to come."

"Had I known this would happen, I still would have come." Rob dropped to one knee. "You need to go back to the hospital."

Tom shook his head. "We've got work to do. I'm not wasting any more time in that place." Tom slowly removed his hat and looked around before handing it to Rob. "Not a bad setup. The ironwork over the windows and doors gives us more security."

"And it's close to the hospital," Caroline said, coming to his side.

"I'm glad to see you're all right."

"I would have died in the swamps if it hadn't been for him," Caroline said, nodding towards Rob.

Rob placed Tom's hat on the table. "It was Mama Rue and Monique who saved you, Caroline. Not me."

"True, but you were the one who rescued me in Houma."

Tom glanced from her to Rob. "Who are Mama Rue and Monique?"

Rob glanced at Caroline and grinned before turning back to Tom. "I'm not sure you would believe me if I told you."

"How is my husband?" Caroline asked.

"I heard he's awake and asking questions, but other than that, nothing has changed."

"I know it's not safe for me to see him, but could I talk to him?"

Rob shook his head. "Caroline. We've already talked about that. The hospital phone lines aren't secure."

"The Kid is right," Tom said. "The best I can do is get you updates on his condition."

"I appreciate that, but you should know I'm not leaving New Orleans again."

Rob looked at Tom and chuckled. "She has no problem speaking her mind."

"I'm willing to hear your opinions, Caroline, but until this is over, I'm responsible for keeping you alive," Tom said as his pager sounded. He took it from his belt and looked at it.

"It's Wiley. Where's the phone?"

"Kitchen wall," Steve said. "You stay where you are. I'll take it."

Tom handed him the pager. "Tell me everything he says."

Steve went to the phone and dialed Wiley's number.

"Wiley, it's Steve. Tom got your page. What's going on?" Steve listened for several minutes. "Damn. Hold on, and I will tell him." Steve pressed his finger to his lips and motioned to Rob to take Caroline out of the room.

Rob took her to her bedroom and whispered to her at the door. "Stay in here and keep quiet. We don't want anyone to know you're here."

"Who's on the phone?"

"It's FBI business, Caroline. Stay in here until I come get you." Rob closed the door and nodded to Steve when he entered the kitchen.

"What did Wiley say?" Tom asked.

"Phillip and Wiley were leaving the docks when they received a call on their service radio. Alligator hunters reported several bullet-riddled vans dumped in the swamp outside the city, loaded with bodies."

"Tell Wiley to take Phillip and get down there. I want pictures of the faces of every one of those bodies."

Steve relayed the message, then said, "Hey man, are you all right?"

"What's wrong?" Tom asked.

Steve pressed his hand over the phone. "Sounds like Wiley's hurt." Steve returned the phone to his ear. "Are you all right?" He listened, then glanced at Tom. "His back is acting up again."

"Tell him to go to a doctor. Phillip can handle the photos. The last thing we need is for both of us to be out of commission."

Steve relayed the message. "He's seeing a chiropractor in the morning."

"That's what he said last time."

"Wiley said Phillip will page you as soon as he has the photos."

Steve hung up. "Do you think those bodies have anything to do with Martínez?" he asked.

"We won't know until Kid looks at the pictures."

"I could go with Phillip to see them in person," Rob said.

"Bad idea. That place will be covered with agents and police."

"Wait a minute," Caroline said, coming into the room. "What's wrong with Kid being around agents and police?"

Tom didn't answer.

"You were told to stay in your room, Caroline," Rob said.

"It's me they're trying to kill. I have a right to know what's going on."

Tom shook his head. "If you must know, Kid is working undercover. It's too dangerous for anyone to know he's here."

"What's he doing undercover?"

Tom leaned forward and glared into Caroline's eyes. "That is our business, Mrs. Broussard. Not yours."

*   *   *

Garden District

Jerome climbed the stairs to Pascal's office and went quietly to Jean-Claude's desk without making a sound.

"*Mon Dieu!*" The assistant jumped when he saw him and pressed his hand to his chest. "Didn't your mother teach you to make your presence known before entering a room?"

"Leave my mama out of this, fancy pants. I'm here to see Pascal."

Jean-Claude glared at the man and pointed to the door. "That's twice you've been rude to me since you came into this office. Do not return until you learn some manners."

"I'm not leaving until I see Pascal."

"You aren't seeing anyone."

"What's going on in here?" Pascal said, coming through the door.

The assistant came around his desk and took his boss's hat. "This impolite swamp rat thinks he can insult me."

Pascal walked up to the man in black and shook his finger in his face. "Apologize or get out."

"I handle your dirty work, Pascal. You need me."

"You can be replaced. He can't."

Jerome turned to the assistant and performed a mock bow. "Please accept my apology."

Jean-Claude straightened his jacket. "Don't do it again."

"Good," Pascal said. "Now, did you kill all of them?" he asked as he went into his office.

Jerome followed him. "They are all dead," he said as he settled into a chair.

"Was Martínez there?"

"Possible, but not certain. But if Martínez *was* there, he's dead."

"What did you do with the bodies?"

"They were loaded into the vans, taken to the swamp, and fed to the gators."

"Are you certain nothing was left of them?"

"I have used this spot many times over the years. The gators have never failed me yet."

"Good," Pascal said. "Now, it's time to do the same to the woman. I need to have her eliminated as soon as possible."

"Do not be concerned. The woman will be easy. I just removed twenty men."

"I'm not so sure. She's managed to elude you so far."

"Only because the man with her is making it difficult to locate her," Jerome said. "I'm looking forward to taking him out with her."

"I don't care what you do to him. Just make sure the woman goes first."

CHAPTER THIRTY

The Safehouse

Caroline took a seat at the kitchen table and crossed her arms. "If Pascal killed those men, then you can arrest him, right?"

"We are a long way from discovering who killed them, Caroline," Tom said. "Even if it was Pascal, I'm not in a position to make the arrest."

"Then report it to someone who can. I need Pascal locked up so I can submit my bid."

Tom glanced at Rob. "What is she talking about?"

Caroline didn't wait for Rob to answer. "If I don't submit my bid to the Levee Board before the end of the week, Pascal wins the maintenance contract."

"What makes you so sure they will give it to you?"

"I know the numbers. My company has at least an eighty percent chance of winning the contract, but that number goes to zero if I miss the deadline to submit the bid."

"Sorry, Caroline. That isn't going to happen."

"Then it's your fault when New Orleans crumbles to the ground."

"Kid, what is she talking about?"

"Tom, she has a valid concern," Rob said, pulling out a chair. "This is the reason Pascal is trying to kill her. Let's all take a seat and at least hear her out."

Everyone settled in, and Tom turned to Caroline. "You have the floor. Start talking."

Caroline leaned in and explained the problems with Pascal's inferior concrete and everything she and Jack had done to win the contract.

Tom leaned back in his chair. "So, if Pascal's companies win this contract and he succeeds in running you and the other independent companies out of business, you think his inferior product puts every structure built or repaired with his materials at risk?"

"That is exactly what I'm saying." Caroline nodded. "Hurricane Betsy took seventy-six lives and cost billions in damage. If another big hurricane hits, many more lives will be lost when the homes, buildings, and levees built with Pascal's concrete are destroyed."

The room went silent for a time before Tom responded. "When is the deadline?"

"In four days."

Tom crossed his arms and glanced at everyone around the table several times before speaking. "If there's a way to submit that bid without you being involved, I'll consider it."

Caroline jumped from her chair and wrapped her arms around Tom. "Thank you, thank you!"

"Don't thank me yet. Where's the proposal?"

"It's in the safe at my office."

"Caroline, there's no way you're going to your plant," Tom said.

"I don't have to. My assistant can bring it here."

"That's not going to work. I don't want anyone to know where you are except the three of us."

"What about someone who isn't from here?" Rob suggested.

"What are you talking about?"

"Caroline has a friend from Philadelphia. I met him at the hospital. Maybe he would be willing to help?"

"Oh, my gosh," Caroline gasped. "I forgot all about C.J. That's a great idea, Kid."

"Not so fast," Tom said. "Who is C.J.?"

"His name is C.J. Moretti. My father hired C.J. to be the operations manager of our plant when I was twelve. He was young, aggressive, and soon became part of the family. My parents even hosted his wedding at our home. I was in my third year of college when he decided to go back to Philadelphia and build his own concrete company. Before he left, he trained Jack to take his place. Mom and I lost count of the times Dad flew to Philly to help C.J. get his business off the ground."

"Wait a minute," Steve said, exchanging glances with Tom. "Does C.J. stand for Cheyman Jacopo Moretti?"

"That's right. How did you know?"

Steve leaned in. "Has he ever used the name Jaco?"

"Never. That's his uncle."

"So you know who I'm talking about?"

"Are you talking about Jaco's involvement with the mob?" Caroline asked.

"That's exactly what I'm asking about."

"Jaco is the reason C.J. left Philly in the first place."

"So why did he go back then?" Steve asked.

"His dad became ill, and he went back to Philadelphia to help care for him. C.J. has no connection to the mob."

"Was his business successful?" Rob asked.

"It's the largest concrete plant in Philadelphia."

"I think C.J. would be willing to help," Rob said. "He seems to care for Caroline and Jack."

"Do you trust him to submit your bid?" Tom asked.

"Of course I do. C.J. handled the entire bidding process when he worked for us."

"Then call him," Tom said.

"I can't. His number is in my Rolodex at my office."

"She doesn't need it," Rob said. "He gave me his card."

"Great, where is it?" Caroline asked.

"Long gone, but I know what was printed on it."

Caroline looked at him. "That was over three weeks ago. There's no way you could remember that."

Steve chuckled. "Oh, yes, he can."

Tom looked at Caroline. "If C.J. refuses to come, it's over."

"Oh, he'll come. I'm sure of it."

"Only one way to find out," Steve said.

The three men hovered near the kitchen counter as Rob wrote down the number for Caroline. She went to the phone, dialed the numbers, and looked at the men while waiting for her call to be answered.

"Good afternoon. C.J. Moretti, please. . . Tell him it's his little sister." She motioned for Tom to join her. When he got to her, she held the phone so he could hear their conversation.

"Thank God," said the man at the end of the line. "I have been going crazy worrying about you. When I heard about the gun battle, I rushed to the hospital, but the police refused to let me in. I stayed for days trying to get information, but no one would tell me a thing, so I came back to Philadelphia. Are you all right? How is Jack?"

"We're good. At least for now," Caroline said as calmly as possible.

"What does that mean?"

Tom shook his finger.

"It's a long story, C.J. One I can't go into over the phone. I'm calling because I need your help."

"Where are you? I'll be on the next plane out of here."

She looked at Tom and held her hand over the phone receiver. "What do I tell him?" she whispered to Tom.

"Caroline," C.J. asked. "Who are you talking to?"

"The FBI."

"FBI? Put them on the phone. I need to talk to them."

She looked at Tom.

"Caroline, are you there? Talk to me."

Tom took the phone. "Mr. Moretti, this is Senior Agent Tom Neal."

"Agent Neal, what's going on there? Is Caroline in danger? Please tell me the truth. I'm worried about them."

"Sir, would you be willing to come and help her with something concerning her business?"

"Yes, whatever she needs."

"Book your flight to New Orleans and call us with the information. I'll have someone meet you at the gate. Mr. Moretti, I insist you tell no one about this call or where you're going. Is that clear?"

"I have to say something to my wife."

Caroline took the phone from Tom. "Tell Evie you're coming back to check on Jack."

"That I can do. I hope I can see him."

Caroline looked at Tom, and he took the phone. "I'll try to arrange that. Are you ready to take this number down?"

"I am."

"This number is only for you. Don't give it to your wife or anyone else."

"I understand."

Tom gave him the number. "We'll be waiting for your call," he said, and hung up the phone.

"If he gets in tonight, it would be safer to go to the plant without anyone being around," Rob said.

"That won't work," Caroline said. "The gate guards won't let you in. It will be far less confusing if you wait until the morning. You can tell them you're there to see my assistant about a shipment order."

"I agree," Tom added.

The phone started to ring. Tom picked it up.

"I have my flight information," C.J. said.

Tom snapped his fingers, and Rob handed him a pen and paper. "Ready."

"I will arrive at 7:45 p.m. on Eastern Airlines flight 307. How will I know who I'm meeting?"

Tom locked eyes with Rob. "Do you recall the man you met at the hospital?"

"The tall guy with an athletic build and stubborn attitude?"

"That's him. He'll be waiting for you at the gate."

"Is there anything else I should know?"

"That's all for now. We will discuss everything when you arrive."

Steve crossed his arms and looked at Caroline after Tom hung up. "I know he's your friend, but he may change his mind after hearing about Pascal's involvement."

"C.J. is well acquainted with Pascal. He and my dad had many run-ins with him in the past. But C.J. has a family now … That may change things."

"We won't know until he arrives," Rob said. "If all he does is get the bid proposal from the safe, that will help. We can figure out the rest."

CHAPTER THIRTY-ONE

The Safehouse

Caroline glanced at the clock on the wall. "They should have been here by now."

"Stop worrying," Tom said. "His plane may have been delayed."

Caroline nodded. "I'm just anxious."

Steve appeared from the small living room. "They're here. I'll go open the door to the garage."

Tom got up from the table. "Get down behind the counter, Caroline." He went to the hallway entrance and took his revolver from his holster. Moments later, Rob came through the door, followed by Moretti, and Tom holstered his weapon.

Caroline rushed past Tom and embraced her friend. "Thank God you're here."

His bags fell to the floor, and he scooped her into his arms. "Of course I came. Hello, little sister." He held her at arms' length and looked into her eyes. "Are you all right?"

Tom stepped forward and extended his hand. "Mr. Moretti, I'm Agent Tom Neal."

C.J. released Caroline and took Tom's hand. "Thank you for watching over her, Agent Neal."

"Call me Tom. Steve is the sandy-haired guy, and you already know The Kid."

C.J. nodded, then turned back to Tom. "When we drove up, I didn't see any men guarding the house."

"There aren't any. Posting men out front would broadcast the fact that we're here."

"Sorry, I'm new to this." C.J. glanced around the room. "When do we start?"

"First, you need to understand who you're dealing with."

"It has to be Marcel Pascal."

"Then you understand how dangerous it is to help us."

"I'm well versed in how a mob boss works, Agent Neal. Has Caroline told you about my uncle?"

"She has."

"Then don't give it another thought. I still don't understand why Pascal or anyone would want to harm Jack, though?"

"He didn't," Caroline said. "The shooter was there for me."

"You?" C.J. turned to Tom. "Is that right?"

"Mr. Broussard took the bullet meant for his wife."

"Did you catch the shooter?"

"We did, but he was murdered while in the care of the local police."

"I'm not surprised." C.J. turned to Caroline. "Why is Pascal after you?"

"He wants me out of the way to win the multi-million-dollar levee maintenance contract."

C.J. took her hand. "Now I understand. You have the only plant large enough to handle that contract."

"And we built an expansion plant to increase our chances of winning the work."

"I know. Jack called me several times to discuss it. He wanted a sounding board about spending that much money before you knew you had the contract. He told me you had several heated discussions over it."

"We did. Jack thought we should wait, but I was certain that the new plant would make it impossible for anyone to beat us." She closed her eyes and shook her head. "Now I would take it all back to keep this from happening to him."

"You have always been a bit bull-headed, little sister, but I blame that on Papa. He made you tough."

"Now that you know who we're dealing with," Tom stated, "why don't you get settled, and we'll discuss how to handle this?"

Steve picked up C.J.'s bags. "Hope you don't mind sharing a room?"

"Not a problem. I spent a few years in the army."

After C.J.'s bags were stowed, the group reassembled in the kitchen to eat. Afterward, they sat around the table and talked.

C.J. rubbed the back of his neck. "So, the deadline for submitting the bid is in three days?"

"Actually, two and a half," Caroline corrected. "It closes at twelve noon on Friday. Abigail will let you into my office first thing tomorrow morning, and you can get the bid out of the safe."

"What else do you need while I'm there?"

"Ask her to give you a copy of our latest financial report. I need to see what's happened while I've been away. The expansion plant cost more than expected, and a few days before Jack was shot, someone destroyed one of the control panels at the main plant. I'm sure it was Pascal, but I can't prove it."

"What's been done to get it running?" C.J. asked.

"Jack had it repaired, but there could have been another break-in while I was away."

"As far as I know, nothing more has happened," C.J. said. "I spent a couple of weeks at the plant to ensure business was not suffering after you disappeared. Since you've been gone, I've been in constant communication with Abigail and your plant manager, David Reese. They've done a great job in your absence."

"I had no idea."

"How could you? You were running for your life."

Tom leaned forward. "Could her financial situation cost her the deal?"

"That's one of the factors," Rob injected into the conversation. "When a project is government-funded, it comes with more restrictions and requirements than the private sector."

Tom crossed his arms and glared at Caroline. "You should have told me this before we had Moretti fly here."

"No. I'm glad I'm here," C.J. said. "I think we can get the contract."

"He's right," Rob added. "Once we get the bid and see the financials, there is a good chance we can make it work."

C.J. looked over at Rob. "I'm a little confused, though. How does a bodyguard know so much about government contracts?"

Rob swapped glances with Tom. "Let's just say guarding people wasn't my first job."

Tom cleared his throat and turned his attention to Caroline. "Is there anything else that might keep you from winning this thing?"

"Actually, there is. The Board making the decision is comprised primarily of men. They might think I can't fulfill the contract and manage the plant operations while also caring for Jack."

"That's a legitimate concern," Tom replied.

"Not for her," C.J. said. "She can handle anything she puts her mind to."

"That's your opinion. The Board is a different matter." Tom shook his head. "I should have said no to this when you brought it up."

"I disagree," C.J. added. "Let's not decide until I take a look at her books."

Tom paused for a long moment, then sighed. "Well, you're here. Might as well see where she stands. It's getting late, and it sounds like you have a full day ahead." He eased out of the chair, and everyone stood.

"Just a second," Steve said. "I hate to be the bearer of bad news, but there is one more thing we need to consider. Even if Caroline wins, Pascal may not stop coming after her."

Caroline put her hand on her hips. "After what he did to Jack, I'm not giving up without a fight."

"Agent Neal," C.J. said. "If Pascal isn't going to stop, can't the FBI relocate Caroline and Jack?"

"The Bureau would only do that if her testimony was needed to prosecute him," Rob answered. "At the moment, there isn't enough evidence to prove he is responsible for this."

C.J. looked at Rob and then Tom. "If you won't protect her, I will."

Caroline shook her head. "No, C.J., there has to be another way out of this."

"Look, guys," Steve said. "We don't have to figure everything out tonight."

"Steve's right," Tom said as he pressed his hand to his side. "Steve, you, Kid, and C.J. will go to the plant tomorrow morning. I'll stay here with Caroline."

"Are you all right?" Rob asked.

"I'm fine. All of you get some rest."

"I'll take the first watch," Steve said.

Tom's pager ended the conversation. He unclipped it from his belt. "It's Phillip," he said, and went to the phone.

"Tell me you found something?" Tom glanced back at the people in the room as he listened. "Sounds gruesome. Glad you got what you did. Where can we meet?" He looked at Rob. "We'll find it. The Kid and I will meet you in half an hour." Tom hung up the phone. "Steve, you're in charge. Kid and I are meeting Philip." Tom turned to Rob. "Hope you're up for this. He said identification was going to be difficult."

"What happened to Wiley?" Steve asked.

"Don't know. Went home, I guess. Let's go, Kid."

Tom and Rob entered a Frostop root beer and hamburger shop less than an hour later. Phillip was in a booth at the back of the room.

They settled in, and Phillip slid the pack of photos across the table. "Hope you got a strong stomach. Some of those men were mangled pretty bad."

Tom looked at the photos and then passed them to Rob.

Rob viewed a few of the images and then closed his eyes briefly. "How long were they in the water?"

"Couldn't have been more than a couple of hours," Phillip said. "Any more than that and there wouldn't have been anything left to photo-graph. The hunters said there were so many gators on the bodies they were afraid they would come after them."

Rob nodded and continuing flipping through the photos. About halfway, he paused at one for several minutes.

"Is that Martínez?" Tom whispered.

"It's possible, but I can't say for certain." Rob looked up from the photo to Phillip. "Where were the bodies taken?"

"They were brought here."

"Is there any way we can see them?"

"Not tonight. I need to find out which morgues have them. There were too many for one location."

"The only way to be certain it's Martínez is to see him myself," Rob said, returning the photos to Phillip.

Tom paused before answering. "Phillip, can you get Wiley to page me tonight? I'm going to need him tomorrow."

"Sure, but he was in bad shape when I left him a few hours ago. What do you want him to do?"

"I need him to run an errand for me."

"Call me in the morning and tell me what you want him to do. If he can't, I'll handle it after I turn these photos into our office."

"Thanks," Tom said as he and Rob stood. "Good job on those pictures. I'm sure it wasn't easy."

"Death never is, but that's part of the job."

"Unfortunately, it is."

When Tom and Rob returned to the house, Steve met them at the door.

"Was one of them Martínez?" he asked.

"The bodies were so mangled it's impossible to be certain," Rob said.

"So, what are you going to do?"

"Phillip is locating the morgues so The Kid and I can view the bodies."

Steve searched Rob's face. "Are you sure you want to do this?"

"I have to. If Martínez is dead, it means my family is safe."

"Not until we have all of them," Tom added. "The other partner in the organization, the one they call The Chemist, is still out there."

"Juan Alejandro Vero? I don't consider him much of a threat," Rob added. "Unless he's changed."

"Doesn't matter," Tom said. "He's the one who knows how to

manufacture the drugs, and I'm not stopping until the whole organization is dust."

Rob nodded. "You two try to get some rest," he said. "I won't be able to close my eyes after those pictures."

The following morning, Rob and Steve were drinking coffee while Tom was on the phone.

"There's been a change of plans," Tom said, hanging up.

"What changed?" C.J. asked, entering the room.

"C.J., you and Steve are meeting Phillip at the plant's entrance this morning."

"Who's Phillip?"

"He and Wiley are local FBI working with us," Tom said.

"Where's Wiley?" Rob asked.

"Phillip said he had an appointment with a specialist about his back this morning. He will page me after he's done. Kid, you and I will stay with Caroline until they return."

"You ready, C.J.?" Steve asked.

"Ready."

Caroline came in just as Steve and C.J. left. "I thought you were going to the plant?" she said to Rob.

"Change of plans," he answered.

"What are we supposed to do while they're gone?" Caroline asked as she joined them at the kitchen table.

"We wait," Tom replied as his pager sounded. "It's Wiley," he said, glancing at the pager. He went to the phone and dialed the number.

"Hey, I was told to page you," Wiley said.

"What did your doctor say?"

"Nothing yet. Waiting for the blood and X-rays to come back. Doc said to go home and take it easy, but that isn't happening. What do you need?"

"I need you to keep an eye on the drugs. I've got a feeling Pascal was behind those killings yesterday."

"You think that had something to do with the drugs?"

"Not sure of anything at the moment, but I want to be ready if it does."

"Got it. I can handle the docks."

"Are you sure?"

"It beats sitting around. If I see anything, I'll let you know."

CHAPTER THIRTY-TWO

The Plant

The plant was a blaze of activity when Steve and C.J. arrived. Workers and trucks with large turning barrels were leaving the plant as other trucks were being filled. C.J. directed Steve to park in front of the main building, and as they exited the car, Phillip pulled in beside him.

"You two go in," Phillip said. "I'll stay out here to keep an eye on things."

"If anyone questions why you're here," C.J. said, "just tell them to call the office. I hired extra security after what happened to Jack, when Caroline went missing."

"Good idea," Phillip added.

"I'll page you when we're done," Steve said.

Phillip stayed behind as Steve followed C.J. into the building. When they reached the top floor, a woman in her early sixties jumped up from her desk and rushed to embrace C.J.

"This is a surprise! I would have had someone meet you at the airport had I known you were coming."

"It was a last-minute decision. How are you, Abigail?"

"Busy as always without the Broussards. I don't know what we would have done had you not stepped in."

"Jack and Caroline are family," C.J. said. "They would have done the same for me."

"I'm sure they would."

"Abigail, this is Steve. He's here to help keep an eye on things while I do some work for Caroline."

"How can I help?" Abigail asked.

C.J. took two pieces of paper from his pocket and handed one to her.

"What's this?"

"A note from Caroline giving me permission to access the safe. She asked me to finish the bid proposal for the levee contract."

Abigail read the note, then clutched it to her chest. "Is she all right?"

"She is, but after what's happened, it's safer for her to stay out of sight for a while."

"Those poor children have been through so much." Abigail went to her desk, took a key ring from her purse, and unlocked the office door.

She and Steve stood back as C.J. went to a tall safe in the corner of the room and opened it with Caroline's combination.

C.J. looked back. "Abigail, there are several file folders in here. Which one has the bid?"

"It's in a large manila envelope."

"Found it," he said, holding up the packet. C.J. placed it on the desk and closed the safe. "I also need a copy of the latest financial report and a list of bills and payroll," he said. "Bring anything that would have changed their financials since Caroline and Jack last worked on the bid. I'll also need a typewriter, paper, carbons, and an envelope to submit the proposal."

"Are you aware of the new extension site? The Broussards invested a lot of money in it, which affected our cash reserve total."

"I am."

"If we don't win, I'm concerned we will have to lay off a lot of our people who have been here for years."

"We're trying to keep that from happening, Abigail."

She placed her hands on her round hips and looked at the men. "Then let me do the typing. I've done every proposal we've submitted for the last twenty-two years. As you may recall, I even did a few for you when you were here," she said, turning to C.J.

"That's a good idea," Steve said. "It will go a lot faster with her help."

"That means we'll have to do it here," C.J. said. "Are you good with that?"

"That's a question for Tom." Steve turned to Abigail. "Is there a pay phone around here?"

"No need. You can use the phone on the desk?"

"Too risky. Your line may be tapped."

"Dear Lord, I never thought of that. There's a pay phone in the break room," Abigail said. "I can show you where it is on my way to bookkeeping."

"Let's go." Steve followed her down the staircase to the employee break room. Fortunately, no one was there. Steve dropped coins into the phone and dialed Tom's pager number. He added the number of the pay phone and hung up. Several minutes later, the phone rang.

"Tom, it's Steve. We have a question for you. It will save C.J. a lot of time if Caroline's secretary types the changes to the proposal while he's here working."

"That will require the three of you to be at her plant until it's done."

"Yes, but it will also make it possible to complete the proposal much faster."

Tom took a moment to reply. "You have a point. All right, but be back before dark."

"If he's not finished, we'll have to come back."

"We'll make that decision tomorrow. Just be back here as soon as you can."

Steve hung up.

"What did he say?" Abigail asked.

"We have until dark to get this done."

Steve and Abigail stopped at accounting and went upstairs with binders and ledgers.

"This is everything since Mr. Broussard was hurt," Abigail said, putting everything on the desk in front of C.J. "There are a couple more coming up from accounting in a few minutes. I'll be at my desk handling calls if you need me."

"Thanks, Abigail."

Steve pulled up a chair next to C.J.'s desk. "You know, even if the finances check out, there's still the problem about her husband. There's no guarantee he will be strong enough to return to work anytime soon."

"I've been thinking about that. That alone could keep Caroline from winning this thing."

*   *   *

The Safehouse

It was late afternoon when Tom sent a message to Steve's pager. The phone rang minutes later, and Tom answered.

"Where are you calling from?" Tom asked.

"The pay phone in the company's break room."

"How close are you to wrapping up?"

"Not sure. C.J. is still working."

"I was afraid of that. Remember what I said."

"I know. Back by dark." A buzzing came over the line. "Sounds like you're being paged."

"I am," Tom said, looking at his pager. "It's Wiley. I have to go." Tom ended the call and made another.

"I got your page," he said when Wiley answered. "What's happening?"

"Looks like you were right. Something is going down. A large group of men just showed up."

"Stay where you are until The Kid and I can get there. We can't leave the woman until Steve returns."

"I didn't know you got her back."

"Sorry. Too much going on. Don't let those drugs out of your sight."

Tom hung up and immediately dialed Steve's pager.

"What's happening?" Rob asked as Tom waited for Steve to call back.

"Looks like someone is coming for the drugs," Tom said.

"Is it Martínez?"

"Won't know until I get you to the docks."

The phone rang, and Tom answered.

"Steve, I need you here as soon as possible. A large group of men just arrived at the docks. If they are there for the drugs, I need The Kid there to identify Martínez in case he's one of them."

"What about C.J.?"

"Have Phillip stay with him. I need you to protect Caroline."

"On my way."

Tom ended the call and spent almost an hour pacing back and forth.

"You are wearing out the linoleum," Caroline said from behind the kitchen counter. There was a knock at the back door before Tom could respond.

Rob motioned for Caroline to get down, and Tom pulled his weapon.

"It's me," Steve called out.

Tom holstered his gun and unlocked the door.

"What took so long?" Rob asked.

"Traffic."

"Kid, where's your gun?"

"Lost it a long time ago."

"I have one in the car," Tom said, tossing Rob his keys. "You're driving."

When they were near the docks, Rob parked out of view as Tom unlocked the glove box. He removed a revolver and gave it to Rob.

"Be careful. It's loaded."

Rob slid it under his belt, and they got out of the car. They went to the hole in the chain-link fence and crept past several warehouses. The pallets of goods that had been there before had been replaced with large machinery covered in plastic sheets.

Wiley was behind a massive piece of equipment, and they eased their way to him.

"What's happening?" Tom asked, crouching next to Wiley.

"See for yourself," Wiley said, handing Tom his binoculars. "Check out the men gathered in that open area."

Tom took the binoculars. "There must be at least twenty-five or thirty of them." He passed the glasses to Rob. "See if you spot Martínez."

"Don't see him," Rob said after a few moments. "Wait a minute. Two large eighteen-wheelers just pulled in." Rob returned the glasses to Tom.

"The back just opened up," Tom said. "More men jumped out. They're passing out firearms."

"Looks like they're expecting a fight," Wiley replied.

"You're right. We need Steve."

"Who's going to protect Caroline?" Rob asked.

Tom lowered his glasses. "Wiley, I need you to change places with Steve."

"That's a waste of time. I'm already here."

"You're in no condition to handle a gun fight if this goes wrong," Tom said.

"And you're not exactly well yourself."

"True, but I'm pulling rank. When you get there, tell Steve to bring extra clips and another set of night binoculars. I'm getting closer to get a better look," Tom said, then slipped away.

"Looks like I've been demoted to babysitter," Wiley said and sighed. "What's the address?"

Rob gave Wiley the address, and he disappeared behind equipment.

Nothing happened for almost an hour, then Rob saw a car approaching. He hid under the sheet covering the equipment. After the car passed, he came out and looked through the night binoculars. The vehicle parked, and two men got out. One he recognized as the man with the silver-tipped boots who had tried to take Caroline. He turned his glasses to the second man and felt his heart pounding in his chest.

"Is that who I think it is?" Tom said, coming up next to him.

"It's Martínez, and the one with him is the man I fought in Houma."

They watched as the group gathered around Martínez. Soon after, a couple of the men appeared with oversized wire cutters. Several men from the group disappeared between two warehouses.

"Where are Pascal's guards?" Rob asked.

"The bigger question is where the dock workers are? Look around. There's not one in sight."

"Someone must have tipped them off."

Minutes passed with no activity. Then the doors to one of the warehouses opened, and a forklift carrying pallets stacked high with gray-looking bricks appeared. The forklift went to one of the trucks and started offloading. A second forklift emerged from the building with another load. When Steve arrived minutes later, the process was still underway.

"What have I missed?"

Tom handed Steve the binoculars. "Take a look. That's Diego Martínez giving directions."

"This is too easy," Steve said. "Why aren't Pascal's people stopping them?"

The words were barely out of his mouth when automobile headlights appeared at both ends of the docks.

Rob lifted the plastic sheet. "Get under here before we're seen." They hid until the cars had passed. When they came out again, they saw that Martínez and his men were surrounded by vehicles and armed men.

Martínez's people quickly closed ranks around him and the man with the silver-tipped boots.

"This is about to get interesting," Steve whispered.

A shiny new Cadillac DeVille came into view and parked outside the circle of cars.

The driver exited the Cadillac and opened the back door. Marcel Pascal stepped out. He was quickly flanked by two armed men.

"Damn it," Tom said. "We're too far back to hear what they're saying. I should have stayed where I was."

Rob gave him a look.

CHAPTER THIRTY-THREE

The Docks

"Well, this is disappointing," Pascal said as he approached Martínez. "I was hoping you were dead."

Martínez pushed through his men, and Salvador followed. "I anticipated your ambush, Pascal. That is why I sent my men ahead."

"So you sacrificed your men in order to steal my drugs?"

"How many times have you done the same? I did it to reclaim what is mine."

Pascal chuckled and shook his head. "You failed your assignments, Martínez. The drugs are mine."

"I would have handled the woman, but you never gave me the chance."

"I don't give chances, Martínez. If you don't handle it right the first time, you pay the price for failing." Pascal gestured to the circle of men before getting into his car and driving away.

* * *

Rob glanced at Tom. "That turned out more peacefully than I expected."

"It's not over. Take cover, now."

Rob, Steve, and Tom sheltered behind the machinery as gunfire erupted around them.

Rob inched upwards with the goggles, and Tom pulled him back with his belt. "Are you trying to get your head blown off?"

"Martínez and the man with the silver-tip boots are escaping."

"Stay down. There's nothing we can do."

Rob shoved the goggles into Tom's hands. "I'm not letting him get away." Rob broke free of Tom's grasp and crawled away.

"Kid, get back here!"

Rob didn't look back.

"Steve!" Tom shouted.

"On it," Steve said, and took off after Rob.

*   *   *

Rob darted between machinery and warehouses until he reached the opening in the fence. He crawled through and scanned the area for Martínez and the man who had tried to kidnap Caroline in Houma. Rob was beginning to think he had lost them when he saw them running alongside the road a few blocks ahead.

He crossed to the darker side of the street and shortened the distance between them. Martínez and Salvador stopped and hid behind a large oak tree near the road's edge for a moment, then darted across the street into an old, deserted-looking house at the end of the block.

Rob crept past other homes that looked to be at least a century old but were well-kept and occupied. The porch encasing the old structure Martínez and Salvador had entered, however, looked to be so rotten that Rob wondered how the columns supporting the house's second story still stood.

Rob was about to slip through the gate of the deteriorating spear-tipped iron fence that surrounded the property when someone grabbed his shoulder. He spun around, ready to strike.

"Easy," Steve whispered. "Is this where they are?"

"They just went in."

"I'll go in from the back and you take the front. Do me a favor and try not to get yourself killed."

"I'll do my best."

Steve disappeared along the side of the house as Rob stepped onto the porch. He took the revolver from under his shirt and heard the wooden planks creaking under his feet as he entered the old house. The only light dispelling the darkness inside came from the streetlight at the corner of the block and the moon beaming through floor-to-ceiling windows.

Rob remained in the shadows, going from room to room, searching the bottom floor. Something moved, and he aimed his gun. Two little eyes scurried across the floor, then disappeared into a hole in the wall.

He went to the staircase and had just placed his foot on the first step when someone pressed a gun nozzle into the middle of his back.

"Toss your weapon, *gringo*," Salvador ordered.

"Why should I?" Rob asked, slowly turning to face the man. "You're going to kill me anyway."

"I said, drop it."

"I have a better idea," Steve whispered, pressing his revolver to the man's ear. "Why don't you hand me yours?"

The man's hands went up, and Steve took his gun.

"Boss!" Salvador yelled.

Rob's fist connected with his jaw, and the man fell to the floor.

"Is he out?" Rob asked.

"Down for the count."

Rob started up the staircase.

"Hey, where are you going?"

"After Martínez."

"Careful. He knows you're coming."

Rob reached the landing on the second floor and saw open doors at each end of the hallway. He went to the one on his right and peered in. The moon's light beaming through the large, paned window allowed him to see broken furniture scattered about the floor, but there was no sign of Martínez.

He retreated, crossed the hallway, and peered in the doorway of the other room. This side of the house was darker, making it almost impossible to see anything except the square of light coming from the house next door through the open window.

Rob entered the room and closed the door behind him, making it impossible for Martínez to escape without him hearing. He pressed his back against the wall and started inching around the room. His foot touched something that caused a noise, and a shot rang out, piercing the wall inches from his head. He reached down and ran his hand over the object. It was a long piece of turned wood. He suspected it had been a bedpost and tucked his gun into his belt before picking it up. He held on to the post at one end, reached out, and tapped the wall with the other end.

Another shot flashed, but this time it was several feet away.

There you are, Rob thought. He quietly retreated to the other side of the room and tapped the wall again. More shots rang out, hitting the wall ahead of him.

"It's been a while, Martínez," Rob said.

"Who are you?"

"Don't you remember? I laundered your drug money."

"That can't be. Roberto is dead."

"Maybe I am," Rob said, quickly taking several steps to the other side of the room. "I took Rojas. Now I'm back to get you."

"Not if I kill you again." Martínez stepped in front of the large window and started firing wildly until he was out of bullets.

Rob dropped to one knee, propelled himself forward like a football lineman, and rammed into Martínez, launching him through the window. Had he not caught hold of the window frame, he would have followed Martínez out.

Rob looked down to see where Martínez had fallen, but it was too dark below to see. He ran down the staircase and out the front door and found that Steve had handcuffed Salvador to a porch column and had a gun pointed at his head.

"Where's Martínez?" Steve asked as Rob ran past him.

"He went out the window."

Rob ran around the house and discovered Martínez draped over the old iron fence. He placed his fingers against his neck, but there was no pulse.

"Is he alive?" Tom asked, coming up behind him.

"He's done." Rob lifted Martínez's shoulder. "Looks like the spears at the top of this old fence punctured his chest."

"Damn, I wanted him alive." Tom's words were barely out of his mouth when a flashlight beam blinded him.

"Stay where you are," a male voice said. "I've already called the police."

"Kid," Tom whispered. "Don't let him see your face."

Rob slowly stepped backward into the shadows.

"What are you doing out here?"

Before Tom responded, his pager sounded.

"What's that noise?" the man with the flashlight demanded.

"I'm with the FBI. It's a device I use to keep in contact with my people." Tom took the pager from his belt, then held it up for the man to see before reading the dial.

"Damn it," Tom muttered. "It's Wiley. There are five X's after the number.

"Caroline's in trouble," Rob said. "We have to get back there."

Tom held up his hands and stepped towards the man. "My partner is right. We have to go."

"Not yet, you don't. I hear sirens. We're going to wait for the police."

"There isn't time. I'm going to reach for my identification." Tom slid his hand into his coat pocket and took out his wallet. He flipped it open to display his badge. "Can you see this?"

"I see it."

"Tell the police there's been a mass shooting on the docks. The dead man on the fence is Diego Martínez. He's the leader of a large drug organization out of Mexico. Another member of his organization is handcuffed on the front porch. Tell the police to contact the FBI and give them that information. Can you remember that?"

"Of course I can."

"Good. Now repeat the man's name I gave you?"

"You said his name is Diego Martínez. But who are you?"

"That doesn't matter. We have to go."

"No, you're not leaving."

"Sir, one of my agents is behind you with a gun pointed at you. He's been there since you arrived. If we wanted to harm you, we would have done so by now."

The beam of the flashlight swung from Tom to Steve.

The man turned his flashlight back to Tom. "I guess you are who you say you are."

"Thanks for your help," Tom said as he and Rob went to the front of the house with their hands raised.

"I heard your pager," Steve said as he holstered his weapon.

"Wiley's in trouble," Rob said.

"We need to get out of here before the police arrive," Tom said.

"What about Martínez?" Steve asked.

"He's dead. We have to get to Wiley and Caroline."

They rushed across the road. Tom stopped abruptly, grabbing his side. "Steve, get to a phone and page Phillip," he said through clenched teeth. "Give him the safe house address and tell him it's urgent."

"What about C.J.?"

"Tell him to make sure C.J. locks himself in at the plant and to stay put."

"Will do." Steve took off in a dead run.

Tom tossed Rob the keys. "Get the car and come back for me."

CHAPTER THIRTY-FOUR

The Plant

Phillip sat across from C.J. as he worked on the proposal. "How's it looking?"

"I can't say until I finish the last report of their financials. I sent the secretary home. There's nothing more she can do until I get this part done."

Phillip's pager buzzed, and he checked it. "Something's happened. I've got to make a call."

C.J. got to his feet. "Is it about Caroline?"

"Don't know. I need to find a pay phone."

"There's one in the break room on the bottom floor, left of the staircase."

Phillip raced from the room, found the break room, and rushed to the phone. "Your code said it was urgent," he said when his call was answered.

"Wiley's in trouble. Lock C.J. in and get to our safe house."

"I didn't know you had a safe house."

"I'll fill you in later. Get there as fast as you can."

"What's the address?"

"It's 817 Neeley. It's near Tom's hospital."

"I know the area. On my way." Phillip returned to find C.J. standing at the top of the stairs, waiting for him.

"Is Caroline all right?"

"Not sure. Lock yourself in and don't come out. We'll get back to you as soon as we can," Phillip said, then ran out the door.

* * *

The Safehouse

Rob and Tom parked at the end of the block and got out. Tom checked the clip in his revolver as they approached the house. "Stay close and keep your eyes open," he said.

"Got it."

They went to the back of the house and saw the screen door ripped off its hinges and the door kicked in.

Rob eased forward and looked in. "There's blood on the floor," he whispered.

"Go."

Rob darted inside and fell to the floor with his gun raised. Tom came in behind him, dropped to one knee, and scanned the room. The kitchen was empty. He pointed to the hallway, and Rob jumped up and checked the rest of the house.

When Rob returned, Tom was nowhere in sight. "Where are you?" Rob called.

"Back here," Tom said from behind the kitchen counter. "Wiley's hurt. Come help me turn him over."

Rob slid his gun into his belt and rushed around the counter.

"Did you find Caroline?" Tom asked.

"She's not here." Rob was almost to the counter when he heard someone near the back door. "Someone's here." He rushed to the end of the counter and pointed his gun at the door.

"It's me," Steve said.

"All clear," Tom replied. "Wiley's hurt."

Steve holstered his gun and rushed in to help.

"Get back, Tom, and let us turn him," Rob said.

Tom slid past them and went to the end of the counter. "Be gentle with him."

They turned Wiley over and discovered his face covered with blood. It was coming from his head, lips, and even the corners of his swollen eyes.

"Wow," Steve said. "Someone really beat him."

"Give me a damp cloth," Rob asked. "Maybe I can revive him."

Steve gave him a damp kitchen towel, and Wiley moaned when Rob put it on his head. Rob was still trying to revive him when Phillip rushed in.

"What happened?"

"Back here," Tom said.

Phillip went to the end of the counter and looked down at Wiley. "How bad is it?"

"He's breathing," Steve answered. "That's all we know."

Rob moved the cloth to wipe the blood from Wiley's head and discovered a large gash and two sizable lumps. Wiley moaned and his eyelids fluttered.

"He's coming around," Rob said.

Wiley rolled his eyes and tried to lift his head. "They took . . . they took her."

"Easy, Wiley. Can you sit up?"

"Think . . . think so." Rob lifted him from the floor, and Steve helped get him to a chair.

"Who did this?" Tom asked.

Wiley's head swayed back and forth as he tried to focus.

"Who took Caroline, Wiley?"

He started to touch the gash in his head, but Rob stopped him. "Best you leave that alone."

Phillip got down on one knee and looked into his partner's face. "Who did this to you, buddy?"

"Don't . . . know. I was knocked out as soon as they broke in. I heard her screaming when I came to and tried to get to her, but one of them started hitting me and I blacked out again."

Tom leaned in. "Were they Mexican?"

Wiley slowly shook his head. "Not sure. I heard one of them say something about Muller's warehouse before I passed out. When I came to, they were gone. I managed to get to the phone to page you before everything went black."

Rob placed the wet cloth over the bleeding gash on Wiley's head.

"He needs a hospital."

Wiley waved his hand. "No. You've got to find the woman."

"Where is Muller's warehouse?" Rob asked.

"It's probably in the warehouse district," Phillip said. "This place got a phonebook?"

Steve pointed to the kitchen.

Phillip went over and started opening drawers.

"Found it." He thumbed through the yellow pages as he mumbled, "Muller, Muller, Muller. Here it is. Muller's Storage Warehouse. 1515 Gaiennie Street."

"Is there a map?" Tom asked.

"Yep." Phillip ripped the page from the phone book. "I know where it is."

"Good, you're driving. Steve, see if they took our extra ammo." Tom looked back at Rob. "Call the hospital and get an ambulance. You stay with him until it comes."

"I'm going with you. Caroline's been my responsibility, and I'm seeing this through."

"It's gonna take all of you to get her back," Wiley said. "You all need to go."

"All right," Tom said. "But The Kid is still calling for an ambulance."

Wiley's head bobbled as he tried to speak. "Okay. Sorry, Tom. I must be getting old."

Tom put his hand on his friend's shoulder. "This could have happened to any of us, Wiley."

Phillip got down on one knee. "Don't die on me, old man. I need my partner."

Wiley patted Phillip's cheek. "Stop worrying about me. Take care of yourself. This is a bad bunch."

"I got the ammo," Steve said, coming from the hallway.

"Don't move until the ambulance gets here," Tom insisted.

"Stop fussing over me and save the woman."

They ran out and got in Phillip's car. He turned on the lights and siren and sped away as the first light of day spread over the city.

"Kill the alarm and lights," Tom ordered as they approached the warehouse district. "We don't want them to know we're coming."

"We're almost there," Phillip said. "Gaiennie Street is just a few streets ahead."

"Pull over here." Tom held up his hand. "Steve, hand me a clip."

Steve took one from the bag and gave it to Tom.

"What else do you have?" Tom asked as he pocketed the clip.

"A Glock and additional clips."

"Take all of it. You and Phillip circle around and get to the warehouse without anyone seeing you. Find a way in from the side or the back. We'll take the front."

The two men exited the car, and Rob got behind the wheel.

"How do you want us to handle this?" Rob asked as he drove.

"We're not. You are staying in the car."

"No, you need help. You just got out of the hospital."

"Kid, I've already put your life in danger enough on this trip. I'm not doing it again. If this goes bad, radio it in. Just don't give your name. Then get to the airport and fly home to your family. Understand?"

"I understand." Rob knew arguing was useless and said nothing more as Tom exited the car.

*   *   *

Tom ignored the burning in his side as he hastened to the door of the warehouse. He stepped inside and stood in the shadows, scanning the area for movement. No one was there. He rechecked his revolver out of habit before going deeper into the building. The warehouse was filled with crates, barrels, and shelves stacked high with boxes.

As Tom inched forward, he heard a faint noise and stopped to listen. He heard it again, but this time, it was a high-pitched, muffled sound. He darted between shelving to see where it was coming from and saw Caroline. She was gagged, with her hands tied behind her back, standing atop a barrel near the edge of a large open pit. She had a rope around her neck.

Tom could see the terror in her eyes and rushed towards her.

"I wouldn't touch her if I were you." A man dressed in black stepped from the shadows. Three armed men also appeared and took positions several feet apart.

"Get her down from there," Tom said.

"Don't think so," Jerome said as he pulled out his gun and pointed it at Caroline. "She would have died weeks ago had it not been for your interference. Drop your gun, or she dies now."

"I don't believe you. You want something, or Caroline would already be dead."

"You're right. This is the part of my business I enjoy, G-Man. I wanted to lure you here so we could play a little game."

"What kind of game?"

"Drop your weapon, or I'll see how close I can get this barrel to the edge before it falls in," Jerome said, nudging the side of the barrel with his leg, causing it to wobble. Caroline screamed behind her gag.

"Wait!" Tom shouted. "I'm putting it down," he said, placing his gun on the floor.

"Kick it away," Jerome demanded. When Tom slid the gun across the concrete floor, he said, "That's better. Now, tell your men to join you."

"What men? There's no one here but me."

"Wrong answer, G-man." Jerome inched the barrel closer to the edge.

"Stop, please, stop!" Tom shouted as Caroline continued to scream. "I'm telling the truth. I'm the only one here."

Jerome placed his hands on the container and gave Tom a sideways grin. "You're lying."

"Stop!" Rob shouted as he stepped into view. "I'm coming out."

"See? I knew you didn't come alone. Get over here where I can see you," Jerome ordered.

Rob walked up beside Tom with both hands raised.

"Damn it, Kid," Tom whispered. "I told you to stay back."

"I wasn't going to let you do this without me."

"Stop talking and get rid of the gun," Jerome shouted.

Rob slowly placed his gun on the floor and kicked it away.

"That's better. Now, where are the rest of you?"

"They are caring for the man you almost beat to death."

Jerome cocked his head. "I'm not sure I believe you, but it doesn't matter. They will be easy to find after I'm done with her and you."

Rob peered intently at Jerome.

"What are you looking at?" Jerome asked.

"Those nasty marks around your neck. You were lucky Mama Rue let you live."

"That old witch. I'm going back to put her down after I'm done with you."

"I'm not so sure you can. I saw you screaming like a scared little girl when you ran from her into the fog."

"You are acting awfully brave for someone about to die."

"Not really," Rob said. "Our odds of getting out of here just improved."

Jerome turned and laughed when he saw Wiley behind him with a gun. "I'm surprised you can still walk, old man. But as you see, our plan worked."

"What is he talking about, Wiley?" Tom asked, but didn't get an answer.

"Your friend sold you out, G-Man," Jerome said, chuckling, as Wiley went to stand beside him. "I guess he wasn't the friend you thought he was."

Tom shook his head. "Damn it, Wiley. Why?"

Jerome laughed. "Go ahead. Tell him."

"I had no choice," Wiley said.

"There's always a choice."

Wiley looked at Rob, then back to Tom. "I didn't know until this morning the deal included all of you."

Gunfire erupted outside the building for several minutes, and then it stopped. "Sounds like my people found your friends," Jerome said.

"Someone heard that and called the police," Rob said.

"Unfortunately, you're right. Looks like our little game has to end." Jerome put his hand on the barrel. "Ladies first."

Rob stepped towards him, and Jerome pointed his gun at Tom. "Or should I start with him?"

"Mama Rue was right," Rob said. "You're going straight to hell."

"Let's see. Good-bye, beautiful lady."

Phillip jumped out from the shadows and began firing just as Jerome was about to push Caroline off the barrel. He managed to take down two of Jerome's men before he was shot by the third.

"No!" Wiley shouted and shot the man who had just shot his partner.

Jerome spun around, knocking the barrel out from under Caroline, and fired, hitting Wiley in the chest.

Tom grabbed Caroline's legs and lifted her up to keep the rope from choking her as Rob tackled Jerome.

The two men fought over the gun until Rob was able to knock it from Jerome's hand, causing it to slide across the floor. Jerome responded with a blow to Rob's jaw, stunning him long enough for Jerome to take the knife from the sheath strapped to his leg and slash Rob across the chest.

Rob fell back, giving Jerome time to get to his feet and run from the building. Rob got up and went after him.

Steve limped in from a side door with blood streaming down his leg and helped Tom with Caroline.

"I've got her. Take the rope off her neck," Tom ordered in a strained voice.

"Got it," Steve said. "I'll untie Caroline and check on Phillip. You take care of Wiley."

Tom rushed to the bleeding man. "Hold on, Wiley," he said as he checked the gushing wound.

"It's okay, Tom. It's better this way."

Tom turned and shouted. "Caroline, find a phone and call for an ambulance."

"Don't bother," Wiley said. "I radioed headquarters of a kidnapping on my way here."

"You need to stop talking."

"How . . . how's Phillip?" Wiley managed to say.

Tom turned. "Steve, how is he?"

"It's bad."

Wiley reached up and grabbed Tom's coat. "Save him, Tom. You've got to save him."

"We're trying, Wiley. Please stop talking and save your strength."

"Doesn't matter. The big C is going to kill me in a few months anyway."

"You should have told me."

"Couldn't," Wiley said as he coughed. "I had to make sure Melanie and Kyle would be okay. That's the reason I made the deal with Pascal."

"You didn't have to do it, Wiley. I will take care of your family."

Wiley gasped for air, then said, "I betrayed you, Tom."

Tom squeezed Wiley's hand. "No, you didn't. We're alive because of you. That's what I'm telling Melanie and the Bureau."

Wiley's lips parted to speak, but he didn't get the chance. Tom gently closed his eyes and held him.

CHAPTER THIRTY-FIVE

New Orleans Warehouse District

Rob saw Jerome on the road next to the levee. He took off as fast as he could, causing the gash across his chest to bleed profusely. He saw Jerome glance back before going up the side of the levee. Rob gritted his teeth against the pain and sped up. He tackled Jerome at the top of the levee and both men went down. Jerome struck Rob across the jaw, causing him to lose his grip.

Rob shook off the blow and grabbed Jerome as he descended down the river side of the levee. They fought as they tumbled downward until both men fell off the bulkhead into the river.

Rob surfaced and spun around. He saw Jerome several yards away, swimming toward the middle of the river. Rob put his long legs into action and quickly caught up with him.

He grabbed Jerome and pulled him under, but Jerome wiggled free of his grasp. Rob resurfaced and swam after Jerome, into the growing current. A horn blast sounded ahead of him, and Rob looked up to see a tugboat with barges barreling towards them.

"Get back! Get back!" Rob yelled, but it was too late. The first barge went over Jerome, and he disappeared. The draw of the barges pulled Rob under, and he swam with every ounce of strength he had to break free of its force. After the boat and barges passed, Rob searched the river as waves from the boat washed over him. Suddenly, he heard Mama Rue's voice in his head.

"The mighty Mississippi has a code of its own. It will choose who to swallow up and who it will spit out."

There was no sign of Jerome anywhere. Rob swam back to the levee and pulled himself from the water. He stood and looked across the river one last time before returning to the warehouse. When he arrived, the place was overrun with FBI, police, and ambulances.

Rob slipped between onlookers and police cars until he was close enough to see Tom in the middle of a group of men in dark suits. Rob fell back, went to where the ambulances were, and saw Steve arguing with the attendants as he was being lifted into the back of one of them. There was no sign of Caroline, so he circled around until he saw her being placed in an unmarked car and driven away. He needed to know who had taken her, but knew he couldn't ask.

Rob walked for miles before seeing an approaching trolley. He started to jog to the trolley stop, but as soon as he did, the wounds across his chest opened up and began to bleed again. He pressed his hand against his chest, hoping to stop the flow of blood as the trolley stopped.

"Man, those are some bad cuts," the conductor said when he stepped on board. "Who did that to you?"

Rob looked down at his blood-soaked shirt. "Never argue with your wife when she's shucking oysters."

The conductor chuckled. "I hear you, man. You best take a seat before you scare my passengers to death."

"Good idea."

The conductor clanged the bell, and the trolley started moving as Rob sat. He took his pager from his pocket and pressed the dial, hoping someone had paged him, but the screen didn't light up. Rob shook the device, and water ran out.

There's no way this is working, he thought. *Looks like I'm out here on my own.*

*   *   *

The Garden District

Pascal appeared at his assistant's desk. "Any word?"

"No, sir. Nothing since Jerome called to say he had the woman."

"I told him to call me after it was done."

"Sir, you know he takes great pride in making his victims suffer."

"The man has no conscience," Pascal said. "That's why he's so good at what he does."

"True, but I will be relieved when this ends."

"So will I, Jean-Claude, so will I. We wouldn't be dealing with this if Martínez had taken care of the woman the first time."

"Yes, sir, but look at the bright side. You now possess six containers of drugs worth millions."

"You're right. The drugs and the contract are a double win."

"Well done, sir." Jean-Claude clapped his hands lightly.

"We'll celebrate when I know the woman is dead."

Pascal returned to his office and sat behind his desk. He laced his thick fingers together and rested them on his protruding belly. *A double win*, he thought. *Well done, if I do say so myself.*

*   *   *

Rob got off the trolley and flagged down a cab. "I need to get to the Crescent City Concrete plant in Kenner."

"That's an hour from here," the driver said, looking at Rob's tattered clothing.

"What will it cost?"

"Almost twenty dollars. You good for that?"

Rob took his wallet from his damp pants, opened it, and gave the man twenty-three dollars. "That's all I have."

"No problem. Get in."

When they arrived, Rob approached the guard at the plant's entrance.

"What's your business here?"

"I need to get to the office."

"If you're looking for work, we aren't hiring."

"I'm here to see Mr. Moretti."

"What's your name?"

"Kid."

"Stay put while I check." The guard entered his booth and picked up the phone. A couple of minutes later, he stepped out. "He's waiting for you in the main office."

Rob got directions from the guard. When he entered the office, a woman at the reception desk gasped as he approached her.

"I'm here to see C.J. Moretti."

"Top of the staircase," she said, staring at his blood-soaked shirt.

Rob climbed the stairs and went into the first office.

"Oh, my gosh," a woman said, jumping up from her desk. "Sit down. I'm calling for an ambulance."

"Don't. It's not as bad as it looks. I need to see C.J."

"He's in Miss Caroline's office. I'm Abigail, her secretary. If I can't get you to a hospital, I insist our plant nurse take a look at you," she said as she led him into the next office.

"Oh my God!" C.J. said, coming around the desk.

"Relax, C.J. I'm fine," Rob said, easing into a chair.

"What happened?"

"Caroline was taken by Pascal's men. She is safe now, but Phillip, Steve, and another agent were hurt getting her back."

"Where is she now?"

"With the FBI, I think. I need you to find out where she is and get her here before Pascal discovers she's alive."

"Dear Lord. I was so caught up in finding three million dollars for the bid proposal that I didn't realize you were going through all that."

"What three million?"

"The company has two million in reserves. If I can show they have five, it will put them at the top of the contenders for the levee bid. I could handle it myself, but there's not enough time to move my assets around."

"I'll take care of the money. You get on the phone and find out where the Feds have taken Caroline."

"How are you coming up with three million dollars so fast?"

"Stop worrying about the money. The safehouse was compromised. This plant is the safest place for all of us now."

"I will make a few calls. I still have contacts down here."

Abigail returned with the nurse as C.J. picked up the phone.

"Let me look at you," the nurse ordered.

Rob flinched as he pulled the shirt from his wounds.

"You should go to the hospital. These cuts are deep and need cleaning before they are stitched."

"I'm not going anywhere. Can you do that here?"

"You're going to need an infusion of antibiotics. The last thing you want is an infection."

"I understand, but there isn't time. Please, do what you can. I promise to take care of it as soon as possible."

"You better. The longer you wait puts you at greater risk of infection."

"I understand," Rob said, nodding, "but I don't have a choice."

"All right then. I'll do my best to minimize the damage. Let's get you down to the infirmary."

"I'll go right after I speak to Abigail."

"While you two talk, I'll go get set up," the nurse said, and left the room.

"I found her," C.J. said, coming around the desk.

"Great. Bring her here, but don't tell anyone where you're taking her."

"I won't." He rushed out the door.

"What do you need from me?" Abigail asked.

"I need your help to save the Levee Board bid."

"What can I do?"

"C.J. said the company needs at least three million more to win the contract. I can make that happen, but to do it, I'll need the tracking and account numbers for the company's reserve account."

"Can't we wait until Miss Caroline gets here? I'm uncomfortable giving that information to someone I just met."

Rob glanced at the clock on the wall. "The money is coming from a bank in Zurich. If we wait, it won't get here in time for the bid submission."

She stood, contemplating his request. "I guess if Miss Caroline and C.J. trust you, I can too. Take a seat and I'll get the information for you."

"I can't call Zurich from here. There's a good chance Pascal has these lines tapped. Where is the closest pay phone?"

"There's one in the employee break room. Let me get what we need, and we'll go."

"One more thing," Rob said, pushing himself from the chair. "I need money to make the call. I used the last I had getting here."

"I'll grab the petty cash bag."

Rob started to rebutton his shirt, but Abigail pushed his hands away.

"You aren't putting that thing back on. Stay where you are." She left the office and returned shortly with a clean, pressed work shirt. "You can change into this after you see the nurse."

Abigail got what they needed from her desk, and Rob followed her to the break room. When they arrived, two women were sitting at a table.

"Sorry ladies, we need this room," Abigail said. The ladies left without a word, and she closed the door behind them. Then she handed Rob several rolls of quarters from the petty cash bag.

Rob opened one of the rolls, dropped a coin into the phone, and dialed the operator.

"Overseas operator, please." It took almost twenty minutes and two rolls of coins before the banker in Zurich answered.

"Eric, this is Robert Chambers. Thank you for taking my call. I know it is almost closing time, but this is important."

"We are never closed for you, Mr. Chambers. How can I be of service?"

"I need three million dollars wired from one of my accounts to an account in the United States, and it has to be done tonight."

"As you wish. Which account and where will it be wired?"

Rob gave him the account number, glancing at Abigail as he spoke. "I have a lady here who will give you the information on where it's to be wired."

"Of course."

Rob placed his hand over the phone. "I'll step out while you speak to him. After you're done, ask him to hold."

Abigail took the phone. A few minutes later, she opened the door, and Rob returned to the phone.

"It's imperative that the money be in that account before you leave your office, Eric."

"Most certainly."

"Thank you. This means a lot to me."

"You are most welcome, Mr. Chambers."

Rob hung up and turned to Abigail. "The transaction will be completed today. I suggest you call your bank to tell them it's coming."

"Shouldn't I do that here, from the pay phone? You said Pascal could be listening."

Rob pondered her question. "No. Call from your office. I want Pascal to hear about this."

"You can tell me why after you get those wounds looked after."

*　　*　　*

It was almost dark when C.J. walked into Caroline's office alone.

"Where is she?" Rob asked, getting to his feet.

"She's here. Abigail grabbed her out in the hallway."

"Did you have any trouble getting her released?"

"Have you met Special Agent Ashcroft? He grilled me for over an hour before allowing me to see her."

"Was Tom there?"

"I never saw him."

Caroline walked into the room and dropped into a chair. "I'm not sure what's worse, being almost hanged or being questioned by the FBI."

Rob smiled wearily. "What did you tell them?"

"Everything. Why Jack was shot, who was behind the hospital attack, and why Pascal kidnapped me. That should be enough to get him arrested."

"I wish it were, but don't count on it."

"Did you have time to handle the money issue?" C.J. asked.

"What money issue?"

Rob took a faxed copy from Caroline's desk and gave it to her.

"This says three million dollars was wired to our account." She glanced from the fax to her old friend. "Why did you do this, C.J.?"

C.J. shook his head. "I didn't. It was him."

"Kid, I'm alive because of you. I can't let you do this."

"It's done, Caroline. The Levee Board has to see that you are more than financially stable," Rob said.

"Even if we win the contract, it could be a year or more before I can repay you."

"That's not an issue."

Caroline shook her head. "I appreciate this, but I'm not sure it will help. How am I going to explain this sudden influx of funds?"

Rob paused a moment. "Tell them it came from a silent partner."

"But the Board will need documentation on this partner."

"Then I'll be that partner," C.J. said. "I'll repay the loan, and we can either make our partnership temporary or official. That's for you to decide."

"Are you sure this is necessary?"

"Yes, Caroline, it is," Rob answered.

"If it's any comfort," C.J. added, "everything else looks great."

"Except for one thing. Jack isn't here."

"I have a suggestion for both of you," Rob added. "What if C.J. takes on the role of business manager during Jack's absence? As a partner, it's a perfect fit. And from what I've seen, he's already been doing it since we left. You two can decide how long he keeps that position after you win the contract."

C.J. looked at Caroline. "I think it's an excellent idea."

"But what about your family and your company in Philadelphia?"

"With you back, I think we can handle it. I know my wife will be thrilled. She's been telling me she wants more time with her family, and they're all here."

"But if you're here, who will run your company?" Caroline asked.

"I've got good people, and so do you. My people will handle things as I go back and forth between plants. It's not forever, Caroline. It's only till Jack recovers."

Caroline looked down at her wedding ring and rolled her fingers over it.

"Jack is coming back," C.J. said. "It may take some time, but he will."

Rob placed his hand on Caroline's shoulder. "What did Mama Rue tell you?"

"She told me all I needed was faith, love, and hope to make miracles." She looked up at him. "Do you believe it's true?"

Rob thought back to what had happened at the river. "Everything she's said so far has proven true. Why not this?"

"Then let's do it."

C.J. picked up the phone and buzzed the secretary. "Abigail, can you come in?"

"The bid is due tomorrow," Caroline said as Abigail entered the room. "I'm afraid we need the entire proposal to be retyped. Can you stay until it's done?"

"I already called my husband an hour ago and told him not to wait up for me."

C.J. gathered up the documents and handed them to Caroline. "Review this stack and give them to Abigail to type while I draw up our new partnership."

Rob went over to C.J. and whispered. "Before you do that, I need to speak with you in private."

C.J. nodded and Rob followed him down the hallway to Jack's office. "What's on your mind?"

"The partnership needs to be drawn up in your full name," Rob said.

"Why? Most of the Board members only know me as C.J."

"I understand, but it's important."

"I'm not following you."

"I'm asking you to trust me on this, C.J."

C.J. thought for a moment before answering. "If you're willing to put three million dollars of your own money into this," he said finally, "you can call me Peter Pan for all I care."

"Not sure that will work with the Board, but thanks."

"I'm surprised we haven't heard back from your friend Tom."

"So am I."

*   *   *

Garden District

Jean-Claude hung up the phone and rushed into Pascal's office. "I just received word that all of Jerome's crew is dead."

"And Jerome?"

"He wasn't one of them."

"What about the woman?"

Jean-Claude hesitated a moment before shaking his head. "The FBI has her."

Pascal pounded his desk. "Damn it, why isn't she dead?" He pushed away from his desk and started to pace. "Who do we have that can clean up this mess?"

"Sir, it will take days to bring another crew in."

"We don't have days. The bid deadline is tomorrow. There has to be a way to stop that woman from submitting her bid."

"We could have some of our men block all the doors to the Levee Board offices?"

"Do it, and tell them to search every person that enters that office, even couriers and mail carriers."

"Sir, tampering with the US mail is a federal offense."

"That is the least of my worries, Jean-Claude. Get it handled."

CHAPTER THIRTY-SIX

The Plant

Rob was awakened by the sound of a ringing telephone. He lifted his head from Caroline's desk and realized it was coming from Abigail's office. He saw Caroline sleeping on the sofa and C.J. snoring in a chair across from him with his feet propped up on the edge of the desk. They were all exhausted after working until three in the morning to finish the proposal.

Rob slipped out as quietly as he could to answer the phone.

"Crescent City Concrete," he said with a yawn.

"Kid, is that you?"

"Tom! Where are you? I've been worried that something happened to you."

"At the hospital. Where the heck have you been? I've been paging you all night."

"My pager died when I went swimming in the Mississippi River. How are our people?"

Tom paused before responding. "We lost one. Waiting for one to be released, and not sure about another. How are you?"

"Nothing that a few stitches won't fix."

"Is this line safe?"

"Questionable."

"Then we'll discuss the rest later."

"How much trouble are you in?" Rob asked.

"Not certain. Stay put until I get there." The call ended.

Rob noticed the date on Abigail's desk calendar as he hung up the phone and realized it had been a month since he had seen his family. Every fiber in his body longed to be with them, but he knew this wasn't over.

Caroline and C.J. were awake when he returned.

"Who was that?" Caroline asked.

"Tom. He's at the hospital with our injured men. He's coming here as soon as he can."

C.J. shook his head. "That means we have to do this without him."

"If you're having second thoughts, I can do it," Rob said.

"No. It's my turn. You're better at protecting Caroline than I am."

"Well, you're not going anywhere looking like that," she said.

"What choice do I have? My suitcase is at the safe house."

"You will find everything you need down the hallway. Jack and I had a bathroom and closet built in the office for unexpected situations like this."

"Then I had better get moving," C.J. said, and left.

Caroline sat on the arm of the sofa and looked at Rob. "I don't understand why you are doing this. Helping me secure this bid with your money has nothing to do with protecting your family."

"In a way, it does. I was the one who set up the introduction between the drug organization and Marcel Pascal."

"I find it hard to believe you would get involved with people like that."

"It wasn't by choice, I promise you," Rob said. "But that's a story I'm not free to tell."

"I'm beginning to think we should just forget about the bid before anyone else gets hurt."

"We went over that last night, Caroline. You, of all people, know what's at stake if Pascal wins that contract."

"I know. I'm just scared."

It wasn't long before the offices were filled with employees. Rob went to the break room and when he returned with a pot of coffee, C.J. was there with Caroline.

"The jacket's a little tight," he said, flexing his shoulders, "but I think it will work."

Caroline went to him and straightened his tie. "Just keep the jacket unbuttoned. You look great."

Rob handed him a briefcase. "Are you sure about this?"

"Like I said, it's my turn."

"I'm certain by now Pascal has gotten word that Caroline's alive. He will stop at nothing to keep her from submitting her bid. If it gets dangerous, don't put yourself at risk. Just give him the bid."

"We've come this far. I'm ready to see it through." C.J. glanced at his watch. "Traffic is a nightmare this time of the morning. It will take me a couple of hours just to get into the city."

"I have a car downstairs waiting for you," Caroline said. "Take care of yourself, C.J."

"Stop worrying. I can do this."

They went with him to the top of the stairs and watched him go out the door.

"I guess all we do now is wait." Caroline sighed.

* * *

It took over two hours for C.J. to get to the Levee Board's office building.

"Do you want me to take you to the door?" the driver asked.

C.J. gripped the briefcase in his lap. "No, drop me off here."

"Are you sure? We are two blocks away."

"I'm sure."

The driver pulled to the curb. "I'll park here and wait for you."

C.J. walked to the building but went to a side entrance instead of the front door. He took the stairs to the second-floor landing and looked down into the lobby.

He wasn't surprised to see two men standing near the doors of the Board offices. One was tall, with dark hair and a muscular build. His shirt clung to him as if he had been poured into it, making his arms and chest look enormous. The other man was short, heavier than the first, and almost bald.

C.J. was about to go down when a woman came in the front door wearing a scarf over her hair. She had her handbag tucked under her arm and was carrying a white box. The shorter man stepped in front of her as she approached the door of the Levee Board office.

"Excuse me," she said. "I need to pass."

"What's in the box, lady?"

"I beg your pardon. That's none of your business."

"I'm making it my business. Now show me what's in the box."

"If you must know, it's my daughter's birthday, and she prefers beignets over cake. So, being a good mama, I've brought her a box of her favorites from Café Du Monde."

"Open it," the muscleman ordered.

"What on earth for?"

"You heard him, lady. Open the box."

"Why? I already told you it's pastries."

"Stop arguing and open the damn box," the shorter man demanded.

C.J. watched from the landing as the woman raised the lid, revealing the sugar-covered squares.

"Satisfied?" she asked.

"Not yet." The shorter man snatched one of the squares, tapped the sugar from the beignet into the box, and shoved it in his mouth. "Now, open your purse," he mumbled, spraying crumbs as he spoke.

The woman closed the lid and placed the box on the floor. The little man snatched her purse from her hands before she could open it. He jerked it open and started digging through her bag.

"You can't do that!"

"I'll do whatever I like to this, and to you, if you try to stop me."

When C.J. heard that, he raced back down the stairs, went around the corner to the building's main entrance, and walked inside.

"Let her go," the muscleman said. "This could be our guy."

The woman snatched her purse from the man, picked up the box, and hurried into the Levee Board office.

C.J. tried to go around the man but was blocked by his beefy arm.

"Please step aside," he said. "I need to get into that office. I'm almost out of time."

"Hand over that briefcase."

C.J. clutched the case to his chest. "I will not."

"We'll see about that." The muscleman snatched the briefcase from his hands and handed it to the shorter man before shoving C.J. against the wall.

"Give it back," C.J. shouted as he tried to break free. "Those are legal documents."

"More reason for us to have a look," the muscleman said.

"I think this is it." The shorter man dropped the case, ripped open the tab of a large envelope, and started to read.

C.J. reached for the document. "Give that back!"

"Hold him," ordered the muscleman as he snatched the document from the little man's hand.

The shorter man pushed his hand against C.J.'s chest and lifted his shirt with the other to reveal a holstered gun.

"Stay put, or I'll use it."

"Well, look what we have here," the muscleman said. "It's the Crescent City Concrete bid."

"You have no right to that. Give it back, or I'm filing charges."

"File anything you like. You aren't getting this."

All heads turned when the doors to the Levee Board office opened. A young woman stepped out, saw the three men, and hurriedly hung a sign on a hook next to the door before retreating and closing the door behind her.

The muscleman nodded to the sign. "What does it say?"

The little man hurried over. "*Bid submission for project 78395 levee maintenance is closed.*"

The tall man grabbed C.J.'s briefcase and shoved it into his arms. "What a shame. Looks like you missed it."

"Give me that bid!" C.J. ordered, reaching for the document.

"Nope. I think my boss will find this interesting reading, especially now that it's worthless." He gave C.J. a shove. "Let's go. Our work here is done."

*   *   *

The Plant

Rob heard familiar voices outside the office and rushed out to find Tom carrying crutches and holding onto Steve as he hopped up the stairs.

"Stop," Steve scoffed. "It's easier if I do this myself."

"Are you all right down there?" Rob called out.

"I have a hole in my leg!" Steve shouted. "There's nothing right about it." Tom stayed behind him as he took one step at a time.

"I'm surprised they let you out of the hospital," Rob said when Steve finally reached the top.

"Steve wasn't the problem," Tom explained. "Ashcroft showed up at the hospital to ask us more questions."

Steve took the crutches from Tom. "For a minute there, I thought he was going to lock us up."

"What changed his mind?"

"Tom told him about the drugs on Pascal's docks, and he rushed off."

"I'm sure he's calling every judge he knows to get a warrant," Tom added.

"He's going to have a hard time getting one," Caroline said. "Pascal has most of them on his payroll."

Tom glanced into the office. "Where's C.J.?"

"I'm here," C.J. said, coming up the staircase behind them.

"Did it work?" Rob asked.

Tom glanced from C.J. to Rob. "Did what work?"

"Let's go into Caroline's office," Rob said. "We have a lot to tell you."

Steve took the sofa, and Caroline pushed the coffee table closer so he could prop up his injured leg. Then she closed her office door.

"What's going on, Kid?" Tom asked.

"C.J. delivered the bid this morning."

"Well, not exactly," C.J. said with a grin.

"Stop," Tom said, raising a hand. "Just tell me what happened."

"Two of Pascal's men snatched the bid from my briefcase and kept me pinned against the wall until the time ran out to submit it."

Steve's face grew dark. "What? You mean we went through all this for nothing?"

"Calm down, Steve," Rob said. "What did they do with the bid, C.J.?"

"They took it. One of the goons said the boss would enjoy reading it."

Steve shook his head. "Dang that Ashcroft. We would have been here to help if he hadn't shown up."

Caroline grabbed C.J.'s arm. "Where's Abigail?"

"I don't know. I thought she would have been here by now."

"Wait a minute," Tom said. "Who's Abigail?"

"My assistant," Caroline said.

"What does your assistant have to do with this?"

"I suspected Pascal was going to do everything he could to keep Caroline's bid from being submitted," Rob explained. "So Abigail was our backup."

"Kid, why on earth would you send a woman into this?"

Before anyone answered, Abigail rushed into the office waving a paper.

"It worked, it worked!" she shouted. "Here's the stamped receipt to prove our bid was submitted."

Caroline wrapped her arms around her assistant and hugged her. "I was worried sick. Where have you been?"

"Wait just a minute," Tom said, waving his hands. "C.J. just said Pascal's men took the proposal."

"They did," C.J. replied. "But Kid anticipated that and had Abigail make two original proposals. She had one, and I took the other."

"I nearly died when that hoodlum snatched a beignet," Abigail said. "I was terrified he was going to keep the whole box."

"Hold on," Steve said. "What's so important about a box of beignets?"

"The beignets were also Kid's idea," Caroline said. "Just let Abigail explain."

All eyes turned to Abigail.

"I went to Café Du Monde early this morning and asked them to let me put a white envelope in the bottom of the box before they lined it with wax paper and filled my order."

C.J. took a step closer. "When I saw that guy snatch a pastry, that was my cue to get down there and distract them."

"And it worked," Abigail explained. "The men forgot about me as soon as C.J. walked in. That's when I grabbed the box and my handbag, ran into the Levee Board office, and turned in our proposal!"

"What took you so long to get back?" Caroline asked.

"I stayed in the office until I was sure those men were gone. The staff didn't mind. I told them I had brought the beignets for them."

"Great idea, making C.J. the decoy, Kid," Tom said, grinning with pride.

"Thanks, but it was these two that made it work."

"Yeah," Steve said. "But now Pascal has Caroline's bid."

"True," Tom said. "And once Pascal realizes he was tricked, he'll come after her with a vengeance, and she'll be worse off than before."

"Then let's hope the other part of Kid's plan works," C.J. said as he removed the snug-fitting coat.

"There's more to this?" Tom asked.

"A lot more," Caroline said. "C.J. has agreed to be the company's business manager until Jack returns."

"That's great for your company," Tom said, "but how will that protect you from Pascal?"

"Kid provided financing to shore up the proposal, and the bid shows the funds came from C.J., our new silent partner."

"Okay," Tom said. "There has to be more to this?"

"There is," C.J. added. "Kid had me sign the document Cheyman Jacopo Moretti instead of C.J. Moretti."

Steve started to chuckle. "I get it. You want Pascal to think the Philadelphia mob's buying into Caroline's company."

"It's a long shot, I know," Rob said, "but it was worth a shot."

"Maybe having the same name as my uncle does have value after all."

"That's great," Steve said, "but what happens when Pascal checks it out?"

"That's the part I haven't figured out," Rob said, turning to Tom. "Do you have any ideas?"

"You just sprung this on me, Kid. Give me a little time."

C.J. glanced around the room. "Now that the bid is in, what do you want us to do?"

"There's nothing we can do except hope that Ashcroft gets his warrants. If he does, Pascal's attention will be on Ashcroft, not Caroline."

"If that's the case, I want to see Jack," Caroline said.

All eyes went to Tom.

"I agree with Caroline," Steve added. "She should see her husband."

Rob flinched in pain as he sat down on the arm of the sofa. "It's time, Tom. They've been separated long enough. Pascal thinks he's won. He's not concerned with her now."

"True, but that will soon change. Before we worry about that, though, let me see how badly you're hurt."

Rob opened his shirt. "It looks worse than it is."

"Dang it, boy. You are being held together with tape."

"It's all we could do at the moment."

"Ouch," Steve said. "I thought my leg was bad. What happened to the guy who did that to you?"

"He's at the bottom of the Mississippi River."

Tom chuckled. "What is it with you and water?"

"So, Mama Rue was right about you too," Caroline said.

Tom glanced from her to Rob. "Who is this woman you keep talking about?"

"I'll tell you when this is over," Rob said, rebuttoning his shirt. "Let's figure out the safest way we can get Caroline in to see her husband."

"Not you, Kid. The only place you're going is home."

"Tom, Steve's hurt, Phillip's in the hospital, and Caroline said Wiley is dead. You need me." A grin crossed Rob's lips. "I'm all you have left."

"Hold on," Steve said. "I'm injured, not incapacitated."

"You know what I meant."

"Ashcroft knows someone was helping us other than Steve, Phillip, and Wiley. He was pressuring us to tell him who you were," Tom said.

"Steve and I managed to avoid answering him, but the longer you're here, the greater the chances of him discovering the truth."

"Wait a minute," C.J. said. "If Kid isn't working for you, who is he?"

The room went silent.

"I'm just someone who has been through the same thing Caroline has," Rob said.

"I asked Kid to help us," Tom said. "That's all you need to know, C.J."

"Well, from where I stand, he's missed his calling. I think the FBI should hire him."

"No thanks," Rob said. "Not my line of work."

Tom took a moment to respond. "Fine. You can come, but you're going to the airport as soon as we're done."

"It's a deal."

CHAPTER THIRTY-SEVEN

Ochsner Hospital

Two cars pulled into the hospital parking lot later that evening. C.J. and Rob were in one, and Tom, Steve, and Caroline were in the other. Tom parked near the rear entrance and got out. Steve opened the passenger door and began fighting with his crutches.

"You need to stay here and watch our back," Tom said. "You'll draw too much attention, hobbling around on those things. If we run into trouble, I'll page you."

"Sure, and I'll just crawl to a phone and call for backup."

"I'm certain you'll figure something out. Let's go, Caroline."

When Tom and Caroline entered the hospital, Rob and C.J. were waiting near the door.

"Find the service elevator," Tom ordered.

Rob went down the hall and returned a few minutes later. "This way." They followed him and took the service elevator to the fifth floor. When the doors opened, they were met by a familiar face.

"Well, this is a surprise," Nurse Bennett said, smiling at Tom. "I was sure you would be dead by now."

"Sorry about that. There was an urgent matter I had to handle."

"And here I thought it was because I offended you."

"Trust me, that wasn't the case."

Rob scanned the hallway. "Where are the agents and police?"

"Something happened in the warehouse district and they were called away. Why are you here?"

"We're here to protect Mrs. Broussard. Can you help us get her in to see her husband?"

"Of course, but only if you agree to allow the doctor to check you before you leave."

Tom shook his head. "I can't. It's best if no one knows we're here."

"Then at least let me check your incisions. But I warn you, if I see you've torn something loose, you're staying."

"Fine, but after Mrs. Broussard sees her husband."

"Agreed. Let's go."

Nurse Bennett took them to Jack's room. C.J. and Caroline went to Jack's side as Rob and Tom stood near the door.

"How are you, sweetheart?" Caroline said, kissing Jack's cheek.

"Caroline, I can't believe it's you. I've been going crazy worrying."

"I'm fine, honey. It's so good to see you."

"You shouldn't be here, sweetheart."

"It's all right. These men are taking great care of me."

"Hey, buddy."

"C.J., is that you?"

"You're a hard man to get to see."

"Definitely not by choice. Come closer so I can see your face."

"We have so much to tell you, Jack," Caroline said.

"And little time to do it," Tom said from the door.

"And I have something to tell you," Jack said, "but you go first."

"We submitted our bid today."

"That's great, honey. But I'm afraid with me in here, there's no guarantee we'll win. The Board will think you'll need my help to complete the contract."

Caroline glanced at C.J., then back to her husband. "We've handled that."

"How?"

"She's not alone," C.J. said. "We'll explain how when we have more time."

"So you think we have a chance?"

"More than a chance."

Nurse Bennett came to the door. "We are about to have a lot of people on the floor. I was just notified a new patient is coming up."

"How long do we have?" Tom asked.

"About fifteen minutes. We are putting the patient in the next room."

"Thank you," Tom replied.

Rob caught sight of the smile Tom gave her before she left.

"Sorry to cut this short," Tom said. "We must go."

"No," Caroline said, gripping her husband's hand. "We haven't heard what Jack has to tell me."

"Not so much tell as show. Can one of you uncover my feet?"

C.J. lifted the sheet off his feet.

"This may take a moment, but watch." Jack closed his eyes and tightened his jaw.

Caroline gasped as Jack's toes started to move. "Jack, it's a miracle." She turned and kissed him. "You're going to walk! You're going to walk."

"It's a start, Caroline. I still have a long way to go. The doctors said months, maybe a year, before I know how much ability I'll have."

"It doesn't matter how long it takes. You're going to walk, Jack Broussard. I know it."

Nurse Bennett came to the door. "They're here."

"Time to go, Caroline," Tom said.

Caroline placed a hand on each side of Jack's face. "As soon as this is over, I'm never letting you out of my sight again."

"I can't wait."

"C.J.," Tom said, "take Caroline and drive her and Steve back to the plant. Kid and I have something to do here before we head to the airport."

Caroline grabbed Rob and gave him a hug. "I'm sorry for all the trouble I gave you while you were protecting me."

"I have to say you did make it interesting, Caroline. Take care of yourself."

Tom motioned to C.J. and said, "Get her to the car."

C.J. ushered Caroline out the door and went to the service elevator.

"Kid, you're coming with me," Tom said.

They went out and found Nurse Bennett waiting.

"Are you ready?"

"We are," Tom said, nodding.

"We?" she questioned.

"He needs your help first."

The door blew open at the end of the hallway. Orderlies pushed a gurney, followed by nurses and doctors.

"You drive a hard bargain, Agent Neal. Come with me."

"Tom. My name is Tom."

She smiled and took them down the hallway.

*   *   *

Garden District
Two weeks later

Jean-Claude entered his employer's office and handed Pascal a large manila envelope.

"What's this?" Pascal asked.

"It's the Crescent City bid proposal. I had our man hold on to it after we got word that the FBI was seeking warrants for our office and the dock warehouses."

"Good thinking. The last thing I needed was the FBI or police finding our competitor's bid in my possession." Pascal opened the envelope. "It doesn't matter what it says, though. It was never submitted."

"True, but this will give you an idea of what the company's worth when you take them over."

"Doesn't matter. I'll purchase them for pennies on the dollar." Pascal flipped through pages of the document until he came to a specific section. "Didn't you tell me she only had two million in her reserves?"

"I did," Jean-Claude said.

"Then why does this say she has five?"

"I don't know. Do you want me to check?"

"Never mind. The Levee Board never saw it." He read a few lines more. "Says here the money came from a partner."

"Who would be so bold as to join her against you?"

Pascal looked up at his assistant. "Cheyman Jacopo Moretti."

Jean-Claude crossed himself. "Dear Lord. Were you aware that the Philadelphia mob was moving into our territory?"

"I wasn't, but this sounds like they may try."

Jean-Claude crossed himself again. "Jaco is known for eliminating everyone in their path, including family members. Sir, what are we going to do?"

Pascal got to his feet and started to pace. "There has to be a reason for him to be coming here. We need to find out why so I can change his mind."

"Yes, sir, but if he is already a partner in the Cresent City plant, he may already own other locations."

"You're right. Book a flight and hotel for my wife and daughters. I want them out of the country as fast as possible. I suggest you do the same for your parents."

Jean-Claude ran from the room.

The Apartment

"I just got a call from the gate guard," Wanda said to Rob as he sat on their living room floor playing blocks with Sarah. "Tom Neal is on his way in. I hope he's not here to ask you to make another trip. It's taken weeks for your wounds to heal."

"Martínez is dead, sweetheart. There's no reason for me to go anywhere."

There was a knock, and Wanda picked up Sarah and followed Rob to the door.

"This is a surprise," Rob said. "I haven't heard from you in months."

"Sorry about that. A lot has happened since I put you on that plane in New Orleans."

"Hello, stranger," Wanda said, balancing Sarah on her hip. "We were getting worried about you."

"It's good to see you, Wanda." Tom handed Rob the bag he was holding and took Sarah from her mother. "How's this little lady doing?"

"She had her second birthday a couple of months ago," Rob said.

"I know." Tom reached into the bag Rob was holding and placed a doll in Sarah's arms. "Happy birthday, little one. Sorry I missed your big day."

Sarah wrapped her arms around the doll and hugged it.

"You spoil her, Tom," Wanda said with a smile.

"She deserves it."

"Something about you is different," Wanda said. "This is the first time I've seen you in anything but a suit."

Tom looked down at his shirt and khakis. "More has changed than my clothes, Wanda. That's the reason I'm here."

"Do I have to leave the room?"

"Absolutely not. Some of this involves you."

"Me?"

"Yes. All three of you," Tom said.

"Don't say anything about us until I return," Wanda said, taking her daughter from his arms. "We are potty training."

Rob gestured to the sofa after Wanda left. "Have a seat."

Tom settled in, and Rob took the chair across from him. "Have you gotten any updates on Caroline and Jack?"

"I have. They are moving to Philadelphia."

"That's a surprise. I was sure their company would win the Levee Maintenance contract."

"Oh, she got it. But after they won, Caroline and Jack decided to merge their company with C.J.'s. Caroline will run C.J.'s Philadelphia plant, and he will run the Crescent City plant. This way, Jack can focus on recovering without having to worry about Pascal."

"So C.J. is staying in New Orleans?"

"He and his family will stay until Jack has recovered enough to return to work. Then they will exchange places."

"That's great news. I'm glad to hear you are still getting reports on them."

"Actually, I'm not. I just returned from there to see Phillip and check on Wiley's family."

"How are they?"

"Phillip is making progress, but complications from his injuries have limited his activities. He was told he would never be in the field again. The Bureau offered him a desk job, but Phillip refused and took early retirement. But I think you already knew that?"

Rob shook his head. "What are you talking about?"

"Not long after you left, both Phillip and Wiley's wife and son received a substantial fund from an anonymous benefactor."

"That's great news."

"Don't play dumb with me, Kid. I know it was you."

Rob paused a moment before answering. "Steve told me that C.J.

contacted him about repaying the money I put into Caroline's account. I told him to ask C.J. to have his attorneys set up trusts for Wiley's family and Phillip and split the three million between them. I made Steve and C.J. promise to keep me out of it."

"Thanks, Kid. They really needed it."

"Don't thank me. You know that money came from the drug organization's accounts we moved before you secured my deal with the FBI. Phillip and Wiley's family deserved it. Did Ashcroft find Martínez's drugs?"

Tom leaned back and crossed his arms. "Nope. Pascal moved them before his warehouses were searched."

"What about the bodies in the swamps and the men killed on the docks?"

"Without Jerome, there was no way to pin any of it on Pascal."

"Not even Caroline's kidnapping?"

"The only way to prove Pascal was behind any of it would be with Jerome's testimony."

"We both know that isn't going to happen. So, this means Pascal remains in control and can continue to torment Caroline, Jack, and C.J. . . ."

"Yes, but I'm not so sure he will. Several days after you left, C.J. called his uncle to tell him that Pascal may contact him."

"If C.J.'s uncle tells Pascal he's not part of the deal with Caroline, Pascal will go after Caroline and C.J. out of revenge."

"Let me finish. A few weeks later, Jaco called C.J. and said Pascal had called him and wanted to know if he was part owner of Crescent City Concrete. Jaco told Pascal that Crescent City Concrete was a family business and to leave it and its people alone, or he would make Pascal regret it."

Rob shook his head. "I wasn't expecting that. Do you think Pascal believed him?"

"Wouldn't you, if you knew Jaco's reputation? Your plan worked, Kid. Pascal hasn't gone near them since."

"That's great news. So everything turned out for the best."

This time, it was Tom who paused. "Not everything. Wiley lost the last few months of life with his family. Phillip nearly died because of my need to avenge my son's death. And I almost got you killed and your family tossed out of the protection program. It's time I let this go."

"Those trips were my choice, Tom. My family is safe now that Martínez is dead. Once the chemist Alejandro is found, we will finally be completely free."

"That's part of the reason I'm here. I heard from Sam."

"Cigarette smoking, CIA Sam in Mexico?"

Tom chuckled. "There's only one Sam."

Before Tom could explain more, Sarah ran into the room with her baby doll, went straight to Tom, and held up her hands. He picked her up and placed her in his lap.

"Baby play," she said.

"I'm a little out of practice, sweetie. What does the baby want to play?"

"Airplane."

"Sorry, Tom," Wanda said. "That's Sarah and Rob's favorite game."

"She's fine," Tom said. "I love her company."

"Have I missed anything?" Wanda asked, taking a seat in a chair next to Rob.

"Your timing is perfect. I shared the information you gave us about Alejandro's family connection with Sam, and he put his people on it at once. The CIA found Alejandro hiding in Mexico City at one of his father's medical clinics."

"Does that mean it's over?" Wanda asked.

"Not quite. Rob still has to testify at his trial, but now that Alejandro's in custody, the Bureau can move you to a new location."

Rob looked at his wife. "Are you ready for that?"

"More than ready."

Rob nodded, then turned back to Tom. "So everyone responsible for your son's death is either dead now or in prison."

"I know. That's why I've decided to do something different with my life."

"Like what?"

"After we left New Orleans, Hoover ordered me back to Virginia."

"It sounds like Ashcroft had something to do with that."

"Oh, he did. He claimed the death toll increase in New Orleans was due to my interference."

"Didn't the director know that you ended the killing sprees Martínez conducted for Pascal?"

"He did, which was why I was told I was too valuable to continue in the field and was given a promotion. Hoover wanted me to oversee all field office operations nationwide, making me next in line to him."

"Tom, I can't see you sitting behind a desk," Wanda said.

"Neither could I, so I thanked him for the opportunity and resigned."

"You what?" Rob said. "Tom, the Bureau is your life!"

"Not anymore."

"What are you going to do?"

"I've lived a rather conservative life, and between savings and retirement, I have enough to open my own private investigation office. After thirty-plus years with the Bureau, I'm ready to pick my own cases instead of being told which ones to work."

"Will you stay in Virginia?" Wanda asked.

"I'm done with that. I've been thinking about opening my office further south."

Rob chuckled. "Does this have anything to do with a certain nurse?"

Tom tried to contain his smile but couldn't. "I have no idea what you're talking about."

Wanda scooted to the edge of her seat. "If you're not with the Bureau, how did you get through our gates?"

"Good question. Before I resigned, I secured a well-earned promotion for Steve. He is now your handler. Steve gave me clearance to see you."

"That's a relief," Rob said as he glanced at Wanda. "Having Steve as our handler will make it easier to give the rest of the drug money to the Bureau."

"Kid, are you sure about this?"

"With Rojas and Martínez dead and Alejandro now in custody, there's no need to keep it."

"It's dirty money, Tom," Wanda added. "We want no part of it."

"If you're sure, then I'll talk to Steve, and we can come up with a way to handle it so the Bureau doesn't question why you kept this hidden so long," Tom said.

"How long do you think it will be before Alejandro goes to trial?" Rob asked.

"That could take a while. I just got word from Sam that the CIA is struggling with the Mexican authorities to get him out."

"That doesn't sound good," Rob said.

"It's not."

Wanda's worried glance went from Rob to Tom. "Are you saying there's a chance Alejandro could go free?"

"Not if Sam has anything to do with it," Tom replied. "Don't worry about him right now. Let's talk about you. Steve suggested the Bureau set you up in a small Colorado community called Ouray. It's tucked away in a beautiful mountain range, away from large cities, with limited access in and out. The other possibilities are Athens, Georgia, and Darlington, South Carolina. Steve asked me to check all the locations and give him my feedback."

"Wait a minute," Wanda said. "Does this mean after we move, we will never see you again?"

"According to Bureau policy, I'm not allowed to have contact with you."

"Tom, you can't leave us! You're the only grandparent Sarah's ever known."

"I hate this, Wanda, but I have no choice."

"Who says the Bureau has to know?" Rob said with a grin. "It's never stopped us before."

"We have broken a few rules, haven't we?" Tom said with a smile.

"Yes, we have. Why stop now?"

Wanda leaned forward and spoke to her daughter. "Sarah, do you want Tom to stay in our family?"

Sarah looked up at her mama and then at Tom. "Tom Tom stay."

Tom laughed and got to his feet. "After an invitation like that, how could I refuse?" He lifted Sarah and her doll into the air and flew her around the room as if she were an airplane.

ACKNOWLEDGMENTS

To Darrell Chitty
Master Photographer and Artist
Thank you, dear brother, for allowing me to use one of your incredible paintings for the cover of this book.

ABOUT THE AUTHOR

Donna Joppie's first novel, *The Memory Trap*, received The Reader Views Five Star Review shortly after its release in 2024.

Donna was born into a large family with seven creative siblings and raised in Houma, Louisiana. Her personal knowledge of, and ties to, Louisiana and its people, culture, and timeline is reflected in this second novel, *Blood Favors*.

Donna has traveled the world, but she and her husband Rick chose the beautiful hill country of Texas as home.